THE BODYGUARD

THE ACES SERIES, BOOK #6

New York Times Bestselling Author

CRISTIN HARBER

DEDICATION

To Team Titan,
Thanks for your patience. Enjoy Sawyer and Angela.

CHAPTER ONE

STOCKHOLM SYNDROME DID not exist. At least, that was the lesson that Angela Sorenson should have taken from her therapy sessions. Her shrink said it. Google said it. Even her mother, the all-powerful senator from the great commonwealth of Pennsylvania, said it, albeit privately and in a whisper far away from the press releases and news conferences that occurred after Angela was rescued from her kidnapper; because, after all, it wouldn't do to avoid using crucial buzzwords that polled so well and created sympathy amongst voters.

But no matter how often that supposed truth had been explained to her, Angela didn't believe it. Here she was, wearing a bulky bulletproof vest during her weekly therapy sessions that required an escort by a bodyguard, wishing she could snap her fingers and remove the puzzling parts of her past that still gave her nightmares and tugged at her heartstrings.

"Angela?" Ibrahim, her therapist, raised his brows. "I asked if you had been reading the headlines."

Oh, she had. Even in her highly secure cocoon that was Titan Group's Abu Dhabi headquarters, headlines from the United States were hard to ignore—especially when they were about her. Most articles included recent photographs of Tran Pham, the man who had her abducted. Sometimes, the articles used law enforcement sketches or AI-generated composites that had been circulated when international agencies argued whether Pham even existed. Until Angela's rescue, he'd never been photographed.

Every image of Pham bothered her. None showed him as the man she knew. He'd been grandfatherly and giving. Logically, she understood how many years of her life he had stolen. Pham, the man who asked her questions and learned about who she was, was different than Pham, the man who had her kidnapped and kept as a political prisoner.

Angela wondered if Ibrahim thought she was a lost cause. Maybe she was. "Well…" *There's no such thing as Stockholm Syndrome. There's no such thing as Stockholm Syndrome.* Her feelings were simply an expected emotional response to trauma. Her relationship with Pham was best described as a trauma bond. There was no diagnosis to be made, and she wasn't supposed to let her years with Pham—years of captivity and mental abuse—define her. Easier said than done.

Ibrahim studied her. He wasn't a fool. He had to know when she commingled the truth with what she was expected to say in the name of therapeutic progress. "Angela?"

She shifted her shoulders back and lifted her chin slightly, needing to find a minuscule level of control. "I've seen the headlines."

"They'd be hard to miss."

Angela nodded. "I don't go searching them out, but with the trial looming…" She gestured toward the window and the busy, bustling city beyond the safe confines of Ibrahim's office. "It's news. International news. And even if it weren't, my head isn't in the sand."

The corners of Ibrahim's mouth rose in a way that encouraged her to continue. When that didn't work, he pressed, "Does that worry you?"

"The news?" She gestured to her bulletproof vest. "Even if that didn't worry me, I don Kevlar anytime I walk out of the hotel."

"The bulletproof vest should make you feel safer."

"No one knows where I am, yet if I leave Titan's property, I have to have my bodyguard with me."

"I thought you liked your bodyguard. Sawyer, isn't it?"

"Yes, of course, I like him. Who wouldn't? He's a good friend. But it's overkill."

"Jared Westin doesn't think so." Ibrahim tilted his head, apparently curious if Angela would counter the orders from her boss.

"Jared Westin thinks about every possible possibility and outcome, then plans for it, then plans for his plans to catch fire and burn to the ground." All of Jared's many, many plans made her feel safe. Bulletproof vests? Not so much.

"You've been wearing the vest in public for quite some time now. It's the intensity of the news cycles that I'm more interested in. With the upcoming trial…" Ibrahim gestured. "It's more of a reminder—"

"It's a reminder of what I already know. I lived it. I survived it. It can't worry me."

Ibrahim waited.

Angela smirked. "The vest worries me. That's what makes my head turn somersaults. Not the trial."

"Only a few weeks are left until you testify against Pham."

"Just like there's only a few more weeks to wear this vest."

His lips quirked. "And then the whole thing's over. You will forget any of it happened. Pham will be gone. In prison. A figment of your imagination, maybe? Is that what he will become after you testify?"

Life after testifying… She hadn't thought about it that way. Pham had stolen the latter part of her twenties and left Angela wound so tight that it was a miracle her head didn't pop off like a bottle rocket. But Pham was the same man who knew her better than her family, who listened when she talked and spent time with her when he likely had a laundry list of to-dos just as long as either of her parents had in their busy careers. Would he feel like a ghost from the past? An illusory friend from a nightmare? "That's a sneaky way to ask how I feel about Pham."

"I'm not trying to be sneaky, Angela. The death threats are real. Testifying could be a paradigm shift for you. You're treading water, and I think you're tired of that."

"That's not true."

"I'd like to see you feeling stronger about yourself before you face Pham. Wasn't that one of the goals you wanted to work on?"

Angela laced her fingers and squeezed them, hoping the pain in her hands would overpower the pain of the past. Why couldn't she get over the whole ordeal? Hadn't enough time passed that she could simply forget who Tran Pham even was? When was the adage *time heals* going to kick into gear and wipe away that mysterious mental burden she couldn't shake? "I wish you could prescribe me a magic pill or something that would fix everything."

"You're not broken. You're healing."

A pain lodged in her throat. "Broken bones heal."

Ibrahim's lips twitched.

"Testifying against Pham feels real," she said. "It will hurt. He hurt me, and now I am going to hurt him."

"He has hurt many, many people, my dear."

"But I never saw it, and logically, I know that makes me sound self-ish—"

"It's a testament to the hold he had on you. Logic doesn't work in abusive relationships."

"I understand that. Logically," she tacked on again. "But the betrayal of testifying against him feels more real than the actual threats against my life. Because I haven't seen it. Again, logically, I know his terrorist network has made clear they won't let me testify. But that part feels like a story-book. Like something that would happen to someone else."

"You're trailed by security and wearing a bulletproof vest because of Pham."

"And I don't need to be." Very few people on Earth knew where Ange-la had disappeared to. Outside of her family, she'd put her complete trust in Titan Group, and with that came a set of rules she'd lived by easily. Stay offline, be careful of her connections in the US, and avoid travel unless it was with Sawyer. "I'm following the rules. Doing what I'm told. What's expected of me. I'm surviving."

"You're treading water. Not moving. Not growing."

"Surviving."

Ibrahim waited for an eternity before offering a slight nod. "Self-preservation is important."

Angela looked out the window. From her spot in the small office of a posh Abu Dhabi high-rise, she could see no way forward. She had to testify, she had to face Pham, and, eventually, she would have to find herself again—but she wasn't there yet.

"Angela, you have to voice your thoughts if I'm going to help you walk away from Pham's trial unscathed."

"I'm already scathed, Ibrahim. You know that better than anyone."

"Let's stick with positive self-talk." He didn't wait for her pithy retort. "You're working on your inside"—he gestured to his head—"as much as your physical well-being."

"Positive self-talk," she agreed, crossing her hand over her heart. Sarcasm and self-control were the reasons therapy wasn't working, but she couldn't let go of her crutches.

Ibrahim waited as though he could read her mind. He waited as though this time, she would say aloud everything she alluded to but wouldn't verbalize. His positivity would let him continue waiting beyond the end of this session, the one after that, and the one after that. Ibrahim had the patience of a saint, and she wanted to scream.

Finally, he broke the silence. "You have so much negativity bottled in your chest."

She almost smiled. Angela tugged at her blouse collar. "Good thing it's well hidden behind the Kevlar."

"Let it go, Angela," Ibrahim said. "What do you have to lose?"

Control. Her throat constricted. If she let go and shared what she really thought, she would lose the memories from captivity that she'd labeled as good—as loving. Ibrahim would force her to label them correctly as coercive manipulation. What would she have then? The good memories, the ones she'd clung to during years of imprisonment, would disappear. She'd be lost and heartbroken like a little kid who wasn't ready to learn the truth about Santa Claus.

"You have to name the struggle before you let it go," Ibrahim said.

"I've been trying to name the struggle." Her throat ached. "Stockholm syndrome. You won't listen."

"Trust me." Ibrahim waited, holding her with an unblinking stare that tried to pry loose what needed freeing. "Trust *yourself.*"

The knot in her throat thickened. "I'm not struggling with the trial, how long Pham will go to prison, the threats..." Emotion choked her words. "But with the man I came to know."

"Pham." Ibrahim nodded once, acknowledging the single most significant source of her pain and confusion.

A tear trickled down her cheek. "He was the grandpa I never had."

Angela pulled a heart-tugging breath. "He was the only person who ever acted as though he cared for me like family."

"It's time to let it out, Angela. Shine a light on the ugly, and eventually, it fades."

She wanted Pham to fade. "Let it out" was so cliché, but it somehow worked. The chokehold on her voice released, and she admitted, "Pham smiled. He cared. He talked to me and asked questions and remembered what I said."

Ibrahim didn't tell her she was a fool or explain the manipulation. He listened to her darkest secrets, which she hadn't revealed in years of therapy—the reasons she couldn't get over her captor.

"That probably felt nice," Ibrahim said.

Validated, Angela let the floodgates open. "Pham knew I wanted steak and scalloped potatoes over barbeque chicken and mac and cheese. He knew I liked retellings of classic novels over bubble-gum-cute fairy tales but preferred entertainment magazines—the ones with movies and shows—over everything."

When she finally stopped talking, silence pervaded Ibrahim's office. Tears had dried on Angela's cheeks. The remnants of her near-manic outpouring made her feel lighter, untethered, and honest but far too raw.

Angela sniffed and ran her fingers under her eyes, summarizing in a whisper. "He spent the time to figure me out."

"No one else did that for you before?" Ibrahim asked, already knowing her answer.

She shook her head.

"Did he do that for you? Or for himself?" An eternity inched by before he added, "He kept you against your will."

"*I know that.*" Memories collided with facts. Her tears welled again. Angela wiped her cheeks. "I know he's a narcissist; I know he's evil. And most importantly, I know I was a replacement for the daughter he lost. Logically, I'm not an idiot. *I know.*"

"Logically." Ibrahim smiled and then cocked his head. "I'm curious; when did you learn that he blamed your mother for his daughter's death?"

"Early. A man like Tran Pham can't abduct you and not connect it to your power-hungry senator mother."

"So you spent years knowing why he treated you like family?"

Angela bit her bottom lip. She was told about Pham's daughter, Quy Long, almost immediately and then quickly realized that, despite Pham's career choice and his daughter's involvement in the criminal world, he loved and missed his daughter. He was a grief-stricken terrorist. "Yeah." Pham's relationship with Angela was never real. She was a replacement for the daughter he'd lost and a punishment for her mother, who Pham blamed. "Nothing was real—but it *felt* real."

"Feelings can be deceptive."

"That might be, but even now, I can put myself into his shoes and, given his worldview and resources, understand how avenging his daughter made sense."

"Tran Pham is a narcissist. That's what narcissists do. They can make you feel things that don't exist." Ibrahim's expression tightened. "You said Pham treated you like family."

She nodded.

"And that you've never had that experience," he pushed. "But what about your boyfriend?"

She balked. "Paul?"

Ibrahim chuckled. "Do you have another boyfriend I'm unaware of?"

Nope. Paul Bane was her only one. Perfect Paul with the perfect hair and the perfect body had been around for years. Paul was pre-abduction. Angela saw her life that way: everything before captivity and everything after. "What about him?"

"You've been together for so long," Ibrahim prompted. "Would you consider him family?"

No. Paul was practically a stranger. He and Angela were a superficial couple. She pressed her lips together and finally confessed, "Pham acted more like family than any other person I have called family. Paul included."

"How do you think Paul would feel about that?"

"That I don't consider him family?" She snorted. "If I ever managed to get a hold of him, he would agree." However, the opposite was true this week. Paul had broken character and tried repeatedly to get a hold of her. She had been busy. Though she should have felt a hint of guilt, his insistence had been aggravating.

Angela sighed, not wanting to dissect her relationship with Paul today. That was more of a conversation to hold with a friend. Not a shrink. Or maybe she would ask Sawyer and not only get a friend's perspective but a man's.

Sawyer was one hell of a man. His opinion was like gold. Her cheeks heated. Angela refocused on Ibrahim and tried to lighten the conversation. "So, Pham is more of a family than my flesh-and-blood family. That's what I've been keeping to myself—man, you have your work cut out for you."

Ibrahim chuckled. "I'm glad you told me."

Angela shrugged with a sheepish laugh. "Now that I've said everything out loud, maybe I'm cured." She crossed her fingers. "Maybe?"

Ibrahim studied Angela for an uncomfortably long moment. She didn't feel as if he were waiting for another profound revelation from her, yet it felt like she was supposed to say more. Feel more. Experience a bigger, deeper revelation, and she didn't have it in her. "I'm tapped, Ibrahim. I don't have anything more to share."

"No…" He stroked his chin. "But I do."

She raised mental barriers and guarded herself for whatever he might share. But she wasn't about to let him know her anxiety needled her. Angela faked a grin and beckoned. "Come on. Hit me with it. I can take it."

He crossed his arms over his chest. "When you put our therapeutic sessions like that, how can I resist?"

Angela laughed. "Come on."

Ibrahim nodded but paused as though gathering his thoughts. "Your struggle isn't with Tran Pham."

"What?" After everything she'd just poured out, this was Ibrahim's dramatic takeaway? "I'm sorry, but Psychology 101 students could figure out that I'm screwed up because of Pham."

He held up his hand. "It's not that simple, Angela. Pham listened to you. He provided for you, and while it was a definite perversion of the act, he cared for you, unlike your parents or boyfriend. *That's* where your burden lies. Not what Pham gave you but what you never received from your loved ones."

CHAPTER TWO

SAWYER CABOT CHECKED the time. Two minutes until Angela's appointment would end. Despite what he assumed was discussed during that standing meeting, she would walk out, picture-perfect, as though she'd spent the day at the office instead of rehashing her nightmare past. Sawyer would escort her back to Titan headquarters, and his on-and-off job of keeping his eyes on Angela would be done.

A door to the small waiting room opened from the main hallway, and a woman entered, her gaze angled toward the patterned carpet. A dark gray burqa covered her head, draping over her shoulders and falling to the floor. Sawyer kept his eyes to himself, shifting his outstretched legs under his chair, and checked his watch again. One minute to go. He'd thought there had always been enough time between appointments for privacy's sake.

The end of Angela's session ticked by. The door didn't open. If Angela was anything, it was on time. She ran a tight ship. Then again, therapy wasn't exactly a conventional meeting. Sawyer trusted Ibrahim to watch the clock if Angela's internal time management had gone off course.

Sawyer's heel bounced. He watched and waited for Angela to walk out at any moment. Then reason caught up with instinct. They were at her therapist's office. She hadn't walked out of the appointment yet because something was happening back there. A breakthrough or an epiphany or whatever caused therapists to go beyond their scheduled time slots. This was a good thing. Sawyer wanted this for Angela.

His gaze shifted from the door to the other person in the waiting room. The woman nonchalantly paged through a magazine. Her oversized designer bag sat in the chair next to her. That bag probably cost more than his first car. He wouldn't put it on the floor either.

Sawyer checked his watch. Angela should have exited by now. Ibrahim never ran long. Perhaps something was wrong. He knew the office layout. There was another way into Ibrahim's office. The entrance opened into a private hallway with the therapist's private office, a file room, and a locked egress point to the public hallway. He knew the blueprints of this floor like the back of his hand. Not that Sawyer had been worried. Memorizing the layout was just part of the job.

Ibrahim had been vetted. He was safe. The office was safe. No one could get in and or out without security-provided access. Still, Sawyer checked his watch. His gaze pivoted from the door Angela would exit to the door that led to the hall and elevators. He glanced at the woman with the handbag and wondered how much time Ibrahim built between appointments. It had never been an issue before.

Then again, maybe she wasn't a client. A sales rep, maybe? Unscheduled drop-in? Unsettled energy corkscrewed up his back. Sawyer tapped his heel. Would interrupting Angela's session cross the line? Ibrahim had a panic button. It hadn't been activated.

Sawyer pushed out of his chair. He paced the tight space. The woman's gaze followed him momentarily, then she settled her bag closer and returned to her magazine.

He checked his watch. Three minutes late. Something was wrong. Sawyer approached the door—but pulled back. Nothing was wrong on the other side. Even if something *was* wrong, Titan had systems to notify the world if Sawyer had to burst through the door. The likeliest situation was what…? Angela was having some deep therapeutic moments that Ibrahim didn't want to interrupt. Or, even more likely, they'd lost track of time. Perhaps Ibrahim's timer or clock hadn't notified him of the session's end.

The door handle twisted with a quiet metallic click, and the tenseness lodged in Sawyer's chest released. He turned toward the voices coming through the cracked doorway. Angela, always polite, thanked Ibrahim for his time. Ibrahim, always quiet, thanked Angela for her hard work in their session.

Behind Sawyer, he sensed the waiting woman now stood. The hairs at the nape of his neck stood as well. A patient wouldn't stand for their appointment before they were greeted. They wouldn't approach before a patient from an earlier appointment had stepped through the threshold.

Sawyer turned.

The door that separated Angela and Ibrahim from the waiting room opened wide, and a rush of cool air kissed his neck.

"I'll see you next week," Ibrahim said.

The other woman moved. She was a blur of a burqa with a pistol in hand.

Sawyer reached for the door behind him. "Get back."

"What—" Angela called.

The heavy door slammed amidst Angela's cries. Sawyer lunged for the other woman. Her pistol-wielding hand jerked hard. Gunfire popped. Sawyer wasn't hit. He wasn't the target. Only a door separated this woman from Angela.

Sawyer attacked as the woman rebounded. Dark fabric flowed like a curtain of distraction. His mind registered the weapon. Compact. Self-loading. It might've been a Russian PSM, made for Soviet officials, with a history for KGB assassins. He'd never seen one before and couldn't see it now. Blindly, he wrestled with the shooter. Her build was slight, but she was strong. Trained. They hit the floor. Gunfire popped again and again; he wasn't the target.

Angela's muffled scream reverberated in his head. Sawyer and the shooter rolled. Heavy office chairs scattered around them. Fabric floated like a labyrinthic barrier. He fought to find the PSM and grappled for a handhold.

The shooter moved like water. She twisted and kicked, and Sawyer finally caught her wrist. Their breaths labored. Her breathing was the only sound she made.

His grip tightened. "Let it go."

She rolled hard. Her head and face covering pulled down. Sawyer didn't lose his hold. His free hand wrapped around her neck. Adrenaline coursed through his system. The pistol fell from her grasp. He pushed it out of reach.

Behind him, the office door opened.

"Sawyer," Angela cried.

"Get out of here." Sawyer flipped the shooter onto her stomach and pinned her legs under his weight. Sweat pricked the back of his neck. "Go."

"Angela," Ibrahim snapped.

"Call Jared," Sawyer demanded.

Angela skirted the perimeter of the upturned office. "Already done."

He ripped a strip of fabric from the burqa, doubled it over, and wrapped the woman's hands behind her back. His racing breath slowed. He repeated the process for her feet. Then he noticed the way Angela hovered. "Ange, what are you doing?"

"What do we do about her gun?" Angela asked warily.

"*We* do nothing. Leave it." Sawyer gave her a stern look, tore another strip of fabric, and tied the shooter to the furniture. He glanced at Angela again. She was too close. Too curious. "What the hell are you doing?"

"I wanted to see..." She crept closer. "The person who wants to kill me."

Ibrahim stepped to Angela and reached for her shoulder. "Angela." He half squeezed, half pulled her back. "She doesn't want to kill you for a reason. You are only a target. A job."

Sawyer ran his hand over the shooter. The quick pat-down produced a tactical knife strapped to her ankle. "Pham sent her. You know that." Sawyer redoubled his pat-down, searching for communication gear. "You work alone?"

The woman didn't reply.

"How the hell she found you, though..." His molars ground. "I'd like to know that."

Angela broke free of Ibrahim. She inched closer and crouched an arm's length from the subdued shooter.

"I'm not a target. I'm a person," Angela said.

"Ange..." Sawyer shook his head. Trying to reason with an assassin wouldn't be productive. Still, Angela leaned closer as though inspecting an oddity rather than a killer. He tried to elbow her back. "Get back into Ibrahim's office."

"Absolutely not." Angela moved closer.

"Come on." Sawyer blocked her with an arm. "Get back, Ange."

"Angela." The color had drained from Ibrahim's face. "Listen to him. Come back with me."

"No."

Sawyer couldn't read her expression, but her mascara was smeared under her eyes. The shooting hadn't made her cry. Angela never cried during therapy—at least, as far as Sawyer knew. He glanced at Ibrahim and back to Angela as she edged in. Her breaths were eerily steady. A cold confidence flared in her dark eyes.

"Angela, can you get an ETA from Boss Man?" Sawyer asked.

"Jared will be here when he's here." The unfamiliar edge in her voice made his nerves tingle.

Sawyer touched her elbow. "You okay?"

"That woman tried to kill me." Angela swatted his hand away and glared daggers at the shooter. "Pham sent you to kill me."

With a thousand-yard stare, the woman's eyes remained straight ahead, as though the other people weren't in the room.

"I'll get an update on Jared," Ibrahim volunteered.

Sawyer nodded. "Thanks." They'd had a major security breach. How the hell had anyone found Angela? They'd gone more than a year since Pham's network had put a hit out on her. After all this time without so much as a blip, a lone assassin found her in Abu Dhabi.

Sawyer picked up the PSM. The lightweight pistol fit in the palm of his hand. He ejected the mag, pulled back the slide and lifted it from the frame, and removed the recoil spring, rendering the weapon temporarily useless. "Give her some room, Angela."

Angela ignored him and poised before her attacker like a rattlesnake focused on its prey. "What did I ever do to you?"

"Nothing, Ange. That's the point." He put the pistol and its parts on an end table piled with therapy and entertainment magazines. "You're not a person to these people. You're a target. A paycheck."

Angela reared her hand back and slapped the assassin. The impact snapped her head to the side—a red welted handprint arose on her cheek.

Ibrahim jumped for Angela. Sawyer stared. Her crisp blouse was partially untucked from her skirt. Stray hairs had escaped her tight ponytail. Those details wouldn't have been noticeable if he hadn't known how exacting Angela was in her appearance and how tightly she tried to control life. "Let her go."

Ibrahim shot him a look. Sawyer nodded. Angela had lost control. Her nostrils flared. He had no idea what had happened in her therapy session. But she was face to face with the threat they had been avoiding. It was real. Everything she tried to ignore, to play off and pretend didn't exist, was very real and deadly.

Ibrahim let Angela go. She balanced in high heels and smoothed a skirt that made her legs go on for days.

The shooter probed the inside of her own cheek with her tongue and slowly faced ahead again, not saying a damn word.

"You want an answer that you're not going to get," Ibrahim said quietly.

Sawyer agreed. Ibrahim understood. Mercenary assassins didn't offer chit-chat. They didn't have experience with capture and forced conversations with their targets. They wouldn't provide answers to questions from their near-kills, and even if they did, they wouldn't be able to explain why they'd taken shots—at least not in a way that would make sense to Angela. Angela Sorenson was a payday.

He walked behind Angela and placed his hands on her shoulders. "Even if she had something to say, it won't be what you want to hear." Sawyer pressed his fingers into the straps of her Kevlar vest. "She's a paid gun. A lone operative. The only thing she's thinking about is her next move." He kept his eyes on the shooter's thousand-yard stare and dropped his voice. "She's calculating how to get loose. How to eliminate everyone in the room. What to expect when Boss Man shows up. What to do when she's moved to transport. How to handle lockup. How to escape."

Angela glanced over her shoulder. From inches away, her eyes searched his. "She tried to kill me."

For the first time, her voice betrayed fear. Anger curled in his chest. "Not if I'm around. Have you ever noticed what we do at work?" He laughed, but it didn't lighten the mood.

Angela pulled away and glared as if she'd never considered that Titan dealt with risks of death on a nearly daily basis.

Sawyer let her walk to Ibrahim.

"Come," Ibrahim urged. "Let's go. We can talk in my office."

"I have had enough therapy today." Angela looked from Ibrahim to the shooter and then to the bullet holes that puckered the walls. Her gaze swept over the upturned furniture and returned to her therapist. "I'm sorry about your office."

Sawyer snorted. The woman had dodged bullets and retaliated against her attacker, and now she offered an apology for chaos. "This isn't on you, sweetheart."

"To the contrary," she murmured. "I'd say I'm one hundred percent the reason."

Sawyer glanced at Ibrahim. They could team up and explain the hell out of the circumstances when she didn't have adrenaline coursing through her blood. Angela was logical. This would make sense. But now was not the time. His only focus was on returning Angela safely to the fortress they called home.

CHAPTER THREE

A FULL DAY had slipped by, and Sawyer remained clueless about the previous day's assault. It didn't require a genius to figure out the motive for the attempt on Angela's life. Tran Pham didn't want her on the witness stand. Looming threats were why Angela had been tucked away in Abu Dhabi. But after years in hiding, how had Angela's location been compromised? With each passing moment of silence and a lack of answers, Sawyer grew restless.

Jared Westin had promised Sawyer an intelligence briefing that morning. Then nothing happened. His boss had gone dark—not a word from Jared about their missed briefing and not a word to Angela, keeper of the schedule and wrangler of their team. If she didn't know where Jared was… Sawyer's stomach churned. Something was wrong.

His heel bounced. Sawyer repositioned on the couch. An undercurrent of tension knotted through his muscles as he scoured the luxurious lobby that covertly housed Titan's Middle East headquarters. He wished he were near Angela. But she didn't require a protective detail on their property.

Titan had eyes all over the building. Cameras covered every square inch of public space and the gated private offices with NSA-level security protocols. Half of the hotel staff had backgrounds that should have made Sawyer feel comfortable when Angela was in meetings on her own. Bellhops with black belts, a retired Green Beret for a concierge, and a head chef with a former life as a CIA asset were within fifty meters of his position. They could be called upon if there were a problem anywhere in the hotel.

The farthest elevator door opened. Liam and Hagan walked out and, seeing him posted like a sentry, walked over.

Sawyer strode forward and met them. "Any word on Boss Man?"

They shook their heads. Liam crossed his arms over his chest. "Strange, huh?"

"Yeah." Sawyer dragged his hands across his weary face. The night before hadn't given him enough sleep to confront an absence of answers.

"Where's Angela?" Hagan asked.

"Upstairs, acting as though no one tried to put a bullet in her face."

Hagan glanced around the lobby and nodded to a surreptitiously hidden camera. "It's the safest place Angela could be." His wife, Amanda, and her associate, Shah, managed the hotel's security and surveillance nerve center. "You know that as well as I do."

"He already knows that." Liam eyed Sawyer. "What do you want Angela to do? Sit in her suite and stay put until we figure everything out?"

Sawyer shrugged. "That doesn't sound like an awful plan."

The guys chuckled as if they had an inside joke. Sawyer wasn't in the mood to suss it out.

"Look, man. The offices are safer than the suites," Hagan said. "But she could be anywhere in either of the towers and be fine."

"I don't think 'fine' is the level of security I'm comfortable with."

Hagan and Liam exchanged looks. Hagan continued, "Amanda would know if a militant mosquito farted on the premises. No one can get to Angela while she's on site."

He was probably right. The problem was that Amanda and Shah couldn't prepare for every possible situation. There would always be a risk. He had planned for a thousand scenarios, and yet an assassin had walked into a secure location and nearly blew Angela's brains out.

As if Hagan had called in for reinforcements, his wife exited an elevator. Amanda didn't look worried for Angela or concerned about security problems, but she did look paler than usual.

Hagan greeted Amanda with a hand around her waist and a quick peck on the cheek. "I didn't expect to see you." He gave her a quick once-over and maybe saw what Sawyer did. "You feel okay?"

"I have a headache. That's all." She rubbed the back of her neck.

Hagan shifted closer to his wife. "Do you want a bottle of water?"

Amanda's color was definitely off. Sawyer motioned for them to give him a minute. He asked the front desk for water stashed in the mini fridge behind the counter and then returned and handed the bottle to a protesting Amanda.

"Really, I'm fine." Amanda inhaled deeply through her nose and exhaled through her mouth before taking a sip.

"Better?" Hagan asked, far more concerned about his wife's headache than threats that might loom over the hotel.

"Yeah." She recapped the water. "But I'm going to lie down."

"I'll go with you—"

Amanda cut Hagan off with a flick of her hand. "I can manage a headache." She eyeballed Sawyer. "Stay with him. He's not looking so good."

"Me?" Sawyer shirked from her scrutiny. "I'm just a guy with unanswered questions and a missing boss. Not to mention a laundry list of security uncertainties."

She narrowed her eyes. "My head hurts, Sawyer. Don't make me shake you."

"Fine," he relented. "Not uncertainties. But…" Sawyer shrugged. Amanda had this place on lockdown. There was no question about Titan's security.

Amanda squeezed Hagan's hand and turned. "If anyone needs me, find Shah. I'm off to nap."

"And don't forget," Hagan said, watching his wife leave, "Angela agreed with Amanda and Boss Man. If she's off-site, she'll wear Kevlar."

"Yeah, as much as she won't like it." Sawyer rubbed the back of his neck. Angela liked clothes and fashion. She wasn't trendy, though. Her skirts and blouses conjured images of timeless models and classic beauties.

"Well, she likes it more than being dead," Liam said. "She seemed levelheaded enough last night."

"More than you," Hagan added under his breath.

Sawyer glared. His phone pinged, and he jumped as though someone had shouted from behind.

Hagan and Liam exchanged yet another glance that Sawyer didn't like. He ignored them and checked his phone. "Not Jared."

"Where the hell is that guy?" Liam asked the question Sawyer had wondered about a thousand times.

"He'll turn up," Hagan muttered.

Sawyer opened Angela's message.

Are you downstairs? I'll be there in one minute.

Hagan shrugged, as relaxed as if they were discussing weekend plans. "Five bucks and a beer says Boss Man's helping interrogate the shooter."

Liam snorted. "I'd take that bet."

Sawyer's jaw clenched. He wanted in on the interrogation but had more pressing concerns. Angela asked if he was downstairs, and she hadn't waited for his reply. For all she knew, he was off-site. Angela had decided to head to the lobby without a plan. He responded quickly.

I'm with Liam and Hagan in the lobby. Southwest corner from the elevators.

He checked his watch. Fifty-nine seconds. If Angela said she'd arrive in one minute, that was when she would arrive. "She's on the move."

"She's changing floors, not being handed off between protective details," Hagan pointed out.

"Bite me," Sawyer muttered.

Liam slapped Sawyer's back. "You'll feel better once you have eyes on her."

"*Again*, a reminder—we're in a fortress." Hagan's eyebrows cocked as if he had more to say.

Sawyer shrugged from the backslap. "I know Amanda has this place on lockdown."

"She does."

"But she and Shah can't mitigate every risk. They can't account for everyone's actions." No one understood how Angela walked around Titan headquarters like she could control the whole damn world with a well-planned schedule and a succinctly worded agenda. "All I'm saying is…" Sawyer shook his head. He didn't know what he was saying. He ran his hand along the nape of his neck. "Maybe she should stay put in her suite until we know where Boss Man is and have some answers."

Liam frowned. "You know yesterday wasn't your fault?"

"I know we have plans upon plans, and yesterday, we proved we didn't have enough."

"We didn't know of an imminent threat."

"She has been living in hiding for years." Tension climbed up Sawyer's spine. "There's a known threat."

"Maybe you want to be assigned to her on the grounds too?" Hagan asked.

Angela had been under his watchful gaze since Jared brought her into the fold. Sure, his role was officially with the ACES team, but he treated both duties equally.

"Give him a break," Liam said.

Sawyer didn't know who Liam was directing that toward. Hagan's wife had a nightmare of a history with protective details, while Liam's wife, Chelsea, had had a taste of Tran Pham and the hell Angela had gone through.

"I didn't mean—" Hagan tossed up his hands. "I meant Angela's safe in this building. I'm not trying to beat a dead horse, but come on, man. You don't need to worry."

Sawyer dropped his head back and drank in a long breath. "I know. I'm just..." He didn't know what. Instead, he kept tabs on his mental countdown. Thirty seconds until she should be in the lobby.

"Distracted," Hagan offered.

Liam elbowed Hagan. "Maybe Angela has an update."

"Maybe," Sawyer hoped.

The group pivoted toward the elevators. His gaze worked across the lobby, registering every person, their baggage and body language. He hunted for threats and searched for out-of-place minutiae, for anything like what he'd almost missed a day ago.

The elevator that serviced only their office floors opened, and Angela strode into the gilded hotel lobby.

"She doesn't look like she has answers," Hagan said.

"No, she doesn't." She wasn't wearing Kevlar either. Sawyer studied her tight-lipped frown and the tension in her jaw. Her bright eyes didn't hold their regular happy glimmer, and her high ponytail of dark raven hair didn't swing with each step.

But she did look like she was trying to control every aspect of her life completely. The relentless bite of her black high heels clicked across the gold-flecked marble floor in a manner that dared anyone to get in her way.

Despite the stress, she still looked like a million bucks. He could never decide if her fashion style was buttoned-up or slyly suggestive. He'd never ask. She would knee him in the groin. They were close, but friendships had a line. Where would the line be for insisting on a bulletproof vest twenty-four hours a day? Kevlar would definitely change how she dressed.

Sawyer rubbed the back of his neck. It wasn't his place to notice how she carried herself in those high heels or that skirt. They were coworkers. Friends. At times, bodyguard and protectee. Not to mention, Angela was in a long-distance relationship. Sawyer swallowed hard. Even if they didn't have a laundry list of barriers that kept a relationship at bay, Angela was the kind of woman who only did serious, long-term relationships. That wasn't something Sawyer was capable of anymore.

He pulled his attention from her and swept the lobby for threats again. Hagan and Liam stepped to the side as she joined them, subtly blocking Angela from the main reception area's view. Like hell they weren't all treating her like she was under their collective protective detail until they knew what was going on.

Sawyer raised his chin.

Hagan crossed his arms. "Where's Boss Man?"

"That's the question of the day." Angela pursed her lips and then let out a long breath. "I have no idea, and it's driving me batty."

"Did you touch base with Parker?" Sawyer asked. Parker, Titan's tech guru, was based in the United States and led the global tech operations. He was in constant contact with Jared.

"We spoke before the sun was up." Angela shook her head. "No dice."

Stress knotted at the base of Sawyer's neck.

"Maybe Parker knows and isn't sharing?" Hagan suggested.

"That would be a good thought," Angela agreed, "except he called me looking for Jared. As did Brock Gamble."

Brock served as Jared's number-two man in charge. If the second in command of all Titan's operations didn't know where Boss Man was, then Sawyer's rising stress level was appropriate.

"Well, hell." Liam frowned. "That's a little unnerving."

Her frown deepened. "Just a little."

Liam's phone buzzed. "It's Chelsea. I'll let you know if she knows anything." He stepped away to answer the call from his wife.

"Well, I'm going to head upstairs." Hagan turned toward the elevators. "Hit me up if you hear anything."

Sawyer rubbed a hand over his face. "Will do."

Angela wandered toward a couch in an alcove sitting area off the side and scowled at her phone. Sawyer followed, grateful to get her out of the public's line of sight, and sat beside her. His gaze continued to pivot for threats. She dropped her phone into her lap and, after an exasperated sigh, slumped on the couch.

Sawyer studied her. "Jared will turn up. We'll get answers." He pretended to relax. Or, at least, he tried. He repositioned his legs and threw an arm over the back of the couch.

"Jared's not the only guy giving me a headache."

He snorted. "Calling Tran Pham a headache is putting it lightly, but it will work out—"

"Not Pham." She squeezed her eyes shut before giving him a pleading look. "Can I show you something?"

He gave up on pretending to relax. Acting wasn't his talent, and her head was in a different place anyway. "Yeah, sure."

"It has to do with Paul."

Sawyer balked. "The boyfriend?"

They didn't talk about her relationship. Sawyer couldn't remember how or when he learned the boyfriend existed. Maybe it had been mentioned in Sawyer's initial safety briefing when he was first assigned to Angela as a security detail for when she left the building. Sawyer couldn't recall Angela taking phone calls from Paul or sharing stories about the guy. Paul never visited, and if he did, Sawyer wasn't sure he'd like him. Paul

Bane looked like a Washington, DC politician. Sawyer was confident that Paul would think and act like one too.

"I need a man's perspective," Angela prodded. "Please, Sawyer. Don't make me beg for your two cents." She pouted, and her pleading face made him laugh. "I can do this all day until you agree."

Sawyer groaned and relented. "Fine. My perspective"—he gestured for to hit him with her question—"I'm ready."

Her cute, pouty face melted into a grateful smile. "Earlier this week, for two days, he was blowing up my phone."

All right, so she and the boyfriend had talked and texted. Sawyer scowled.

"But I was absurdly busy and running around to secure a safe house in Libya."

He nodded, recalling an incident in Tripoli that called upon their team to haul ass across the Mediterranean Sea.

"I told him that I couldn't respond."

Sawyer leaned back. "You think he's upset you blew him off? He'll get over it."

"I told him that unless he was dying or something, I'd call back later this week." Her gaze flicked to his. They both knew that the Libyan safe house issue took only a few hours to figure out. "That sounds harsh. But it's sort of how we've always operated."

"All right."

"Don't judge. Okay?"

"I'm not judging." Except he was. At least, he was analyzing. Angela, who was completely involved and invested in her friends and work, didn't blow off conversations. Sawyer lifted his hands. "This is a no-judgment conversation."

She picked up her phone and scrolled. "Then yesterday happened."

"That was a hell of a day for you."

"Yeah, someone tried to kill me, and I thought, 'Gee, this is something I should tell Paul.'"

Sawyer had spent all day with Angela. She yelled and cried and decided she wouldn't let the assassination attempt get the better of her. Chelsea and

Amanda had huddled with and hugged her. Hagan had organized their teammates and support staff to meet at one of the hotel restaurant bars for a nightcap to top off the crappy day. Sawyer hadn't seen Angela on her phone.

"I wasn't dying," she continued. "But, ya know, one bad shot away from dying. Closer to dying than any other time in recent history." She didn't ask a question, but she stared at him expectantly.

He shrugged because what else was he supposed to do? "I'd want to know if someone tried to kill my girlfriend."

"Exactly." She forced a laugh. "I tried to get a hold of him. Not like he did the other day with the flood of calls and texts. But I tried, and I made clear it was important."

"Okay...?"

"I haven't heard from him."

Sawyer's brows furrowed. What did she need that he and Titan hadn't been able to give her? Then again, there were many things that a boyfriend could give her, even through a long-distance phone call. Pressure ticked in Sawyer's jaw. "Okay..."

"You're pausing and thinking a lot before you say anything," she accused.

"Well... yeah." He half laughed. "Is this more of a Chelsea or Amanda conversation?"

Her eyebrows reached toward the sky-high ceiling. "Absolutely not."

His own eyebrows arched. "Because?"

"They each have a lot on their minds, and I don't want to share my silly burdens. It feels trivial. But I can talk to you about anything. I trust you without reservation."

He didn't know what to make of Angela's choice to avoid her friends. "We've never talked about your boyfriend."

"There's never anything to talk about. I don't remember that I have a boyfriend half the time." She shook her head. "Forget that. What I mean is—I want to know this: do you think he's not answering because I wasn't answering earlier this week?"

Damn, there was a lot to unpack in just a few words. "I mean... that would be childish."

She fiddled with the delicate gold bangles that peaked from the cuff of her blouse. "He's not childish."

The tension in his neck tightened again. "So he's just as busy as you are."

"Sawyer, I said it was *very* important."

"Look…" He sucked in a deep breath that did little to ease the discomfort corkscrewing his trapezoids. Sawyer searched for a diplomatic answer. "He doesn't know what's happened. You didn't say, and, tit-for-tat, you both ignored each other. So…"

Angela's lips pursed.

What was he trying to say here? Defending Paul wasn't on his agenda. Then again, Sawyer didn't have an agenda. "I don't know, sweetheart."

She deflated as though he'd punctured the last reserve of hope she'd been guarding.

"There are a million things that could be going on," Sawyer tried. His semi-defense of Paul ratcheted up the ick factor. He pinched the bridge of his nose. There was no reason to neg on the guy when Sawyer didn't have both sides of the story. "I don't think I'm a lot of help."

She held her phone up to him. "Will you look at this and tell me if it reads as crazy as it made me feel?"

A small picture of Paul Bane was at the top of the message. The image looked like a corporate headshot. Or a political one. The type in which the guy smiled as though he was trying to portray his trustworthiness and relatability. The churning in Sawyer's stomach double-timed. "You don't want me to read that."

"Yeah, I do. I need some perspective." She shoved the phone closer. "There's no one else in this entire building that I would ask."

He cut her a glance. "Talk to Chelsea or Amanda. What about Jane?"

"I already explained that I can't."

"They're your girlfriends."

"I can't. Sawyer, come on." She repositioned on the couch, sliding closer, and made the pouty face that knocked out his defenses. "I'm going to beg again, and no one wants that."

The faint, familiar hint of her perfume enticed him to steal another glance at her effective pout.

"I almost died yesterday."

He pulled back and laughed. "I was there, Ange."

"That's gotta count for a favor or two. Please?"

Sawyer shook his head but gave in. He browsed her message to Paul. It read like a business email, complete with a subject line.

Important: Need to discuss.

When is a good time to connect?

"Give me a break." The corners of his lips lifted. "That doesn't exactly read like 'someone tried to kill me. Answer the phone.'"

"No." She held up her hand and then pointed at Sawyer. "I would send you a message like that. But him?" She shrugged. "That would be a little over-dramatic."

His brow furrowed. No wonder she hadn't asked Jane, Amanda, or Chelsea. Their response would be far less diplomatic than his. "To say to your boyfriend? After someone tried to kill you? Is there a better time to throw on the theatrics?"

"He's…" She bit her lip. "A little more buttoned-up than us. And he's busy."

"You're about the most buttoned-up, closely controlled person I've ever met," he muttered. "If we're being honest."

She elbowed him. "Not in all circumstances."

Sawyer chuckled. Angela wasn't a stick in the mud. Last night was proof of that. The ladies hadn't even bothered with a glass of wine. They danced. Played trivia. Goofed around. All in all, Angela seemed to let the assassination attempt disappear from her mind. And he never saw her checking her phone for a missed call or text message from Paul. "All right. Not in all circumstances."

"Sawyer, scroll up."

He thought twice, took a shallow breath, scrolled, and read Paul's messages, which asked when she would come home. Sawyer cleared his throat and swallowed hard. He ran his hand into his hair and then shrugged. "That's pretty self-explanatory, Ange." He offered her phone back. "He wants to see his girlfriend."

"Not-uh." Angela scoffed. "The only time I'm asked to go somewhere is for some kind of political reason, something or other that my mother needs to trot out her stolen-and-returned daughter for. He's asking as her staffer, not as my boyfriend."

Sawyer shifted and repositioned his legs. Angela wanted an honest assessment. He didn't have any context about the boyfriend or know her to be unreasonable. Still... "That's kind of harsh."

"It's not. It's—" Just as suddenly as she'd thrown this conversation onto his lap, she tried to back away. "It doesn't matter anyway."

His eyebrows cocked. "Why's that?"

"I can't show up in the US without a proper plan and lots of planning. He knows that. Besides, I'm not returning to the US until I have to testify."

His chest tightened at the idea of Angela walking around without him to keep her safe. But there was a US-based team that was more than capable. Boss Man would put Angela inside an armored bubble and not let her out until the risks were erased. That should have been a small comfort, but now it was one more thing needling Sawyer.

"Maybe I am being harsh. I don't know. This is why I need your perspective." Angela pushed her phone back. "But you have to read the whole thread," she pleaded. "Please."

He frowned. "I don't know, Ange."

She pressed her lips together. "This will drive me crazy if I don't hash the whole thing out with you. Once you read the thread and I get this out of my system, I won't ask again."

Sawyer took the phone and read Angela's most recent messages after those asking for a good time to connect.

Can you call me when you have a chance? Today was a lot.

The time stamps on the two messages were about an hour apart. Sawyer pinpointed them as having been sent after he had deposited her safely in her suite following Jared's briefing. He hadn't asked her if she wanted to talk. He should have.

Sawyer gave her a quick side glance. "You said yesterday was 'a lot'? That's a bit of an understatement."

"I already explained how Paul and I are. Besides—" She gestured to her phone. "I'm not interested in what I said. I want your thoughts on what *he* said. Scroll up."

Sawyer returned his attention to her phone and scrolled for a moment but paused. "Did you touch base with your mother about what happened?"

"Not in a million years would I bring that up to her. Someone else will tell her."

"But it's not going to be you?" he laughed.

"No way, it's not going to be me. Someone else."

That someone would most likely be Boss Man—if he hadn't already, which might relate to his radio silence. Sawyer turned the possibilities over and watched Angela to see if she had made that connection.

"We can figure my mother out later. Can we focus on this first?"

If she'd connected Jared's absence with telling her mother, Angela wasn't sharing. He returned his attention to Paul's messages.

Babe. What would you think about coming home?

Babe? You never got back to me.

I think you should come home.

Move home.

Babe?

We're all busy, Angela. The Senator agrees with me. You should come home.

I need you to call.

Angela. Pick up the phone.

Never mind, babe. We'll talk this out very soon.

Sawyer smirked. "Babe?"

Angela mirrored his smirk. "I hate that." Her lips pressed together. "Luckily, I don't have to hear it very often."

"You should tell him that."

She shrugged as though she didn't want to invest the effort. "What do you think about his messages?"

When she'd mentioned several messages, this sort of thread wasn't what Sawyer had envisioned. "The messages are… a little pushy. Especially when you said you'd call him later in the week."

Angela nodded. "It's also out of character."

All right. He could now understand why she wanted an opinion on Paul's messages. "Are you thinking about going home?"

"*This* is home."

He'd never thought about her leaving. Joining Titan felt like Titan for life. Once you were in, you didn't walk away. "You like working here, right?"

She stared as though he'd sprouted a third arm and another head. "Of course I do. I'm not going anywhere, Sawyer."

He chewed the inside of his cheek. "You might want to when the trial is over with." Things might change once Pham was in prison for the rest of his life and no longer a threat to Angela. Jared had built the ACES team to function together in perpetuity, and Angela, in her administrative position, was part of that team. They worked together seamlessly. But she arrived because of trauma and danger. "Your family's back home." He lifted her cell phone and handed it back to her. "Your boyfriend is seven thousand miles away."

"Boyfriend?" She took a deep breath and let it out slowly. "We write subject lines in our text messages, and he calls my mom *the Senator*."

"That's a little kinky—"

Angela smacked his arm. "We're having a serious conversation, Sawyer."

"Right, right. Okay, so *the Senator*? That's weird, but ya know…" Sawyer shrugged. "Respectful?"

"We've been dating for the greater part of the last decade. He can call her Samantha."

Sawyer laughed. "Apparently, I don't know that he can."

"Maybe he could try calling her Sam?" Angela suggested, stifling a laugh. "Mom?"

"Do you even call her Mom? *The Senator* doesn't seem very mom-like."

Angela smacked his arm again. "Don't call her that."

"I'm sure not going to call her Mom, *babe*."

She shook his arm. "Seriously, Sawyer. He wants me to come home—why? I have no idea."

"Because he misses you?"

Her nose wrinkled. "I already told you. That's not why." Angela hummed. "I bet there's a fundraiser or a television commercial for her campaign. Why else would he ask me to come home? It's really freaking me out."

"I don't know."

"And then," she continued, ignoring him, "when I need to talk about this huge thing, he's not to be found." She threw her phone into her purse. "You know what I think? I think his life revolves around *the Senator* more than—"

"You?" Sawyer asked.

"No!" But her recoil softened into agreement. "Yes? Maybe? I don't know." She buried her face in her hands.

For one gut-wrenching moment, Sawyer feared she would cry over Paul. He wanted to knock the guy into orbit for making her cry as much as he wished Paul didn't exist in the first place.

Angela picked her head up. Her face didn't show tears. Just pure frustration. "You know what?" she whispered. "I don't want his life revolving around me. Maybe he can just..." She bit her bottom lip again. "...not revolve around me. More like sort of near me? Or something."

Sawyer leaned back. He rolled his lips together, not knowing how to feel.

"Say something, Sawyer."

He didn't need to. She already knew but needed to hear someone say it out loud. Sawyer didn't know why he was that someone. The messages were manic, but her thoughts were easy to decipher. Chelsea, Jane, or Amanda could've handled this in their sleep. "You and Paul need to have a serious conversation about many things. That's my take from your texts."

Angela's lips pressed together again. "No."

Perhaps this was why they'd never had much of a Paul discussion. Finally, Sawyer asked, "Why wouldn't you tell him how you feel?"

Her gaze dropped to the floor. "I just wanted you to translate. Guy speak and all that."

"Angela... that's not guy speak. He wants you to come home, and you think it's for your mother's political campaign. That's..." He raised a shoulder. "Something you need to think about."

Her chin dropped. Angela's mood shifted, melancholy and miserable. She trained her eyes on the lobby floor as though it might hold the answers she was looking for. "He missed my birthday," she said.

His stomach dropped. Had Sawyer missed her birthday too? No, her birthday was in a couple of months. The team had celebrated in one of the hotel's fancy restaurants that the guys never wanted to go to but women and wives all but demanded to visit. Champagne in crystal flutes and meals that arrived in installments called plates weren't his cup of tea, but he had been there and didn't call any attention to his decision to go out for greasy burgers with Shah and Camden after that fancy meal.

"Actually"—she rolled her lips together—"he's never remembered my birthday. Not while I've been out here and not before I was abducted."

Sawyer grimaced. He hated the role of defending Paul. But he couldn't let her think the guy didn't care based solely on missed celebrations. "Some guys forget birthdays. Holidays. That kind of stuff."

Her eyes narrowed. "He never forgets a political event where he wants me by his side." Angela sucked her cheeks in, and whatever fight she had retreated with a deflated sigh. "It feels as though he wants to date Senator Sorenson's daughter, but not me."

Whoa boy. Every time Sawyer thought he had a handle on this conversation, he was dumped on his ass.

Angela turned to him, head tilted, needing someone to promise that all would be okay. She needed her boyfriend's attention. She needed to feel important.

Sawyer squeezed her shoulder and offered the best he could give. "Paul's an idiot, all right. He sounds self-centered, but, I don't know, also obtuse? He's been with you this long..." He scrunched his shoulders and didn't know what to say. "If he wanted to date the daughter of someone important, there are easier ways to do that." Given her expression, his best two cents weren't doing much to alleviate her concerns. "Am I making any sense?"

"Sure," she said unconvincingly.

He blew out a long breath. The advice she wanted to hear and the advice she needed to hear were so far apart they might have been split by the same distance as Angela and Paul. "Give me your eyes for a second."

Her chin rose before she lifted her gaze. Her eyes were more watery than he wanted to see. Despite the threat of tears, Sawyer saw trust. Just like she'd said repeatedly, she trusted him, and it was evident. He'd earned it, starting on the day she arrived in Abu Dhabi. The threats were real and deadly and far closer than anyone realized. But keeping her safe could have many meanings. Right now, it meant answering her questions and guarding her heart. "The real question, Ange, is this: Do you want to be with him?"

CHAPTER FOUR

ANGELA HAD ASKED herself that question more times than she could count. But there was a better question that Sawyer wouldn't have known to ask: was Angela actually dating Paul?

The answer was convoluted. Technically, yes. They were dating. But in name only. They hadn't been intimate in years, nor had they regularly been on the same continent. She supposed they were occasionally confidants, but they hadn't been yesterday when she wanted to process the shooting.

"I haven't mentioned Paul to you very much." Angela bit her lip. "There hasn't been much to say." There had been plenty of opportunities to mention her relationship problems and get Sawyer's advice. It wasn't that she shied away from the conversation—more like she never thought about Paul.

"That wasn't what I asked you." His intense iceberg-blue eyes locked onto her, patient but persistent, refusing to yield the conversation in another direction. He'd wait her out all day, but Angela didn't have the strength to admit every problem in her relationship. If she did, Sawyer might not look at her the same way again, which would cut deeper than any slight from Paul.

"Do you want to be with him?" Sawyer pressed though he shrugged nonchalantly. "You've almost said as much that it seems like an easy answer."

"Relationships are never easy." She offered a fake smile that Sawyer didn't seem to notice. "Nothing is as simple as yes or no. It's not black and white."

"You two have been together long enough to know if you want to do it for the long haul." He studied her in a way that seemed to read her mind and search her heart. "The Angela who I know isn't indecisive."

"I—" Her throat ached. *I... never thought about Paul. Don't want to rock the boat. Avoid upsetting my mother.* Breaking up with Paul would do those things. "I don't know."

"Sure you do."

Sawyer wasn't wrong. She and Paul had grown apart. They didn't have a spark. She'd grown up. Her interests had changed. Angela was never lonely. Titan kept her busy. The last few years of keeping her head down and processing the years she'd been Pham's hostage had siphoned any thoughts of romance or longing. She was content with her personal relationships. Paul wasn't a part of her life and didn't try to be included.

The front desk bell chimed three times, a code for an incoming VIP arrival. The crystal-clear call resonated through the lobby and beckoned bellhops, breaking the question-induced freeze that had stolen her words.

Two bellhops rushed across the lobby. The call bell rang again, three times. Angela straightened. A second call was never needed. Staff appeared out of nowhere. Security stood taller. The atmosphere shifted. Her skin prickled. "I wasn't aware of any VIP arrivals today." Angela glanced at Sawyer, sure he could sense it too. "You?"

"Nope." His gaze tracked from the bellhops to the reception desk to the gold-accented bulletproof glass doors. "Hang tight a second. I'll find out what's happening."

Sawyer motioned for her to stay. She ignored the request, stood, and followed. They walked along the window wall that overlooked the entryway.

A black Suburban sped into the hotel's main drive. Sawyer waved Angela back, but she moved to his side. The vehicle stopped as if the driver owned the place—her stomach catapulted—because he did own the place.

"Boss Man's here," Sawyer said.

Her heart tangled with the knot in her throat. "Where the hell has he been?"

Valets and bellhops rushed to the vehicle in a way that was less like the expected speedy service and more hustle-and-go. Neither he nor Angela had a visual confirmation yet, but Sawyer was correct. Jared Westin's own-the-world attitude made her feel safe. Usually. At that moment, her gut screamed there was a problem. That wasn't how Jared made an entrance, especially after he'd been MIA for hours. "Something's wrong, Sawyer."

Sawyer's stance changed. He stood taller, broader, tensing on high alert. "Not necessarily."

"You don't sound very convincing."

He didn't try to change her mind.

They waited. Jared didn't materialize. Anxiety crackled down her spine. "Do you see him?" Angela stepped to the side. "The landscaping is blocking my view."

Sawyer held out his hand again to caution her. "Hang tight, Ange."

She stepped closer to his side, partly shielded from whatever loomed inside the blacked-out SUV. Angela couldn't discern movement beyond the valets unloading bags. "Jared wouldn't have luggage."

The bellhops and valets blocked the view as the passengers exited. Their group moved toward the lobby doors.

She wasn't at the correct angle to see anyone. "Scoot over."

Sawyer ignored her elbow and didn't budge. Angela leaned against him.

The group bypassed the reception desk. It had to be Jared. He had to have been meeting about the assassination attempt. Perhaps he'd been involved in the interrogation. But that didn't explain his flashy entrance or the dread cementing her in place.

The bellhops split away from the group and unblocked Angela's line of sight. Boss Man powered toward the elevators. His purposeful stride covered the floor like an alpha wolf leading a bloodthirsty pack.

Then she saw them. "Oh God." Her stomach bottomed out. "No. This can't be happening."

Two men Angela had known most of her life tried to keep pace with Jared's angry march. "They want to turn yesterday into a political talking point."

Sawyer glanced down. "What?"

She slunk back and considered hiding behind an oversized plant, but before she could, life sucker punched her again. Angela swayed. Sawyer's steadying hand rested against her back, and then he followed her gaze to her mother and Paul, who trailed several paces behind the other men.

The entourage would see her at any moment. There was nowhere to hide.

Jared saw them but didn't slow the procession. "My office. Now."

Still struggling to keep pace, the two men inclined their heads in greeting as they passed.

"This is very bad," she whispered, unable to look away from her mother's approach. "Very, very bad."

Her mother, the Senator, always looked the same. It was part of her persona, along with her crisp power suit, coordinating accessories, and coiffed hair dyed the same color it had been the first year she was elected to office. Mother had always said she needed to match the image voters had in their minds, that in the court of public opinion, women weren't allowed to age as gracefully as their male counterparts, that life wasn't fair, but she wasn't in the position to act on any of her feminist principles because she was busy enacting laws for the greater good.

Her mother breezed by, offering, "Angela," by way of greeting.

Paul smiled but remained silent. He didn't break from the group or greet Angela or explain why on Earth he was in Abu Dhabi. He had to know that one of Pham's lackeys had tried to kill her, and yet, Paul didn't step from the group to ask how she was. Paul didn't care—and she didn't care if he did or not. Her shock had morphed into grade-A, top-shelf anger.

Sawyer checked the lobby for anyone else struggling to keep up with Jared's posse. "What in the hell is happening?"

The small distance between her and Sawyer was too much. She was alone in a way that she couldn't explain, drowning and suffocating in the middle of Titan's hotel lobby. Angela needed to sidle against Sawyer. She needed his protective hand on her back and calm promises that everything would be okay. But all she could do was watch the entourage board an elevator.

The elevator doors finally closed. Angela released her breath.

"Are you okay?"

She shook her head. "I can't do this. I don't even know what they want, but I can't."

"All right. Take a minute." Sawyer guided her to the alcove again. "They're not monsters. They're family."

"There's some overlap in my family's Venn diagram." Her pulse raced as fast as her thoughts. "Whatever they want, it's something they decided to blindside me with."

He pulled her onto the couch. "Jared's not going to blindside you—"

She grabbed onto his arm. "Jared has been MIA all day and has probably been trying to head off whatever is about to happen."

Sawyer covered her hand, which had a death grip on his forearm. "You don't have to worry—there'll be an explanation."

"An explanation won't make this situation okay."

He pursed his lips and glanced toward the elevators as though he might be able to make sense of the last two minutes. Finally, he shook his head and said, "I don't know what's happening, but Boss Man doesn't look happy. He'll deal with it—"

"Whatever it is, they're here for work. Not for me." She dropped her head against his bicep and groaned. "Nothing good is about to happen."

He draped his arm over her shoulders and squeezed. "There's no point in getting upset before we have the slightest clue about what's happening."

Her eyes pinched shut. "I know enough."

Sawyer patted her back. "Well, I know that Jared's mad enough to piss lava."

She couldn't help but laugh. For the first time in what seemed like hours, Angela grinned. "He did kind of look that way, huh?"

"Yup, and they didn't look smart enough to know they were in trouble. Who were the guys behind Jared?"

"My mom's campaign manager and her political consultant."

"Ah…" Sawyer said, sounding as though he had a more nuanced understanding. Then his forehead tightened. "How long does it take to get out here?" He knew what she knew. The departure location and aircraft were the main variables. For a moment, Angela ran calculations in her head and saw Sawyer do the same.

"Huh." His eyebrows arched. "That's some amazingly shitty timing for a surprise visit, or they gathered their posse and jumped on a private jet pretty quickly."

Her phone pinged. Angela pulled it out and held it so Sawyer could see the sender's notification. "Another text from Paul."

"At least he's texting you again," Sawyer muttered.

She snorted and then opened the message.

What's your ETA?

Sawyer inhaled deeply then let out the breath as if trying to remain calm. After a moment, he laughed.

She tipped her head back to see his face. "What?"

"He's a little off-brand right now, isn't he?"

Her eyebrow arched.

"Shouldn't it read something like, 'What's your ETA, babe?'"

A smile crept onto her face.

"Babe," Sawyer teased.

"I don't even know when he started calling me that." Angela elbowed him. "It's not like he thinks I'm a babe."

Sawyer gestured to the phone. "Obviously, he does."

She rolled her eyes. "Maybe he means it like Babe Ruth? Did they call him in during the clutch or something?"

He laughed. "What, like you're a pinch-hitting girlfriend?"

Angela's eyes widened. "Oh my God, I am." She tipped her head back. "That makes so much sense."

"No, it doesn't. You're nuts. That's what you are, *babe.*"

Laughter was the best medicine. Everything was wrong with her world, but at least Sawyer could make her smile. Angela stood and pulled his arm. "Come on. If I'm going into the lion's den, so are you."

CHAPTER FIVE

THE WAR-ROOM DOOR was a simple conference-room door. Angela had bustled in and out of it a hundred times without thinking. She wasn't a team leader and had never gone into the field for military operations, but this conference room was her domain. However, now she was stuck outside of it, high heels cemented to the carpet.

A headache that she didn't want to confront waited on the other side of the door. Sawyer patiently waited behind her. She wasn't sure she could walk in if he weren't her backup.

Then again, Jared wouldn't let anything happen to her. She'd always done a good job as an administrator for the ACES team. Her position went beyond the secretarial role he'd probably envisioned—a job only offered to her out of pity. But she'd surpassed everyone's expectations, including her own.

Angela handled the normal ho-hum business of paperwork but also scheduled private jets, coordinated safe houses, and arranged for aliases. She shopped for supplies for undercover assignments and managed an assembly of clandestine players and surreptitious clients.

She loved her job.

She was good at it.

But she was never the topic of conversation. That would change when she walked into the war room.

There were three roles Angela could play: Jared Westin's assistant, Senator Sorenson's daughter, and Paul Bane's girlfriend. Each one had expectations heavy enough to drown a whale.

"Don't let 'em scare you," Sawyer said under his breath, tacking on, "*Babe.*"

The corners of her mouth quirked. "Funny, I don't want to throat-punch you when you say that."

"It's all about the delivery." He turned her around and squeezed her shoulder. "You got this, Ange." Then Sawyer stepped back for her to make an entrance. "Head up. Shoulders back. *You've got this.*"

Her hotter-than-the-Sahara bodyguard was giving her a pep talk to face her in-name-only boyfriend. Nothing weird about that...

She glanced over her shoulder. Sawyer winked. Her stomach and confidence jumped. That was what she needed. Her head was up. Shoulders back. Angela channeled the person Sawyer believed she was and grinned. "Here goes nothing."

She opened the door and paused to take in the players.

If Angela considered the total length of time she had known each of them, her mother had the most claim to her, but Angela wasn't often her mother's top priority. Their relationship was practical, though not without their version of love.

Paul had been in Angela's life since she was a hospitality major in college. They'd met when he'd interned in her mother's senate office. He had remained committed to Angela throughout her ordeal with Pham, apparently never losing hope that she'd be found someday. She was. He seemed glad. Their relationship had never been a torrid love affair, but did those things really exist?

How did Jared see Angela? He had the slightest claim on her yet the strongest gravitational pull in the war room. He and his Abu Dhabi-based team had her loyalty. They'd rescued her from Pham. Boss Man provided her with a job in a secure location and the ability to control the minutiae around her. But she never forgot that she hadn't earned the position in Titan. Someone gave it to her because of her last name.

Jared sat at the head of the table. Her mother and Paul sat on one side. Rich and Rob, the campaign manager and political consultant, sat on the other. The imposing table had never seemed to unnerve Angela before now.

Sawyer followed her into the war room.

Her mother eyed him. "We don't need anyone else but Angela."

Sawyer didn't hesitate as he proceeded next to Rich. "Given that Angela mentioned she has no idea what's going on"—he looked to Jared—"I'll defer to my boss."

"Sit." Jared gestured to the seat Sawyer was about to take.

Nervousness masked, Angela sat next to Paul and across from Sawyer. Her boyfriend seemed like an old acquaintance, neither friendly nor comfortable, more like the landscape on a road she'd driven a hundred times.

She took a pen and small notebook from her bag as she would have if called into a meeting with any other client. She waited, poised to take notes or handle anything Jared asked of her.

"Good to see you, Angela," her mother said.

Angela's grip tightened on the pen, but she painted an acceptable expression on her face. "It's a surprise."

"It is," her mother agreed. "You know how trips like these are. Under the radar."

Angela demurred and refocused on Jared.

Paul sighed as if he were a petulant child not given attention. "If you had responded to my texts, you wouldn't be completely in the dark."

Annoyance rocketed up her neck. Angela pressed her lips together, wondering if now was an appropriate time to mention the text messages from her that he had missed. Instead, she kept her eyes on Boss Man.

Tension ticked in Jared's jaw. Irritated lines etched over his darkening expression. "Give me a break, Paul." Jared snorted. "No bullshit in my war room. You understand me?"

Her pulse thumped in her ears. Angela's gaze skipped from Jared to Sawyer then back to Jared again.

Her mother cleared her throat. The gold bracelets on her wrist clinked. "I'd suggest business first. Then, Angela, you and Paul can discuss personal details afterward."

Jared's scowl deepened. "Samantha," he growled, "I do not have time for this bullshit."

"So you keep saying," her mother returned. "If we did this my way—"

"Your way," Jared fumed, "nearly killed my people."

"I wouldn't call Angela your people."

The blood drained from Angela's face. Her veneer threatened to crumble. She focused on Jared and ignored the hurt that sliced into her chest as though her mother had thrown a ninja star with surgical precision.

"First." Boss Man's quiet voice reached a deadly baritone that rumbled like thunder across the war room. "You don't know your ass from your elbow when it comes to my team." He squeezed his right fist with his left hand, and the knuckles cracked. "Second. You don't know your ass from your elbow when it comes to your daughter."

Watery emotion surprised Angela, but she kept her expression cold as untouched gun metal.

"And third, if you ever"—he pushed out of this chair and towered over the table—"and I mean *ever*, Samantha, interfere, involve, or otherwise include yourself in my domain again unless I expressly request it, I will end you."

Mother's bracelets clinked as she shifted. Her iron-clad posture didn't slip, but her silence spoke volumes.

"Are we on the same page, Samantha?"

Angela's mother lightly cleared her throat, pressed her red lips together, and relented. "Fine. You have my word."

Jared turned his attention to Angela and drew a measured breath. Slowly, he let it out as though he were counting to ten. "Angela…"

Panic curled in her gut. Her gaze flicked to Sawyer and then locked back onto Boss Man. She gave him her full, grateful, albeit nervous, attention.

"This foursome"—Jared gestured between Rich and Rob, Paul and her mother—"has been here for a few days."

Angela's jaw dropped. "What?" She pivoted in her chair to stare at her mother and Paul. "And you didn't tell me?" They didn't answer. She turned to Jared. "You knew?"

Boss Man sneered. "That'd be a big, fat negative."

"If you'd answered your text messages," Paul added.

Jared's fist slammed into the heavy wood table and made the quartet jump. The corners of his lips quirked. "Watch yourself, kid."

Kid. The jab had the intended effect. Paul's irritation was palpable and probably close to how she felt about his *babe.*

"They have been here?" Sawyer's anger mirrored Jared's. A tightening fury shifted over his face.

"Yeah," Boss Man confirmed.

Her slow brewing rage shifted from the secret visit to the implications. She looked between Sawyer and Jared and asked, "Did they blow my cover?"

Jared nodded curtly.

She turned to Paul and her mother. "You blew my cover!" The ramifications snowballed. "Someone tried to kill me—Sawyer's life was in danger." Anger skewed her vision. "Because of you two?"

"Babe—"

"Do not," she hissed, "ever call me that again."

Undaunted, Paul reached for her hand. "Angela," he tried.

She smacked his hand away and swung her attention to Rich and Rob. "Why are you here? What do you two need?"

"Well," Rich said, confidence shaken, "we thought we had a few weeks to discuss this with you—"

"Spit it out before I do," Jared warned.

"I'm going to run for president," her mother offered. "And Paul's going to run for my Senate seat."

Angela's jaw dropped. Her mother never wanted to leave the Senate—and Paul? A senator? "What?"

Her mother was unfazed. "It's not unheard of for a chief of staff to step into a senator's—"

"Chief of staff?" Angela jerked to Paul. "Since when?"

He reached for her again. "If you were home—"

"I am trying to stay alive until this stupid trial wraps."

"About that," her mother said.

Angela's heart lurched into her throat. "What?"

"We have a problem with the Pham trial," her mother said with the quick, sharp rip of an unseen metaphorical Band-Aid. "You may have noticed delays in the news."

"I try not to watch the news." The pen in Angela's hand trembled. She let it drop onto the table. "What kind of problem?"

"Pham wants to cut a deal," Paul said. "The Feds are considering it."

Her mind spun. She wanted to testify. She wanted Pham in prison. But the insane part of her cared about the old man who cared—*pretended* to care—for her. He listened. He knew her likes. He spent time with her. He kidnapped her and kept her for years but acted more like family than the two people at her side. "The Feds have to talk to me first. They told me that. They would do nothing unless they talked to me first."

"Well, lucky you, with a mother in high places," Jared muttered.

Her mother snarled at Jared but then softened for Angela. "Dear, look, there's more to it. We can turn this into a good situation."

"Samantha," Jared warned.

"What does 'more to it' mean?" Sawyer asked in a voice that mimicked Jared's. "A good situation?"

Paul and her mother exchanged glances.

"Oh, for fuck's sake." Jared waited then shook his head. "Angela's not going to break. Spit it out."

She wasn't so sure about that. Since the day of her rescue, she'd tried to control every part of her life. "What is it?"

"Pham has offered something too good to ignore," Paul said.

Mother put on a practiced, patient expression. "There might be someone else out there, Angela."

"What does that mean?" she asked.

The gold bracelets clinked. "Like you."

Angela's stomach dropped. "Someone else…" Her throat knotted. "Like me?"

"We don't know for certain," her mother said softly. "Negotiations are ongoing. But Pham says he has another person, and his lawyers are tough negotiators."

Angela faced Sawyer. She wanted to leave the war room and for Sawyer to leave with her. She needed a break. Fresh air. Anything but sitting in here, learning that someone was still going through the hell she had been rescued from.

"You okay?" Sawyer asked.

She shook her head.

"Maybe..." Sawyer looked to Jared. "...You all wrap this up without her."

Jared's jaw flexed. "Give them another minute."

Angela felt her stomach bottom out again. "Oh God. There's more?"

"Actually," Paul said. "Yes, but it's on a brighter note."

Paul's faux chipper tone warned she wouldn't like whatever he said next.

"You can come home. Pham cuts a deal. You won't have to testify." Paul smiled. "We could get married, announce the Senator's presidential run. I'll—"

"Get married?" She jerked back an arm's length from Paul. "Are you insane?"

"A political dynasty in the making," Rob suggested, smiling. "The numbers look great."

"You polled on this already?" she shrieked.

"Angela, would you calm down? You're overreacting," her mother scolded.

"Yes. The numbers look great," Rob continued, apparently unable to read the room. "We tried a couple of different options, different timelines. A few variables: Do you change your last name? How close to the presidential announcement should we have an engagement? Et cetera. Et cetera."

"*We?*" Angela choked over their subversive casualness.

"Enough," Boss Man barked. He pointed at Rich and Rob then hooked his thumb over his shoulder. "Get the hell out of here."

Both men shrank back in their seats and eyed her mother. Angela didn't care who they feared more. She wanted them to disappear. No, she wanted everyone to disappear. None of them seemed to notice how deeply they'd violated her. A deep sound rumbled in Jared's chest. His fist slammed onto the solid wood conference table like Zeus smacking a mountaintop.

The two men jerked to their feet and stumbled over one another on their way out. The conference room door closed with a deafening finality. The air had thinned as though the atmosphere had escaped with the running men.

Jared's dark scrutiny swung to Angela's mother and Paul. A sheepish frown pulled at Paul's features, but her mother didn't flinch.

"The important thing," her mother said without a hint of shame, "is that you'll be safe and at home."

"I'm not getting married!"

Paul looked at her mother and then back at Angela. "Why don't we talk somewhere more private?"

"Good luck with that," Jared muttered.

"They need a moment," her mother reiterated.

Jared dropped his head back with a disappointed shake but then eyed Angela. "What do you want?"

She balked. "A minute in private isn't going to change my mind."

"Five minutes," Paul suggested.

"They can have five minutes," her mother agreed.

Jared waited.

Angela nodded. "But my answer is not changing," she said.

He stood and checked his watch. "Five minutes, the clock starts now." Jared nodded for Sawyer to walk out with him. Begrudgingly, Sawyer moved to Jared's side. "You, too, Samantha. The clock is already ticking."

The corners of Sawyer's tight glare ticked as her mother pushed from the table. Without saying a word, Angela understood the strength he wanted to convey. Whether Sawyer wanted her to use that strength to knock Paul back to the United States or just hold it together during a conversation, she wasn't sure. But his message was loud and clear: he was on her side.

The room emptied, leaving her alone with Paul for the first time in over a year. The man was absolutely insane if he thought they should talk about marriage. Angela crossed her arms over her chest. "Have you lost your mind?"

"Have you?" Paul rolled his chair closer to hers. "This is everything we've planned for."

She shirked. "I never planned any of this."

"We've been together for almost ten years. You're acting like marriage isn't the next step."

"We have been apart most of that time."

"But you're safe now, and we can fix the proximity problem."

"We haven't had sex in the last—"

"Jesus Christ, babe." His cheeks turned pink. "Since when does sex make a relationship? You want to have sex? Let's go have sex."

She threw her hands into the air. "I don't want to have sex."

"I know. It's never been your thing. *I know you.*"

She blanched. "You know me? You don't know me."

"If that's what you want, Angela, that's fine. Tell me what you want, and it's done."

Her mind spiraled. Never her thing? What was his thing? He'd never wanted to flirt and cuddle. He'd never tried or initiated—she usually hadn't either. But *not her thing?*

"Babe—sorry. *Angela.* See. I'm listening, and I'm telling you what I want. That's what we do. I need this. You need that. We operate as a team." He looked at her funny. "I thought that we'd be on the same page."

The only thing she recalled him asking for was scheduling appearances. A headache punched behind her eyes. Paul didn't want her. He wanted access to her mother. Was that what he always wanted? She knew that. She'd just told that to Sawyer. But hearing it out loud, sounding as cold and lifeless as a stock report, was sickening.

Her stomach dropped. Did he ever want her—or had he always seen her as a means to an end? "What did you mean by 'that's never seemed like my thing'?"

Paul faltered, and his blush returned. "We all have our things."

Her brow furrowed. "What are your things?"

"I mean, damn, babe—"

"Stop calling me that."

"Damn, *Angela*, I'm trying," he snapped. "You're getting a little personal."

"Paul, you just asked me to marry you. That's about as personal as it gets."

"We're a team. I asked you to continue our partnership."

She pressed her fingers to her temples and wanted to curl up in her chair and disappear. "Oh my God."

"Angela, if sex is important to you—"

"Is it important to you?" she hissed.

He blinked as if seeing her for the first time. "Yeah…"

"With *me*?"

He didn't answer.

"Oh my God," she repeated, shaking her head. "You need to leave."

Paul ran a hand over his face. "This isn't going the way I thought it would."

"Leave."

He stood, towering over her, and rested his hands on her shoulders. The inauthentic touch was repellent.

His audacity fueled a fury in her veins. "Do not touch me."

"Fine." Paul crouched in front of her. "Look, Angela, from day one, I thought, I don't know. You and I were a team. We had the same end goal."

She smirked. "And here I thought I was your girlfriend."

"Now you can be my wife." He smiled and squeezed her knee but saw the gesture hadn't landed like he'd hoped. "We'll have sex."

Her stomach roiled. "You're going to say whatever it takes to get me to say yes, aren't you?"

Paul stood up and paced. "I didn't think I had to sell you on this." He scrubbed his hands over his face and returned to his chair again. Upon regaining his composure, he scooted in front of her once more. "I didn't think we had a romantic relationship. I thought we had a pragmatic one."

Her eyebrows rose.

"You never complained," he pointed out.

"I wasn't around to file grievances," she countered.

"But when you were around…" He crossed his arms, deciding to change tactics. "I'm going to be completely honest, okay?"

She lifted her hands in exasperation. "Yeah. Spit it out, Paul."

"I didn't think you were that into, I don't know…" He had the good sense to appear sheepish. "Doing it."

Angela blinked, unsure what to say.

"Like," Paul continued, "you know how some women are, hell, I don't know what it's called." He rubbed the back of his neck. "Frigid?"

Her jaw fell open.

He gestured toward her. "I thought maybe… that was you."

"Maybe it's you," she snapped.

"Babe—"

"For God's sake, stop calling me that—do you even find me attractive?"

"Of course I do. You're an attractive woman. We make an attractive couple."

How much of that attraction was her mother's Senate seat? They could be an attractive couple printed on campaign mailers and sitting on the steps of an attractive house in a campaign commercial. Angela grabbed her purse and breezed by Paul at the table. "I hope you didn't buy a ring. We're through."

CHAPTER SIX

S AWYER DIDN'T DO politics. He didn't care for the gamesmanship and relentless twenty-four-hour news cycles, and he couldn't imagine what growing up might have been like in the Sorenson household, the inhabitants of which valued victory and power over anything else.

To Angela's credit, Sawyer had never seen in her a shred of the manipulative, combative woman that he knew of her mother. Angela didn't hunger for the limelight or grandiose titles. He couldn't imagine Angela marrying someone for politics. He couldn't imagine her doing anything that wasn't genuine.

Then again, she thrived on controlling her surroundings. He'd always believed that was because of what had happened to her with Pham. An arranged, low-contact marriage, one even suggested out of the blue, might be more of what she wanted.

"Stop fidgeting," Jared ordered from the other side of his oversized desk. "She's not marrying that fuckwad."

The two men were alone, having deposited the Senator and her political staff in an adjacent conference room. Sawyer blew out his cheeks and tried to relax. "The office would be weird if she left."

"She's not leaving."

Boss Man's confidence did little to ease the gnawing tension in Sawyer's chest. Angela made the place run like a well-oiled machine. She'd come into their group as a woman who needed space and as a witness who needed security. She was far more than a capable administrator. She'd become Titan.

Sawyer wondered if she knew that.

He studied Jared's office. Angela had hung his accommodations and awards on the walls. When Jared had thrown a fit, she'd laughed. It was, she said, as if he wanted people to think he had been conjured out of nowhere or was maybe a machine built for special operations.

"What are your parents like?" he asked Boss Man.

Jared snorted. "Nothing like Samantha Sorenson." He cracked his knuckles. "The Senator is a helluva person to have on your side, but I wouldn't call her maternal."

"What about Angela's dad?"

"Never met him. Lobbyist, I think. He does his thing. She does hers." Jared shrugged. "Again, nothing like my folks."

"That's pretty generic," Sawyer pushed.

Jared's eyebrows inched up. "You want me to ask questions about your loved ones?"

Sawyer drew a quick breath. "Not particularly."

But Jared leaned back in his chair and flashed the slightest smile. "My folks. There were times when they literally held each other up. Good people. Salt-of-the-earth-type people."

"My parents, too. Nothing like the Sorensons." At one time, Sawyer knew what type of family he wanted. It had looked a lot like how he'd been raised. Loving parents. Happy childhood. But he didn't want to think about that. "You've known the Senator for a while?"

Jared nodded.

"Did you know Angela?"

"Not until we rescued her and Chelsea."

"I bet the Sorenson household was a weird place for a kid."

Boss Man nodded. "Angela grew up adjacent to the watchful eye of her mother's protective detail. There was never any need to put Angela in her own protective detail. At least that's what they thought."

Congressional families didn't receive security unless there was a threat. Then Sawyer realized that the Sorenson gaggle was missing people. "Where is Sorenson's security detail anyway?"

"Haven't seen much of them." Jared shook his head. "I think this political stunt was very much under the radar."

Someone rapped on the door. Sawyer jumped as though he'd been caught gossiping. Angela walked in, expression unreadable, as if he and Jared weren't waiting for her personal family drama to wrap. "I'm sorry that took so long."

Boss Man glanced at his watch. "It's been less than ten minutes."

She lifted her shoulders. "You gave us a countdown clock of five minutes." Angela sat in the chair next to Sawyer. "Can we talk?"

"Sure," Jared said.

Sawyer stood. "I'll let you—"

"No." She waved him back into his chair. "I'd like to talk to both of you."

Shit. Worry pooled in the pit of his stomach. Sawyer glanced from her to Jared then reclaimed his chair. Anxiety needled through his veins. If Angela bailed on Titan to marry Paul... She wouldn't. Would she? No... Still, nervous energy rioted in his chest like his heart wanted to escape into his throat.

Angela smoothed a hand over her skirt and took a long breath. "I want to know the details of Pham's negotiations."

That was not what Sawyer thought she would say. His eyes darted from Angela to Jared.

"We can get you that." Jared rested his elbows on his desk and laced his fingers. "What else?"

Sawyer repositioned himself on the stuffy office chair. He wanted Angela to discuss the more important topics of marriage and leaving Titan.

"If there's someone else kept captive like me..." She rolled her lips together and inhaled slowly through her nose like she didn't want to get sick. "If Pham has someone else out there, I want to help find her."

"We don't know the person's a woman," Jared pointed out, not addressing her request.

"She's a woman. Everyone beside me was tortured and killed. If Pham kept her, she's a woman." Angela paused. "Just like his daughter."

All the FBI profilers in the world couldn't have an inside track on Tran Pham like Angela did. But Sawyer wasn't sure that she was correct. "Pham's done a lot of harm to a lot of people, men and women."

Jared nodded and leaned back in his chair. "You can't discount that this could all be bullshit. Delay tactics until they find you."

Her lips pressed into a thin, angry line. "Well, my mother helped Pham with that one."

Sawyer's molars ground. Endangering Angela's life, trying to marry her off for political clout? That mother-daughter relationship was one he couldn't fathom.

"Speaking of her and"—Jared thumbed toward the office wall—"her entourage…"

This was what Sawyer needed to talk about. His stomach turned. Angela wouldn't marry Paul. She couldn't. Sawyer was just asking her if she wanted to date the guy. Now marriage was on the table?

"Am I gonna hear wedding bells anytime soon?" Jared asked.

"No." Irritation furrowed in her brow. "Absolutely not."

Relief spread through Sawyer's chest. Of course she wouldn't do it. But the idea that she might, that there was even the slightest chance she would cut bait and head to the US, was too much.

Jared chuckled as though the proposal were low-key comedy. "How'd the kid take it?"

Sawyer ran a hand through his hair. Thank God for Boss Man asking the questions. He didn't trust himself to remain as calm as Jared.

"For starters, we're not together anymore."

Another flood of relief calmed Sawyer's nerves. The corners of his mouth lifted. This was great. She didn't need that kind of man dragging her down.

"Paul can hash out a new political strategy with my mom. I want nothing to do with it."

"All right, then." Boss Man grinned. "Shall I send them packing?"

"I already said goodbye. They should be on their way out if not gone already."

"All right, then." Jared rubbed his hands together. "Let's see what we can learn about Pham." He reached for the phone. "Parker's been working his contacts since about an hour before we arrived at the hotel."

Her eyebrows rose. "He had been trying to find you."

"As had everyone else. I needed time to figure out what your mother was up to."

"How did you know?" she asked.

"Very few options made sense after you were attacked." Then, into the phone, he said, "Hey, Parker. "Got anything good yet?" A moment later, "Hang on." Jared put Parker on the speakerphone. "Sawyer and Angela are here."

Greetings were exchanged. Parker began, "We've got a lot of unsubstantiated hot air."

Angela retrieved a notepad and pen from her purse. "Sounds like Washington, DC."

Parker continued, "Pham's attorneys are negotiating for something analogous to a political prison exchange. He shares where the person is, and then he returns home."

Sawyer glanced at Angela. "As in no jail time?"

"None other than time served," Parker confirmed. "That's what they're asking for."

"*No.*" She looked from Jared to Sawyer and then leaned toward the phone. "Absolutely not."

"I'm just the messenger," Parker said. A keyboard clicked in the background. "Regardless of negotiations, the Feds are investigating. Their working theory is—if someone's still out there—that person worked the military operation where his daughter died."

"So not like me," Angela added quietly.

"They wouldn't rule that out. I don't think they know much," Parker replied.

Jared rubbed his temples. "Anything else?"

"If there is, they're not letting me know."

Parker had more connections and ways of discovering information than almost anyone. "Do you think your mom knows more?"

"Maybe." Angela bit her lip. "She's power-hungry, but she doesn't want me dead. She wouldn't have concocted this marry-Paul scheme if she thought I would come home and Pham was still a threat."

"She came out here and put a bull's-eye on you," Sawyer pointed out.

"True…" Angela considered for a moment. "She might know more and isn't telling. She always holds her cards close to her chest."

Jared grabbed his cell phone and pressed it to his ear. "Samantha, have you left?"

Sawyer glanced at Angela's unreadable face. Was she upset about Paul? The faux marriage proposal had blindsided her, but she hadn't answered his question about wanting to date Paul.

"Leave the bozos and meet us back in the war room." Jared tossed his phone onto the desk. "Parker, get patched into the war room, and let's get everything on the table."

Angela faltered. "I'll stay here."

"Yeah, that's not gonna work." Jared beckoned her out of the chair. "Get up."

"I already said my goodbye."

"And then you marched in here and told me you wanted to help find the woman. This is how you're going to do that."

Angela glanced Sawyer's way.

"I'm with Boss Man." Sawyer held out his hand. "You can do this."

Her wheels turned as her frown deepened.

"Don't leave me hanging, Ange."

Angela squeezed her eyes shut and then relented. Her hand met his. "Only because I trust you guys."

CHAPTER SEVEN

A NGELA SMOOTHED HER pencil skirt and tucked her purse under her arm as if the bag were an armored shield that could repel her mother's disdain and disappointment. Jared was correct; they needed to pick her brain and discover the details that only she would know. Angela's heartbeat quickened. She glanced over her shoulder. Sawyer and Jared were waiting for her to make the first move. Jared wore his usual scowl, but she couldn't read Sawyer's expression.

"If she says something that upsets you," Sawyer said, "Boss Man can send her packing again."

Jared chuckled. "You got that right."

Angela forced herself to stand taller. With two of the strongest men she knew at her back, she led the way to the war room.

They rounded a corner and saw her mother, who had mastered the power walk after years of scuttling around the Capitol. Angela didn't have that kind of strut, but she wasn't demure.

She opened the door and first let Sawyer and Jared into the war room. Her mom held back, eyeing Angela. "I'm glad you caught me when you did."

"I bet." Because her mother would have hauled herself back home without so much as a hug goodbye. "You should have called."

"Paul reached out."

"You're my mother."

"And Paul?"

Angela held firm under the scrutinizing glance. "I guess he's your chief of staff."

They glared for an extra moment, but the slightest hint of a smile surfaced on her mother's face. She wasn't an awful mother. More like a power-grabbing politico who held a tinted view of what was best for their family. "Despite everything, you're looking well."

Angela almost smiled, gestured for her mother to enter the conference room, and shut the door after she walked in. Jared reigned over the war-room table with Sawyer at his side.

Parker waited on screen as her mother took the seat she'd occupied earlier. "Good afternoon, Senator," he said.

"It's nice to see you again, Parker."

He smiled as if to say "bullshit" but minded his manners.

Angela sat next to her mother, took out her notepad, and tried to pretend this event was an ordinary meeting as Parker recapped their recent discussion in Jared's office.

When Parker was finished, Jared leaned forward, a hand cupped around his fist and a don't-bullshit-me bluster darkening his scowl. He fixed his attention on her mother with a laser focus. "All that's to say, Samantha, you know more than you're letting on."

"Do I?"

"Spit it out."

Her mom focused on Angela. "Honey, I'm trying to do what's best for the both of us."

Angela cleared her throat. "That's not what we're here to discuss."

"Samantha," Jared groused, "move on."

Her gold bracelets jangled. "If we make an exchange with Pham, this chapter of Angela's life will be over. No testifying. No threats on her life. It will be done."

"Mother—"

"And we'll accomplish your goal," her mother added. "We'll have rescued someone else who might still be in the same predicament you lived through, Angela." She faced Jared. "I think we can all agree that's a win-win."

Jared's frown lines deepened. "This isn't one of your political negotiations."

"Pham needs to go to prison," Angela spat out. "Don't you get that?"

But even as she said that, waves of shame at her hypocrisy rolled through her chest. If only Ibrahim would give her a magic cure to wash away her lingering empathy for her abductor.

"Angela, dear…"

"Stop that." She hated the patronizing way her mother could say her name. "He *needs to* go to prison. If not for me, for all the people and families he hurt." Her lips pursed, and she smirked. "That would make one hell of a press release and photo op for you to capitalize on."

"Watch yourself, young lady."

Angela jutted her chin out. "If not for me, then to send a message to other terrorists. Mess with you, get prison time. Rich and Rob could make posters and T-shirts."

The gold bracelets clinked again. Her mother wanted the debate. Angela could see it in her eyes, along with the deepening frown that she held back. "What you're asking for only makes sense in an ideal world, and we don't live in one of those." Her frown deepened further. "Believe it or not, I'm looking out for your best interest."

"You're so invested in yourself that you can't see where our interests intersect and diverge."

"That's not fair, Angela."

"We don't live in a fair world, Mom." Angela turned to Parker. "If there's someone else out there, can we find them without Pham's assistance?"

Parker's dark brows furrowed. He took off his glasses and rubbed the bridge of his nose. After considering, he searched for an answer before saying, "That's a tough one."

Jared's lips pursed, apparently in thought. "We don't know a who, where, when…" He glanced at Parker. "Do I have that correct?"

"If they exist at all…" Parker suggested.

"But if we did," Angela pressed, "we could find them and kill the trial negotiations."

Sawyer looked from her to Parker and Boss Man. "I mean, that's what Titan does. Find people. Manage situations. More or less."

Her heart squeezed. *Thank you, Sawyer.* "We could do so much more if we had more information." Angela turned pointedly to her mother. "Which we could probably get."

"That doesn't keep you safe," her mother pointed out. "I might have an agenda, but I don't want Pham to hurt you again."

"You did blow her cover, Samantha," Jared growled.

"I had a plan," her mother snapped.

"Stop." Angela waved her hand at them. "Can anyone tell me if I'm safe *here*?"

Sawyer crossed his arms. "I won't let anyone get that close to you again."

He couldn't blame himself. They had no idea she'd been compromised. "I know."

"We could put her in a safe house somewhere," Jared mused.

Dread crawled up Angela's neck. "I don't want to go to a safe house."

"Here or at home?" her mother asked as though Angela hadn't protested.

"I'm not going to a safe house," Angela reiterated.

"Do you have places in Canada? I'm unaware of Pham's network up there."

They weren't listening to her. "I want to help find this person."

"Well, Samantha, you put a fuckin' bull's-eye on her in Abu Dhabi," Jared spat. "Though here with us is still safer than Canada or wherever else you have in mind."

Sawyer caught her eye, his brows rising. They had never seen Jared spar like this with someone before.

Angela slapped the table. "Enough." Jared and her mother finally turned their attention to her. "Surely the Feds didn't hear what Pham's people had to say and decide to sit and wait for more information." She faced Parker on the video conferencing screen. "Could you find out if they've made plans to gather intel?"

"It'd go faster with a little help." Parker eyed her mother.

"*Fine.*" Her mother picked up her cell phone and sent off several messages.

Jared gave the Senator an appreciative nod and told Parker, "We'll wait."

Parker's video feed remained on but muted. He pressed a phone to his ear and turned to face another computer screen, typing as he talked.

Angela's gaze dropped from Parker to Sawyer. The corners of his mouth lifted in a stealthy smile that made her feel like a million bucks.

Parker continued to work. Her mother returned to her phone and typed away. Jared and Sawyer had far more patience than Angela, though she'd guessed they'd had enough special forces gigs that required them to wait in places far less comfortable than Titan's war room.

Finally, Parker returned and unmuted. "Good news."

That phrase hadn't lived up to all it could have so far today. She hoped he wasn't just saying that.

"They have a possible informant, someone who shared a cell with Pham while his lawyers were kicking around the idea of an exchange."

That news wasn't especially great. Prisoners offered jailhouse gossip in exchange for better deals. That didn't mean the gossip held a kernel of truth. Vetting the information would take more time than they had.

"They've also been trying to ferret an agent or two into Pham's network, but no one's confident they know enough about his system to make it work." Parker frowned. "In short, we don't know what Pham's thinking. It's a work in progress."

Everyone looked as though they'd hit a dead end. She waited in disbelief for the moment that Parker, their resident genius, or Jared would realize the resources she possessed. They wanted to know about Pham's network? She didn't know the specifics yet, but she understood them completely. "The Feds can profile his thoughts, but I understand them."

Her mother's jaw ticked. Jared's brow furrowed. And Sawyer—she couldn't read his expression. Of everyone in the room, he was the one whose opinion she wanted to know. "I know Pham better than any agency. I lived his operations." Angela inhaled deeply and mustered the courage to ask for what she needed. "I can do whatever the Feds are trying to do. I should be the one who's in the thick of his network, hunting for someone who might be going through what I lived through."

Sawyer's brow furrowed. "Ange, his network is trying to find and kill you. You're not the person that should step into this role."

She deflated but only for a moment. He didn't say she couldn't do it, only that she would be spotted. But he was wrong. Angela shook her head. "If that's what everyone thinks, then that shows how little you understand his network. Pham's network is like a corporation. Like a bank. The people who specialize in murder are not the same people who work on money laundering."

No one said anything.

"He had an entire staff of people who took care of me. They brought me meals. Books. Everything I could think of. They were housekeepers and chefs, assistants. Those are not the people on high alert, searching for me, trying to kill me." She eyed each person in the room. "Whatever undercover identity the Feds have, I can do it better than what they're trying for without even being read into the profiles they're creating." Angela faced Boss Man. "I want in on this. I need it."

"Angela," her mother warned under her breath.

But she didn't look away from Boss Man. "Let me in on this. Please."

"Angela," her mother said more forcefully. "You're asking for a lot. You're *risking* a lot. And I don't know if you know what you're doing." She shook her head. "This isn't who you are."

Her heart lurched.

"With all due respect, ma'am," Sawyer said, "I don't think you know Angela, who she is, or what she can do." He focused on her. "Is this who you are? What you want to do?"

His defense had tied her throat into a double knot. From the moment that Titan had rescued her from Pham, she had controlled every aspect of her life. Now, she'd asked Jared to let her work a nonexistent assignment, searching for an unknown person, without an hour of operative training. She had no idea who she was at the moment.

"It's what I need to do," she replied.

CHAPTER EIGHT

THE HOTEL HAD several pools. This one was for staff. It was slightly larger than what might be in a suburban backyard. Swimming short laps didn't lessen Angela's frustration. She'd planned to swim laps until Jared was ready to talk about infiltrating Pham's network, but her mind had other plans. Paul took center stage as soon as she sliced through the water.

He called her frigid. That bothered her more than the marriage proposal. A marriage proposal could be expected after more than a decade together. But frigid? The accusation was a cheap shot at the very least and, in the worst case, something he believed.

Angela reached the end of the pool and kicked underwater to turn. Maybe she thought he was frigid. Paul didn't flirt. He never said sexy things. He didn't make a move. Their intimacy, however stilted it might have been, progressed appropriately initially. Dates. Kisses. A weekend away. An overnight meant sex. They had sex. There had never been an overwhelming desire. They weren't a tear-your-clothes-off-and-screw-against-the-wall kind of couple. Angela wasn't even sure that existed outside of movies.

The pool water rumbled behind her as someone jumped in. She hoped they would stay out of her way. Angela threw every ounce of her power into her stroke. Her biceps burned. Every kick hit harder than the last. Her breaths came with every other stroke, not nearly giving her enough oxygen for what she needed.

The other swimmer fell in line beside her. They were too close, and she would have panicked if she hadn't realized who was by her side. Sawyer.

She faltered, pushing her head up with a gasping breath. He stood easily and held out his arm. She grabbed hold of him, still trying to catch her breath as he walked them toward the shallower end of the pool.

Angela pulled back her goggles and wiped her face. "What are you doing here?"

His blond hair was dark against his forehead. Sawyer raked the tousled strands back and took a few steps toward the shallower water. "You look like you're trying to kick the pool's ass."

Her feet found purchase on the pool floor. The water bobbed at her chin. Angela half stood there, half treaded water. "More or less. It's far more legal than strangling my ex."

They moved to the side of the pool. "I thought you might be waiting out Jared," Sawyer said.

"That too." She hooked her elbow over the concrete edge and rested her head on her tired arm. The water came midway up his chest, lapping against well-cut muscles. Rivulets fell down his shoulders, gliding on their mad dash to the pool. Sawyer extended his arms so that his hands skimmed over the top of the water. He made small waves, back and forth, as he studied her.

"Do you think Jared will come around?" she asked.

Sawyer's jaw tensed before he drew in a chest-expanding breath and let it out as though unconvinced of what to say. "I think he'll weigh the risks and make the right decision."

She pushed off the wall and half floated, half walked to deeper water.

"So the ex is on your mind." His eyebrows rose. "The breakup is a good thing, right?" Sawyer asked as if he knew there was more to the marriage-proposal breakup.

Embarrassment curled down the length of her spine. Sawyer would never call a woman frigid. However, she couldn't imagine any woman who received his intense attention would be able to resist. There was more to him than six-packs and sex appeal. He had the most easy-going, trusting demeanor she'd ever met for someone who jumped out of helicopters or ambushed enemy tangos for a living.

"It's a very good thing," she agreed.

Sawyer sank under the water and swam a wide circle around her.

When he surfaced, water dribbled down his face. "Do you want me to find Jane? Chelsea or Amanda or someone?"

"Why?"

His shoulders bunched. "Girl talk or something?"

Angela laughed and splashed water at him. "I don't want to stress them out and make this a big deal."

"You want me to go and let you finish your pool massacre?"

She laughed again and shook her head. "I can't believe he expected me to go along with this stunt. I mean, can you imagine proposing to someone? That's wild to begin with."

His face skewed.

"But suggesting marriage like that? It's essentially a business proposal. Could you imagine me saying, 'Yeah, this is a great idea'?"

"Absolutely not."

She flicked the water and glared. Paul had called her frigid. Humiliation took the gusto out of her anger. In a softened voice, she asked, "That's insane, right?"

His eyes narrowed. "But that's not what's bothering you, is it?"

She hid her embarrassment and splashed him once more instead of answering.

Sawyer played with the water in front of him, reaching out and running his hands just under the surface. "Was he surprised when you said no?"

"Defensive."

"Huh." He crossed his arms. "Why?"

Warmth curled up her neck, and ashamed, she looked at the empty pool deck. She didn't want to share Paul's accusation. If Sawyer knew how long it had been since she and Paul were intimate, he might agree and would probably judge. Not because Sawyer was anything like Paul, but what kind of person stayed in a dead relationship and did nothing about it?

Sawyer floated closer. The water rippled between them. He brushed wet strands of hair off her cheek. "What is it, Ange?"

The warm touch on her cold cheeks made a shiver run down her back. Angry, humiliated tears burned in her eyes. "I'm embarrassed." She couldn't look at Sawyer and turned toward the wall. "Damn, the chlorine is starting to bother my eyes."

His hands rested on her shoulders, and slowly, he pulled her toward him. Her tears fell, burning hot on her pool-dampened cheeks.

Sawyer squeezed her shoulders then turned her around with a half-cocked smile. "You want me to go beat him up or something?"

She laughed. "Of course not."

Then he saw the tears. That made them fall faster. "Breakups suck. Even ones that you want."

She swiped her cheeks. "God, this is so embarrassing."

"They sure as hell are nothing to be embarrassed over." He wiped a tear from her cheek and left a trail of pool water where the tears had been. "Don't let a little prick like that bother you, all right? You can do so much better."

"It's more than that."

He waited, as still as a mountain in the center of the empty pool room. Water lapped. Silence hung heavy until she had to break the quiet.

"Paul said that he thought we had a pragmatic relationship, not a romantic one."

Sawyer's eyebrows drew together. "Why would he think that?"

Her chin dropped, and Angela stared into the pool water. "We never acted very much like a couple." She flushed, and a scorching blush ran down her neck. "We haven't been *together* in a long time."

She could've sworn he would have jumped away, but the water between them remained still. Sawyer didn't say anything. What was there to say? Her long-term relationship had been based on the hope of establishing a political dynasty.

Sawyer touched his index finger to her chin and lifted her face. "You have had a lot going on. Nothing is embarrassing about that, Ange."

The back of her throat burned. "We haven't—" She corrected herself. "I haven't been with him in a romantic sense since before I was abducted."

Sawyer's lips parted. Pity darkened his eyes, but he rolled his lips together and steadied. She bent her knees until the water lapped below her bottom lip. If only she could disappear into the bottom of the pool and resurface after he left. But Sawyer didn't move. Her dark hair floated around her shoulders. "Kind of pathetic, huh?"

The silence said so much.

"Yeah," she continued, breaking the silence. "Pathetic. I get what you're thinking, but you have to understand—"

"Why the hell would I think that?" He dropped his head back and stared at the rafters before taking a deep breath. "Trust me, Angela, you have no idea what I'm thinking."

She hated the pity. If only Sawyer would get out of the pool, they could forget that she'd said anything.

"I want to understand. He asks you to marry him. You don't have a physical—or really, any relationship. It ends. You're upset." He cocked his head to the side. "But there's something more that I'm missing. Why are you so mad?"

"I think he's been with other women."

His eyes narrowed. "There's more. That's not why you're upset."

She tried to sink underwater.

Sawyer caught her. "Am I wrong?"

He wasn't going to let it go. She could walk away, but he'd wonder. She'd eventually tell him, and all of the buildup would multiply her embarrassment. No, it was better to mimic her mother's style of awkward news delivery and just rip off the Band-Aid. "Paul said I was frigid."

Sawyer's forehead furrowed as if he didn't understand what she had just said or what Paul had meant.

She backed away from him, cheeks hot and eyes burning. "I was with him for years. It didn't bother me because I didn't want to see him. But not having sex? That wasn't my problem. I never thought, 'Oh, gee. I wish I could have sex with my boyfriend.' So maybe there is something wrong with me." She rubbed her eyes. "You know what? Maybe I'm just angry because he might be right."

CHAPTER NINE

SUCH DEEP RAGE vibrated inside Sawyer that he was surprised that the water didn't shake around him like he was the epicenter of an earthquake. He struggled to find the right words. If he let loose what he wanted to say, he would scare Angela out of the pool and into hiding. Finally, he managed a stilted, spitting, "There is *nothing* wrong with you."

Her eyes stayed on the water. "After Titan rescued me, after the FBI debriefed me, after Jared offered me a job, a place to recover, and I moved to Abu Dhabi…" She shrugged. "It just never happened. And…" She lowered her voice. "I never thought about it."

Angela had been through hell. For years. So what if she didn't want to jump in Paul Bane's bed? But Sawyer couldn't imagine being in Paul's position and not doing everything in his power to help his woman recover. Sawyer couldn't fathom, after finding and rescuing the woman he loved, that he wouldn't have held her tight until the nightmares subsided and thanked God he had her home again.

His throat ached because worse than that, Sawyer couldn't imagine everything Angela needed and didn't receive. If he had any idea that Paul hadn't stepped up to the plate and cared for Angela in that way, Sawyer might have ruined their friendship and interfered.

"I can't handle your pity," she whispered.

He let out another deep breath. "Shit, Angela. I'm not pitying you. I'm a lot of things, but that's not close to one of them." He reached for her arm and gently pulled her closer. His fingers slipped over her skin protectively, promising that she had nothing to fear from him. "You could've talked to me."

"I never thought much about it," she admitted.

"Ibrahim?" he asked, knowing he was prying more than he should.

Finally, she turned and faced him again. A blush pinked her damp cheeks. "No." She lifted a noncommittal shoulder. "I've had more important things to figure out."

Sawyer stymied the urge to bring her to his chest and wrap her in the strength that she should have been surrounded by over the years.

"The thing is," she said. "I never…"

Tension drew tight in his chest. Waiting her out was killing him slowly.

"I never wanted him," she whispered. "It felt like we were so young, like we were so inexperienced. He never got my blood racing. I never had butterflies. I think I liked the stability and normality that he offered." Angela studied the water as though she could find the answer floating between her stomach and Sawyer's. "That's what I wanted from my connection with Paul. Stability. And that's what I had before I was abducted. Since then?" She frowned. "I've been busy working on me—but I have never been… frigid." She bit her lip. "I don't think."

"Paul should've offered you anything, everything. He should've known what you needed and worked to find the rest." Sawyer's heart thudded heavier when her eyes met his. He should've known, should've asked. But he hadn't. "Angela." He needed to tiptoe through this minefield. His thoughts weren't clear except that he had a responsibility to her as her part-time bodyguard and friend. "The breakup is done. You can move on and decide whatever you want your future to look like."

"You look angry," she whispered.

Damn, he hated Paul. "I am."

"Don't be. That's not why I told you."

"I am anyway. He didn't stand up and be the man you needed. Fuck him for that, and fuck him for taking a cheap shot when you left him. Fuck. Him. You dumped him, and he lashed out like a child."

"Wow." Angela laughed quietly. "It never ceases to amaze me how different the two of you are."

Sawyer bit his tongue. There was no comparison. "You are an amazing woman. Do you understand that?"

Angela rolled her eyes. "All right, all right. Don't lay it on too thick."

"I'm telling you the God's honest truth. Do you know you're amazing?"

She wouldn't meet his eyes. "If I say yes, can we change the subject?"

He pulled her close. "Do you believe me, Ange?"

She rested her cheek against his chest, and, finally, she tilted her head up and met his gaze. Goose bumps prickled down his arms. His breath became shallow.

"I'm too tired to believe anything right now."

His molars ground. Sawyer couldn't stand in a pool and convince her of all she deserved. "Come on." He scooped her into a cradle hold. "We need to get out of the pool."

She laid her head against his chest. Her hair fanned over his shoulder as he walked them toward shallower water. He summited the stairs and stopped next to the pool chaise with her belongings. Sawyer snagged her towel and wrapped it around her shoulders. "You deserve far more than most men could give on their best day. One day, the right guy will come along, and you'll know that."

CHAPTER TEN

ANGELA STILL SHIVERED, though she hadn't been cold in hours. Sawyer had left her to sit in the sauna. After she was sure he'd left the pool area, Angela relocated to her suite, where she soaked in her tub. The entire time, she'd been thinking—and shivering. Emotionally, she was tapped out. Physically, her goose bumps were like a low-humming adrenaline jitter that she couldn't shake. But she wasn't sure if her inner trembling came from the drama with Paul and her mother or from baring her secrets to Sawyer.

If she was any less screwed up in the head, Angela might confuse the closeness she had with Sawyer with romance. They had a solid friendship in which she could reveal her ugliest embarrassments, and he would tell her she was awesome. That kind of connection was rare.

A knock sounded at her door, and a fresh round of shivers rolled down her spine. No one other than Sawyer would stop by that late at night, but Tran Pham's band of merry assassins had taught her to double-check assumptions. She picked up her phone. Sawyer hadn't reached out.

Is that you?

A moment later, three little dots danced on her screen. It was taking him longer than necessary to type, "Yup." Finally, he confirmed he was at the door with a "yeah." What had he been writing?

She glanced down at her favorite pajamas. She'd chosen them tonight to feel beautiful and happy, to remind herself that she didn't need toxic relationships and wasn't newly single; she'd been single for years without realizing it. The pajamas lay over her skin like a soft whisper. Although she usually loved silky pants and frilly tops, they suddenly felt too thin.

Angela made a quick pit stop at her bedroom closet, found the matching robe, and tied the sash around her waist as she walked to the door. Her shivers hadn't stopped. The pajamas were too thin. Her heart slammed in her chest. She paused at the door and checked for Sawyer through the peephole. He leaned against the wall, and the fisheye lens made him seem even farther away.

She rested her forehead on the door but couldn't stop her racing heart. Today had been too much for her to handle. After a long breath, she opened the door and smiled. "Howdy, stranger."

He stood at an arm's length from the threshold to her room, his own arms crossed, with a serious look. "You okay?"

The spastic, hiccupping pace of her heart stuttered. "Of course." She cocked her head. "Is that why you stopped by?"

"It took you a while to answer."

"It took you a while to say that had been you knocking."

Sawyer rolled his lips together and nodded, not explaining. "You weren't asleep."

"You knew I wouldn't be."

He raised his chin. "Night owl."

This conversation didn't feel right. His body language screamed that he would rather be in a million other places. She wasn't sure why he didn't stride in—or, for that matter, why she remained shivering against the door jamb, not letting him inside. "Do you want to come in?"

The corners of his lips tightened. "Sure."

She backed against the door and let him in. "I haven't heard from Boss Man. You?"

He shook his head as he walked past her. Their apartments were hotel suites. Hers had two main sections. The living area had a small kitchenette, desk, couch, and television. The bedroom and bathroom were through a door she'd left propped open.

Sawyer seemed larger than normal. He appeared to take up more space in the room than he had the last time he'd been in her suite, and he sucked up more of the oxygen too. He moved to the dark window and stared.

"You didn't have to check on me." Angela perched on the edge of the couch farthest from him. "Today was a lot." She crossed her arms and rubbed the silky fabric against her skin. "But I've been through worse." She half laughed. "Yesterday was quite the doozy."

He turned from the window, and his eyes narrowed. "Are you cold?"

"No. I have a shiver I can't get rid of."

He nodded as though he understood and paced before the large window—the backdrop of city lights illuminated around him. Sawyer stopped and opened his mouth as though to say something, but he shut it without a word. He paced again.

Did he want to talk about Paul? The breakup? That horrible word Paul had called her? Had Sawyer ever encountered a woman he'd been with who didn't make his world spin? "Have all of your relationships had a spark?"

He stopped cold. "Yeah, sure." Sawyer caught himself and shrugged. "More or less." He ran a hand into his hair and let the thick blond locks thread through his fingers. "I don't know, Ange."

What was normal? Why didn't she notice a massive red flag in her relationship with Paul, which was already draped with them? "Are sparks all the same? They can't be, right?"

"I haven't thought about it before…" He shrugged. "But I guess not."

Relationships were confusing. They were a type of friendship but *more*. However, *more* didn't always come with a friendship. "I think I'm…confused." She rolled her eyes. "Or maybe I'm programmed wrong."

"Don't be ridiculous, Ange. Paul's an idiot."

She moved onto a couch cushion, pulled her feet up, and wrapped her arms around her shins. "Both things can be true."

"Maybe so, but not in this case."

She ducked her head between her knees, trying to parse out what she wanted to say. "Have you always had a spark in a relationship?"

"You mean, have I ever kissed a girl that didn't get my blood rushing?" He shrugged sheepishly. "Yeah, probably. But not that I can remember."

He'd probably kissed more than his fair share. A spark for everyone seemed too much. "What about that you've slept with?"

His eyebrows arched, and Sawyer laughed. "I don't know." A blush colored his cheeks. "There may've been times I thought there was a spark, but really, there was booze."

She laughed in return. "You're adorable when you blush, you know that?"

He gave her a funny look. "I don't know that anyone's ever called me that."

She couldn't decipher his expression. "I didn't mean to insult you."

"Didn't say you had, sweetheart."

Still unable to get a read on him, she moved on. "Fine. I still have questions."

He laughed again, shaking his head. "I don't know if I have answers for you."

Angela ignored him. "There have got to be levels. Like, no spark would be a zero. Maybe a smidge of a spark is a one. Lots of sparks, a six?"

He stared blankly.

"Or maybe a five-point scale would be better."

"Give me a break, Ange. I've never ranked anyone. I haven't quantified how they made me feel."

"Never?"

He shook his head.

"Maybe not with a scale," she said. "But I bet you have. If you were to marry someone, she would probably set off your sparks alarm meter. You just don't know it yet."

He put up his hand and waved the idea away. "I can't—that's so—" He shook his head. "It doesn't work like that."

"It might. Maybe sparks are on an innate spectrum of interest. I'm sure there have been some women who made you smile, but they are different than women who you couldn't wait to get in bed."

"*Angela.* You make me sound like the kind of guy with a new woman on my arm constantly."

"No, sorry, that's not what I meant." Angela squeezed her legs and stared out the big window. The lights glittered. She loved this city. If Pham hadn't taken her, she wouldn't be able to sit on her cute yellow couch and let the lights dazzle her. "Earlier tonight, I was thinking about my parents. Their relationship is very much like mine with Paul. Business.

Small talk. Maybe I'm a product of my environment." She refocused on Sawyer, who was posted against the window, surrounded by the lights. "Then I thought about Liam and Chelsea, Chance and Jane, Hagan and Amanda."

"If you want to look at winning couples, you can't go wrong with them."

"They have deep connections and sparks." They weren't just couples. They were families.

He rolled his bottom lip into his mouth and nodded. "That sounds like the winning formula."

"Have you ever had both?" she asked.

He faltered and then crossed his arms over his chest. "I came by to check on you. Not talk about me."

"I know. I'm sorry." She walked to the window and stood by his side. "It's been a weird day."

They watched the Abu Dhabi skyline side by side. His arm brushed hers. Angela leaned against him and rested her head on his bicep. The night sparkled. She shivered again.

"I think…" he whispered in a low rumble. The bright lights glittered. It was as though time paused and an eternity passed. He inched back. "That you should get a good night's sleep."

The floor seemed to tilt. Angela's throat ached. Sawyer draped his arm over her shoulder and ran his hand along her arm. Finally, the shivers she'd been unable to shake subsided. She could breathe, even if she couldn't catch her breath. Angela squeezed her eyes shut. "I'm grateful you're in my life."

His hold tightened. "Same." Sawyer placed a chaste kiss on her head and lingered against her hair. "It wouldn't be the same if you left."

She wasn't going anywhere.

Finally, he said, "You should get some sleep."

Angela didn't move. So much more was left to say, but she came up completely blank when she tried to think about it. Sawyer let her go and walked away, leaving Angela again to shiver.

CHAPTER ELEVEN

THE BRIGHT AFTERNOON sun poured into Angela's office. She stared at the notebook on her desk. She hadn't known that haiku and iambic pentameter would have been part of her job description. Yet here she was, trying to forget the last few days and write snarky poetry for Boss Man.

She was creative to a point, and she had passed that point many, many moons ago. If she hadn't been waiting for Jared to discuss her request with federal investigators, Angela would have been in her suite, staring out the window she and Sawyer had half hugged in front of, where he dropped a perfectly benign kiss atop her head, wondering if she just experienced her very first spark at more than thirty years old.

Her cheeks flushed hot. Distractions were tantamount right now because there was no way in hell she would let herself think of Sawyer Cabot as anything other than her very good, very platonic friend. Angela refocused on her semi-teasing literary riddle and made absolutely no progress.

Jared knocked on her half-open door and walked inside. His expression was unreadable, and he did not say what his final decision would be.

The best situation might be if he said no. Her safety would be ensured; she'd continue with her everyday job. She might even pull another wordplay message out of nowhere.

But if Jared said yes, her world would turn upside down. That would be hell for a control freak like her. However, she'd asked for the upheaval. She needed to help find Tran Pham's last victim.

Angela tried for an uninterested look and asked, "What rhymes with bazooka?"

"Crapula."

"That's so helpful. Thanks, Boss Man."

"Literary elements are not my forte." He sat opposite her and propped his feet on the other chair. "I didn't expect to come in here and interrupt a psy-ops session."

She closed the notebook. "The way I figured, if you came in and said we're a go, I'd need to get ahead on work I won't have time to do." She shrugged. "And, if you say we're a no-go, I'll bury my disappointment in bad poetry."

Jared ran a hand through his short-cropped dark hair. "You know what your mother said was bullshit, right?"

She groaned. "Which part?"

"When she insinuated you weren't part of Titan."

Angela shrugged. She was more than aware of the circumstances behind her hiring.

"You are Titan." Jared's jaw flexed. "In every sense of the word."

She wasn't sure if that was true. "Thanks."

He did not attempt to hide his study of her face but moved on when Angela remained quiet. "I'm worried that Pham is playing a game of mindfucks like a 3-D chess grandmaster."

She snorted. "He probably is. That's a good description of his style."

"And," Jared continued, "I'm concerned that we don't know anywhere near enough to make this an effective assignment."

Her heart sank.

"Parker's working on more intel, but we're fishing in a black hole. Lots of nothing is weighing us down." Jared shook his head. "I don't want to disappoint you, Angela." He gauged her reaction. "I think you might need this."

"I do," she confirmed, barely trusting her voice.

He grumbled. "I can't send you somewhere when I don't have a clue what direction to start."

She refused to lower her head, but disappointment crept into every inch of her body. She wanted to cry but didn't dare sniffle around Boss Man. Besides, she'd wept more than enough tears yesterday.

He rubbed the back of his neck. "Don't give up yet. Okay? Let Parker dig. Once that guy finds the smallest hint of intel, he's like a cat pulling the string on a sweater. The whole thing will be a ball of yarn when he's done."

Parker as a cat? The corners of her mouth rose. "A ball of yarn, huh?"

"Yeah, a big pile of possibilities. Okay?"

Parker wasn't a cute kitty. He was more of a stealth hacker cat. That might be the inspiration she needed for one of the little notes that she wrote for Jared, which he occasionally left for the ACES team to find. He said the notes were psychological training to help a new team build camaraderie. Honestly, Angela was ninety-nine percent sure that Boss Man enjoyed theatrical moments. He'd never claimed to love drama, but he was in the thick of it sometimes.

"You can't think of anything that might help Parker?" Jared asked. "Anything from years ago, from conversations with investigators or the prosecutor's office? Anything."

An old idea came to mind. She chewed the inside of her cheek.

Jared scrutinized her as buried thoughts tried to surface. "What is it, Angela?"

"Nothing, really."

His face pinched. "That look on your face doesn't look like nothing."

Angela shaded the corner of a Post-It note, weighing whether she could handle a second day in a row of judgment. "I've been told it's nothing."

Jared took her pencil and tossed it down. "Why don't we let Parker be the judge of that?"

"I've been told it is a big ole nothingburger."

Jared cocked his eyebrow. "Like what?"

"I brought this up years ago. The investigators treated me like a moron—and they might have had good reason."

"Angela, you have to trust us. We're here for you. You know that." He waited until she left the Post-It note alone and raised her eyes to him. "I wasn't blowing smoke up your ass. You're Titan. You know what that means?"

"That I'm good at my job."

"It means that I believe in you. Parker. All the guys." His pointed look tightened. "Sawyer. Trust in us like we trust in you. If what you say is a nothingburger, we'll let you know. If not, we work on it. But we're not going to treat you like crap because you gave Parker a lead to smoke out."

Trust in Titan. That was always the mantra, and she did. She believed in the team and their work. Angela took a deep breath. "After you guys came in and saved the day, investigators grilled me for weeks. They wanted to know everything they could about Pham."

Boss Man nodded. "I hired you as soon as they let you out of their claws."

"There were parts of my story that they ignored. It was as if they were only listening for certain details, and the ones I found noteworthy were…" She made a face. "Not of interest to them."

"What kind of things?"

"Mostly about how the abduction happened. Faces I saw more than once. Sometimes again later…" She shook her head. "They were very certain that my recollections were off."

His eyes narrowed. "Why were they so certain?"

"Because the faces—actually, it was only one face. A woman who I swore I would randomly see throughout the years, she was…" Angela shrugged. "Just a face. They told me she was a vision, like an imaginary friend, that I conjured up as a rescue daydream."

She could tell that her vague explanation failed to make sense to Jared. "I told you. It's a nothingburger."

After a beat, he shook his head and asked, "Can I get Parker in on this conversation?"

"We shouldn't waste his time." Her cheeks warmed. "I was told more than once that I didn't see what I thought I saw."

His lips pursed, and then Jared smiled as though he detected a challenge. "You've known me long enough to know that I like to double-check the bureaucratic types."

"I know, but—"

"Angela, I've known you long enough to believe in your gut instincts."

Uncertainty crawled down her neck. If he only understood how awful her instincts were. "Honestly, if I tell you the details, you'll think it's ridiculous."

"Life's ridiculous."

Wasn't that the truth? She couldn't help but laugh. Still, if Jared thought she was a moron also, that would significantly decrease her chance of helping investigate and find Tran Pham's remaining hostage. "All the investigators thought I was a moron when I brought her up. They thought I had…" She twirled her finger by her head and whispered, "…a few loose screws."

"If you close your eyes, can you envision what they said you made up?"

Without a doubt. Angela could still see the woman's face in her mind as clearly as if she had seen her in person that morning.

Jared leaned in to Angela. "I have trusted you with my teams. They have trusted you with their lives. My life. It might not be the same way they rely on one another to stay alive, but it's just as important."

"Jared—"

He held up his hand. "Like I said, the past few years have taught me that you have a hell of a good instinct." Jared settled back into the chair. "If you want to wait to rope in Parker, just tell me what you told them. No matter how ridiculous and wrong they said you were. And if what you said is some crackpot bullshit, I'll tell you."

She could agree with that. "And we won't waste Parker's time?"

"And we won't waste Parker's time," he confirmed, "but I'm willing to bet Parker will be very interested in what you say."

Angela trusted Boss Man's instinct and ability to cut through the bull-shit. She trusted him enough to risk another day's embarrassment. "I saw a woman before I was taken," Angela admitted. "I saw her often."

Jared's expression remained scarily focused.

She continued, "Federal agents said they'd checked surveillance footage from when and where I reported seeing her. They'd worked the streets, asked questions, and even brought in people for interrogations. But for all their work, they'd turned up absolutely nothing." She bit her bottom lip. "They think she didn't exist."

He kept quiet.

"Pham didn't always keep me in the type of place you found me. He would bring me on these family vacations." Her voice had lowered. "He'd pretend I was his daughter, though he never called me her name. But it was like… like he wanted to spoil me—her, the daughter—but I was the stand-in. We'd go scuba diving and stay at these opulent resorts, relaxing at isolated beachside cabanas where no one else was on the island except for his entourage and resort staff. Mostly butlers." No one could understand the two sides of Tran Pham. "It's strange to explain how I could have been both a captive and a sunbather at a high-roller resort. The kind of place where billionaires vacationed and no one ever asked questions—where no one would ever talk to a federal agent about who or what they saw." Again, she bit her bottom lip, uncertain that Jared's lack of reaction weighed in her favor. "This is when you start asking why I didn't ask for help or run away."

He barely shook his head.

"Or maybe tell me that my years with Pham weren't so bad."

Once more, his expression tightened. "You know better than that, Angela. No one in Titan would do that."

"Sometimes I don't hate Pham." Her gaze dropped. "Even when he kept me at the warehouse like a pet in a cage, he ensured I was provided for." Then her chin jerked up. "But just because that's true doesn't mean I don't want him to stay in prison."

"I know." Jared's jaw worked while the wheels in his head turned. "Bring me back to the woman. Give me more."

Angela took a deep breath. "The same woman was always in the background, almost as if forced to watch us. I saw her on vacation, set to the side, positioned toward us. She wasn't security. She wasn't acknowledged. I don't know how she arrived or when she left. But she was there." Angela searched his eyes for a reaction and, finding none, continued, "I can't tell you why. We didn't interact with her, and I never saw her at home—I mean, where he kept me," she amended. "She wasn't one of the employees who delivered food or magazines. She didn't wait on Pham like his other employees had. She was simply, sometimes, just *there*. Watching."

"Did Pham ever interact with her?"

Angela shook her head. "Never."

"Never," he muttered under his breath. "Like I said, that bastard plays some serious 3-D mind-fuck chess." After a moment, Jared rubbed a hand over his face. "Yeah, this is the kind of yarn ball Parker can dig into."

She slumped in her chair, relieved to have been believed and unsettled at the thought of going through the search for her again. "Nothing will come out of it."

"So you've been told."

"So I've been told," she agreed.

"Do you believe there's nothing to her?" he asked.

"Boss Man, I don't know—"

"That's first-rate bullshit, Angela. What do you believe?"

She leveled with Jared. "I am one hundred percent certain that woman is out there." Angela closed her eyes and remembered the woman's haunted eyes and listless body. "Do you think she's the person over whom Pham wants to negotiate?"

"I don't want theories yet. I want intel." Jared reached over and lifted the handset from her office phone. He punched a few numbers and waited for an answer. "Yeah, it's me," he said into the phone. "We're about to unload one hell of a puzzle for your genius brain to tear apart."

CHAPTER TWELVE

TREADMILLS WHIRLED. THE sound mixed with the heavy footsteps of grown men running to nowhere. The monotonous rumble surrounded Sawyer and thundered in his head. He'd thought the run would clear his mind of the memory of Angela under his arm, of the way she leaned against him, and how he kissed the top of her head. It didn't, and now he had a headache that pounded in time with the pace of his run.

Boss Man walked into the gym and stopped in front of the row of treadmills. He ignored the men flanking Sawyer's sides and threw him a look that hit Sawyer like a grenade. Something was wrong. Sawyer smacked the stop button and hopped off the machine before the belt finished revolving.

"Let's go," Boss Man barked over his shoulder, not waiting for him to catch up.

Sawyer pulled off his shirt and toweled the sweat from his face, hustling to meet Boss Man's pace. "Gimme a second."

"No."

Sawyer's gut churned. His pulse jumped and drummed in his ears.

"Good luck," Hagan called as he passed.

Sawyer needed it. This had to do with Angela and everything that spiraled from the moment Pham's bullshit had shown up in Abu Dhabi.

The private gym was on the far west side of the same floor as Titan's office suite. Usually, Sawyer didn't head toward Boss Man's office in athletic shorts with only a sweat-drenched shirt wrapped around his neck, but nothing had been normal this week.

Air conditioning and uncertainty poured over him. The hair on his arms stood on end. The silent, sterile hallway closed in around Sawyer.

Boss Man wasn't exactly known for his manners, but that he'd hightailed out of the gym with only an order to keep up gave Sawyer heartburn.

Jared's office door had been left ajar. Sawyer strode in to find Boss Man behind his desk. Parker was on the big screen facing a different screen in his lair, clacking away on a keyboard.

As Angela sat across from Jared, her lips parted. "Guess I know where Boss Man found you." Her gaze flitted to his chest then jerked toward Parker.

"All right." Jared cracked his knuckles. "Let's go over this again. This time for Sawyer's benefit."

Angela sat with a ramrod-straight spine. Her ankles were crossed underneath her chair. She didn't have a hair out of place. Her simple white blouse was starched. A slender black skirt covered her knees. Rocking the uptight librarian getup, she didn't appear any different than usual, except her face made it look like she might shatter.

Parker turned from the other screen and greeted Sawyer with a chin lift. "This is what we know."

Sawyer kept Angela in his peripheral vision. He wasn't sure she was breathing.

"Mylene Hathaway," Parker said as the screen switched to a headshot of a woman in a U.S. Army uniform. "She was a communications analyst coordinating with the National Intelligence Office, acting as a principal advisor to the director. She played a crucial role in Operation Red Gold, where Pham's daughter Quy Long was killed."

"Mylene Hathaway. That's who Pham has?" Sawyer looked from the headshot to Jared and back again. "And no one knew?" He scowled. Mylene Hathaway sounded like someone who would be on the army's shortlist of missing people. She was young and beautiful—a poster child for a public-relations nightmare if the public knew she was AWOL. "How is that possible?"

"You know how Pham operates," Jared growled. "He doesn't kill the people he wants to hurt."

"Yeah." Sawyer nodded. "He inflicts suffering when he kills their loved ones."

Jared nodded. "The sadistic fuck."

Parker reappeared on the screen. "We have a mile-long list of people who he has ordered killed in the name of retribution. Most of them… It took years to figure out they were Pham's victims."

"Pham did that to Mylene Hathaway?" Sawyer asked.

Parker crossed his arms. "Maybe."

Maybe wasn't a very Parker-like answer. He was likelier to mention statistical deviations and binomial distributions. Sawyer glanced at Jared and Angela. "Maybe?"

Jared pursed his lips, and after a century-long second that was answer enough, he confirmed that they didn't know shit. "Maybe." He tilted his head to one side, cracking his neck, then the other. "Parker, explain."

Sawyer braced for an explanation flush with terminology that would go right over his head.

"Mylene Hathaway has been AWOL since the year before Angela's abduction. She returned from the DNI's office outside Washington, DC, and, as we understand it, learned that her husband and sister were having an affair."

Despite Parker's far less-than-expected technical answer, Sawyer emitted a low whistle.

"Yeah," Parker agreed. "They were found murdered, and shortly after that, a warrant for Mylene Hathaway was issued but never served." He cleared his throat. "No one could find her."

If he didn't know better, Sawyer would've guessed Mylene had knocked off her husband and sister and gone into hiding. Given that Pham was part of the conversation, that was far too easy. Sawyer stole a glance at Angela, who was as still as a statue. "They never found her?"

Angela didn't answer.

"They did not find Mylene," Parker confirmed. "There was a manhunt, but it didn't last long. Bureaucracy and internal politics. She fell off the radar."

Sawyer shifted in the chair. His thighs stuck to the leather cushion. He didn't want to study Angela and her lack of conversation and reaction, but it was unnerving. "So… it's a cold case…" He tried to read the room.

Parker and Jared were clearly unimpressed with the military's investigation. Angela was stock-still and unreadable. Sawyer ran a hand over his face and sifted through what he knew of Pham. "So, do we think Mylene killed her husband and sister or not?"

"Someone did," Jared snarked.

"The evidence points to Mylene," Parker said.

Then what was the catch? And why the hell was Angela stone-cold and ignoring his questions?

"But," Parker added, "this is the picture a sketch artist drew after meeting with Angela. After she first reported the unknown woman to the Feds." A profile sketched in pencil replaced Parker's face on the screen. "And this is the sketch from a forensic artist Angela spoke with this morning." A near replica split the screen. Side by side, the drawings were shockingly similar. "Now, for good measure." A photograph appeared next to the two drawings. "This is Mylene Hathaway in civilian clothes in a photo dated just before her husband and sister were murdered."

"Holy crap." The woman in the photograph was smiling. That was the only difference between the picture and the two sketches drawn years apart. Goose bumps ran down his back. He faced Angela and repeated the obvious, "That's the same lady."

"Yes," Angela finally said. "And she's been under Pham's thumb since before he took me." With her statue-act shattered, she turned to Sawyer. A terrifying storm of devastation and cold fury brewed in her dark eyes. "She's been there, stuck in hell, with no one trying to find her."

Sawyer couldn't fathom the years that Pham had stolen from Angela, but he could hear and see the trauma that bubbled so close to the surface. Despite that, her fight for control was stronger. He wanted to comfort her, though nothing he could think of was adequate. His fleeting thoughts felt selfish and hollow. Unspoken words—platitudes—caught in his throat. There was nothing to say about Mylene or the situation.

"What now?" Sawyer managed.

"This is the thing." Boss Man grimaced. "We know squat."

"Technically..." Parker reappeared on the screen. "Not squat."

Jared gave Angela a stern look that promised they weren't at rock bottom. "Parker has strings to pull."

"That's good," she whispered.

Sawyer leaned back, his skin stuck uncomfortably to the chair. He crossed his arms. "All right. Until Parker works his magic, we know squat. That's not nothing." He studied Angela. "It's a holding pattern."

Jared nodded, eyeing Angela as though sizing her up for a task. "Parker can only do so much without new intel."

Sawyer didn't like the mental gymnastics he could see on Jared's face. Nor did he like the way Angela's position stiffened a degree more. His glance ping-ponged between them before he finally determined the question that he already knew would have an answer Sawyer would hate. "How do we get more intel?"

"On a years-old cold case that no one wants jurisdiction over?" Jared's eyebrow arched like Sawyer had asked to search for life on another planet. "There's not a lot of resources."

"Yes, there is," Angela countered. "If Mylene is who Pham wants to trade for a deal."

"We don't have any indication that's who Pham has or is willing to trade in exchange for a reduced sentence."

"I don't want Pham to trade on Mylene." Angela clutched the chair arms. "I don't want him using her for one more thing."

Jared nodded thoughtfully. "I get that, Angela…"

"But what?" she pushed. "If we tell them what we know, they'll either continue to ignore me, as they always have, or use it in negotiations."

"Then where does that leave us?" Sawyer studied Boss Man and tried deciphering what the hell was running through his mind. "If we give whatever we learn to the Feds, we give up control."

Jared nodded.

"They'll want to run point," Sawyer continued. "Which isn't something you like to do."

The corners of Jared's lips quirked, and he gave a slight nod. "This is what I'm thinking." He studied Sawyer and Angela. "You two go into the field and dig where Parker says to dig."

"What?" they both said, his voice laden with confusion, hers with hope.

Angela perched on the edge of her seat, hands still tightly grasping the chair's arms, but now, it was as if she held on to keep from springing into the air. Sawyer was the polar opposite. Trepidation pooled in the pit of his stomach. "What do you mean? Both of us dig?"

"You dig. You find out what's out there to learn."

"Field work? In the U.S.?" Sawyer did a double take. He understood Angela had asked to be involved, but this assignment didn't make sense. Angela didn't leave the office for work. She didn't go anywhere dangerous. That was the point of Angela's job, far, far away from her home base, where she was safe from Pham's network.

"Yeah," Jared said. "Get in the field. Dig around. Learn what there's to learn." He focused on her. "You can do it."

"I can do it. Absolutely," she replied.

"I'll get you everything we have," Parker said. "Mylene Hathaway's full history. Army. National Intelligence Office. The files from the murder investigation. Anything I can find." Parker turned from their screen to work on his computer. "And I'll dig on this end. We'll see if we can find anything that points to Pham's involvement in the murders."

Sawyer's jaw jutted. "What? Now we're cold-case investigators? I don't think so."

"We're not trying to exonerate Mylene," Jared said. "We're researching, trying to confirm Pham's involvement."

"We can do that from here."

Angela glared. "I don't think so."

"Parker is in the U.S. We're here with NSA-level technology—"

"What happens when we prove he's involved?" Angela asked.

Jared pursed his lips and shrugged as if he hadn't just suggested the most ludicrous assignment Sawyer had ever heard. "Once we do that, if we're right, one thing begets the next."

"Begets? What the fuck, Boss Man? We're not—"

"There will likely be one of two outcomes," Parker said, finally sounding the slightest bit data driven. "She's dead or held against her will."

"Parker, man, this doesn't sound like anything we—Angela, especially—need to get near. Right?"

Parker ignored him. "Killing his targets hasn't been Pham's typical M.O."

Were they really having a conversation about Angela working in the U.S. when someone had just attempted to kill her? How was he the only one who didn't see sky-high red flags?

Jared nodded. "That leaves us with the option of finding her alive."

"So she's out there." Angela released the chair from her death grip, letting hope infiltrate her words. "We can find her."

Possibility lit her sweet, innocent face in a way that gutted Sawyer. He didn't want to tell her no. Hell, the two other people in their conversation should be putting their feet down with absolute hell-nos. Sawyer's heart galloped. There was no way he would gallivant around the world with Angela to find Mylene Hathaway, and there was no way he would endanger Angela to find another of Pham's victims.

His molars ground again. Jared needed to shut down this half-cocked idea, but he didn't. "Wait." Sawyer glanced from Parker to Angela and then to Jared. "We can't—are you all serious?"

Jared nodded.

Sawyer did another double take. "In what world is this a good idea?"

"In the world we're living in," Angela snapped.

"Look, Ange, I didn't mean—" Honestly, though, he did. He couldn't imagine what she'd gone through. If he had been in her position? Yeah, he'd want to do what he could to help someone living in that same hell. But this wasn't how they needed to handle the situation with Angela. "Neither of us is the right person for this job."

"It's the job I need."

Sawyer waited for Boss Man to back him up, but silence loomed. "I'm not an investigator—"

"Sure you are. I know what you do, Sawyer."

He pinched the bridge of his nose. Titan specialized in getting the job done. What the job might be? Every time, it was different. He'd worked hostage recovery situations as many times as he had infiltrated behind enemy lines. That was Titan's bread and butter. If it involved helicopters, ammo, and need-to-know intel, Sawyer was your guy. But cold case... research? Intel gathering? He didn't even know what to call it.

Sawyer shook his head. Angela knew what they did, and she knew enough to understand that out of everyone on the ACES team, he was the least qualified. Hagan liked to figure out puzzles. Liam specialized in surveillance. Sawyer just wanted to get in and get out. He'd walk into hellfire so long as it was on his to-do list.

He rubbed his hands over his face as though he could scrub away the mental contradictions. If his job meant he was supposed to smoke out a missing woman, that shouldn't have been a problem. But doing so with Angela when they knew precisely nothing? That idea didn't sit well with him. His eyes pinched shut. "This is a bad idea, boss."

"You want someone else to go with her?"

Sawyer's eyes flew open. "I didn't say that." He tried to ignore Angela's glare boring a hole in the side of his head and failed spectacularly. "If we find her, then what?"

"Focus. Bull's-eye on the problem first." Jared's forehead furrowed. "We don't know what we don't know. I can't tell you what we'll do with it once we know."

Sawyer scowled. "If she exists."

"She exists," Angela hissed.

"If she's still alive," Sawyer corrected.

"She is." Angela's confidence scared the hell out of him. It was almost enough to quell the anxiety thudding in his chest. "Pham wouldn't be trying to negotiate—"

"We don't know that is who he was going to offer up in exchange—"

"Then we find them all," Angela roared. "Like we should have done before."

The truth was enough to suck the oxygen from the room. Sawyer didn't disagree. But that didn't change his mind about who should do what. He rolled his lips together and stared at Jared. Angela shouldn't be involved. She was untrained and emotionally too close. For the same reason a surgeon shouldn't operate on their loved one, Angela shouldn't search for a victim of the same abductor, even solely to gather intel.

"Spit it out, Sawyer," Boss Man ordered. "You think I'm wrong? She's wrong? Whatever you've got to say, say it so we can move forward."

Sawyer glanced at Angela.

"Angela's not going to bite," Jared muttered.

Her eyes narrowed. "You don't know that."

Sawyer ran his hand over his face and into his hair again, where his knuckles tightened. "I don't understand why you would let her do this."

"Because I asked, Sawyer," she said.

"I've asked for a hell of a lot of things over the years, and you," he said to Jared, "didn't bother entertaining any bullshit requests." Sawyer raised his eyebrows. "And now something comes along that puts Angela in danger, and you're all 'let's go see what happens'?"

"Her location has been compromised," Jared pointed out. "She's gotta go somewhere. Why not go somewhere that no one would expect?"

"Let's not forget," Angela added, "I want to do this. I *asked* to do this. I can't just sit here and do nothing."

"Yeah. You can." The muscles in Sawyer's jaw ticked. "What if shit hits the fan? What if we find Mylene surrounded by Pham's ghouls? We're unarmed. Unprepared." He motioned to Angela. "Untrained."

"We've talked about that," Parker said.

"*What?*" Sawyer had walked into the conversation too late, powerless to the decisions made without his input.

"We mitigate the dangers. Prepare for the unexpected, arm you both appropriately, and provide training as needed."

"Arm us both?" Sawyer repeated incredulously. Had he ever seen Angela hold a weapon?

"Sawyer," she said. "I'm doing this with or without you."

Jared didn't dispute her words.

Frustrated, Sawyer pushed back into his chair. He didn't have a good understanding of the job requirements and wasn't making a good argument. No for no's sake wouldn't cut it. Suddenly, Sawyer was acutely aware that he was half-dressed. No wonder he wasn't convincing anyone. He looked like an idiot.

"Give me a chance, Sawyer," Angela said.

He had a hundred reasons to say no, but damn when her voice pained him. On top of that, this investigation might happen without him. There was no one else he'd rather send in his place. Sawyer rubbed the back of his neck. "So, where would we go?"

Angela's small smile hit him straight in the chest.

"Her last known location was in North Carolina," Parker replied. "A little island off the coast called Emerald Isle."

"That's where she lived?" Sawyer said.

"No. That's where Mylene's husband and sister were murdered. She didn't live too far from there, though."

"What the hell are we going to find there?" Sawyer asked.

"Probably not much," Parker answered. "But it's a good starting point. From what we know about Pham, if he took Mylene, she wouldn't be that far from her home base."

Sawyer needed more convincing. "You're blowing me away with all the intel."

"Statistically speaking," Parker continued, "this is our best bet. We start there. I'll milk the system for what else the Feds might know but haven't shared. I'll see what I can do to eavesdrop on Pham's communication network. You two will be working the ground game until I have something more for you to follow up on."

"Sounds like we'll have nothing to do." Sawyer chewed on the inside of his cheek. "Boring."

"First, it's too much, too dangerous." Angela sighed. "Now it's too boring."

Sawyer didn't know what his problem was. Angela's involvement felt grossly unnecessary. Titan could move her to a different safe house, and Senator Sorenson could move heaven and earth so the Feds could follow up on the Mylene Hathaway lead.

Angela rolled her eyes. "Fine. Let's ask someone else. Camden?"

"No." He side-eyed her. "You're not going anywhere—"

"Excuse me?"

"Not going anywhere *with Camden*." Sawyer blew out a deep breath. "Don't cut me off, Ange. You know that's not what I meant." Except that *was* what he meant.

She shrugged. "Camden is always looking for reasons to travel."

"This isn't 'a reason to travel'. It's putting yourself in danger—"

"Or boredom," she quipped. "You never know."

He rubbed his temples. "You're driving me crazy."

"Sawyer, look, man. She's doing this." Jared studied Sawyer. "You're the one who's kept her safe since the day she arrived."

This week? Barely. Sawyer ground his molars again.

"So what's it going to be?" Jared asked. "Are you gonna let someone else pick up your responsibilities?"

"I'm not his responsibility," Angela said, though her voice sounded far away.

Anyone on their team would keep her safe. Sawyer trusted the ACES team with his life every damn time they left on a job. But did he trust them with her life? Yeah. Of course. But at the same time, he couldn't imagine letting them step into a role that was his. "I'm in."

CHAPTER THIRTEEN

ANGELA HAD ONLY thought this long day had ended, but when she heard the knock on her door, she knew Sawyer would be standing on the other side. It didn't take him long to knock a second time. Angela touched the mud mask caked on her cheeks. It had already hardened. Sawyer's knocking would wake half the floor if she made him wait for her to wash it off.

She grabbed the silk robe off her bed, secured the sash around her waist, and peered through the peephole. Fully dressed, he had donned a shirt since the last time she'd seen him, but that didn't make him look any happier.

"What do you want?" she called without letting him in, though since the mud mask had dried her face in place, her question sounded more like *hut-da-oo-wunt.*

He scowled toward the peephole. "We've gotta talk shop."

Wanting to talk shop was a slight change in his attitude. She cracked the door and peered out, her greenish face hidden in the shadows of her dark entryway.

"If we're doing this"—he stepped close as though she were about to open the door—"you have to know how to fire a gun."

She would've made a face if she could have. "I can fire a gun."

His brow furrowed. "What?"

Angela sighed and then let him in. "Come in."

"*What?*" He strode inside and followed her down the short hallway to her sitting area. "Why do you sound drunk?"

After the day she'd had, who would blame her for having a glass or two of wine? Angela turned on her heel and smiled. The face mask cracked on her cheeks.

Sawyer jumped then caught himself. "What's the matter with your face?"

"I wasn't expecting company." Now that she'd cracked the mask, Angela didn't sound like cotton balls were shoved in her mouth. At least, not as much as before.

"I guess not."

She waved for him to have a seat. "Give me a minute."

"That looks like it will take an hour with a jackhammer."

Sometimes, the aloof way the guys on Titan's team acted made her wonder if they'd ever spent time with women outside their office walls. Obviously, the married ones had, and she understood that Sawyer had dated. Maybe they'd never reached the level of face-mask seriousness.

Had Paul ever seen her in a face mask? Had he ever done anything with her that wasn't to facilitate his now-apparent end goal? Probably not...

The television turned on as Sawyer made himself comfortable. She had no doubt that tonight he was there for business; tonight would include no long, swaying hugs by the window. He wanted to talk shop. She would talk shop. Operations were a whole new ball game. Hence Sawyer's gun-shooting concerns. She decided to rush through the mask removal process.

Face scrubbed clean, she returned to the living room. A soccer game was on the television, but it didn't hold his attention. He was studying his phone when she padded back in. "Who's playing?"

He tossed the phone and turned off the game. "No idea."

Oh, man. Sawyer's stress level was palpable. "I've fired a gun before."

His eyebrows rose. "Like a water gun?"

"Oh, don't be an ass."

Quiet laughter rumbled in his chest. Maybe he wasn't as tense as she thought. "Earlier tonight," he said. "I realized there's a lot I don't know about you."

Angela had just been thinking the same thing. "You know me better than I know you." She held up a finger. "You know where I work. How awesome I am at my job."

Sawyer laughed again, this time a little louder.

"You know my family," she continued, "my ex, the major trauma that I've survived, the greatest hits of my most embarrassing life moments." This time, she raised an eyebrow. "Pretty major stuff."

"True," he agreed. "Yet, I don't know if your weapons experience is more backyard games or tactical preparation."

"Tactical preparation? Yeah, no, not that."

"So, water guns?"

"Those water cannons that you use to win prizes at a carnival? I've won the biggest stuffed animals you've ever seen."

The corners of his mouth curved upward. "So you're saying you're good?"

Angela sat on her yellow couch and tucked her feet underneath her. "Are you still upset with me?"

"I was never upset with you."

She side-eyed him. "I call bullshit."

"More like concerned." He rubbed the back of his neck. "I was caught off guard. But I've had time to process."

"What's there to process?"

"You, Angela. You know jobs can go from ordinary to bat shit in the blink of an eye. I don't want to see that happen when you're involved."

"Why?"

"Because…" He twisted his lips. "The idea of you walking into danger? That makes me uncomfortable."

"Not doing something makes me more than uncomfortable."

"Yeah, I've gathered that." He stretched, acting as though he were buying time to gather his thoughts. "We debated. I heard the pros and cons, and now I'm on Team Let's Do This."

"Total buy-in?"

"Complete." He nodded. "But we should prepare for the unexpected."

"I have shot a gun before, all right? A water gun *and* a handgun, but not in a long time," she admitted.

"All right, that's good."

"I've never been trained, but my dad showed me more than once when visiting the Poconos."

Sawyer crossed his arms and nodded, taking all the information in. "I never hear about your dad."

She laughed. "Me either. He's a good guy. Busy. Very busy."

"Busier than your mom?"

Angela considered. "Equally busy." She shrugged. That lifestyle wasn't one most could imagine. "My parents sort of live their own lives."

"Was that a good thing or bad?"

She shrugged again. "It's the only thing I know."

He sat next to her on the couch. She liked him close. The conversation didn't feel like an interrogation when they were side by side.

"What about your parents?" she asked.

The question seemed to catch him off guard again. He considered for a moment. "They're very normal."

"What does that mean? Happy? Not happy?"

An honest smile touched his lips and met his blue eyes. "Very happy. Good parents. Good role models. I had a very normal upbringing, and they wanted me to have a happy, normal life. It's something that comes up when I visit—" The light in his expression faltered, and he forced a smile. "They would have been thrilled if I was settled down near them. But that's not the path life gave me."

"They think you're married to the job?"

Sawyer pressed his lips together. "Yeah." He cleared his throat and pretended to laugh. "Married to the job. I'll never be like Hagan, Chance, or Liam. It'll just be Camden and me, single until the end of days."

She'd never seen Sawyer fake a smile and force laughter. He wasn't all that good at it. "If I get dressed, do you want to go to the range and practice?"

According to the guys, the shooting facilities were one of the best parts of Jared Westin's hotel headquarters. That wasn't an amenity that she enjoyed. Lap pool and saunas? Check. World-class dining? Check. Training facilities for ACES? Nothing but the best. She used Titan's gym. Sometimes, she'd watch their tactical training. But she'd never had a reason to go to the gun range. Until tonight.

"Are you up for it after your spa night?" he asked. "Or do you have some kind of lotion routine that will take hours?"

She laughed. "So you *do* know a thing or two about the secret lives of women?"

"Ha." Awkwardly, he checked his phone and stood up. "You know what? I didn't realize how late it was. I'll let you get back to whatever you were up to."

"It's okay. I don't have a lotion routine." Shooting guns hadn't been how she envisioned spending the end of the night, but she didn't want Sawyer to leave.

He rechecked the time. "It's late."

Late nights were never a bother before. If she wanted to run errands at night, Sawyer had accompanied her. Arbitrary timelines never confined their social schedules. "Did I say something to upset you?"

"Nah, I'm just exhausted." He pushed off the couch and headed for the door. "Good night."

"Sawyer?"

He glanced over his shoulder. "Really, Ange. I shouldn't have shoved my way into—"

"You didn't. I let you in."

"And now you can let me out." He turned around but still retreated another step. "I'm tired. That's all. It's been a roller coaster of a day, and it just hit me like a Mack truck."

She didn't believe him. "I may be a newbie in the field, but even I know we need to communicate well."

"We do, Angela," he said, taking another step back, "and everything's fine."

Her lips flattened. "That's a load of BS, my friend."

His head lolled back as though it were too heavy to hold up. Sawyer stared at the ceiling for a long minute. "I thought of something that has nothing to do with you or this job." He crossed a hand over his heart. "I swear."

Then, with a reminder to deadbolt her door, he was gone.

Angela replayed the conversation in her mind and didn't see where she'd gone wrong. She had a busy, abnormal family. He had a happy one. She'd worn a mud mask. He and Camden were perpetual bachelors.

Angela deadbolted the door and dragged herself toward her bedroom. She could go to the gun range and practice. That would show Sawyer she meant business, that he could take her seriously. But the range held no interest now that he wouldn't be by her side. Her bed was calling.

She cinched the robe sash tighter and crawled under the covers. The bedroom was her sanctuary. Jared had let her work with an interior designer to furnish her apartment. After living on a cot in a fenced-in cage in a warehouse for the better part of her twenties, she'd painstakingly chosen bright colors, luxurious fabrics, and plants that she couldn't kill.

But, as she forced her eyes closed, the carefully appointed room felt lonely. Abandoned. Sawyer had left disingenuously, and she didn't know why.

CHAPTER FOURTEEN

ANGELA'S PHONE RANG. For a single, panicked moment, she thought she'd slept through her alarm. She scrambled to answer the call despite the ungodly hour. "Hello?"

"Up and at 'em," Sawyer demanded as though it weren't the middle of the night.

"What?" She fought the invading wakefulness. This had to be a nightmare. "It's still dark outside." Not even a crack of daylight shone from around her bedroom curtains. "Go away."

"You can sleep when you're dead."

God, what time was it? She'd been up all night, trying to fall asleep. Now that she had, Sawyer was torturing her. Angela fell back into bed, phone pressed to her ear, and grumbled. "What do you want?"

"Breakfast."

She groaned. "Microwave a breakfast burrito."

A knock pounded on her front door. She would have closed her bedroom door if she had had the presence of mind last night. That might have muffled Sawyer's attempt to roust her. "You're such a bully."

He pounded on the door again.

"You're going to wake the neighbors."

He scoffed. "I brought coffee."

Angela rolled onto her side. "You're lucky I'm a caffeine junkie."

"That's what I was counting on."

She hung up on him, tossed the phone, and tied her robe around her waist. Finger-combing her hair into something that bore less resemblance to a banshee's, she answered the door and snagged her coffee.

Sawyer followed her inside. "You're looking well-rested."

"Bite me."

He parked against the wall and sipped his coffee while she guzzled hers.

"Sawyer." Her patience was short. The caffeine hadn't had nearly enough time to hit her system. "Why are you here?"

"To get you out the door. Go get dressed."

Angela's eyebrows arched.

"Go get dressed." He shooed her toward her bedroom. "Get ready to go Stateside."

Angela maneuvered past him. What was he talking about? Right now? She had to get dressed to "get ready"? *Come on, caffeine.* She needed her brain to kickstart. "That's not helping."

After a minute of sitting on the edge of her bed, she heard his footsteps approach the bedroom. "You dressed?"

"If you mean not naked, then yes."

He walked in. "Get out of bed."

"I'm not in bed," she protested. All of fifteen seconds had passed. What more did Sawyer expect of her before the sun had risen? "I don't know what we're doing, so I don't know what to wear."

Sawyer plucked her coffee from her hand—if she were more awake, she'd have protested or at least defended herself—then took her hand and pulled her to her feet.

"I don't think I like you very much right now," she muttered as he dragged her toward her walk-in closet.

They stopped in the middle of a small room. Shoes lined one wall, dresses another. Angela had her skirts and blouses near a vanity that held accessories. A fainting couch and matching upholstered bench held court in the middle of the space.

Sawyer let out a low whistle. "There's a ton of crap in here."

"Not how I'd describe it, but yes."

"You're very organized."

"Very," she agreed. "But it's not helping me out right now. I don't know what we're doing, so how can I dress for success?" She cringed. The sentiment was true, but her control-freak personality was coming on a little too strong.

Sawyer snorted and turned from the rows of skirts arranged by length. "There's not an outfit in here that's going to make everything run smoothly."

"You don't know that." She tugged haphazardly at a couple of options. "We need an agenda. How else am I supposed to know what to wear?"

He snickered. "Who knew you were so dramatic before coffee?" He took a long sip and wandered toward the vanity counter, where he studied the granite as though their day's agenda were hiding in the flecks of white stone. "Look, I'm sorry I took off like that last night."

She no longer needed caffeine to wake up. Her brain jolted to an unfamiliar level of hyperawareness. Angela smoothed her hands down the side of her robe as a wave of last night's abandonment crashed over her. She tried to ignore it. "It's fine."

He scrutinized the vanity. "My head went to a dark place, and I just needed to roll."

She hated he wouldn't face her. Hated that she wanted him to explain more. But more than that, she wanted to bury the emptiness that arrived when he'd left and kept her tossing and turning all night long.

He looked into the vanity's oversized mirror and studied her.

"Let's forget it," she offered then retreated for her coffee. Angela used the seconds-long reprieve to settle the disjointed tension in her chest and returned to her walk-in closet.

Sawyer perched on the edge of her vanity. He held her gaze and then looked around. "Your closet is the size of a living room, you know that?"

She laughed, happy he'd moved on. "Working for Titan has its perks." Angela folded herself onto the fainting couch and tucked her legs underneath her. "All right, we're getting ready to go to the US. Why don't you tell me everything you know? Then I can get dressed and pack a bag."

"Parker pinged me. We have briefing books ready and a jet booked to take us to North Carolina."

Her mouth parted. Booking planes and organizing briefing books? Those responsibilities were her job. "Who did that?"

Sawyer shrugged. "What's the matter?"

"I'm supposed to do that."

The corners of his lips lifted upward. "Actually, right now, you're not."

Disentangling herself from her regular job was worse than figuring out how to dress for the unknown. She didn't know how to handle the situation. Jared wouldn't know the first thing about making transportation arrangements. Parker was too busy. Angela often worked in proximity to Amanda, but their jobs didn't overlap. Even if they did, Amanda had too much on her plate at the moment.

"Ange." Sawyer watched her. "You can't do both jobs well. You have to let Titan do what Titan does."

She agreed—but who? How? Suddenly, the immensity of her haphazard job switch hit her. Angela pressed her hands against her temples. "Oh my God. What have I gotten myself into?" She didn't know a damn thing about gathering intel. She knew how to arrange for safe houses—and, oddly enough, that was because she'd studied for it in a way. Her college degree had been in event planning and hospitality. She was an organizer. She could manage agendas and facilities. Could she do what Jared needed her to if she hadn't spent four years studying? And somehow, she thought she could just hop into the field and investigate? Sawyer had been right.

Their phones pinged. It was too early in the morning for a message to be related to anything other than the job. She hurried out of the closet and found her phone. "It's Parker." It was getting close to the middle of the night on the east coast of the US. She returned to the closet and saw Sawyer's expression had darkened as he glanced up from his phone.

Her stomach lurched. "That look doesn't bode well."

Sawyer's eyebrows arched, apparently in agreement that it wasn't good.

She opened Parker's message.

The Feds were sniffing around. Your mother looped them in.

Angela could've predicted that would happen, and her mother could've held out for longer, but Angela didn't expect much from the woman who day-traded information.

"Keep reading," Sawyer grumbled.

Special Agent John Patterson will be in the hotel lobby in an hour to meet with Angela.

"Great. The Feds want to tell me I'm wrong and crazy all over again." She tossed her phone aside and groaned. "At least that helps me figure out what outfit to wear."

Sawyer snorted.

The phone pinged again. Angela rolled her lips together. Intuition said that the news would only worsen. "What's it say?"

Sawyer quickly skimmed the message. His expression landed like a sucker punch into her gut.

"What?"

The muscles in his neck tightened, turning the crank on her punched stomach. "Sawyer?" She didn't wait and grabbed her phone.

Special Agent John Patterson is a shrink.

Angela's chin snapped up. "A shrink?"

Sawyer blinked as though the message had been written in an alien vernacular. "What the hell?"

Her breathing quickened. "I cannot believe she's doing this."

"Your mother? What—why?"

Angela pressed her fingertips to her temples and calculated when the federal agent would have left the United States if he intended to meet with her in an hour. "She had other plans for me. Remember? Getting married, yada, yada." An ache drilled at the back of her skull. "They can't keep me from this job."

"Maybe that's not why they want you to meet with someone."

"Wishful thinking."

ANGELA SAT AT the conference table as the orange glow of the morning sun rose over Abu Dhabi. The rich aroma of expensive coffee filled the well-appointed office suite. She tried not to fidget. Every minute felt like five.

Amanda, filling Angela's typical role, opened the conference room door and escorted their guest inside. John Patterson was lanky. His rumpled suit matched his tired eyes. She stood to greet him as Amanda ushered him into the conference room.

"Angela Sorenson," Amanda said by way of introduction, "this is Special Agent John Patterson, FBI."

"John." He extended his hand. "Thanks for meeting on such short notice."

They shook. John's firm, sure grip was far more enthusiastic than she expected for a man who had hopped on an airplane and gotten halfway across the globe before she'd gone to sleep the night prior.

Did her mother and the Feds mean to catch Angela off guard, or was this simply a matter of miscommunication? She'd spent the last hour talking herself into a tizzy and back to a calm, rational explanation. "I'm sorry that you had to take the red-eye. I'm sure we could've handled whatever you need to know over a video conference."

"Call me old-fashioned, but…" John gestured for her to take a seat. "I like to sit face to face."

The hand motion irked her. This was her world. Angela handled agendas, booked the meeting rooms, and indicated when guests should take their seats. She pivoted. "I'm going to pour myself a cup of coffee." She walked toward the coffee service set up along the far wall. "Would you like any?"

He seemed to understand her move. But, of course, he was a shrink—for the Feds, no less. The man was likely hyper-analyzing her every breath. "I'm fine," he said. "Bouncing back to my regular schedule is easier when I avoid caffeine."

"Sounds like hell." She fixed herself a larger cup than she needed. "I guess you're here because of my mother."

"She had something to do with it," John acknowledged. "But we're more interested in the intel that Parker brought to us." He sat at the table and waited until she returned. "I understand you'd given it to us before, and we dropped the ball."

Angela smiled sardonically. "Dropped the ball *and* made me feel like an idiot."

He nodded, removing a small notepad and pen from his suit jacket pocket. "I'm sure they didn't mean for that to happen, but I'd like to apologize that it did."

She settled in the chair across from John. "I know you didn't fly here to issue apologies."

He clicked his pen as if to agree.

Angela kept her back straight and chin high. Confidence had always been her shield. It hadn't let her down even when she had to fake it. "What are you looking for that Parker hasn't already told you?"

"You're aware that I am a profiler."

"That you're a shrink." She nodded. "I'm aware."

John's lips turned upward. "Guilty as charged but not like you might think." He weighed her silence and then took it as permission to continue. "We build psychological profiles that are used in a variety of ways. For our purposes, I'd like to see what I can do to help narrow the search for Mylene Hathaway."

"I've already shared everything I can think of."

"But *we* haven't spoken before."

Tension needled on her forehead. "And what makes you different from the other profilers and analysts who took what I said, shredded it, and made me feel like a first-class idiot?"

Now, it was time for him to wait in silence. Finally, he shrugged. "I've never met or worked with most of the analysts you spoke with previously." He offered a gentle grin. "I'm not your enemy."

Her mother's standard operating procedures had turned Angela bitter and slightly paranoid. With that mood compounded by too little sleep and maybe too much coffee, she needed to ease up on the guy. Her stiff shoulders dropped. "Understood. Sorry."

John nodded with professional understanding. "From what I gather, you've had a lot on your plate this week."

"You can say that again." She sipped the unneeded coffee. "How can I help? You're interested in Mylene Hathaway?"

John pressed the top of the pen open and closed. "I want to talk to you about the day Pham's associates took you." He click-clicked the pen again. "Is it all right with you if we review the details?"

Angela wanted a pen that clicked too. They could communicate like dolphins and be just as capable of learning anything new. "That has pretty much been talked to death."

He pressed the top of the pen with his thumb again. Click, click. "Humor me."

She took a deep breath and recounted everything that she'd said before. This many years later, sharing her recollections of the abduction was robotic. She made sure to add details that hadn't initially occurred to her years ago but that investigators always asked on follow-up. Weather? Sunny. Sounds? Normal parking lot sounds. Gut feelings or intuition about what was about to happen to her? Nonexistent.

After she wrapped up, Angela waited for the surefire follow-up questions meant to double-check her memories. But John Patterson reread his scant notes.

"Are you recording our conversation?" she asked.

"No, no." He circled something on his notepad, click-clicked his pen, and laid both objects on the table, squaring them to the edge. "Besides, if I didn't tell you I had been recording, the ethics on that…" He waggled his hand from side to side. "Not great."

Angela snorted. Life with her mother had made her a little mistrustful about people in power and their ethics. "Didn't look like you wrote much."

"I didn't."

Her eyebrows arched.

"I've been studying Pham's case for years."

Now her stomach tightened. "You're one of the Feds working on ways to infiltrate his network."

John Patterson nodded. "And I've been told your thoughts on my work."

Angela flushed. Had he heard her opinion on the ineptitude of the agents studying Pham? "Oh boy."

"You're not wrong." He studied her. "When you said that I can only know as much as I can research, that's true and infinitely less than someone like you who has lived it."

Her cheeks warmed again. She nodded, not thrilled that someone had shared her thoughts on his job. Angela didn't want to knock the man's work now that he was in front of her. "Please don't take what I said personally."

John leaned against the back of the rolling chair and click-clicked his pen. "I didn't, and you're right. It's one of the reasons I'm here, talking to you in person. I don't want to miss a single detail. An eye tic. A quick intake of breath. My notes are basic and only serve to re-capture your thoughts on Pham, not analyze them."

"Then what is it that you're really interested in?"

"I want to analyze what you're not saying, what you might not even realize you're avoiding."

"Well, then, the man you need to see is my therapist."

"Your appointment this week had some fireworks."

She snorted. "You can say that again."

"You don't seem scarred, if you don't mind me saying."

Angela paused, unsure how to explain that her scars were ugly, but they were hers. "I don't know that anyone could go through everything that I have and not operate outside the lines of what's expected."

"Trauma affects everyone differently. Some overreact. A mouse farts, and they dive for cover. Others might slap the woman that had tried to kill them."

Angela blushed. "I was upset. But, between Sawyer and Ibrahim, I was safe."

"Ibrahim is a therapist who you regularly see?"

She nodded.

"And Sawyer Cabot is a Titan operative?"

Was that the best way to describe Sawyer in this conversation? He'd acted as her bodyguard so long as he wasn't on the job when she needed to leave Titan's premises. But he was also her good friend. "Yes, he's based here."

Again, John clicked his pen.

"If Ibrahim has notes on my Pham recollections, you can have them," she offered, pivoting from the topic of Sawyer.

"That's not a bad idea. Do I have your permission?"

"On Pham details? Sure. Go for it. I want to do whatever it takes to ensure Pham stays behind bars." And rescue Mylene Hathaway, but she didn't want to share that with John Patterson. "Be warned, I'm quite the case study. He might not have notes on Pham. I'm more than enough to keep him busy."

"Everyone feels like that after living through your kind of hell."

It was scary that enough people had lived a similar life experience that John could generalize. "We could have him meet you here today."

The pen clicked again. "That would be helpful."

An awkward silence spread between them, as if he expected Angela to continue sharing. "I don't understand exactly what you're looking for," she said.

"The most interesting details emerge in casual conversations. Simple ones after simple questions. Like, do you enjoy working here?"

"Yes, of course."

"Do you feel safe?"

"There are probably fewer safe places in the world, given what my life is like."

"What's your life like?"

"You know most everything. Abduction. Captivity. Relocated for work. Someone tried to kill me because my mom blew my cover."

"Is sarcasm one of the ways you handle stress?"

"That, coffee, and clothes."

John's lips flattened. "How familiar are you with different types of shock?"

"I have no clinical expertise. That's Ibrahim's bailiwick."

"How familiar are you with an M-16 rifle?"

Her face skewed. "What? I'm not."

"Mylene Hathaway," John segued.

Angela refocused to keep up with the questions.

"You have Titan's full support with your involvement, wherever that may take you. Whatever circumstances you find yourself in."

"I know," she agreed. "And I'll be with Sawyer."

"He's a co-worker?"

Hadn't they just been over this? "Yes."

"And a friend?"

"Yes—"

"Romantic—"

"No!" She leaned forward. "Why would you even ask that?"

"How strong would you consider your family's support network?"

"My what?"

"Your family's support. Let's talk about Paul Bane."

Angela's mouth opened. "Paul isn't my family or a part of my life. Even when he was, he wasn't supportive." Or even interested in her in any way other than the connection to her mother. But that wasn't the Feds' business.

John made a quick note. "How about your parents?"

Her dad was semi-easy to reach, but she hadn't leaned on him. Most often, the easiest way to reach her mother was the scheduling office. But again, why did the FBI care? "What does this have to do with Pham?"

"Have you ever thought about killing Pham?"

Angela jerked back. "That is none of your business."

"You want him to remain behind bars?"

"Yes."

"If you were asked to do something you didn't want to do, if it came to Pham, would you comply?"

"That depends."

"Have you ever been high up and thought about falling off?"

Her lips parted.

"Jumping off?" he prompted.

"No."

"How do you deal with stress, Angela?"

"Well, apparently, I glare at it from across a conference room table."

John chuckled and wrote a note.

"Let's circle back to Sawyer Cabot."

She narrowed her eyes. "Why?"

"I didn't get a clear answer. Is he, or has he been, a romantic partner?"

"Are you crazy? No."

"How do you feel about that?"

"What does any of this have to do with Mylene Hathaway—" Her stomach bottomed out. "Are you doing a psych evaluation on *me*?"

Once more, John clicked his pen.

Son of a bitch. This whole meeting was a sham. "Are you kidding me?" She pushed out of her chair. Did Parker know? Boss Man? *Sawyer?* Humiliation drove daggers up her spine. Did they have concerns about her interest in Sawyer?

Was she interested in Sawyer?

Was Sawyer concerned? Titan? Or had her mother come up with this scheme to understand why Angela hadn't fallen in line with the campaign plans? That was the only answer that made sense. Heat rippled from her neck into her cheeks. This interrogation had been bought and paid for by her mother.

John tossed his pen onto the table. "What about this makes you uncomfortable?"

"You didn't answer my question."

"Everyone who goes into the field needs a risk assessment."

She knew but had to ask, "Who sent you?"

"We already covered that your mother asked me to visit you."

Her nostrils flared.

"Angela, what makes you uncomfortable with this discussion?" he asked again. "Given your work at Titan for the last few years, my line of questioning is normal operating procedure."

"This is not how they're done." Her molars gnashed. "Not to mention, they're never done surreptitiously."

"I apologize if it came off that way," he said casually, studying her.

This back-and-forth, she realized, was part of his psych evaluation also. "You want to know what makes me uncomfortable?" she scoffed. "Everything."

"That's a throwaway answer. Give yourself a second and see if you have a different answer."

God, this man infuriated her. "Don't talk to me like I'm a toddler."

"I'm aggravating you," he suggested.

"Yeah, not to be rude, but—"

"Dig into that, Angela. Why not be rude? You're safe. You have loved ones. A job that you enjoy and protects you—"

She squared her shoulders. The lack of control in this pointless conversation was enough to unravel her, but wasn't that what John Patterson was looking for? What her mother wanted? Absolutely. "We're done."

CHAPTER FIFTEEN

YLENE HATHAWAY STARED at the blank computer screen like it was a blank canvas. In her time under Tran Pham's thumb, she had learned to do magic with the dance of keystrokes and lines of code. Sometimes, she daydreamed of posting on social media or even anonymously on message boards, asking for help. She could tell the truth and explain why she lived as a prisoner in this cute little house. Then again, why would she do that? She had nothing to gain from freedom, so she stayed where she was, doing as instructed.

Each day, Mylene followed the same routine. She woke up in the same little bedroom with bare walls and a single chest of drawers, pulled the worn duvet over her tiny thin twin bed, ate her breakfast of plain Greek yogurt, granola, and honey, worked on her tedious assignments from Pham's organization, ate a midday meal at which her creativity was limited to lunch meats and various breads, continued working on her assignments, prepared dinners that let her lose herself in the chopping and cooking, and, once again, worked on her assignments.

If she faltered or in any way deviated from her standard work output, Pham's people would take away her privileges—fresh groceries and full-bodied coffee—and without those, life was merely a continual task list, broken only by dreamless sleep.

She'd hoped that with Tran Pham imprisoned, life would change. It hadn't. She'd hoped that with him behind bars, she might walk away. She couldn't.

Her little beach house had a shabby picket fence instead of razor wire. The building wasn't much to look at from the outside; it was slightly run down but not jarringly out of place for the neighborhood. The grass, dominated by weeds, was always cut before it became a nuisance, and, she reasoned, the lack of a manicured lawn was a native ecosystem and good for the bees. That wouldn't exist if Pham kept her elsewhere. Dandelions pocked the sidewalk cracks. Leggy purple and white weed flowers spotted the yard. She supposed it was nice, though she didn't look out her windows and never dared to step out her front door. The outside world was almost as terrible to look at as were the walls inside her house.

Her little prison of a home offered safety so long as she kept her eyes pinned to the ground when she was outside the kitchen, her office, or her bedroom. She wasn't a flight risk. Pham didn't require bars or guards. Their weapons were far more powerful: fear and shame.

CHAPTER SIXTEEN

S AWYER CLOSED THE hardcover and ran his thumb along the worn fabric and title imprinted along the book's spine. He rarely visited the administrative arm of Titan's executive office suite unless he was visiting Angela's office. Most often, the team met in the war room or the hotel's lobby. Until today, Sawyer had never sat in the formal area that greeted the bigwigs and head honchos who hired Titan for covert operations worldwide.

Across from him, Amanda Carter waited, legs kicked out across the cushions of an uncomfortable-looking couch, her laptop resting on her thighs. She didn't appear to be working. At least she was less pale than the last time Sawyer saw her.

Amanda raised her gaze from the screen and chewed on her bottom lip. "What do you make of the Fed?"

He turned the book over and over again. "I don't like unplanned visits."

She nodded. "Angela doesn't like unplanned anything."

He agreed. "It bothers me that the Feds thought it was okay to fly across the world without giving us a heads-up. That doesn't sit right."

"They didn't want her to have time to prepare."

Those were his thoughts exactly. "Prepare for what?"

Footsteps approached.

"We're about to find out," Amanda said.

Alone, Angela walked into the reception space. Her angry eyes gave a clue to how the meeting went.

Sawyer stood. "That must've been fun, huh?"

She gave him a hesitant once-over and kept her distance. "Nothing like

someone asking questions that don't have black-and-white answers."
Angela frowned at Amanda. "I stormed out."

"That bad?"

"That bad." Angela nodded. "If you're feeling up to it, would you
mind escorting John Patterson to the lobby?"

Amanda unfolded her legs from the couch and closed her laptop.
"That's why I'm here." She gave Angela a reassuring touch to her arm as
she passed then added over her shoulder, "I need to take him out this way
if you two want to disappear first."

Sawyer nodded and guided Angela from the corporate reception area
to the elevator. Her arms were folded over her chest as she walked. An
awkward distance hovered between them, as if she didn't want to stand
beside him. "Where to?"

"Are we friends?"

He stopped abruptly. "Yeah, of course."

After another stride, she turned toward him. Her folded arms remained
up, guarded. She almost said something but shook her head and looked
everywhere but at him.

"What happened in there, Angela?"

Uncertainty had softened the anger in her eyes. "A mind screw."

He wanted to close the gap between them and absorb whatever doubt
and hesitation colored her thoughts. He also wanted to throw John
Patterson out of the hotel. Instead, Sawyer shoved his hands into his
pockets. "We need to go somewhere before Amanda and the Fed arrive."

"Do you think we're going to find Mylene?"

"I think we're going to give it our best." He checked his watch.
"Where do you want to go?"

Voices flitted down the hall. Angela glanced over Sawyer's shoulder,
squeezed herself, then dropped her arms. "I want to pack."

He smiled. "For North Carolina?"

She nodded. "I want to leave as soon as we can go wheels up."

He called the elevator. "Parker has a jet on standby." The elevator
arrived as if it knew they had to make a quick escape. Sawyer pressed his
thumb to a nondescript print reader and eased back into the corner to

watch her.

"Don't look at me like that." Angela tucked her chin down and squeezed her eyes shut. "I can't take any more judgement—"

"None of my thoughts had a damn thing to do with judging you, Ange."

Her eyes darted upward. "Then what were you thinking?"

"That you've had one hell of a week. Starting with the shooting, dealing with your mom, the ex-boyfriend." Sawyer gestured to the floor they had just left. "The Fed digging for who the hell knows what."

"A field readiness test." She bit her lip. "Or some kind of relationship psych exam."

His eyebrows rose. "Say again?"

Angela sighed and then met his gaze. "You heard me. My mother wanted a reason to bring me home or, at the very least, keep me from this job. But Jared could've been involved. I'm not sure. The guy wanted to know a lot about Paul and…" She blushed. "Relationships."

The elevator doors opened, and Sawyer ushered Angela toward her apartment. He wasn't sure what to say. Field readiness evaluations weren't unheard of. They all underwent psych evals and a battery of readiness tests—but not moments before an op. The questionable timing crossed Jared off the list of instigators. Boss Man didn't pussyfoot around a healthy, well-functioning team, but he never surprise-tested mental acuity like they were playing a game right before a job. "Why do you think Boss Man might be involved?"

"Does anything happen in this building that he doesn't know?"

Sawyer could think of a few events, starting with the time Hagan and Amanda began dating and the poet ninja who posted funny-but-antagonizing flyers around the building to drive Boss Man crazy. "He doesn't butt into people's personal lives."

She shrugged as they stopped in front of her door. "Of course, he knows John Patterson was here." Angela unlocked her apartment and let Sawyer in behind her. "But even if he knew the line of questioning, Jared probably didn't think twice because, all things considered, it's not a big deal. I'm blowing this out of proportion."

"I don't know about that."

Tension pinched at the corners of her lips and eyes.

"Something happened in that meeting that you're not telling me about."

She wrapped her arms over her chest. "My entire body aches."

"Stress is a physical thing."

Angela squeezed her eyes shut.

"You're avoiding my question." Sawyer hesitated but then stepped closer. He didn't like the unknown and hated that she wasn't sharing her burden.

"I know." She released a deep breath. "He had questions about you."

Surprised, he faltered. "What kind of questions?"

Her cheeks turned pink, and just as she had at the elevator, she looked everywhere but at him. "I don't know. If we're friends."

Sawyer cocked his head. He shoved his hands into his pockets again, restless that she had to ask, restless in a way he couldn't pinpoint. "And you didn't know?"

Angela side-eyed him, looking half defensive, half annoyed. "Of course I know."

"But you just asked me in front of the elevators if we're friends."

She hesitated. "I—uh, he started to ask if we were more than friends." She tried to laugh, but it sounded more like a wheeze. "I know. Crazy."

Sawyer stood very still, able to hear his heartbeat. "You were in a relationship."

"A nonexistent one, but yeah," she agreed. "But the idea that you and I were…" She wouldn't meet his gaze. "That doesn't make sense."

His thoughts scrambled. Sawyer considered his words and struggled to keep his tone even. "Why wouldn't we make sense?"

"Because you're you, and I'm me."

"What does that mean?" he pressed.

"I have no idea." Her laughter didn't ring true. "I need to pack. Make yourself at home."

She sidestepped Sawyer. He caught her arm. Her breath lurched. He heard it the same way he had heard his heart jerk. More than that, he felt her gasp in his chest. A heady hunger that damn near blinded him took hold.

His hand stayed on her elbow. The pad of his thumb skimmed against the fabric of her blouse. Nerves jumbled in his throat as a charge of electricity radiated up his arm and down his spine. Angela watched him, beautiful, with wide eyes so overwhelmed that guilt punched him in the chest.

Sawyer stepped away. "I'm already packed." He released her arm and swallowed hard. "We'll leave when you're ready."

CHAPTER SEVENTEEN

S PORTS PLAYED ON the television in Angela's living room. She sat on the edge of her bed. Alive. Terrified. She didn't know what to do with John Patterson's questions, but worse, she didn't know what to do with Sawyer. Or with herself.

Angela had never felt more alert than in the ten seconds that Sawyer held her elbow. If this was what desire was… then Paul had been right. She'd been frigid—with *him*. She wasn't cold or unfeeling or uninterested. But she was far, far out of her element and experience.

And she was embarrassed. Sawyer had touched her arm, and she could hardly catch her breath.

Her phone chimed. The noise was an instant antidote to the heady fluttering that left her unable to think straight.

Angela dug her phone free. The text notification from her mother hit as if a bucket of ice-cold water had been dumped over her head.

The messages grounded Angela in the present, reminding her of their family's dysfunction. They repeated that the breakup with Paul was a mistake and that her mother worried for Angela's mental well-being. The texts kept coming. Paul's name and her mother's disappointment continued message after message until Angela couldn't handle it. She typed one word—*ENOUGH*—then muted the conversation and tossed the phone aside.

She should've been angry. The text-message diatribe confirmed why John Patterson had arrived in Abu Dhabi and grilled her. But the anger didn't come. Angela was still floating, high as a kite because she wasn't broken inside.

Angela quickly packed a bag appropriate for investigative work in

North Carolina: shorts and casual shirts. A bathing suit and cover up, just in case they found time to hit the beach. No pencil skirts, starched blouses, or high heels for this trip. Her toiletry bag was on the light side. Everything fit neatly inside a small duffel bag. It wasn't the go-bag that Sawyer would have, but she was ready to leave town for an unknown length of time.

"All right," she called, slinging the bag over her shoulder. "I'm ready."

He appeared at her bedroom door. "Is that what you're wearing?"

Apparently not. She kicked off her heels, shooed him out the door, and changed into something more like she packed. But not before making a mental note that Sawyer did not seem fazed by their conversation and hadn't noticed how she reacted when he'd touched her arm. Thank the Lord for that miracle. There was no need to make her first field job more complicated.

Besides, he didn't have long-term relationships. She was just out of one. He wouldn't be interested in her anyway. They were friends, and she wouldn't screw that up.

"All right, a second time." Angela waltzed out in flats, jeans, and a black cotton shirt with three-quarter-length sleeves and a boat-neck collar. Chic and comfortable. "Do I look okay?"

"You always look good." He pulled the bag from her shoulder. "But now you look more comfortable."

Her stomach flipped. The light and airy feeling had to stop. She didn't have time to understand and manage it. The sensation might've shocked her, but, as with every other uncomfortable feeling, she could control it. Angela refocused on what Sawyer had said. She was comfortable, which was the only thing needed for a fifteen-hour flight.

Just as Sawyer said, the arrangements had been made. An SUV waited to take them to the airport, where a private jet waited on the tarmac. Their luggage was taken as they were shown into the cabin. Blankets, snacks, and drinks were offered as they chose an L-shaped couch, and before Angela could open her book, the captain was taxiing down the runway.

HOURS LATER, ANGELA awoke to dim lights and white noise. She wasn't sure what time it might be, but it was dark outside the windows. She had stretched onto the long part of the couch. On the shorter chair section attached to the couch, Sawyer had fallen asleep next to her. His arm rested by his side, his hand close to her face. His legs draped across a footrest as he reclined. His blanket dangled off his lap. Angela reached over to right it.

"Thanks." His eyes remained shut. He didn't move.

She pulled her hand back quickly. "I didn't realize you were awake."

Sawyer repositioned himself onto his side, looking down at her. "On and off. After dinner, you were out like a light."

She laughed quietly. "Are you comfortable?" There were other couch configurations. He didn't have to sleep in a reclining chair.

He brushed strands of her hair off her face. "I'm good." His fingers lingered, skimming over her cheek as her pulse thundered. His eyes weren't on hers but where he touched until he pulled away. Then they locked onto hers.

The intensity stole her breath. She didn't know what to say, and even if she did, Angela couldn't speak above a whisper for fear of shattering the warm, all-encompassing hold between them.

A flight attendant walked through the cabin and asked if they needed anything. They didn't, but the warm moment disappeared. Sawyer took a long drink from a water bottle. Angela turned onto her back and stared at the curvature of the aircraft's sloping ceiling. Why didn't Sawyer do relationships? Why did she want to know? More importantly, how could she have gone her entire life without someone touching her arm or cheek like he had? Familiar and gentle?

Fewer than forty-eight hours ago, Angela had cried tears after a man had called her frigid. As it turned out, she was simply a woman who hadn't been in the right situation yet.

Sawyer wasn't a situation, though. He was a friend. But knowing that didn't keep her mind from replaying how his touch rocked her body.

He didn't do relationships. Romantic relationships were complicated. Her next one needed to have no agenda. No strings. Casual flings at work were a horrible idea. She closed her eyes and tried to ignore Sawyer. It wasn't working.

In the future, when she was ready, an agenda-free relationship would be nice. One that made her lungs stop working as Sawyer had earlier. How would she find someone like that?

"You have a lot on your mind," he said. "Don't you?"

Startled, she felt a blush crawl up her cheeks. "More than I know what to do with."

"Want to talk to me about it?" he asked.

Ha. Absolutely not.

"Wimp," he teased.

Angela curled into her blanket. "Why don't you have someone?"

His gaze narrowed as if that wasn't where he thought the conversation would go. "Like a girlfriend?"

"Yeah. You said you don't do relationships. It seems like such a final statement. I've seen you date beautiful women. No one sticks. Why?"

He stared at the ceiling as though a good answer might have been hidden in the panels that concealed the oxygen masks. "Never enough time. Not enough interest. You know how it goes."

"No, I don't."

His intense gaze dropped to her. "I don't think that's what you were thinking."

"Don't change the subject from you to me. I'm curious."

"You're much more interesting."

"Did you have a bad breakup?"

"Are you thinking about Paul?"

"He's the furthest thing from my mind." Her nose scrunched. "I wonder if he had his political plan from day one. Like back in college. I mean, why did he want to date me? To rule DC one day?"

"I doubt it was that diabolical." Her question appeared to catch Sawyer off guard. "It's because you're hot."

Fire swept across her cheeks again. "Come on! I'm serious."

"So was I. You're beautiful." Sawyer counted off with a finger, adding, "Kind, funny, smart, resilient." He lifted his other hand. "Interesting, trustworthy, a good listener with sky-high integrity—and"—he winked—"you're hot, sweetheart."

"All right, Sawyer. Enough."

"You asked. I answered." He shrugged. "If that idiot never mentioned your finer points—"

She scoffed. "People don't walk around listing their significant other's attributes."

His eyes locked with hers for a long moment. "Maybe they should."

White noise hummed around them.

"I don't want to talk about him anymore," she said.

He nodded.

"Promise? Because he keeps coming up. I've thought and talked about him more in the last couple of days than I have in years. We can pretend he never existed. That no one exists outside this plane."

Sawyer pulled in a chest-expanding breath and let it out slowly. He kicked off the blanket and stood up.

Again, her stomach dropped. She'd said the wrong thing. "What are you doing?"

He held out his hand.

"Sawyer?"

"Give me your hand."

She did. Her blanket fell as he pulled her up. His hand hooked around her waist, pulling her stomach to his, lingering. Gone was her control. Gone was any barrier that would hide her racing heartbeat.

"What are you doing?" she asked.

He tugged his bottom lip into his mouth as though considering a thousand possible answers. The corners of his mouth teased her. The seriousness in his eyes promised more than she could handle. Somewhere in between, his warm, hard body tangled against hers, and there was nothing but vulnerable truth. "Pretending that no one else exists."

He reached to the floor, grabbed her fallen blanket, and then lay on the couch where she had slept. Sawyer pulled Angela down and folded her against his side, spooning her body. Her head rested on his bicep as though it were her pillow. Sawyer laid the blanket over them, as calm and cool as possible. His rock-hard body enveloped her as his arm draped over her hip possessively. Breathless, she tried to make sense of his actions.

"Good night, Ange."

The easy lull of his breath slowly melted away her surprise. She puddled against him, confident she'd never fall asleep while jumping through the mental calculus needed to understand what was happening. One thing was sure. She wanted to be kissed.

He slept. She imagined. He held her close. She dreamed. What if his confidence and her lack of experience were balanced? What if their friendship was good enough that she could tell him what she wondered, what she needed?

What if…

What if…

"What if" was enough of a lullaby that she let herself fall asleep and dream of possibilities.

CHAPTER EIGHTEEN

T HE CABIN LIGHTS were still dim as the sweet scent of shampoo and a woman's soft, supple body coaxed Sawyer awake. Taking even breaths, a warm, safe Angela slept under his arm. He wasn't sure what to make of pulling her to his side, but he couldn't imagine a better way to wake. A long time had passed since he last fell asleep beside a woman. An even longer time had elapsed since he'd *wanted* to fall asleep next to a woman. The appeal hadn't been there in far too long.

Was it here now? That didn't matter. Sawyer couldn't break his rules. Not even for Angela. He breathed deeply and realized the piling tension of the last few days had dissipated, replaced by an entirely delicious pressure in his chest that he wasn't sure how to handle—or ignore. This wasn't fair to Angela. Hell, he wasn't sure it was fair to him.

The jet bumped as the pilot navigated turbulence. Angela stirred and sighed, burrowing into Sawyer's fragile hold. He didn't want her eyes to open. Her mind would go into overdrive, fixing and correcting and explaining what he wanted to simply stay.

After another rumble of turbulence, the jet angled up and changed elevation. Sawyer prayed for smoother skies. Too many more jolts might force the flight attendant to ask them to buckle up. He waited, wishing for more than he had a right to request, and when the aircraft leveled smoothly, he stayed awake. How much longer did he have? They were scheduled to touchdown at five in the morning local time. He couldn't check his watch without possibly waking Angela. Sawyer tried to savor what wouldn't happen again. His eyelids shut, but he never drifted back to sleep.

Then, her soft posture became rigid. The easy rhythm of her breaths stilted. If he could've read her mind, Sawyer would have been certain the wheels were spinning at a breakneck speed.

"Morning," he whispered, not moving a muscle. She could turn to face him or run away. He wasn't sure which option was better.

Her body straightened, but she didn't flee. Instead, with her head still resting on him like he was her pillow, she asked, "What time is it?"

He exhaled as if he'd been holding his breath for an hour and finally checked his watch. "A little after four."

She lifted her chin, offering him her sleepy, semi-panicked eyes. "We'll be wheels down soon?"

He nodded. "In forty-five minutes or so." There was a fifty-fifty chance that Angela would not acknowledge how they slept. The situation would be easier that way, if he were being honest. If she peppered him with questions, all the vulnerability and unknowns would dissolve. He didn't want her to say a word.

The sleepiness faded. Angela eyed their bodies and then studied him. "Sawyer…" The questions were about to start.

"You're very good at scripting a narrative," he said.

Her eyes widened at the apparent accusation. "Oh, really?"

The corners of his lips quirked. "Yup, and I'm wondering how that will work out right now."

Angela tried to elbow him, but that only brought their bodies closer. She blushed. "Well, I'm feeling a little out of my element at the moment. Scripting might help."

She wasn't wrong. Still, he didn't want her to explain away what had drawn them together. "You know what I think?"

"I have absolutely no clue."

In truth, he didn't know what to think. "Me neither."

Maybe, subconsciously, pulling her to sleep at his side had been an unspoken offer to handle their conversation and erase what she hadn't wanted to face. She had ceded her tight grip on her world and melted into his. He had her. He'd held her. He'd protect her. Like he always had—but more so.

"Should I move?" she finally asked.

That question wasn't easy. He couldn't be anything like she needed. Safe. Secure. Stable. In it for the long haul. The realization made his empty heart ache. Still, he couldn't stop himself. "Do you want to?" Hope, unfamiliar and unwelcome, danced in his chest. He'd asked too much. "I mean." He cleared his throat. "If you're comfortable, stay. No big deal."

She scoffed and shook her head. "No big deal..." She repositioned herself and stared blankly at the wall. Her walls of control and scripted narrative would arrive shortly. Sawyer hated them and was just as annoyed at himself.

He closed his eyes. Soon enough, the plane would land, and everything would return to normal. He hated it even as much as he needed it.

"Sawyer?"

Her no-nonsense tone made him smile. "Hm?"

"I have a proposition for you," she said.

His curiosity was piqued. A proposition wasn't what he had on his bingo card. "What's that?"

She propped onto her elbow and rested her head in the palm of her hand. "Well, don't decide right now."

He grinned.

"You don't do relationships—"

"Ange—"

"Don't interrupt either." She waved him to shut up. "Like I was saying. You don't do relationships." She gave him a stern look to keep his mouth closed.

Sawyer managed to stay quiet.

"And I have a lot of figuring out to do," she said.

Angela paused, waiting for him to slip up and ask questions before she was ready. But this wasn't his first rodeo when it came to her speeches. He didn't take the bait, though he was curious as all hell.

"We're on this trip where everyone has already told me we'll hit dead ends and have nothing to do..." She blushed in a way that went straight to his groin. "What if we mess around?"

Straight, straight, straight to his groin. The woman had knocked the air from his lungs without moving a muscle.

"Like for practice or something," Angela tried to explain as if he hadn't heard a word she'd said. "Or fun. I don't know." Her blush intensified. "I don't have practice doing this. But you do."

Was that insulting? He couldn't parse underlying meanings and possible jabs when all the blood in his body had caught fire. Sawyer swallowed hard and arched his eyebrows, failing to assume the unaffected manner he'd hoped to achieve. "I do?"

"Yeah. Sure. Your dates. No relationship. That kind of stuff."

Everyone he'd dated casually was very different from her.

"For a finite amount of time," she continued. "For the duration of this job."

He blinked and tried to match her words to meanings, but his brain wasn't operating as expected.

"We'd have rules. Expectations. Safe words?" Her brow furrowed. "No, that's probably not what we're going for."

She was negotiating a contract for them to go to bed, and he hadn't managed to speak yet.

"So that's my proposition." Now her face skewed. "If you could say something, I'd feel less like an idiot."

"Ange..." The warmth from lying beside her was gone. She was leaning into her role as the queen of control, asking for a time-boxed friends-with-benefits situation, all while he'd been enamored with—and confused by—the fact he held a woman while she slept. They'd inched close to something very personal, and she ran. Hell, worse than that, Angela was asking for a walking, talking vibrator to teach her the ropes. A distant cousin of disappointment bubbled thickly in his chest. "I don't think I can do that."

Her face fell. She played her change in mood off with a shrug. "It was just an idea."

She wanted a teacher? Why didn't she want romance? Angela deserved to be swept off her feet after a ho-hum time with the ex who should not be named. Not that Sawyer was the right guy to shower her with attention. "I'm just... not in the right headspace for something like that."

"Seriously, Sawyer. A simple no is all that's needed. You don't have to make up excuses." They were still so close, but she wouldn't meet his gaze. "Can you forget what I said so this isn't weird?"

"It's only going to be weird if you move to another seat."

"Don't patronize me. Okay?" Angela wriggled and repositioned herself to face away from him but stayed on the couch.

"That wasn't my intention, sweetheart."

She hmphed, and he could practically feel her eyes roll. But after a minute, she added, "You're a very good big spoon, Sawyer. Never would have guessed it."

"Not so bad yourself, little spoon." He hid his regret in a forced laugh against the back of her head. "That's just one of my many talents."

An hour later, coffees in hand, they had landed, stepping off Titan's jet and into a waiting SUV. The drive to Emerald Isle wouldn't take long. Angela was eerily normal. The same couldn't be said of himself.

Their driver left them at a safe house on the beach that came with a car and a fully stocked refrigerator. An updated briefing book sat on the kitchen counter. Sawyer didn't know who'd made the arrangements, but they'd done a great job.

He bypassed the kitchen and living room and proceeded upstairs. The floor had two bedrooms, the larger one with an ocean-facing balcony. He tossed Angela's bag onto that bed and dropped his belongings in the bedroom across the hall. "Good view up here."

He didn't hear a peep.

Sawyer wandered to the main floor again and found Angela at the kitchen table with papers spread before her, pen in hand. "You don't want to see your room?"

"I want to find Mylene." She had grouped the crime scene photos next to those taken from a vacation rental website. Law enforcement notes were categorized by agency: Local PD. Military police.

He walked around the table and read the notes she'd scribbled in her little notebook. Her proposition was apparently a distant memory. At least it was for her.

Angela dropped her pen on the table. "We're a block away from where the murders took place." Her eyebrows arched. "I don't know what we're going to find, but we should take a look."

"Yeah. Sure." Sawyer grabbed an apple from a fresh fruit bowl. "Can you imagine staying at a vacation rental where a woman killed her husband and sister?"

"Except Mylene didn't kill them."

He bit into the apple, chewed, and swallowed. "That's our working theory."

Angela glared.

"What's that look for? If you keep an open mind, the truth will be easier to spot."

"What? Now you're Sherlock Holmes?"

He took another bite of the apple. Not only was her proposition a distant memory, but work had her full attention. She wasn't in the mood to question their working theory. Sawyer reminded himself to let the investigation do the talking. He polished off the apple while she took notes.

What was there to write down? That was the point of a briefing book. Someone had done that already. Sawyer glanced over her shoulder. "You're making us an agenda?"

"Why wouldn't I?"

Good question. He was neither Sherlock Holmes nor Dr. Watson. At least Watson knew when to ask questions and listen. Sawyer could only twiddle his thumbs. "I'm going to look around."

He left her to investigate the provisions in the pantry and searched for secretly stashed weapons throughout the house. After a minute, he'd completed his search and returned to the kitchen. "Did you pack a vest?"

She glanced up and stared as though he'd asked permission to dance like a fool. "No one knows where I am."

He shrugged. "Things change."

"It doesn't blend in on the beach." She smiled as though the discussion had ended. "But I did pack SPF and a sun hat."

He read over her shoulder. The timeline on the note started in fifteen minutes and wrapped with their return at eleven in the morning. "I think we need to compromise on some things."

"Like?"

"Fifteen-minute increments of planning? We need to get a lay of the land before we check out the other beach house."

She pursed her lips. "But…"

"But?" Sawyer knew what was happening. She was filling in every second of the day to control the narrative and ignore what she'd said. That might be possible for her. Not so much for him. "Go get dressed in something beachy. We're going to wing this one."

"I don't want to waste time."

He sighed and opted to compromise. "We'll walk up from the beach and cut over."

"We can look at the other house?"

"Sure. We'll scope it out."

Angela tapped her index finger on her pen and then relented.

Fifteen minutes later, she returned to the kitchen table, perfectly on an internal schedule. Her dark hair was tied back. A large-brimmed hat covered her face. Angela's black one-piece curved over her figure and short-circuited his brain. This choice of clothing wasn't the athletic bathing suit she wore for laps. A black knit cover-up dangled over her hips.

He cleared his throat. "Very beachy."

She eyed his board shorts and flip-flops then busied herself with the paperwork on the table. Angela gathered the reports and photos and put them neatly in her beach bag. She slid her sunglasses on and returned to hiding behind the oversized sunhat; then she and Sawyer were off.

From the deck, they followed the small boardwalk, which deposited them on the beach. The early June morning hadn't brought out sunbathers or families yet. A woman threw a Frisbee for her dogs. They galloped into the waves and fought over the toy before they raced back for another throw. The occasional lone runner loped by. An older couple walked hand in hand.

Sawyer and Angela carried their shoes while walking on the damp sand. The occasional wave lapped over their feet. Angela was very quiet. Hell, so was he. Mylene had Angela's focus. Angela had his. He hoped the sun would bake sense into his brain as they strolled through the lapping waves.

Angela grabbed his forearm and stopped. "There it is."

This beach house was as close to the water as theirs. He wrapped an arm around her waist and pulled her close. "Easy, Ange. We don't need to stare."

But if anyone glanced their way, they might have a problem. She was stiff as a knife and stuck out like a woman who needed an escape plan. "You okay?" he asked. His hand smoothed over her hip and skimmed up the smooth swimsuit. "I'll let you go if you need me to, but you can't stare at the house."

She licked her bottom lip. "No. It's fine. You just caught me off guard."

"Sorry…" He should have repositioned them to get a better look at the house, but he couldn't.

Her chin dipped. "I'm—" Angela shook her head. "What I said on the plane…" She raised her eyes to his. "I wish I could take it back."

Sawyer cinched her closer. "Regrets are no fun."

"That's me. Life of the party. Throwing caution to the wind."

That was what she'd done, and he'd shot her down. Now, who was the one with the regrets? His reflection in her glasses showed his frown. Sawyer forced a grin. "Put your arms around my neck."

That she did was the slightest balm.

"Look like you can stand me," he said. "I'm going to get a good look at that house."

Angela laughed, and he repositioned them.

"What do you see? Anyone staying there?"

No car sat in the driveway. "Looks like nobody's home." The shades were drawn. The covers for the grill and hot tub were in place. "Probably no renters right now."

"Then can we go over and check it out?"

"Give me another minute to be sure." Sawyer surveyed the area and moved them closer. No people were watching. No security cameras were in sight. "I think so. Let's go."

Angela all but yipped. Despite her control and agendas, she didn't approach anything involving Mylene with an ounce of hesitation, and it would give him heartburn.

"Are you going to try the front door?" She grabbed his hand and pulled for him to move faster. "Break a window?"

"Option C. Scope the deck and see what our opportunities are." He needed fewer chances for neighbors or nearby security cameras to catch them.

They walked onto a deck that could have used a handyman's attention. Rickety and in need of bracing, the deck mirrored the beach house, which had good bones but was desperate for upkeep.

Two lockboxes hung on the deck railing. Rental guests and cleaning staff, he guessed. Both were well used. The beach house wasn't abandoned. The duo's timing had been lucky.

Sawyer tried the back door. Its lock was simple and standard. He pulled a lockpicking kit from his wallet.

"Option D," Angela said. "You had a plan to get inside all along."

He winked and got them through the doorway. The place smelled of musty beach house and lemon air freshener. Sunlight crept around blinds and the sides of drapes. He didn't know what they were looking for. "What do you want to see?"

Angela twirled as though inspiration would magically hit her but then pulled the crime scene photos from her beach bag. She lined them on the kitchen counter. Law enforcement had done a good job at documenting the entire house. Windows. Doors. Dirty dishes.

"The interior's the same." He opened a cabinet. "Same dishes."

"I don't know why that would change unless someone sold the place."

True. The house had the same couches. Probably the same bed where the husband and sister had spent the night before they were shot. Sawyer and Angela walked into the living room. The only difference from the crime scene photos was a new area rug under the coffee table. The original rug had probably been taken into evidence, given the proximity of the bodies.

Angela held up a photograph in which luminol lit up a blood-splattered wall. "That's there." She shuffled another picture. "And that's right here."

Sawyer wondered if the walls had been repainted or scrubbed with bleach. A little luminol and a black light would likely light them up like the Fourth of July. "Want to go upstairs?"

Her frown deepened. "Yes."

The layout was not dissimilar from their beach house's. The same builder likely constructed every house in the neighborhood. Angela stared at one bedroom and then the next.

He didn't see anything interesting. Did she? "What do you think?"

Angela shrugged.

That look had more to it—or maybe not. Studying crime scene photos and walking around a house that hid a dark secret could weigh heavy. "You okay?"

"Yes, it's just…" They stood between the two bedrooms. "Why did you give me the room with the balcony?"

"It was the nice thing to do?" He raised a shoulder. "Nicer room for the fairer sex."

"Imagine if you were married, having an affair, and renting a beach house with your secret girlfriend."

He frowned. "That'd make me a piece of shit."

"Yeah, I know." Angela gave him the side-eye. "But just imagine. Okay?"

"Fine. For investigative purposes, I'm a cheating asshole."

"And you're staying at a beach house for an affair. Which bedroom would you choose?"

"The one with the balcony."

"Right," she agreed, directing them into the bathroom. "What about your toiletries? Where would you put your stuff?"

"Is this a trick question?" he joked. "I have no clue."

"Have you ever lived with someone before?"

"Uh—"

"Yeah, me neither." She stared at the bathroom counter and then shuffled through the photographs. Then she held up the corresponding picture. "I think this is weird."

He glanced at the crime scene photo and didn't see whatever she wanted him to. "What am I missing?"

"Look at how everything has been arranged."

He stared at the toiletries on the counter in the picture and then at the blank counter in front of him. "What?"

"Look at the toothbrushes and toothpaste."

Again, Sawyer stared at the counter and then the photo. "I don't see anything noteworthy."

She pointed at the counter. "The two toothbrushes are right beside each other, a half inch apart, hanging off the edge into the sink. Who does that?"

"What?"

"No one lines their toothbrushes side by side, a half inch apart. Not even if they have been married for years. It's too precise and unnatural."

Sawyer scowled at the photo. "Really?" He used an electric toothbrush that had a charger. But before that, he couldn't remember thinking about the placement of his toothbrush on a counter, much less whether he put it next to or opposite someone else's.

"If you're new into a relationship, it'd be too June Cleaver to line up toothbrushes. If you're cheating and sneaking around and not used to sharing a bathroom, it's a bold statement to line them up."

A skeptical look crossed his features.

"You're proving my point, Sawyer. No one does this."

"Okay, say you're right. What's the point? It has nothing to do with whether or not Mylene killed—"

Loud, excited voices poured into the beach house.

"Shit," he muttered. They inched out of the bathroom. The voices didn't sound threatening, but he wouldn't take a chance. Sawyer tucked Angela behind his back. He wasn't armed, and she wasn't wearing a Kevlar vest. Sweat broke out on the back of his neck. "Did you leave anything downstairs?"

Angela shook her head but caught herself. "My hat."

What sounded like two kids and a shepherding adult boomed from the first floor. Bags were dropped. Kids squealed.

"Forget it." They had to get out. The kids sounded like a herd of buffalo as they explored the beach house. "The back door is still unlocked—come on."

"What's upstairs?" one of the children called.

They stopped short. No-go on the back door. Sawyer took Angela's hand and beelined for the bedroom balcony as little feet raced up the stairs. He threw open the sliding glass door and flung it closed just as he was certain the kids hit the top of the staircase.

A two-story beach house on stilts meant Angela and Sawyer were three floors up. Directly below, two women unloaded a minivan on a crushed-shell driveway. A concrete patio extended on both sides. Neither would make a pleasant landing zone.

The second-story deck was just off to the side, several feet away. Sawyer could make the jump. He wasn't sure how Angela would fare.

"No way," she said, reading his mind. "Absolutely not. I'm going to break my neck."

"I'm open to suggestions, sweetheart."

"Maybe we stay up here until they leave?" she half joked. "Or maybe they'll head straight to the beach?"

The sliding glass door flew open. They froze against the side of the house.

"Whoa," a kid squealed from inside the doorway. "We are so high up!"

"We're not supposed to open doors!" a younger-sounding kid chided. "I'm telling."

The sliding glass door slammed shut.

"Oh God. Okay," Angela managed. "I'll jump."

"This will be easy, Ange."

"Do not blow smoke up my ass."

He couldn't help but smile. "We crawl onto the other side of the rail. I'll jump down. You lower yourself and then I'll grab you and pull you over."

"That simple, huh?"

"Then we stroll off the back deck while the moms bring in their stuff through the front door."

This situation was a far cry from the most dangerous one he'd ever found himself in, but it might have been the most stressful. If he maneuvered to the second-floor deck and Angela lost her nerve, he'd have a hell of a time getting back to her without catching the eye of someone below.

"Do you trust me?" he asked.

"I don't have a choice."

"That is a bullshit answer, Angela, and this won't work if you don't trust me."

"Of course I trust you. Go on. Be Spider-Man."

"Atta girl." Then he didn't give her a chance to back out. Sawyer jumped to the lower deck. His landing was smooth, albeit louder than he liked as the entire house groaned. The women below him stopped speaking for an eternally lengthy moment before their cheerful banter rebounded.

Another century-long moment passed before Angela peeked her head out from her hiding spot on the top balcony.

Sawyer nodded. "It's go time."

Whether she heard him or not, she hooked her leg over the railing. Her flip-flop dangled precariously over the edge. She maneuvered onto the rail but pulled back entirely. The dangling flip-flop disappeared, and his heart stopped. But he waited, not letting a shred of doubt jinx her determination to get off that balcony.

"Come on, come on, come on," he whispered. "I know you can do this."

Then, two flip-flops landed next to him, followed by her beach bag. No one below noticed the raining accessories. Sawyer took a breath and grinned.

Angela hooked one leg and the other over the edge and pulled herself over the rail. She squatted, twisted, and crouched until she apparently trusted the deck railing to hold her weight. Carefully, Angela lowered herself until she dangled. Sawyer snaked his arm around her knees before she had a moment to panic and lowered her bottom onto his shoulder. They weren't graceful, but they were efficient. He placed her bare feet on the deck and hauled her against the wall.

She picked up her flip-flops and bag. "That was an adventure."

He had a feeling they were just getting started. "Never a dull day on the job."

The kids ran outside and scurried around the driveway.

"No one is inside." She nudged him. "Get my hat."

Not a bad idea. They were by the door with the lock he'd picked initially—although he was surprised she didn't want to haul ass home. "Give me a sec."

Hell, by now, if the renters caught them on the deck, they could feign embarrassment and pretend they'd wandered to the wrong cookie-cutter-style beach house.

He braved a quick visit inside, grabbed Angela's hat, and, with his hand at the small of her back, guided their escape back to the beach as though they were a beach-faring couple out for a stroll.

Adrenaline-fueled laughter overcame Angela by the time they neared the sand that was still damp from a receded high tide. "That was insane."

He grabbed her hand and walked toward the waves. "It was something." What exactly? He didn't know. Certainly not on his top one thousand list of close calls. Still, his heart hammered in his chest. He wasn't ready to let her go.

Angela scooted in front of him, walking backward, with a smile that reached from ear to ear. "And you saved my hat."

Sawyer tugged her back to his side. "All in a day's work."

They reached the water, and she danced over a retreating wave. "This is such a buzz."

He laughed.

"Seriously, Sawyer. I feel like I'm high right now."

He kept laughing and shook his head. "Have you ever done drugs?"

"Nope." She held onto her hat but tipped her head back for a moment. "But this has to be the feeling people chase after. Because, oh my God. I feel like I could fly." She tossed her bag and flip-flops out of the reach of the waves. "Get in the water with me." She untied the cover-up from her hip and flung the garment onto the sand; then she threw her hat like a Frisbee into the vicinity of her discarded clothes.

Angela headed toward the water, casting another big and beautiful smile over her shoulder. "Don't be a scaredy cat, Spider-Man. Come on."

CHAPTER NINETEEN

A LIGHTNESS FLOATED inside Angela's chest. Adrenaline painted the ocean and sky vivid blues and made her feel invincible. Her heartbeat and thoughts were still too fast. She hadn't been kidding. This experience must be what flying high, completely untouchable, was like.

The ocean was cold. The waves pulled back, but Angela was deep enough that the water covered her knees. She held out her arms as if to soak in all the warmth the world had to offer.

Another wave rolled toward her. Sawyer splashed as he ran into the water. The rolling wave crested, churning sand on its path. Sawyer scooped her as a wave hit. Laughing, Angela hooked her arm around his neck and squealed through the roaring onslaught of cold salt water.

Farther out, another wave formed. Sawyer cradled her to his chest and plunged deeper into the water.

"It's coming." She kicked her legs and waited until the last moment to bury her face in his neck.

His laughter and roaring water surrounded her. He waited until the last second before turning their backs to the wave. Her wet hair clung to her cheeks. The salt burned her eyes. But she didn't care as he jumped the waves and dodged seaweed.

"Are you used to the water yet?" he asked.

"Nope." Every time the water retreated, the wind blew over her skin. She held out her arm. "Goose bumps."

"Then we have to go deeper." He carried her until the water lapped at his chest. "Past the waves."

Water pulled around them. "Sawyer…" He carried her until it reached his shoulders. "How deep are we?"

Angela kicked her legs again and tried to stand. The water covered her face. She pushed off the smooth sand and wrapped her arms around his neck. "I can't stand here."

"But are you warmer?"

She considered. "Yes."

His handsome grin made her insides wriggle. "Then mission accomplished."

"If I let go, I'm going to drown."

He laughed. "You know how to swim." But his hands found the backs of her thighs and wrapped her legs around his waist.

The heavy thud of her heart drummed louder than Mother Nature. The crystal-clear adrenaline high that had her rollicking with laughter had been replaced with a heavy feeling in her lungs and arms, a sensation so wonderful and terrifying that she was certain she might drown if Sawyer weren't there to hold her up. Then again, Sawyer was the reason she couldn't breathe.

This man was her friend. Her protector. Her bodyguard. She shouldn't have a loopy, lightheaded desire to be this close, craving more. And the way he watched her made Angela's stomach hit the sea floor and roll like a pummeling wave.

She should say something. Laugh. Joke. Hell, disappear under the cold water. But she couldn't. His damp hair clung to his temples. Rivulets of salt water slid down his skin.

They were so close and not moving—until his palms skimmed over her thighs and ass and slid up her back. Angela could see her chest rise and fall in the water. Her breaths were too deep, but the oxygen wasn't clearing her sun-kissed brain fog.

"You okay?" he asked.

She had to swallow before her voice allowed a small "yes."

His forehead dipped to hers. His breath tickled her cheeks, and with her eyes closed, she felt his heartbeat thunder in his chest just like hers.

Angela opened her eyes. He was watching her. This close, she could see the flecks of ice blue in his irises. Her mouth watered for his, and she tilted her head as if too quick a move would change everything.

Sawyer's soft lips brushed hers with a saltwater kiss sweet enough to boil her insides. His hungry hands kneaded into her sides, but his kiss tortured her. She melted in his arms. His mouth moved over hers, teasing, parting her lips with his tongue.

Desire rumbled in his chest, tangling with their kiss. Her tongue touched his. Electricity and insanity spiraled down her spine. She'd never known need this intense.

And then it ended.

Sawyer gently kissed her again. Chaste and sweet. He squeezed her close and then relaxed his grip. Angela wanted to scream. Her eyes opened. He was watching her again. This time, his eyes had a different look, one she hated.

His eyes pinched, and a sad smile hung on his beautiful face. "Sorry."

The apology was too much. Her arousal morphed into anger. She wanted to ask questions, but all she could do was push away and tread the water. "Don't say that."

His grin hitched. "Then I'm not sorry."

She didn't like that either. Her lips pursed.

Sawyer grabbed her arm and pulled it to his neck. "I can't let you drown."

"I'm a strong swimmer," she protested, looking to bicker. "I don't need your help."

Sawyer ignored her and guided them back toward the shore.

SAWYER DIDN'T WANT to let Angela go. When they reached shallower water, he could have given her space. Actually, he couldn't. He didn't want her angry and running off. But he let her go.

They walked out of the water, inches apart but miles away. Salt water slid down her face. The sun had turned her cheeks pink, and her hair was wild. But gone was the carefree happiness she'd radiated earlier. That was his fault. He should say something, but nothing had come to mind since the moment he realized he had crossed the line.

She'd crossed it with him.

That didn't matter. They were in two very different places. Angela was rebounding from Paul, and Sawyer… Sawyer had a past that would always haunt him.

Years had passed since he'd been in love, not to mention in pain. That he could see similarities between the two women who were nothing alike terrified him, and it wasn't fair to either woman.

Even thinking about that made him feel ill. There was more to his friendship with—and attraction to—Angela than he wanted to admit. The last week had avalanched over him in a way that he couldn't have predicted and didn't know how to make sense of.

"I'm exhausted." She cupped a hand over her eyes and searched for the belongings she'd tossed. "And I'm shriveled up like a raisin."

They had drifted. He spotted her hat and shoes but let her lead the way to where they had started. The water excursion hadn't been planned. They didn't have towels or chairs, but she sat in the sand at the edge of the waves' reach.

Neither of them talked about what had just happened. He made himself comfortable at her side. Their legs extended in front of them.

Angela leaned back on her elbows. Should he say something? Sawyer didn't know what to say, so he lay down and let the sun beat against him.

Maybe he should have let her pull together an agenda for the day because he didn't know what to do next.

A football skidded across the water and bumped against his knee. Sawyer palmed it, saw the kids who had been throwing it—they looked very similar to the kids from the beach house—and lofted the ball. They squealed in delight and were definitely the same kids.

"I know those shrieks," she said.

He glanced over his shoulder and saw the canopy that the family had staked up. A woman raised her arm to thank him for throwing the ball.

The ball sailed back toward Sawyer but fell short a few yards. Grateful for the distraction and unable to resist a football, he lumbered off the sand and returned the throw.

A kid threw back with increased accuracy.

"Nice throw," Sawyer called.

Angela pulled her hat on and then leaned onto her elbows again. "Looks like you made a friend."

Her voice didn't have the slightest sound of irritation as after he'd kissed her in the ocean. Partly relieved but semi-disappointed, he laughed and lofted the ball back.

Delighted shrieks ensued again. Angela smiled. He did too.

"Give me a minute. Football duty calls."

"Take your time," she replied. "I'm going to dry off and search for my dignity."

So she hadn't forgotten about the kiss. He didn't know what to say, so he winked. "It's probably with mine."

Angela laughed. *Thank God.*

He jogged toward the kids. "You guys wanna throw the ball?"

They mostly screeched and shrieked instead of talking, but he rolled with it, tossing the football back and forth. Sometimes Sawyer pitched it high toward the overhead sun and let it divebomb straight into the sand. Other times, he jogged circles around the kids, faking them this way and that. Most often, the kids didn't come close to landing a catch. But when they did, Sawyer joined in the celebration like they had caught Super-Bowl-winning touchdowns.

He bowed out of another round of toss when the kids were called for more sunscreen, and his stomach growled.

Angela clapped for him as he jogged back. "Who knew you had such skills?"

Sawyer held out a hand and helped her up. "I grew up playing with anything with a ball. Football. Basketball. Soccer. I'm a regular jack-of-all-trades."

"No, I mean with little kids. You're a natural."

He glanced over his shoulder. The kids squirmed as their parents slathered them in sunblock. Yeah, he was good with kids and had always thought so. "They're fun."

"Do you have any younger siblings?

"Nope." He gave Angela a once-over. "You look like you could use sunscreen too."

"You always change the subject when it comes to you," she chided.

"Do I?" He shrugged. "Are you hungry?"

"See?" She pointed at him but admitted, "I'm starving."

"Then let's go eat."

They picked up the pace toward their beach house. His mind drifted in circles, from kissing Angela to avoiding conversations. He checked over his shoulder again but couldn't see anyone they'd left behind on the beach. If life hadn't broken him down, would he be one of the families who dotted the beach, playing in the sand and surf? Sawyer didn't see why not.

They arrived at their beach house and used the outdoor shower to wash off the sand.

"Oh, that's cold." Angela rubbed sand off her legs where his hands had just been. Sawyer bit his tongue before offering to help and then took his time with his much-needed cold shower.

As sand-free as they could manage, they sluiced off and dripped inside into the air conditioning. Shivering, Angela rushed upstairs. "I need a minute in hot water."

He walked into the bathroom on the main floor, confident she'd take more than a minute. Sawyer showered away the salt water and was dressed before the water in the upstairs bathroom was turned off. He studied the law enforcement reports while he waited.

They held nothing but the facts. Two dead bodies. Gunshot wounds. Identification had been found for Mark Hathaway and Tabby Foster, Mylene's husband and sister.

Mark and Mylene. He played the married couple's name over in his head. The names sounded good together. Mark and Tabby? That sounded just as nice but would have been a shit move.

Sawyer picked up a photo dated a year before the murders. Mark and Mylene looked good together too, though looks could be deceiving. Had this man been sleeping with his wife's sister? The photograph wouldn't tell Sawyer anything. Neither would Angela's toothbrush theory.

As he tossed the photo onto the table, footsteps came down the stairs.

"Okay, that took more than a minute," Angela said, entering the room. "But I rushed." Damp hair hung over her shoulders. "Sort of." Her cheeks were too rosy from the time she and Sawyer had spent on the beach. "I need to go buy a bottle of aloe after we eat. My shoulders." She peeled the neck of her shirt down. "Might hurt later."

Angry skin surrounded her fair tan line. "Ouch," he said.

"Could be worse." She scanned the table. "Has anything jumped out at you?"

"A whole lot of nothing."

Looking further at the table, she eyed a binder labeled Welcome Guests that had an illustration of their beach house. "Did you find a place for lunch?"

As if on cue, his stomach rumbled again. "There's a food truck we can find up the street." Sawyer grabbed a set of car keys hanging from a hook near the door. "I checked the reviews. All pretty good. Most say to order the crab cake sandwich and let them dress it their way."

Angela picked up her sun hat. "Sounds tasty."

They arrived in the parking lot where the food truck had been permanently set up, and they weren't the only ones who had searched out the well-reviewed crab cake sandwiches. A long line of locals and tourists waited. "That bodes well," she said.

Tables and umbrellas occupied several parking spaces. A long, umbrellaed table held coolers of drinks and condiments. Sawyer eyed the line. Very few people in the world knew where Angela was at the moment, but it still made Sawyer nervous for her to be without a Kevlar vest, surrounded by strangers.

Angela found a table and stayed out of the sun while Sawyer ordered more food than they could eat. Under the guise of scanning for threats, he watched her while he waited. She was magnetic. Even though her face was hidden under a sun hat, he could picture her dark eyes and smile. The memory of her lips had imprinted itself in his brain. With instant recall, he remembered the way their legs had tangled and their stomachs had touched. He could almost feel her soft curves wrap around his waist.

"Number five-eighty-two."

The announcement of their order number pulled Sawyer to reality. He released a breath. How in the hell had he said no to Angela's suggestion on the plane of no-strings-attached get-togethers? He rubbed the back of his neck, more than a little disappointed in himself.

He retrieved their food and delivered enough to feed a small family to the table where Angela sat. They chowed down. The reviews were correct. The sauce on the crab cake sandwich was perfect, and the hush puppies and fried shrimp were the real deal too.

Sawyer hadn't realized how much energy the sun had taken out of him until he started to eat. Hunger morphed into sleepiness. Now, he wanted a nap.

Better than that, he wanted to fall asleep next to Angela, just as they'd slept on the jet that morning. But given... *everything*... that wasn't a good idea.

Hell. His desiring her like this was getting worse by the second. Sawyer threw a fried shrimp into his mouth. Maybe his approach was wrong. Maybe she had the right idea. They kissed. He'd pulled back because he was much too in his head. They *could* get physical so long as they didn't become intimate. Exactly as she'd suggested.

That was what she wanted, after all. Who was he to say no to Angela? With parameters, he could box himself in and be cautious. "Let me ask you a question."

She recapped her water bottle. "Shoot."

"It has to do with your question on the plane."

Angela's eyes jerked toward him, but she feigned unaffectedness in a way that left him wanting to peel back her layers. "Hmm?"

Sawyer took another bite of his crab cake sandwich and chewed slowly. Perhaps he should've considered exactly what he wanted before bringing it up. "You said practice."

A blush further reddened her sunburned cheeks. Angela maintained a forced, practiced calmness that made his heart gallop laps around the parking lot.

"That's what I said," she agreed.

"Do you want to tell me more about what you were thinking?" he asked.

"Not really."

"I asked nicely," he teased.

She glanced at the busy tables around them. They weren't close enough to be heard, and even if they were, most people were involved in touristy conversations or glued to their phones. "Why?"

He shrugged casually, belying the nervous electricity tightening in his chest. "You caught me off guard."

"*You* caught me off guard in the water."

His lips curled. "I don't know. That felt like it was going to happen whether we liked it or not." He crossed his arms and cocked his head. "I liked it, in case you were wondering."

"You apologized."

He couldn't help but laugh. "I apologize for the apology, sweetheart."

She glared, but he could've sworn she did so only to hide her smile.

"Will you tell me more?" he asked again.

"No."

"Ahh." He put a hand over his heart. "That hurts."

"Give me a break, Sawyer. When I said that…" She wrapped both hands around her water bottle. "We were in this dark, warm, safe cocoon." She chewed on her bottom lip. "In the light of day… that seems like a crazy ask. An inappropriate one."

He eyed her. "Inappropriate is subjective."

She blinked hard, and pink tinted her cheeks again. "True…"

Angela had said "practice." That idea had an end goal he could work with. They would return home and stay friends. "Not exactly friends with benefits. But more like a situationship."

Her unreadable stare offered no answer.

"Ange?"

"I don't get the difference between the two."

"Friends with benefits is more, 'I'm bored, let's hook up,' and this would be more, 'Kissing you at the beach was better than my vivid imagination, and I want to do it again.'"

Her jaw fell open.

Sawyer added his last selling point. "Given what happened in the water, I think it would be very, *very* fun."

Her face broke. She half laughed. "Yeah. But here's the catch, remember? I..." She pushed her loose hair behind her ears. "Have no experience with any of this. My last relationship was such a dud that it was a business plan I didn't notice."

"Ange, you fuckin' stopped my heart with that mouth of yours. So let's consider that you may not realize you know what you're doing, but"—he inched closer and lowered his voice—"you're amazing at it."

Her jaw fell open again, and her pink cheeks turned scarlet. "Oh my God, would you stop?"

"Only because you asked." She had no idea what it was like to be wanted. His pulse strummed in his neck.

"Kissing you." She shook her head and avoided meeting his eye. "That was the exact opposite of Paul or anything in my past. And I don't—I can't—"

"You sure as hell did something earlier." He finally caught her gaze. "You can do that again."

"I don't know what I did. It was nothing like with—"

"We're not talking about the past, remember?" That was one of the reasons this arrangement would work so well for him too. "We're talking about a here-and-now situation that's..." Mutually beneficial? No, he wanted more than great sex.

"Exploratory," she offered with an endearing mixture of nervous energy and excitement. "*Experimental*—"

His eyebrow arched. "Fun."

Angela inhaled and squared her shoulders. "Fun."

He grinned. "You suddenly look terrified."

"I kinda think I'm going to pass out or puke."

He couldn't stop from laughing. "That's the way to get into my pants."

She smacked his arm. "Sawyer Cabot."

He didn't miss his moment. Sawyer tugged her out of her chair and into his lap. Just like in the ocean, her arm slid behind his neck as though they'd fallen into bed a hundred times before. Sawyer was acutely aware of his heartbeat. It drummed slowly and heavily in his chest, mismatched with his breathing, which now felt like a tornado in his throat. He had to think to breathe, which was a hell of a problem. "All jokes aside. Do you trust me?"

Her breath hitched. "Without question."

So neither of them could take a steady breath. He liked knowing that what was happening to her was the same as what was happening to him. Sawyer wanted to be back at the beach house and carry her off to bed. He wanted to overwhelm her world so that all she could do was think of him. But something in her eyes told him they weren't there yet. "What is it?"

She closed her eyes and kept them shut while she sighed. Finally, she refocused on him shyly. "I don't want to disappoint you."

"Ange—"

"Or bore you—"

"*Angela*—"

The piercing ring of a cell phone made her jump. She sucked in a quick breath and pulled out of his arms to retrieve her ringing phone from her bag. "It's Parker." She answered the call. "Hey."

Sawyer studied her switch from curious and uncertain to the no-nonsense woman who set agendas for fun. He liked both sides of her. Just then, though, he really wished she were back in his lap.

Angela pulled her notebook and pen from her purse and scribbled as Parker peppered her with information. Finally, the call ended.

"What's Parker have to say?" Sawyer asked, suddenly uncomfortable with the possibility that this trip could wrap up quickly.

"Well," she said, still in business mode, "he confirmed what we already knew about my mother blowing my cover. Pham didn't know I was working for Titan. They only found out because Pham's network had been trailing her for years. When she arrived in Abu Dhabi without a public agenda, they put two and two together and posted people all over the city."

Senator Sorenson should've known better. But Sawyer didn't have to say that. Angela knew. "What else?"

"Mylene's and Mark's family still live in the area. We could go talk to them."

Talking to relatives? That wasn't Sawyer's bailiwick. No one wanted a heartbreaking past to knock on the door without warning. "What else?"

"Parker has learned more about Pham's public-facing business network. There are several shell companies semi-associated with his network in the area. They follow the Interstate 95 corridor from North Carolina to Delaware."

"What do we do with that?"

She shrugged. "I don't know. Parker's trying to find any real estate associated with them that might raise red flags."

Sawyer frowned. What constituted a red flag? They didn't have the resources to check everywhere, and even if they did, red flags were often red herrings. Angela had been rescued from a commercial warehouse in a run-of-the-mill industrial complex. Titan had rescued many people from locations that would not raise red flags. Pham's people could hide Mylene Hathaway in the backroom of a burger joint or the basement of an office building. "I guess that's a start."

"Parker has his ways," Angela said, sounding like she needed the encouragement as much as Sawyer did. "We could go talk to Mylene's parents."

Back to dredging up people's pasts. What would the two of them learn that wasn't in the investigative reports they'd yet to comb through? "What are our other options?"

"We could try to find Mark's family?"

Sawyer bristled. "Talk to the family about their dead child? Not unless we have to."

"Yeah," she agreed. "Back to the paperwork?"

Or the beach. The ocean. Seclusion... But Angela's attention was focused on Mylene. His was stuck on the conversation prior to Parker's call. "That's probably best."

Angela adjusted her hat and gathered her trash. The only redness left on her cheeks was from the sun. He tossed the car keys in the air and caught them, deciding to bring that heat back as quickly as possible.

CHAPTER TWENTY

THE AFTERNOON HAD been filled with more paperwork than either Sawyer or Angela wanted to read. Folders held newspaper clippings and copies of every report Parker could find. Receipts and rental guest history began years before the night of the murders, starting when Mylene Hathaway had first been assigned to the DNI. Parker had scrounged every speeding ticket and toll booth payment between Mark Hathaway and Tabby Foster. The paper trail was never-ending.

Angela stretched and watched Sawyer fill his water glass and return to the table. "Should we take a break?" she asked.

"I can't look at this anymore. My eyes are crossing." He reached from behind her and pushed the papers away. "It can wait until later."

Her eyes were probably crossing too. Somewhere in the records of phone conversations and bank transactions was the answer she needed. But she was so tired of reading through the piles of paper that she might miss the answer even if it were in front of her. She stood up and stretched. "You're right."

His warm hands rested on her shoulders, his thumbs pressing into the muscles that had tightened while she was hunched over the table. His fingers squeezed.

Angela's eyes slipped shut. Shivers cascaded down her arms. "That feels so good."

Sawyer massaged the base of her neck, slowly moving until his fingertips brushed the back of her hair pulled into a ponytail. He tugged the band out and threaded his hands into her loose hair. Tension dissolved from her body.

"That's heavenly," she said.

She turned around in his arms. His hands slid down and fell away.

Was he going to kiss her again? Was she ready for them to cross the line beyond all talk? Angela's breath shook. She didn't care if he saw her chest rise and fall like she'd never been touched by a man before. She hadn't been. Not really. Nothing in her past rose to the level of this powerful man simply standing close. This was what desire felt like. She'd lived too long and not known.

Sawyer positioned his hand on her hip and secured her in place. "You are beautiful."

The gravelly deepness of his voice rumbled through her nerves. Shivers cascaded from her chest to her toes.

His hand skimmed to the small of her back and pulled her close. The bulge of his arousal was a shock. She hadn't touched him. She hadn't tried to act sexy. Angela turned him on by merely existing.

"I like your hair like that." He grinned. "Loose and a little crazy."

"Well, I'm feeling a little crazy," she admitted.

His free hand ran up her spine and into her hair, which he gave a tousle. "That makes two of us. I'm feeling a little crazy for you."

She wrapped her hands behind his neck, and he brushed her hair off of hers. He nuzzled against her. Warm breath tickled under her ear. The stubble on his cheek scratched gently under the curtain of her hair. Angela prayed for his lips to touch her skin. She tilted her head. He bent closer, breathing her in.

Sawyer was awakening parts of her body that she didn't know existed. A deep arousal swirled through her. "I didn't know I could feel this alive."

"Me either," he whispered, lips barely touching her cheek.

A quiet moan escaped from her. Maybe she should've been embarrassed, but the same hungry groan sounded from him. It was more than she could stand.

The soft touch of his lips brushed over hers. The gentleness was almost too much to take from this muscled, massive man. His patience nearly made her cry—and then everything changed. Softness became starvation. Her hands knotted in his shirt, his in her hair.

His sweet mouth opened to hers and devoured. Their tongues teased and danced until need purred in her throat. Her body hummed. Angela needed this man so much she hurt.

And then he slowed again. He gave her gentle, careful attention, and it was just as good. Angela opened her eyes. Sawyer was staring down.

He stroked her cheek. "Are you okay?"

"I don't know how I'm still standing."

His chest jerked with silent laughter. "Come out on the deck with me."

A protest formed on her lips. But the sexy way his smile curved stole her dissent away. He led her out the sliding glass door to an oversized lounge chaise that faced the ocean. A flower-covered lattice blocked them from the neighbors' sight. The view overlooked the rise of grass-covered dunes and the ocean. As long as they weren't standing next to the deck rail, no one could see them. They were in an oceanside oasis.

The setting red-orange sun sank on the opposite side of their house. Pinks and grays reflected in the puffy white clouds over the ocean, and the waves crashed rhythmically. Sawyer sank onto the lounger and pulled her alongside him.

This was why couples honeymooned at the beach. She'd never thought about it before and would've guessed the allure was more like bathing suits and drinks. But she would've been wrong. Profound awe welled deep in her chest. They were just tiny specks in the great cosmos. Yet they had feelings as powerful as nature—and that was just how she felt before he kissed her.

The wind blew warm and salty. A sly grin hung on his chiseled face. Maybe he noticed that she'd been floating.

Angela could feel her own silly look curving on her kiss-swollen lips. "Why'd you drag me out here?"

Amusement danced in his eyes. "Because I needed fresh air."

"I don't know. I forgot to breathe and was still standing," she teased. "Barely."

"I was holding you up."

"Okay, probably."

"Who's going to hold me up?" he joked.

She patted the lounger. "Now you don't need to worry about that."

"What about you?" Sawyer played with her hair. "What do you need?"

"That's a big question, Sawyer."

"That's the way I roll."

She pressed her forehead to his. "This." From the inside out, she was shimmering. Confidence bubbled in her chest. Arousal pulsed. She was drunk on him and had barely had a taste. "You."

He would give and take in ways she couldn't conceive. That was the trust she had in Sawyer, and in return, she would give him everything he wanted.

He scooped her onto his lap, and their mouths met again. Sawyer rubbed his hand over her knee, rubbing her thigh. Her sex throbbed. A building ache deep in her core dropped lower and lower as his strong hand inched higher.

"I want more than that," she whispered against his lips.

He nipped her bottom lip. His fingers slipped under her shorts. Her breaths raced as his touch crawled closer and closer to where she wanted him. Her legs shifted apart. His knuckles grazed the silk that covered her mound. The tease had just enough pressure. Again, Angela couldn't breathe.

"Like that?"

Did he have to ask? "I might kill you if you stop."

He laughed against her mouth. "That's not the way I plan to go, sweetheart." Still, he moved his hand. "Lift up." Sawyer tugged her bottoms off. His fingertips fluttered over the triangle of hair between her legs. "Better?"

Lost for words, she nodded.

"Tell me what you like."

Angela didn't have the first clue. "I don't know."

He inched her legs apart and, this time, without the barrier of clothes, stroked the back of his knuckles against her again. His arm around her back held her in place. Her eyes pinched shut as his knuckles skimmed across her folds, playing against her slick skin.

"This?" Careful fingers teased and spread her until the cool ocean air danced with his rhythmic touch. The pads of his fingertips circled her clit with a delirious pressure. "That's good?"

Her head dropped back. "Yeah."

"Good." Sawyer kissed her neck.

Angela squirmed and lifted her hips. The incoming climax would be too much. His fingers abandoned her throbbing clitoris.

"No, no, no…"

But he moved to her opening, and her mind changed instantly.

"God," she gasped.

Sawyer retook her mouth. His tongue moved against hers. His fingers pressed into her tight entrance. The filling pressure brought needy gasping sounds from deep in her body. "Sawyer."

He worked her into a frenzy. Angela couldn't catch her breath. Her hips flexed. A desperate low cry roared through her as her climax exploded.

Angela floated in his arms. Her limp legs tangled with his, and Sawyer held her close. Inexplicable tears lodged at the back of her throat.

He stretched them both out on the loungers so they lay face to face. Sawyer stroked her hair. He didn't hurry her along, didn't rip off his clothes. He just held her as the sun dropped lower in the sky and the day fell into twilight.

Finally, she took a deep breath and raised her eyes to his. What did a person say after a world-shifting experience? She didn't know.

But apparently Sawyer did. "That was fuckin' amazing." The corners of his mouth curved up as though he meant it.

CHAPTER TWENTY-ONE

THE MORNING SUNLIGHT bounced off the bleached roads. Sawyer squinted behind his sunglasses and checked his blind spot, merging into traffic. Parker had given him and Angela a list of people who had known Mark and Tabby. Fortunately, the list didn't include family. Sawyer wasn't sure if he could stomach a conversation with a parent who had lost their child. He and Angela were starting with Dwayne Chavez, Mark's closest known friend and drinking buddy.

"Have you interrogated people before?" Angela pulled the paper farther down on her breakfast sandwich and took a bite.

"We're not interrogating anyone."

She swallowed quickly. "I know. Just wondering what those tense conversations are like."

"I haven't in the sense you're thinking."

She grinned. "More like in an action movie, huh?"

He snorted and laughed. "Maybe so."

"After Titan rescued me, the Feds let me read my case file from when I was first abducted."

"Oh, yeah? Interesting?"

She shrugged. "I read the conversation transcripts and summaries between law enforcement and my friends from the initial investigators. From when no one knew why I disappeared into thin air." She fidgeted with the paper wrapped around her breakfast. "Sort of strange. People are so worried that they don't hold back details. It showed who really knew me." She considered, tilting her head. "And who didn't."

Sawyer had a good guess as to who didn't have the faintest idea about Angela, but he didn't want to hear Paul's name. Possessively, Sawyer's thoughts replayed the previous night. Her orgasms were seared into his thoughts. If she hadn't climaxed to the point of exhaustion, he might never have stopped.

But he had, and that had been almost as much fun. Sawyer made her dinner and tucked her close on the couch. She fell asleep under his arm, and in the morning, stiff from sleeping on the couch, they worked through the load of information Parker had provided overnight.

Sawyer refocused on the highway and squeezed the steering wheel, checking his mirrors. Habit had him monitoring the vehicles behind them for tails. Interstate 95 had him vigilant for idiots driving while using their cell phones. He didn't see either right now but wouldn't drop his guard.

"Most everyone thought my abduction was related to politics." She chuckled. "Though I had a college girlfriend who swore on her grand-mother's grave that I had skipped town and assumed a fake identity to avoid living in my mom's shadow." She snorted and took another bite of her breakfast. "When I first read that, I was offended."

"How come?"

Angela shrugged. "I wasn't unhappy. I didn't think some overpowering force loomed heavily in my life. Certainly not one that I had to run away and hide from." She polished off the last of her breakfast. "But now? Moving to Abu Dhabi, where no one knows where I am? I might have been hiding from Pham, but I reaped the benefits of living far away and on my own—even if everyone knew I was *the Senator's* daughter."

He glanced over at her. "No one looks at you like that."

"Sure they do. How could they not? ACES literally pulled me out of captivity before Jared gave me a job. I'm the traumatized girl with the screwed up past and bossy mother."

"Trauma isn't who you are. It's what you've been through." He re-checked his mirrors then studied Angela and cracked a grin. "And you're pretty awesome." He watched her sun-pinked cheeks instead of the road. "Everyone sees that."

She crumbled the breakfast wrapper and shoved it into the fast-food bag. "Do you have a good opening question for Dwayne Chavez?"

He shrugged. "How about we open with 'we're not cops'?"

"And what then?"

For a second time, he shrugged. "'Got anything more you want to say than what you've told the cops?'"

She gave him a funny look. "That's a little generic."

"Mark's drinking buddy deserves a bullshit-free conversation. That's the only way these interviews will work. If we separate ourselves from the other investigators and let him say whatever he might still have to say after all these years."

"Dwayne will want to know who we are and why we're asking."

"True." Sawyer raised a shoulder. "But that doesn't mean you have to say. You only need to give him enough so much."

"What if he says nothing?"

"Then maybe there's nothing left to say," Sawyer replied. "We can't make him talk if there's nothing he hasn't said."

"What if we get the feeling there is, but he doesn't want to tell us?"

Sawyer drummed his thumbs on the bottom of the steering wheel and mulled over her question. "Then we turn our questions around from 'what haven't you told us' to 'do you want to know the truth about what happened?' He'll say 'yes.' We'll say, 'Answer our questions.'"

"Why would anyone trust us?"

He chortled. "Why not?"

Forty-five minutes later, they found an office complex with Dwayne's mud-spattered truck parked under the shaded corner of the lot. Sawyer pulled into a spot a few cars over.

She peered toward the small building. "Do we go and ask for him—?"

A gaggle of men exited the office.

"Or it might be our lucky day," he offered. They tried to pick him out of the group and didn't. "Let's go see if he's available."

The receptionist questioned why they wanted to see Dwayne. He didn't see clients, and they couldn't produce badges. But Angela smiled and briefly mentioned a painful connection they shared with Dwayne and their hope to touch base with him for only a moment. Her charm worked, and Dwayne came out to meet them.

They stepped outside. Introductions were awkward, since Sawyer and

Angela were less than forthcoming. But Dwayne made himself clear. No matter what Mark's crazy, homicidal wife had thought, he wasn't a cheater.

They thanked him for his time.

"One more thing," Angela asked and nodded to his hand. "Are you married?"

Dwayne lifted his hand and showed his wedding band in confirmation. "Five years and counting."

"Do you share a bathroom?"

His brow furrowed like she was an idiot. "Yeah."

"Where do you put your toothbrush?"

The lines on his forehead deepened, and Dwayne gave Sawyer a confused look before answering Angela. "On the counter." Dwayne looked at Sawyer again. "Why?"

"Next to your wife's toothbrush?" Angela pressed.

Dwayne shook his head incredulously. "What? I have no idea. On the counter." He gave them a dubious look and left.

"No one lines toothbrushes together," she said. "I'm telling you, the whole thing was staged."

Whether that was right or not, Angela believed it.

"Is that question going to be our calling card?"

She gave a quick laugh as they returned to the car. "Maybe it should be."

CHAPTER TWENTY-TWO

MYLENE WASN'T PROUD of her work. Her assignments were punishment, similar to how Tran Pham had forced her to live with the constant reminder of the loved ones she'd lost.

For the first few years, Mylene hadn't understood the far-reaching effects of her seemingly insane projects. Pham's associates would give her names and current events. They'd ask her to pit people against one another or conjure up conspiracy-riddled stories. At first, she thought that was part of the punishment, some sort of creative writing torture that would force Mylene to live in the headlines and denigrate the country that she loved so much.

She was wrong. They'd needed a native English speaker who understood the idiosyncrasies of current events and who had nothing to lose. That was her, trapped in her house of hell with time on her hands.

Mylene proliferated misinformation. Pham's colleagues fed her storylines to bot farms. Sometimes, she assumed his people sold her stories and code to the highest bidder. After all, information warfare couldn't come from one source. That would be too easy to spot and clean up.

Once she understood how they were using her, she waited to feel guilty. Regret never came for anything except Mark and Tabby, so she worked like their robotic cash cow.

Her production value had to be a reason Pham's goon squad hadn't decided to kill her now that he was locked in a federal penitentiary. It wasn't as if Pham was in a position to enjoy her suffering.

ANGELA AND SAWYER had days of interviews under their belts. She was more convinced than ever that Mylene Hathaway was one of Tran Pham's victims. They'd found no indication that Mylene's husband and sister were having an affair. More than that, Angela sensed that except for two dead bodies and a missing Mylene, no one who knew Mylene, Mark, or Tabby could fathom the tragedy that had unfolded years ago. It pained Angela not to tell them what she thought had happened and that, perhaps, Mylene could be found and exonerated.

Back on the beach, the receding tide rolled out quietly despite the darkening storm forming miles offshore. Angela let the quiet waves lap over her feet. Her mind drifted. She and Mylene were the same age. Pham had connected them. Their connection was different, however. Mylene was one of the many persons Pham blamed for Quy Long's death. Angela was a victim. Her mother was the focus of Pham's anger, one of the people he most blamed for what had happened to his daughter. Angela could have been dead like Mark and Tabby. Instead, she was a fill-in for Pham's daughter.

"Hey, Ange."

She jumped. The sand had muffled Sawyer's approach. Her heartbeat didn't slow down, though. Tension had crackled between the two of them since their rendezvous on the deck and slumber party on the couch. They had worked nonstop since, hunting down the leads that Parker gave them and rehashing every conversation. They hadn't had a break until now, when she wandered to the beach, waiting for Sawyer to wrap up a phone call with Parker and Jared. "All done with calls for the night?"

"All done." His hands clasped to her waist and pulled her close. "And nothing to do except pay attention to you."

God, Sawyer made it easy to melt. Her arms wrapped around his neck. The pair came together with effortless ease. She had never known the magnetic pull of a kiss, and as his mouth took hers, she melted all over again.

The wind lifted her hair off her neck, and his kiss deepened. They weren't alone on the beach, but she didn't care. They could kiss until sundown and then take advantage of the dark.

"Damn," he whispered against her lips. "You are fun to kiss."

She grinned. He was the most fun she'd ever had, period.

"Come on." He led her to dry sand and sat down, reading her expression. "A little sand on your clothes won't hurt."

Sand could get everywhere; she would rather go inside and keep kissing. But Sawyer petted the spot next to his side and smoothed the area flat. She couldn't resist.

"Not so bad, huh?" he teased.

"What are we doing?"

"Relaxing." He lifted his chin to the ocean. "Give it a chance."

"I was before you arrived."

"Nah, I could tell from your body language something heavy was on your mind."

Angela sighed. "You're not wrong."

He extended his legs and leaned back on his elbows. "Mylene?"

As she watched a bird swoop into the water and fly away with dinner, she wanted to ask if she could tell him the truth, to say her thoughts aloud, even if they were dark and crazy. Angela knew he'd answer with his favorite question: did she trust him? She did, but that didn't make sharing any less scary.

"I think…" Rain fell miles offshore. "I thought Mylene and I were similar." Angela crossed her legs and ran the palm of her hand on the cool sand. "But we're not. I was collateral damage. She was a target."

He nodded as though he'd understood that from the start.

"Mylene probably hates him without reservation, and I…" Her fingers pressed deep into the sand. She smoothed the spot and dug the small hole again. "I sort of get him."

"Him?"

"Pham," she whispered.

Distant thunder rumbled from the ocean. A hidden crack of lightning lit up the storm clouds. "In what way?"

Angela pushed sand into the hole she'd made, smoothed the surface, and dug it once more. "He lost his daughter." She packed the sand. "Even if he's a horrible person, responsible for horrible things… I can see both sides. Horrible person and grieving father."

The dark clouds were illuminated with lightning. "Yeah." His voice sounded as far away as the storm clouds. Maybe even more distant.

Her heart sank. He didn't understand, and she couldn't explain. "Have you ever known a parent to lose a child?"

After an eternity, he answered, "Yeah."

Angela waited for more, but Sawyer had locked his unfocused gaze on the water. The tide was out, but the calm, retreating waves now frothed with white surf. The storm wasn't close, but its effects had reached the shore.

Finally, he tore his gaze from the ocean and studied her. "You're empathetic."

She snorted. "I wouldn't call it that. I've been trying to tell Ibrahim I have Stockholm syndrome."

Sawyer's deep frown broke, and he chuckled. "What's Ibrahim say to that?"

She laughed with him. "That I'm wrong."

His laughter faded with a resigned head shake. "You're something, that's the truth." He hooked his arm over her shoulder and kissed the top of her head. "There are many ways that your time with Pham could have left you. Empathetic is one hell of a way to be, all things considered." He pulled her toward his chest. "You're better than most." His chin rested against her hair. "Better than me. That's for damn sure."

Sawyer lay on his back and pulled her on top of him. She squeaked. His unguarded smile returned.

"Am I squishing you?"

His hands drummed on her bottom. "You couldn't if you tried."

Angela kissed him. Her dark hair fell, hiding their faces from the world. Lazily, his hands roamed her back. She liked being on top of him, how he made her feel petite when she was anything but. Angela teased his lips with hers. She nibbled and played with the sexiest man to walk the earth—and he liked it. His erection thickened beneath her. Sawyer's searching hands slipped under her shirt to smooth his palms over her skin.

She slipped her tongue into his mouth and explored what made him groan and tighten his fingers on her sides.

Sawyer moved a hand to the back of her neck. His fingers threaded into her loose hair, holding her against him and driving her mad.

"It's time for you to take me inside," she murmured against his lips.

"Anything you want." He lifted her to her feet and rolled to his. Not bothering to brush the sand off his back, he took her hand in his and retraced the path to their deck.

At the door, he pulled his shirt off over his head and shook the garment out.

Angela leaned against the siding. "Your shorts are pretty sandy too."

His eyebrows arched, and with a devilish grin, Sawyer dropped his shorts down and kicked them to the side, standing in front of her in boxer briefs to display his lean, hard-muscled body. Heat flared in every part of her.

"What about you?" he asked.

She bit her bottom lip and moved closer.

He pulled her shirt over her head and tugged her shorts down. They piled at her feet. He inched back and drank her in. Her nipples beaded behind the lace bra. Moisture pooled between her legs.

"Goddamn, you're gorgeous." Sawyer shook his head as though he had to shake himself out of a trance. He opened the door and pulled her inside.

He headed straight for the bathroom, her hand in his. She wouldn't have guessed him for a hand holder, but it seemed that this man never wanted her to walk anywhere without his hands on her. Once inside, he shut the bathroom door and turned on the water in the shower. Hunger flared in his expression when he focused his complete attention onto her.

Angela shivered. He was an intense, gorgeous man, tan and blond and muscled. His hair was just long enough to thread her fingers into. His body was hard, lean, cut, and could fulfill her every daydream. She didn't know what to do with herself when he came toward her like he couldn't live without her.

Steam swirled around them. Sawyer backed her to the wall. His nuzzling became a nipping kiss.

Electricity rushed in her blood. Her insides pulsed. His erection thickened between them. Angela scratched her fingernails down his back. She teascd along the waist of his boxer briefs and then slid them over Sawyer's muscular ass.

Every part of him was hard and hot. She didn't want clothes between them.

Sawyer's mouth met hers. He unfastened her bra and let it drop. His hands ran to her hips and toyed with her underwear. "These have to go."

She agreed.

He slid them down until they dropped at her feet. His palms teased over her butt and squeezed while his mouth nuzzled her neck.

Angela's breath raced. Her hands ran over the short, coarse smattering of hair on his chest. She explored the muscular cut of his pecs. His breaths were as erratic as hers. As her fingertips teased down his stomach and across the ridges of muscle, their breathing seesawed.

She ran her knuckles along his waist and cupped him through his boxer briefs, and he sucked in a deep, chest-expanding breath. She pulled the rigid heat of his shaft free and slid the last shred of their clothes away.

Everything about him was hard muscled and more than she could have imagined.

Sawyer grasped her hips. Their bodies came together, stomach to stomach, lips on lips. He wrapped her to him and backed her into the shower, never taking his mouth from hers.

The water was almost too hot. Somehow, shivers ran down her back. Sand washed off her body. His kisses were all-consuming, holding her up, keeping her alive. Sawyer threaded his hands into her hair and pressed his chiseled body to her softness. They were a contradiction of experiences, but their need was a universal leveler. She wasn't shy. She didn't feel uncertain or nervous. Desire guided her hands. Caution didn't hold him back.

He kissed and nipped down her neck, massaging her breast until his mouth covered her nipple. She cried. The demanding sensation made her legs shake.

His tongue lashed. His teeth played a dangerous game of teasing. Sawyer slid a hand between her legs and stroked her sex. Too many feelings were present. Her brain couldn't map all the pleasure at once.

With a deft touch, he found her clit. Angela swayed. His kisses trailed to her other breast, offering the same onslaught of tongue lashes and mind-numbing attention.

"Sawyer…" Her head lolled to the side. He was too good to her. This was too much for her to experience. Her climax ripped through her before she could cry his name again. And he didn't stop, matching the thundering pulse of her orgasm until she couldn't move.

She was limp, sated, and still so desperate for more of him that she could not focus on anything beyond bringing him to orgasm.

She wrapped her hands around his cock, and Sawyer nipped her bottom lip. She smiled lazily into his kiss, still floating on a cloud. Her hands stroked him. Approval rumbled in his chest.

Hot water and his need pulled her from her hazy aftershocks. She liked his breaths and the way he groaned. Her thumb brushed the head of his erection. She gripped his muscular thickness, making his hips flex.

Sawyer's eyes were closed, his head tipped back. Pure bliss showed on his face. She'd put it there. Confidence multiplied her need.

She dropped to her knees and rubbed her cheek against his muscular thigh.

"Ange," he managed. "Not yet."

The shower water hit his back, which protected her from the raining spray. Still, droplets ricocheted around them. Angela looked up. Their eyes met. She never wanted this more.

Gently, she caressed his shaft. "I don't think that's the right answer."

Her tongue teased his smooth skin.

His chest expanded, his eyes slipping shut as he breathed her name.

"Yes?" she asked, lips teasing a sensitive spot.

He wasn't hard to convince. After another exploratory kiss, his no transformed into an emphatic yes.

Angela's hand slid to his crown and back. Her lips wrapped over him.

Sawyer gasped. His hands tangled in her hair.

Taking and releasing him, she slid her mouth over Sawyer. Power curled through Angela like an aphrodisiac. Sawyer fought for restraint, and she wanted to make him lose control.

"Ange…" His fingers knotted in her hair. "God…" His hips flexed.

"Sweetheart—" Sawyer pulled from her mouth. His hand wrapped over hers, working his cock until his head dropped back. His release came, falling onto her breasts. He shuddered and stilled. Shower water fell around his shoulders. Pleasure carved a deep, satisfied expression onto his face.

Angela watched, amazed by their connection.

Finally, he opened his eyes, lifted her onto her feet, and wrapped her in a soul-touching embrace.

CHAPTER TWENTY-THREE

WRAPPED IN A towel, Angela let Sawyer lead her upstairs. His towel hung dangerously low on his hips. The chill of air conditioning and of anticipation pricked over her flushed skin.

They entered her bedroom. Without a flicker of uncertainty, Sawyer pulled back her covers.

She didn't have his unflappable confidence. Maybe that was one of the many reasons why her pulse pounded. Angela let her towel fall to the floor in a pile around her ankles.

His eyes flared, and he nodded toward the bed.

She dove under the white sheets.

But he didn't join her. "Give me a minute." Sawyer pulled the soft linens over her naked body and then padded out of her bedroom.

Solitude washed over Angela. It wasn't as much a cold shower as it was a second of clarity. She'd never been in a relationship that ignited her deep within her body and soul. She'd never experienced a desperate need to touch and be touched, to give and give and get then give some more.

Uncertainty seized deep in her chest. She'd never known that in any relationship, reaching back to her earliest crushes and flirtations. And here, she'd found it, but it had an expiration date. The situation with Sawyer was built on a timeline. They had stepped out of their normal day-to-day and into an alternative reality in which exploring lust was *almost* as important as the reason they had traveled across the globe.

That *almost* was damn close.

A moment later, Sawyer returned, and with him, all the uncertainty subsided. Angela needed their legs tangled and hands searching.

He tossed a box of condoms on the nightstand.

Anticipation replaced any last remnants of doubt. She reached for the towel at his waist. It dropped next to hers.

Sawyer joined her in bed.

Angela giggled. "Oh my God. How are you so cold?"

He rolled on top of her and kissed her laughter away. She liked how they played together, that it wasn't an itch-scratching of wham-bam-thank-you-ma'am.

"You're a lot of fun," he said.

"Glad you think so."

His mouth dipped below her ear. "I could have fun with you all night long."

She couldn't stop smiling. This wasn't how she pictured falling into bed with anyone. Comfortable and charged. Giving and taking. She and Sawyer asked what worked and tried new things. They smiled. Holy God, did they smile—when they weren't gasping.

Sawyer kissed her neck, nipping to her collarbone. His strong hand cupped her breast. He thumbed and stroked her tight nipple. He inched lower and kissed her other breast. The dual teases matched tongue and touch, gentling, deepening, and fueling her fire.

"Please." Her back arched. "I need you inside of me."

He laid his head on her pillow and let his fingers dance down her stomach until they gently dipped between her legs, like he'd done on the deck. "I don't want to rush you."

Enough restraint. She crawled on top of him, straddled the thick ridge of his cock, and rocked her sex against him. "Maybe I haven't been clear." She kissed his cheek. "I have been ready for this since you walked onto the beach."

Well before that, if she was being honest. The day before? Yes. The days before the day before? Yes. On the jet? Absolutely, yes. Before that? She wasn't going to be any more honest with herself.

Sawyer flipped her onto her back. Their lips locked around laughter. This was more than arousal. This was *the life*.

He removed a condom from the package and covered himself, and nestled between her legs, he held her eyes. The head of his cock pressed against her opening.

Angela gave herself to him. His body flexed. Hers gave.

As if they had eons to lie together in bed, Sawyer sank deeper and deeper. Their breaths shortened.

An all-consuming ecstasy expanded inside her. She couldn't fathom how he could give her so much. Angela's eyelids closed.

Sawyer feathered kisses along her cheeks until her eyes met his again. He grinned in the most beautiful, soul-clutching way. Then his expression turned roguish.

When Sawyer slid from her and back again, her legs climbed his. Their mouths locked. Swirling desire and burning kisses blinded her from the world outside their bed. He drove her higher and higher, stealing kisses and breaths and calls of bliss. An unrecognizable climax beckoned. She was already too far gone to explode. But Sawyer didn't know that. He pushed her understanding of pleasure past what she could comprehend, and when she couldn't take another dazzling second, Angela called his name.

Sawyer gathered her close and buried his face against her neck. His release hit as her violent eruption rolled toward a lazy, lust-drenched contentment.

Angela stroked his back. Then he collapsed against her and caught his breath.

She pressed a kiss to his temple.

Finally, he carefully withdrew and rolled onto his side. Sawyer removed their protection and then gathered her to his side, big spoon once again.

"Definitely very fun," he whispered just before kissing the back of her head.

"Very," she agreed. Now wasn't the time to explain how trivial the word "fun" was. She'd never known this level of satisfaction existed. Now was too precious a moment to contaminate with revelations. But she did want him to know how special he made her feel. Angela turned in his arms.

Sawyer brushed her hair off her face. "What?"

She couldn't find the words to do justice to the glittery happiness that had grown in her heart. "Thanks."

He cocked an eyebrow. "For what?"

"Being you." She shrugged. That was a far cry from what she wanted to convey. "For letting me be me."

His lips quirked upward, and he snuggled her close as if he understood that the right words were impossible to find. She could have fallen asleep to the rhythmic beat of his heart, but her body had other plans.

"Are you hungry?" he asked of her growling stomach.

"Yeah, but I don't want to move."

Laughter rumbled through his chest. "I was just thinking the same thing. But…" He propped himself onto his side. "I bought steaks for the grill."

Her mouth watered. "Yum."

"Do you want to stay here while I get the charcoal fired up?"

The mundanity of making dinner plans struck her as strange. Did other people live lives filled with mind-blowing sex and then go about their regular business? If she'd thought about it before, it would have sounded like the stuff of fairy tales for adults. "What did you get to go with the meat?"

"Corn on the cob and potatoes for the grill and salad stuff in a bag."

"What do you want me to do?"

"Relax." He rolled out of bed. "Got a book or something?"

"Am I living in some kind of dream world?"

Laughing, he walked out of her bedroom. "Maybe you need to readjust your expectations of the real world, sweetheart."

He was joking, but the sentiment hit home. He didn't think their day was out of the ordinary. It was almost sad how much of life she didn't realize she'd missed.

Sawyer returned, wearing shorts. "What's that look?"

Angela scooted against the headboard with the covers tucked to her chest. "You're lucky, ya know. Having known fun like this was possible."

Again, he cocked his head. "What are you talking about?" But he seemed to recalibrate his thoughts and strode to the end of the bed. Sawyer grasped her ankles and pulled her until she was on her back again. Then he crawled over her. "I have never had this much fun in my life." He studied her as if trying to read her mind. "Do you hear me loud and clear, Angela?"

Her heart, doing jumping jacks and making jazz hands, certainly did. Her mind wasn't so sure. "You know what I mean."

"No, I don't. Because what I said about relaxing with a book? You deserve that. You deserve everything." After taking a deep breath, he gently kissed her lips until she melted into the mattress.

She wasn't sure how long she had remained in bed after he left. He'd never had this much fun? Neither had she. She'd been hesitant to explain that. Sawyer hadn't. Nothing fazed him. His mental strength was just as durable as his physical power. Angela had always known he was a rock-solid force of nature. Now she had the bonus of knowing how much he could care. She could fall in love if she weren't careful to mind the parameters of their situationship. Love would be incredible and then devastating and leave a friendship in ruins—or, they could explore what a situationship might look like as a relationship. Except he had always been upfront with her, even before she'd floated the crazy idea of a physical fling. Sawyer didn't do long-term relationships. At all. For whatever reason, he'd never wanted to share. But it had been an immovably firm boundary.

Of all the respect he'd given her, she would give him that one thing he'd made clear. Maybe that dulled her sparkle, but it was still much brighter than it had been at the start of the day. That was okay. They— and all their fun—were okay.

CHAPTER TWENTY-FOUR

MYLENE WAITED IN the kitchen for the men to leave her house. Today was different. Nothing different had happened since Pham was arrested more than a year ago. But this time, the men who delivered groceries and task lists remained in her living room.

Unless Pham had ordered Mylene to be taken somewhere as a punishment, her schedule followed a strict routine. Mondays and Wednesdays brought food and her weekly objectives. The Friday deliveries included newspapers and magazines for her to study over the weekend. She could see where her work had penetrated the public's perception of an event or purpose. Alternative facts threaded into flame-throwing discussions. She could see how her work ripped families apart, tearing at the basic fabric of communities and trust. But she couldn't stop.

Could she?

No. She didn't know anything other than the instructions they gave her: study what didn't work, avoid the same mistake twice, and find new places to fuel a public uproar. If not, Pham's people would punish her.

How would they punish her now that Pham was behind bars and couldn't watch? When he brought Mylene somewhere as a punishment, she always thought he hurt more than she did. He liked to bring her on family trips—with Angela Sorenson, the woman he used as a stand-in for his dead daughter. Pham made Mylene watch Angela, maybe hoping she would imagine what her life would have been like with Mark.

No matter Pham's intention, the pseudo-family trips never hit her as they did him. Her house of horrors was much worse because it was real. Mark was dead. Tabby was dead. Their murders were her fault.

★   ★   ★

SAWYER HAD SPENT the night in Angela's bed and woken with her naked body draped over him. He hadn't been this content in years. That bothered him, but he refused to let dark thoughts creep into this moment.

Sun peeked from behind the curtains. They hadn't done a great job of covering the sliding glass door because they'd had no thoughts of anything after dinner except for getting naked all over again.

Angela stirred. He kissed the top of her head. She curled into his side and then stretched. "What time is it?" she asked.

He didn't care. "Did you sleep well?"

Her smile was answer enough. "Like the dead."

"You snored like it too."

"I did not." She tickled his chest. "You know I didn't—"

He rolled on top of her, muttering, "Kidding," amongst his kisses.

And just like that, he wanted her all over again. Sawyer barely had enough thought to slide on protection before he nestled himself inside her body again. This woman needed him as much as he needed her.

Last night was couldn't-get-enough sex. This was lazy-wake-up sex. He didn't want to pull orgasm after orgasm from her. Sawyer simply needed to be in her, to feel her, to watch her face, and see her breathe. He wanted to feel her pussy quake with the slow roll of his hips.

Her soft kisses mixed with quiet, needy nuzzles. Instead of digging her nails into his back, she wrapped her arms and legs around him and let his strength drive her into heaven.

Angela came and came. Finally, he didn't have it in him to hold back. With their lips and legs tangled, Sawyer buried himself deep and let himself fall into her like he'd never let go before.

Afterward, they lay together. Not even the need for coffee pulled them from each other's arms. His lips rested against her temple. How had he known her for this long without realizing what they would be like together in bed?

Their phones buzzed. He pinched his eyes shut. The real world was calling, and he didn't want to answer.

Angela tensed in his arms. She wasn't bounding out of bed either.

"Guess we have to get out of bed sometime," he muttered.

Their phones rang again.

"Who will it be? Jared, Brock, or Parker?" she asked.

"I'll start the coffee."

"God, you're a good man."

He kissed her cheek and left her bed. Ten minutes later, they had coffee and a quick breakfast at the kitchen table and called Parker back.

"We have a problem," Parker said instead of saying hello.

Sawyer grumbled. "Do you always call with problems?"

"Yeah—mostly. Did you not realize that?"

Sawyer ran a hand through his hair. This trip had been too easy. Too good to be true. He should've known better. He looked at Angela, who sat straight as a board. Her breakfast spoon dangled in her hand over the ignored instant oatmeal. He tried to remember that problems were expected. Problems were what they fixed for a living. This conversation wasn't Sawyer's first encounter with Parker's all-work grousing. It wouldn't be the last. But this time, the unknown problem packed a hell of a sucker punch.

"Well, don't kill us with anticipation." Sawyer tossed an apple between his hands and tried to relax for Angela's sake. "What's up?"

"Intel analysts have picked up some chatter."

Impatient, Sawyer set the apple down and frowned. "About?"

"Angela's location."

He exchanged looks with her. Not many people could announce her travel with this kind of speed. Sawyer assumed the Senator had told the ex-boyfriend. There was the FBI special agent. No one from inside Titan would have known enough to share, but even if they had, that wouldn't have been a concern. They were trustworthy. "Her location as in 'Angela is Stateside'? Or her location as in 'camped in a safe house on Emerald Isle'?"

"Closer to the latter. Intel says North Carolina."

"What the fuck?" His eyebrows arched. That kind of information was more than whispers from the FBI's offices. "How does that happen? Her mother?"

"I don't know. It could be a couple of things."

Angela set down her spoon. "Like?"

Parker sighed. "Anything from someone you spoke with this past week to perhaps the Senator has a security breach in her communication network. The intel's kind of fuzzy. Not to mention we're a few hours behind. They have a tactical advantage. But we need to take it as a serious and immediate risk."

Sawyer tossed the apple again. His mind raced to map the possibilities. "So we need to go?"

"Go where?" she asked. "We haven't talked to everyone on our list."

"There's a silver lining," Parker said. "If they're talking about you, that's something we can look and listen for. If Mylene Hathaway is alive and anywhere close to you and they put two and two together, they're going to do two things."

"What?" Angela asked.

Sawyer felt a churning in his gut. "Move Mylene and go after you."

Tension washed over her expression. "Neither of those sound helpful."

He pinched the bridge of his nose. "I guess you've run the statistics on the likelihood either of those will happen?"

"Yup," Parker confirmed.

"I'm not going to like it, am I?"

"Nope."

"Wait a minute." Angela perched on the edge of her chair. "This is great news. They're changing their behavior. That opens us up to a chance for them to make a mistake. If they make a mistake, we can swoop in and find her."

"I don't know about swooping," Sawyer grumbled.

"But I'm right, aren't I?" she asked.

A shadow passed along the outside of the closed blinds. Sawyer's stomach dropped. He turned off speakerphone and pressed the phone to his ear, holding a finger up to his mouth. "We might have company. Call you back." He ended the call. His gaze swept the windows for the shadow. "I need you to sit still and be quiet."

"But—"

"Ange—" He shook his head. "Quiet. Don't move." Carefully, he padded to the kitchen window and tried to peer out the edge of the drapes.

He had no line of sight.

Sawyer's ears burned to hear who was outside. Someone who'd accidentally stumbled up to the wrong beach house would have made his day. If it had been a property manager who had an incorrect beach house address, they would have tried to jam their keys into the door. Neither of those situations had been the quiet shadow that made the hairs on his arms stand at attention.

He opened a kitchen drawer and retrieved the handgun he'd spotted after they'd first arrived. A Titan Group safe house was well-armed if a person knew where to look. Another bonus feature of the safe house was the multiple ways in which they could see their surroundings. Nondescript mirrors hung on the walls. Windows overlooked the points of entry. There were several ways to exit each floor. The décor on the deck offered reflections to check angles.

Angela's chair scratched the floor as she pushed from the table.

He lifted his hand. "No one has a shot on you if you stay put."

Her lips parted, but she didn't protest.

Sawyer quietly inspected their exterior surroundings while mentally kicking himself in the ass for dropping his guard. His primary responsibility in all of this was Angela. No matter what they'd agreed to work on, her safety was the priority.

He didn't see anyone else, but he also didn't see the person who had just skirted by the window. Even though he had a good look at the house's exterior, he certainly didn't have a thorough one.

When Sawyer made his way back to the kitchen, he saw Angela waiting in her chair, frozen in place.

"I think there's only one of them," he said.

Her eyes darted to the windows and door. "But there could be more?"

"Possibly." He wished he had a better view of their surroundings. "They likely have several ideas that they're following up on."

"Maybe he thinks no one is home," she offered.

"Doubtful." Upon reading her body language, he added, "The grill's been used recently. Depending on when they first pinged the house as a possibility, they've seen the car move." He had always checked their surroundings when they left and when they arrived. Sawyer consistently scanned for tails when they were out. It wasn't as if he'd been negligent. Just not on high alert.

"So is there someone out there or not?" she finally asked.

"Probably."

"Are we just going to hide in here until they leave?" She tossed up her hands at his silent, incredulous expression. "I don't want someone to shoot at us again."

"Me neither. My best guess is they're new on the scene and trying to ascertain if we're home."

"The car's here. We're obviously home."

"We're quiet with the windows covered," he countered. "Either way, I want to get the hell out of here."

Someone tried to twist the deck door's knob. Another shadow hovered by the window. All right, Sawyer needed to contend with two people out there. At least they weren't shooting their way inside. He decided it was time to roll. "Let's go."

Angela followed Sawyer, crouching when he did, hurrying toward the front door. They donned the flip-flops they'd left on this floor. It wasn't the footwear he wanted at the moment, but it was better than none. He double-checked the nearby windows and inspected as much of the space as he could see of the front. Sawyer snagged the car keys from the hook but wasn't sure if he and Angela could reach the vehicle without being spotted.

Theirs was a tricky situation. The people outside didn't want to take Angela. They wanted her dead. He had to limit her exposure.

Sawyer turned the deadbolt open. The click sounded in his head as though he'd hit a gong to announce their position. His hand rested on the doorknob. "Stay close and behind me."

"Where are we going?"

"I haven't figured that out yet."

"Good thing I trust you."

He laughed. "Good thing." Sawyer twisted the doorknob and allowed an inch of daylight to fall inside. Semi-blinded but mostly sure they were safe, his ears pricked at the sound of the opening door on the other side of thc house. He grabbed her hand, and out they went.

A man yelled from the street that they'd slipped out the front door.

Sawyer jerked to his left then his right, dragging Angela. A bullet splintered into the side of the house. She screamed. Another one popped.

The man called for his partner.

Sawyer made it to a tiny plastic storage shed that would do nothing to slow a bullet. "You okay?"

"I lost a shoe."

"Given the situation, I'll take that as a yes." A bullet thumped the storage shed. They didn't have many options of where to go. One way would leave them wide open and in the middle of the street. The opposite way would head toward the beach. They'd be sitting ducks, as would anyone else who had the misfortune to start their beach day nearby. The last option was to go onto their neighbor's property, where ideally someone would have left the keys in a car. Not likely, but they didn't have any time for another plan. "Time to move boots."

Sawyer lifted her over a nasty patchwork of thorns and cactus, cursing every flip-flopped step he took. The chasing voices stayed close—and fire exploded in his arm. His hold on her faltered.

"Sawyer!"

Son of a bitch. Angela dangled, half supported in his good arm, half running to keep up. He threw them behind the concrete foundation of the house.

Angela cried in pain. Blood coated her.

"Damn it—Angela?"

"Thorns," she explained. "They're everywhere."

He hadn't noticed and jerked her off the ground. The blood—was his. Good. But they still needed an escape vehicle fast.

Then he saw the dune buggy. It offered next to no protection. They'd be open targets, unable to zig and zag from a bullet's trajectory. But, if Sawyer was able to drive toward the beach and use the dunes as a barrier, they could get distance from the shooters and figure out their next steps when no one was firing.

"See the dune buggy? We're running over there." He pointed. "Jump on and get down. Curl up as little as possible."

That was as much time for instructions as they had.

"That?"

"Yeah. That's the plan. Go."

Sawyer hustled, half carrying Angela, and prayed the dune buggy would be functional. They jumped into the seats. "Get down. Get down."

Angela's knees were on the floorboard. She curled into a ball.

Sawyer inspected the dashboard. No keys required. All he needed was a little luck. He punched the Start button. The electric motor turned over. "Halle-fuckin'-lujah."

The dune buggy beeped in reverse. A bullet lodged itself in a beer can abandoned in the center console's cup holder.

Sawyer slammed the buggy into drive. They bumped and rolled from behind the beach house and zipped toward the steep sand dunes. "We're gonna see how much this bad boy can handle. Hang on."

Angela screeched. The buggy raced up the dune and crested. This vehicle was a beast. They were going to catch air on the downside.

He let off the gas and called again, "Hang on!"

"I am trying!"

Sawyer jerked the steering wheel. They banked right.

"*You* are going to kill me."

He laughed and threaded the buggy through a beach walkway and onto the wide expanse of sand where the routine patrol of lifeguard trucks had made it easy to navigate tracks.

Sawyer checked over his shoulder. "I think we're in the clear."

Angela pulled herself upright. "You're bleeding all over the place."

"Shit." He glanced at his arm. "I'd forgotten about that." He could wash the drying blood off in the ocean, but he didn't relish the idea of cleaning his wound with salt water.

Not a lot of choices, though. They didn't have supplies, much less a first aid kit. He'd lost the gun somewhere between the cactus garden and the dune buggy.

Maybe their attackers grabbed it as an early Christmas present. Free ammo. Either way, once Parker had been updated on the situation, Titan would send in a clean-up team to return the two houses to their original state sans bullet holes. The clean-up team would even return the dune buggy after Sawyer ditched it. When and how were his most significant concerns.

"Where are we going?" she asked.

They couldn't return to their beach house. Neither of them had a cell phone or cash. Angela was missing a shoe—and a quick glance told him she was the worse for wear. "I don't know yet. You okay?"

"I could use a cup of coffee and a pair of tweezers." She grimaced. "There are a lot of cactus spines all over me."

"Come to think of it, same," he admitted.

He slowed down and drove along the beach. If there had been more people along the water, he could borrow someone's cell phone while they were distracted by the waves. But not enough people were out for him to pull off that trick for at least an hour.

"What are we going to do?" she asked again.

Sawyer turned toward the waves. "I have to wash the blood off before someone notices."

Angela stayed in the dune buggy, apparently inspecting her arms and legs for barbed prickles. He removed his blood-stained T-shirt and cleaned up the best he could. The pain increased as his adrenaline cooled.

When he returned to the dune buggy, a scowl creased Angela's forehead. "You need to go to a doctor."

He rotated his arm and tried not to tighten the muscle. "It's mostly a flesh wound."

"Sawyer—"

"I'll get it checked out later." He rolled his shirt into a bandage. "Will you tie this on?"

Her frown deepened.

"I promise I'll get someone to look at it later." Blood leaked down his arm.

"Someone *with a medical background?*" she pressed.

"Yes," he agreed.

"You might need stitches."

He sat behind the wheel of the dune buggy. "I don't need anything right now except for your help." He offered the shirt again. "Can you tie my arm up?"

She relented and took the shirt.

Sawyer placed his arm on the dashboard and let her wrap the shirt around his bicep. "Tighter." He sucked in some air. "Little tighter."

"Oh, come on, Sawyer. I feel like I'm hurting you."

He dropped his head back as the pain fired through his arm muscles. "Gotta do it, babe." He caught himself. "Sorry," he amended. "Ange."

Angela tucked the end of the tight bandage into itself. "I don't care if you call me that." She checked her work while Sawyer studied her. "There isn't anything pompous or pretentious in how you talk to me." She raised her eyes to him. "I probably would have called you worse if the situation was reversed."

His lips curled into a slow smile, and with his good arm, he pulled Angela in for a kiss. She was a balm to his wounded arm. Her presence erased the morning's troubles and wiped away his worries. She soothed a lonely, unsettled part of him that he'd been ignoring for years. She made him happy. It was very simple. Scary. But simple.

Their kiss lingered. His racing mind calmed, and for a moment, it was almost as though they were on a day trip to the beach and not in need of a first aid kit while sitting in a stolen dune buggy.

He placed a soft kiss on her cheek and combed her wild hair back. "How are you doing? How many cactus spines are we talking about?"

She held out her arms and gestured to her legs. "About a thousand."

Angela wasn't exaggerating very much. "That's going to take a while."

"Yeah. Do you have a plan?"

"Find first aid and then loop headquarters in."

"If Boss Man were here, he'd bark something about those being objectives, not action strategies."

Sawyer grinned. "Good thing he's not—" His eyes narrowed. "I need to ask you a very important question."

She side-eyed him. "How important? Because I'm not letting you off the hook about seeing a doctor—"

"Someone with a medical background," he corrected.

She rolled her eyes.

"But that's not what I'm talking about."

Looking wary, she waited. "What?"

"You're the note bandit, aren't you?" Over the course of years, someone had left jokes and poems for Jared to find. They usually made the veins in Boss Man's neck stand out. The content was very in the weeds, sometimes hinting at inside jokes that only ACES would know, other times busting their balls. At one time or another, everyone had been their target, though the focus had been on Jared ninety-nine percent of the time.

"Of course not."

The corners of her eyes tightened. Was she blinded by the sun, or had bullshit made her twitchy? Writing those jokes and poems would be out of character for her. Then again, Sawyer had learned more about her in the last few days than he had watching her back over the previous few years. "If you say so."

"Can we go back to the beach house?" she asked. "I have a pair of sunglasses that I love. Not to mention all of the work we've accomplished."

He would let the note-bandit question drop for now. "We don't need any of that paperwork." Pham's people had probably swept through the house already and bagged the intel to pore over. "I'll get you new sunglasses."

"All that work's gone," she said, pouting.

"You know all of it without having it in front of you."

After a moment, she seemed to agree. "Then are we off to find a first aid kit? Doctor? Something?"

He restarted the dune buggy. "We'll find a store and figure everything out from there."

CHAPTER TWENTY-FIVE

A NGELA HADN'T BELIEVED Sawyer planned to find a store and wing it. She'd been wrong. They walked into a dollar store as it opened for the day. Well, Sawyer walked. Her motion was more of a limp as they shuffled by an entrance decorated with a surplus of beach toys and ice chests. With a flip-flop on one foot and cactus spindles in the bare flesh of the other, she tried to blend in beside a shirtless Sawyer, who had a blood-soaked, bandaged arm. It wasn't working.

A teenager operated the self-checkout area. When they approached, he took a step back. "Er, welcome to Dollar Island."

Sawyer painted on his most endearing grin. "Could you help us out?"

The teenager's jaw dropped. "Er. Uh." His eyes jumped from Sawyer to Angela and back again. "Are you okay?"

"Not really," Sawyer said.

"Yeah. It doesn't look like it."

"Could I use your phone and first aid kit?"

"I guess."

The teen's bloodshot eyes fell to Sawyer's bloodstained bandage. "You going to call an ambulance?"

"No."

Angela wasn't sure that their appearance was all that clouded the clerk's mind. Maybe he smoked a bowl before they arrived and was now trying to figure out what was happening.

"Um. Phone and first aid kit." The teen pivoted from one side to the next as though he didn't know where either item might be. "Yeah, over there." He pointed at a phone behind the counter. "That's a phone," he said as if they might be unfamiliar with the kind of telephone that was attached to a wall. "And, uh." He looked at Sawyer's arm again. "The first aid box is in the backroom. I'll..." The clerk sidestepped them as though they might bite. "Go get it."

"Thanks," she said.

Sawyer rounded the counter, made a short call, and returned to her side. They waited for the teenager to arrive with the first aid kit.

"Did you call Parker?" she asked.

Sawyer nodded, wincing as he inspected his arm.

"What did he say?"

He tugged the makeshift bandage higher on his bicep and didn't look satisfied with the result. "An Uber will pick us up in less than ten minutes."

Angela could see why the teenager's eyes had bugged out at Sawyer's arm. It didn't look good. "We're going to a hospital?"

"No, we're going to that food truck from the other day. He's calling in and paying for an order."

"I'm not hungry, and you need a doctor."

"You will be hungry when the adrenaline wears off," he said, ignoring the mention of medical treatment. "By the time we finish eating, someone will drop off a bag of clothes, shoes, and"—he grinned, though the expression was tight and failed to hide his discomfort—"sunglasses."

Her eyebrows arched. "There's a team nearby already?"

"No, he has a slew of gig apps to choose from. Like DoorDash from Target or something. I don't know."

An app? Who needed handlers when they could find an app to take care of the tedious work? That wasn't how she operated from their Abu Dhabi office. Then again, managing sunglasses and food wasn't Parker's job. "Huh."

The teenager returned with an old blue-and-white plastic kit. "Um. Here."

Angela took it and thanked him.

"All right, let's see what we've got." Sawyer popped the lid open and set the kit on the counter.

"Did you call an ambulance?" the teenager asked again.

"An Uber."

"On the phone?" the teen inquired. "The one attached to the wall?"

"A taxi," Angela amended.

Sawyer read the labels on the tiny ointment tubes, collected a few Band-Aids, and held up the tweezers. "Could I borrow these?"

Some kind of calculus played across the teen's face as he studied Sawyer's wound, the tweezers, and the paper-cut-sized Band-Aids. "Yeah, buddy." The boy snort-laughed. "That's fine. You can have 'em."

"We appreciate it," she said, limping behind Sawyer as they left the store. "He's going to have questions."

"Maybe." Sawyer moved his arm too fast and winced. "But who's going to ask him about it? Pham's people don't know where we went. They won't canvass the island and draw attention to themselves."

"He could call the police?"

"I don't think so." Sawyer studied a car that rolled into the parking lot with signs reading UBER displayed in the front and side windows. "Think this is us."

The driver's window rolled down. He eyed them with a heavy level of uncertainty. "Sawyer?"

"That's me." He opened the back door for Angela. "Thanks for the ride."

Angela ducked under his arm and into the air-conditioned back seat—and immediately winced at the cactus spines embedded in the backs of her legs. Delicately, she scooted over.

Sawyer closed them in, and after another once-over from the driver, the car rolled out of the parking lot.

"Let me see your arms first." Sawyer focused on removing the spines while the car headed for the food truck.

The driver watched the back seat more than he watched the road. But fewer than five minutes later, Angela and Sawyer were safely deposited in another parking lot.

Angela limped to the table they'd previously used. The lunch crowd hadn't arrived yet. She wasn't certain that the food truck was even serving up meals, but Sawyer returned quickly with two bags of food and two lemonades.

He set up their breakfast spread, raised one of her legs, rested her bare foot on his thigh, and went to work on the spines again. She ate hush puppies and fed him fried shrimp while he removed the prickles methodically. Once he did the fronts and sides of her legs, he had her stand so he could do the backs. The food truck guys must've thought they were quite the spectacle. Their heads peeked out the order window every few minutes.

She sipped her lemonade. "Do you think they're going to call the cops?"

"Do you think Parker would have taken care of that?"

Of course he would have. "It's hard to be on this side of things."

"Being shot at is a game changer," he deadpanned.

She laughed. "I mean, I know what I would've said to make sure they wouldn't call the cops, and Parker's IQ is off the charts." Angela shook her head. "I don't know."

"Yeah, you do. It's hard to give up control." His fingertips ran over her skin, searching for missed cactus spines. "That's all I can see," he finally said. "Any more?"

Carefully, she ran her palms up and down her legs. "I don't think so."

He handed her the tiny tube of ointment. "You should smear this on the worst spots."

She'd thought the tiny tubes were for him. "What about you? Your arm?"

"I'll get to it, but I'm starving."

A car rolled into the parking lot, and a woman stepped out of the vehicle, carrying two bags from Wal-Mart.

Sawyer stood.

"I've got it." Angela shooed him back to his food. "Eat."

She approached the other woman, and, given how the woman's eyes rounded, Angela had a solid idea of her own appearance: crazy hair, irritated red splotches covering her body, and one shoe.

The delivery woman stopped several paces away, set the bags down in a parking space, and backed away. That was fair. Angela likely appeared to have a contagious disease. Still, she smiled and thanked the other woman for the bags.

Her foot was still sore, but without the cactus needles, Angela didn't limp back to their table.

"Anything good?" he asked then popped a hush puppy into his mouth.

"Hope so." She dug through the bag and found the sunglasses. The UV-blockers did almost as much for her as the food. "I will feel like a new woman before we leave the parking lot." She donned the new glasses. "What do you think?"

"You're beautiful."

"Aw." She grinned, her stomach fluttering. "About the sunglasses."

His grin hitched. "They look like the last ones."

"Not at all." Still, though, she beamed. He'd called her beautiful when she was a mess. Angela kissed him on the cheek. "You're beautiful too. You know that?"

Sawyer blushed. She wouldn't have believed it without seeing it with her own eyes. Something in society kept a certain kind of compliment away from men. Sure, they could be manly and tough. Sawyer was the living, breathing definition of that, not to mention hot and sexy, but he was also beautiful. What else didn't men hear enough of? "You're also sweet and kind."

"All right, Ange. Enough, or I'm going to have you checked out for head trauma."

"Oh, cool your jets. Beautiful, kind, and sweet, in a jumps-out-of-helicopters-and-saves-the-day kind of way." It wasn't that she wanted to embarrass him, but she wanted him to know.

He rolled his eyes.

"And I appreciate everything you've done for me."

"Angela. Enough—"

She kissed him on the cheek again. "All right. Enough." She sipped her lemonade. "What will we do about a vehicle and a doctor?"

He relaxed now that she'd turned the subject away from him. "Wait until something shows up."

"From Parker? We just wait?" No phone. No updates. Angela didn't handle an absence of tasks very well.

He shrugged. "Everything that we need has shown up when it was supposed to. Why question it now?"

He didn't mean those words the way she immediately took them. But Sawyer had shown up for her in so many ways. As much as she could help it, Angela wouldn't question what appeared right before her.

CHAPTER TWENTY-SIX

A CERTAIN LEVEL of assumption and bravado came with working for Titan Group. Angela had seen it from the posh high-rise office in Abu Dhabi. Sometimes, Titan's teams would waltz into hell zones. Other times, they would disguise themselves and hide under deep cover. No matter the occasion, Angela's job was to ensure that ACES had the necessary resources for it.

Now that she was on the other side of an assignment, she realized fieldwork required enormous confidence in Headquarters. The operations team had to believe their support team would cross hell and high water to make sure what they needed would appear. That was the only way she could understand how Sawyer drove their rental car into the horseshoe drive of a swanky hotel without batting an eye.

She wasn't an idiot. Angela knew Pham still had teams searching for her, but the drive from Emerald Isle into mainland North Carolina seemed starkly different from the chase that morning.

Sawyer exited the rental car, giving instructions for the valet to leave the vehicle alone, and guided Angela into the hotel lobby. Her new flip-flops whacked the gleaming floor. Sawyer's arm was newly bandaged and hidden under a new shirt. But they were a far cry from spit-shined and ready for a five-star hotel appearance. Angela didn't have a purse. Neither she nor Sawyer had a wallet. They stood out, but Sawyer didn't appear to notice.

The person behind the counter greeted them warily. "Good evening. How can I help you?"

Sawyer scanned the modern furniture. "Checking in."

"Name?"

"It would be under Titan Group."

Another person stepped forward. "I'll take this from here, George." Her name tag identified her as a manager. "I have your reservation ready. Your luggage already arrived and is upstairs." She typed quickly then produced two key cards. "If you need anything, charge it to your rooms. You're on the tenth floor." She handed them a map and an envelope for their key cards.

They thanked the manager.

"Again, if you need anything at all, we are here to help." She smiled at them and offered a business card. "If you have any problems, this is my direct number. Have a wonderful stay."

And that was how it looked on this side of things. Of all the times that Angela had made arrangements like this, she'd never imagined what it would be like to walk in and know someone else had taken care of the logistics.

Sawyer pocketed the card. "I'll move the car and be right back." The woman behind the counter knew enough not to offer the valet. A few minutes later, Sawyer emerged from an elevator. "Ready?"

The same elevator's doors reopened. He guided Angela inside, hit the button for the tenth floor, and, with his hands on her hips, backed into the corner. He squeezed possessively. "You've had a hell of a day."

"I wasn't shot." Her eyebrows arched. "Unlike someone else I know."

The corners of his lips turned upward. "Flesh wound."

"All the same, it came from a gun, and you need to see a doctor."

"I already saw a guy."

She made a face. "I'm not crazy about a guy who met us in a parking lot."

"I am, if he was Parker-approved."

The elevator slowed, and, Sawyer, always her bodyguard, protectively urged her to his side before the doors opened to the unknown.

"You're always on alert," she noted, wondering if that was exhausting.

An empty hallway was all that greeted them.

His expression faltered. "Doesn't feel like it lately."

She wanted to protest, but he took her hand. She liked the way he did that, first on the beach, then at their beach house, and now. The hand-holding was temporary, but for the time, she felt claimed.

"Here you are." He nodded to the door across from hers. "I'm right there if you need me."

Two rooms. Of course. The manager had said "rooms," plural. Parker would never guess of her situationship with Sawyer, and Sawyer would never breathe a word.

He opened her door and quickly inspected the small space. She followed him. A suitcase waited to be unpacked. She wondered what she would find—good shampoo and conditioner, she hoped. A cell phone waited for her on the desk.

Sawyer handed her the key card to her room. "Knock or text if you need anything."

She needed him to stay as much as she needed a shower to wash away this crazy day. The memory of showering with Sawyer replayed quickly in her mind. Hot water and hotter kisses. Their touches. Angela shivered. "If you're not tired of me, we could get dinner later?"

He grabbed her waist like in the elevator, but this was a thousand times needier. She tilted her head back and waited for whatever he might say. His face promised it was a lot. Instead, he pressed a kiss to her forehead and let his lips linger there. His palms ran up and down her sides until he released her. "We'll get dinner."

Then he was gone.

CHAPTER TWENTY-SEVEN

WITH A TOWEL wrapped around Sawyer's waist, he stepped out of the steamy bathroom and heard his new cell phone buzz. Angela's name was the only one he wanted to see on the screen, and it wasn't lost on him that he couldn't shake the warm and needy feeling when he saw that it was her.

"Ready for dinner already?" he answered.

"No." She made a sound as though he had a screw loose. "Sawyer, there's a gorgeous dress in my closet."

He laughed. "Oh yeah?"

"I mean, it's *gorgeous*. Please tell me that you and Parker have worked out some secret rendezvous point at an opera house or something."

"Not that I know of, sweetheart."

"I have to wear it somewhere."

"Well…" He opened his closet and glanced at the options hanging in it. They were far more interesting than the standard-issue pants and shirts he'd found in his suitcase. "You could wear it to dinner?"

"Where are we going?"

"The hotel restaurant? I don't know."

"You're killing me, Sawyer. Please don't do that. You've done too much to keep me alive. Now you have to take me somewhere to show off this dress."

He laughed and eyed the suit hanging in the closet. It wasn't as if he hadn't had to wear nice clothes for the job before. Sometimes, it felt as though the security gigs in Abu Dhabi and Dubai required him to wear a tuxedo or dark suit more often than not. But Sawyer didn't know why there would be anything like that for this job in North Carolina. "Let me figure out if Parker has some grand plan first."

"I'm going to shower with all my fingers and toes crossed."

"What for? That Parker's sending us to the opera, or I figure out something for dinner other than the hotel bar?"

"Both."

He laughed and then eyed the suit hanging in the closet. Sawyer had no desire to dress up. He'd be happy to wear sweats and order room service. Then again, he'd be more than happy to see Angela in a dress that made her giddy. That laughter of hers did amazing things to him. Sawyer meandered to the closet and eyed the suit. It did nothing for him. Angela did a lot. He called Parker. "The rooms are great."

"They should be. Great location. Excellent security."

Everything that Sawyer would want in a temporary holding location. Still, his thoughts were drawn to leaving the hotel for a night on the town. He rolled back on his heels, still eyeing the closet. "I didn't see new weapons or Kevlar."

"Ha," Parker snorted. "Contrary to popular belief, I can't make everything arrive immediately."

All things Sawyer knew, just as he knew they were safer inside their hotels. Then again, he expected they would have been safe inside a *safe* house. "Have you figured out how we were compromised?"

"No," Parker lamented. "But you better believe I'm working on it."

"Any new Mylene intel?"

"Actually…" Parker drew out. "Maybe. But I don't want to get Angela's hopes up. Let me wait a little longer and see what turns up."

Sawyer should have pushed, but he didn't want the real world intruding again. "All right."

"All right?" Parker asked, keen to what should've been Sawyer's line of questioning. "What's up with you?"

"Nothing."

"Is your arm worse than what you've shared?"

"No, it's fine enough." As if on cue, his bicep ached. "Nothing else."

"That sounds like a load of shit, Sawyer. Is Angela okay?"

"Why wouldn't she be?"

"Because it's the second time she's been shot at in a little over two weeks."

"Well, yeah. Okay. That. She's fine." Sawyer worked through how he sounded. Like an idiot. Or a caveman. Probably an idiotic caveman. He rubbed a hand over his face. The last thing he wanted to do was draw attention to his and Angela's situation. It'd be unprofessional, and she deserved more than speculation about her private life.

Sawyer stared at the suit and rubbed the back of his neck. He was overthinking a conversation about his wardrobe. "So, nothing on the agenda until you know more?"

"Nothing at all," Parker confirmed.

"Great."

"Are you bored or something?"

His mind flashed to the room across the hall and the woman who was likely standing naked and alone under the hot, steamy shower at that moment. "No, I'm surviving." Again, he ran a hand over his face.

Parker waited for a beat. "Something's wrong, bud. I can hear it."

"No," Sawyer said too quickly. "This is the thing. I don't have a weapon, but the clothing options hanging in the closet say we're headed for a night on the town."

Parker laughed. "Oh, okay. I asked Amanda to make the luggage arrangements, since I don't have Angela's sizes on file. She probably put more thought into the clothes than I would have."

That made sense, but Sawyer still didn't understand the suit and dress. "Thanks, man." Sawyer considered calling Amanda, but it was the middle of the night in Abu Dhabi. "Let me know when you're ready to share new intel."

"Roger that."

Sawyer tossed the cell phone onto the bed and stared at the lonely king-size mattress. He didn't want to sleep alone tonight; he didn't want to sleep without *Angela*. She burrowed against him and made everything right in the world. He released a breath and knew he was falling hard.

Sawyer walked to the window. Their agreement was temporary. They would either find Mylene or they wouldn't. Then they would return to their usual routines in Abu Dhabi after Angela testified against Pham. They wouldn't be together as they were now.

That was a good thing. He didn't have it in him to fall in love. Sawyer pinched the bridge of his nose. He wouldn't think of the past, of what he lost, and he refused to compare Angela to—his cell phone buzzed. Sawyer dropped his head back and inhaled deeply before answering Parker's call.

"I changed my mind," Parker said in greeting. "I think I know where Pham's people are hiding Mylene."

An unreadable edge growled underneath what Parker had said and what he hadn't. "What aren't you telling me?"

Parker grumbled. "It's not you…"

"Something you don't want to tell Angela?"

"Yeah," he finally admitted. "How's she doing?"

Sawyer snorted. "All's apparently fine if you have a closet filled with pretty clothes. So hell if I know."

Parker chuckled. "Good idea on Amanda's part. Give Angela surface-level diversions for a distraction."

Was their hookup a surface-level distraction? Sawyer's gut churned. Two shootings and a breakup? That made a scary amount of sense. He paced the length of the hotel room. "What don't you want to tell her?"

"I'm unsure if Mylene is Pham's victim or *employee*."

The answer sucked all the oxygen out of the room. "Well… hell."

"Yeah," Parker said in another grumble. "That changes things, huh?"

It certainly did. "How do we figure the truth out?"

"Without walking in to see for yourselves, I don't know, man."

"Walking in where?"

"Don't know that yet either."

Sawyer rubbed the back of his neck. "None of this sounds right."

Parker sighed. "No. But if there's one thing this job has taught me, the truth is never what it seems."

Wasn't that true in life? "Yeah."

If they were wrong about Mylene, Pham's people were trying to negotiate over someone else Titan Group didn't know about. Where did that leave Sawyer and Angela? "I assume the Senator knows?"

"That's above my pay grade." A keyboard clacked on Parker's side. "The more important question is where Mylene is. It's killing me that I don't know yet."

"When do you think you'll know? Today? Tomorrow?"

"Given the chatter and communication pings that I'm triangulating... I might by morning. Or, at least, I think we'll have pinpointed the players in Pham's US-based operational hub."

"That's always good."

"Don't sound too excited," Parker chided. "So, what are you going to do with this information?"

Sawyer squeezed his eyes shut. "That Mylene is a possible employee?"

"Yeah."

He recalled Angela's excitement over a dress. "Nothing can be done right now?"

"Nothing," Parker agreed. "So, you'll hang tight and wait for more intel before we tell Angela?"

She would kill them for keeping this from her. "Sounds like a plan."

The call ended. Sawyer sat at the desk by the window and batted the cell phone between his hands. Holding off until morning was the right move—and not just for him. They could learn nothing more about Mylene tonight. He set the cell phone down, picked up the room phone, and punched the zero button. "Concierge, please."

The line was transferred, and when the concierge picked up, Sawyer was more confident in his decision. A mirror reflected the smile he hadn't known was hanging on his lips. "I need a dinner reservation tonight for a beautiful woman in a gorgeous dress."

CHAPTER TWENTY-EIGHT

SAWYER DID A double take in the full-length mirror. His suit looked sharp. He ran a hand over the stubble on his cheeks and wondered if he should've shaved. Then he decided that expensive threads *and* smooth cheeks were too much. Sawyer tousled his hair but didn't know much more he could do for that. All in all, he was more himself than ever when forced to wear designer duds for the job. The only thing missing was a gun holstered at the small of his back for an extra layer of protection in case their location had been leaked.

He checked his watch and knocked on Angela's door. His heartbeat skittered with nerves he wouldn't admit to. Tonight was far outside of his comfort zone. Feeling like he couldn't hide a goofy grin, he mused that the situation was like going to prom as an adult.

Angela opened the door a crack and barely poked her head out. "You're not early."

"Nope," he confirmed, having built time into their schedule after her two demands: surprise her, but don't rush her.

"Thank you," she said, staying behind the door. "Will you tell me where we're going now?"

His nerves jittered again. The anticipation was intoxicating. "Open up, and I will."

Her shy smile blossomed. "Be warned," she said quietly. "It's quite the dress."

"Good thing you're quite the woman."

She opened the door to let him in, but he had to take her in before he could move. His heartbeat thundered. White noise buzzed in his ears.

"You look..." He didn't have words. Sawyer was rough-and-tumble.

Even when they lived in luxury, he dealt with harsh realities. He didn't pay attention to the glitter and glitz that came with living in Abu Dhabi because his job so often made him stroll through hell. So he didn't have it in him to find the right words. "...perfect."

And she was. Absolutely perfect. But it wasn't even because of the dress. This perfection was far beyond a sexy dress on a gorgeous woman. He didn't know how to explain it. A rush of possibilities flooded his mind. He could take her to bed. He could take her out. He wasn't sure it would be possible to be as close to her as he needed. Sawyer would do anything she asked of him so long as he was by her side.

She rolled her full pink lips together. "You're very handsome, Sawyer."

"I've got nothing on you, sweetheart." He took her hand and held it up. She twirled, giggling, as her fingers twisted in his. His nerves dissipated. The anticipation of the night was suddenly gone. He didn't care if they stayed in and he watched her spin all night long, so long as she laughed and smiled as though she didn't have a care in the world.

"What do you think about the dress?" she asked.

The green velvet dress reached from the floor and tied around her neck, leaving her shoulders bare. A slit ran up to her thigh but showed skin only when she jutted her hip or walked. "You make it look good."

Angela grinned. "What about these bad boys?" She pointed at the emerald earrings dangling from her lobes.

He strode closer as though he wanted to take a better look but instead trailed his fingers up the slope of her neck. "Those baubles are no joke."

"I know." She tilted her head and murmured, "I found them in the safe."

She smelled amazing. He dipped his lips to her neck and listened to her sigh. "Do you want to stay in?"

Her head lolled back. He kissed her neck.

"Very tempting offer," she whispered. "But I want to go out before we stay in." Her hands ran up the front of his jacket. "God, your mouth..."

His tongue teased behind her ear. "Give me just a minute. I won't even mess up your hair."

Sawyer backed her to the wall, and her face tipped up to him. He took the kiss that she offered. Her mouth brushed his. Gentle. Sensual. He savored the way she tasted. The way their mouths molded together. The way they played and teased.

Carefully, he lifted her dress until he had access to the skirt's slit. His fingers feathered over her thin silk underwear. Angela's chest hitched as he touched. Her soft kisses became stronger.

He slid the fabric to the side and stroked over her folds. He could feel her arousal and heat. Angela shifted. Her lips parted with a panting breath that promised he was touching her the way she liked.

Sawyer caressed her sex until she inched her legs apart. Need made him delirious. Restraint was all that kept him from tearing her dress open. What wouldn't he do to throw her on the bed? Instead, he dropped to his knees.

"Sawyer…" she whispered.

He kissed the inside of her thigh, climbing higher and higher until he reached the apex of her leg and let his tongue flick over her heated skin. He groaned. In two swift moves, he pulled her underwear down to her high heels and scooted the skirt up over her ass. "Fuck, Angela." His tongue worked between her legs. "You taste good."

Her hands threaded into his hair. "I—"

He needed more of her. Sawyer raised one of her legs over his shoulder, exposing everything he wanted. His tongue stroked her, fingers circling her clitoris.

"More," she whispered.

Good girl. That was what he needed to hear from Angela. What she wanted. How she liked it. He kissed her clit and sucked, sliding his fingers inside her body. Wet, clenching muscles welcomed the intrusion. Her hips flexed, grinding her pussy to his face for more. He couldn't get enough. Sawyer withdrew his fingers and then gave them to her again. His tongue worked the swelling bundle of nerves. She tried to thrash into him and then away from him as though she might explode, and he belted her against the wall and gave her everything he had. Licks and nips and kisses and sucks. She fucked against his face. He hammered into her body.

"Sawyer—God—"

Then she exploded and tasted like nectar. Her heat rippled around his fingers and tongue, rolling through him as nothing ever had in his life.

"Do you have a condom?"

He met her fiery eyes. "I do."

Flushed, Angela pulled him to his feet, unfastened his belt, and backed him toward her bed. He let her call the shots, and before he could thank God for this woman, she had him on his back and was rolling protection over his erection.

Angela moved over him as though they'd been lovers for years, and with the confidence of a woman who had no questions about her needs, guided his cock inside her body.

God. He arched as she took him. Her slick heat had been brought on by his kisses, and now, just like a goddess, she rocked and rose over him, finding herself, driving him to oblivion.

Her orgasm hit him like pulsating lava, and he had no choice but to climax with her. White lights and explosions. That was how she made him feel. Nothing was better.

His eyes opened. Their breathing raced.

She grinned. "Just like you promised. You didn't even mess up my hair."

He laughed, hooked his arm around her, and laid her to his chest, kissing her quiet, kissing her to ground himself.

Finally, she slid away from him, excusing herself to the bathroom. Other than her glowing color, Angela didn't look as if she and Sawyer had fucked until they'd exploded. Even that deceptive slit in her skirt looked modest.

They took a few moments to pull themselves together. She eased back into his arms and smoothed her hands down his suit jacket. "Thank you."

"Right back at you."

She downplayed him with a quiet laugh. "I'm serious. Thanks for agreeing to my crazy idea. The practice, the playing pretend to teach me the ropes or whatever. This has been a lot of fun."

Playing. Pretending. Sawyer probably gave her the correct response. But the reminder of the temporary nature of their situation landed on him like a wall of cold water.

CHAPTER TWENTY-NINE

SAWYER'S HEAD WAS in a fog as he and Angela went through the motions. In the elevator and out. He scanned the lobby and assessed potential threats. She'd asked about their rental car. He'd said they could walk.

Outside, hand in hand, they walked down the street. But Sawyer remained underwater even as he scoped out possible danger. He tried to focus on work and volleyed the idea of sharing what Parker might have learned about Mylene Hathaway. He even thought about why he didn't want to be in a relationship—but cut those thoughts off quickly. That wasn't where his head needed to be while he walked Angela into a Michelin-star restaurant.

"Reservation?" the hostess asked.

He told the hostess the pseudonym and caught Angela's wide eye of approval. The sight was almost enough to clear Sawyer's head.

They were seated at a secluded table. Ensconced candlelight danced across distressed brick walls. He noted details like an analyst would write a report: white tablecloths, crystal glasses, and waitstaff who disappeared until needed.

She ignored the menu. "Sawyer."

His eyebrows rose. He couldn't shake the robotic stiffness that had him in a chokehold.

"What's wrong with you?"

Lying to her wasn't an option. Neither was telling her what had set him off—mostly because he couldn't explain why. They had a time-boxed relationship. He didn't want it to end, but he knew he couldn't continue outside the parameters they'd set. He couldn't even explain why.

Funny how he could jump out of planes and climb through destroyed buildings while bombers flew overhead, yet he was physically incapable of opening up.

"We should leave." She folded her napkin on top of her menu.

He balked. "I don't want to leave." Hell, he had committed every second to memory not even an hour ago. Now, he wondered when this feeling would vanish. "Why do you want to leave?"

"Because you're a zombie." She analyzed him. "What happened?"

Her anger did a poor job of hiding the hurt in her voice, and he hated himself. "I'm sorry." He shook his head and glanced around as if the walls might hold a script. "I—" Would he tell her about his past? He wasn't sure that was a good idea, even if he could.

The waitress appeared. "Good evening. Would you like flat or sparkling water?"

"Could you give us a minute?" Angela asked.

"Of course." The woman backed away and melted into the shadows.

"Look, Ange... I haven't shared everything with you."

Her eyebrows arched.

"And I can't," he added, trying to do right by her and his past. "But you need to know that despite this—us—this crazy idea that you need to practice, or however you put it..." He needed to be completely up front with her. She was worth it. "I haven't been pretending a single damn time."

Her eyes widened.

"Everything I've said. Every kiss and touch. Every single fuckin' moment with you has been as real as it gets." He swallowed hard. "And I hate that I can't be the guy that gets you forever."

An eternity passed.

The waitress returned with the same question.

"Flat," Angela answered without emotion, "if that's all right with you."

Sawyer didn't give a single fuck about the water. "Sure."

The water was poured, and the menu was explained. Sawyer watched Angela, only half hearing the details of the dinner options.

When they were alone again, he offered her a way out. "I ruined the night. We should leave."

Angela chewed her bottom lip.

"You probably have questions," he said. "And I can't answer them. Not now. Later…" He hated how screwed up he was. "Maybe, but I don't know. I'm sorry."

"You don't have to be." She smiled, but it didn't reach her sad, dark eyes. "And I don't want to leave."

"You're sure?"

"Fancy dress and amazing restaurant." She was trying to act like he hadn't dropped a bomb, but Sawyer knew her too well. "I'd be crazy to leave."

"Angela—"

"Don't." She held up her hand. "I created this problem between us, and I can fix it."

Their waitress arrived again, but it wasn't hard to read their table. She backed away with a promise to give them more time.

"Everything I've said and done has been real, too," Angela admitted. "But I'm not deaf. I heard you and knew this was temporary. If I didn't absolutely know that, then I would fall in love with you. So I get it."

The wave of cold water hit Sawyer again. He couldn't breathe.

Her brow furrowed. "You can't be mad at me for how either of us would feel if things were different."

"I'm not mad." At least, not at anyone but himself.

"We're friends. We're going back to the real world soon enough. Everything between us has to return to how it was before, because if not, if I lose any part of what I had with you, it will kill me."

Disorientation skewed his vision. Burning confusion rang in his ears. Her declaration was exactly what he needed to hear and what he should've known was coming, and yet, all Sawyer could think was how in love he was with Angela.

There was no falling to do. It was done. If only he could put his hands on her. If he could remind himself that they could have a physical relationship separate from their partnership, he could be able to make sense of his world.

"Please." Desperation in her eyes matched the whisper in her plea. "Tell me you understand." Angela rolled her lips together. "That we're okay?"

Words wouldn't convey what he needed to explain. There were so many other forms of communication he required that were unavailable to him at a restaurant. He needed more than to hold her close and make promises. He needed to be with her, *in her*, promising more than he had the capacity to say.

The waitress interrupted with an expectant, time-is-ticking expression. "Might I suggest the tasting menu?"

Sawyer wanted to send her away.

Angela tore her glance from his and nodded. "That sounds lovely."

"Sure," he agreed. After the waitress had asked about wine pairings and left, Sawyer stood. "Can you please come with me?"

"We're leaving?"

"No." He nodded his head out of the dining room. "Come on."

She clutched his extended hand. It took a mere moment to find a quiet place in a dimly lit hallway catty-corner from the hall for the bathrooms.

"What are we doing, Sawyer?"

He backed into the corner and, with his hands on her hips, possessively pulled her close. "I fucked up your night."

Her eyelashes fluttered, and he didn't know if that was a prelude to tears, a threat of anger, or him overreading the moment.

"And I need my hands on you when I apologize." He squeezed her waist. "I'm the idiot. I fucked up. I need you to forgive me."

She smiled, and this time, it reached her eyes. "Only because you're good in bed."

He laughed. Relief flooded his soul. She wasn't upset if she could make jokes.

Her head tipped back. "I'm going to need you to kiss me."

Slowly, a smile curled onto his lips. "And I'll be forgiven?"

"I don't know. You haven't kissed me yet."

Sawyer nipped on her bottom lip. An instantaneous fire lit between them. Her tongue slid into his mouth, and he held her tight. The kiss promised everything would be as it was earlier in the night. The possibility thrilled him, but he didn't know what Angela would think. "What's the verdict?"

Her arms wrapped around his neck. "You definitely have a way with me." She gave him a peck on the cheek. "And we're going to have a great night."

CHAPTER THIRTY

THE RESTAURANT DESERVED all its stars and ratings. The tasting menu was more than Angela imagined, and she had to give Sawyer credit. After they'd worked through their drama, he dined on tiny portions of skillfully considered cuisine without complaint. His eyebrows might've risen when he was presented with a single squash blossom drizzled with pureed garlic and pine nuts, and he might've swallowed the brioche Wellington with foie gras and tenderloin in a solitary bite. Still, he did so without taking away from her experience.

The meal, the wine, and everything about the night were too good to be true. She floated on air in her gorgeous dress as they walked into the warm summer night. Unlike their time during the walk to the restaurant, he tucked her protectively under his arm, raining attention on her as though she were the center of the universe. Between that kind of focus and the wine, Angela glowed from the inside out.

"Back to the hotel, or do you want to explore?" he asked.

Not many people were walking on the brick sidewalk. Gas streetlamps flickered over the street. Cute shops and closed storefronts lined their path. "Let's see what there is to see."

It wasn't that she wanted to window shop. She just wasn't ready for the night to end.

They made their way onto a busy street. A more vibrant nightlife beckoned as they neared the town hall. Horse-drawn carts waited to give rides to tourists. A woman surrounded by drums held a few people's attention as she sang and danced. Food trucks lined the street across from a square centered around lighted fountains. Mouthwatering aromas floated in the air. If those scents called to her, then Sawyer was probably dying.

"Are you hungry?"

He chortled. "I mean, how could I be after twelve plates of food?"

She laughed.

"There wasn't even a breadbasket. Did you notice that?" He kissed the top of her head. "Would it be rude to grab a burger and fries?"

"Not unless you didn't get me a hot dog too."

Sawyer scoured the area for where to sit. The many options she saw didn't pass his muster. One she declined because it would involve her somehow climbing up a stone wall in her evening gown and heels. Finally, he parked her on a granite bench that backed to a stone building and had a decent view of the fountains. In short order, he returned with his food, a hot dog for her, and fries to share.

The twelve tiny plates had been a nice appetizer. She ate the hot dog carefully as he polished off the burger and fries.

There was something comfortable about how they could transition from high-roller dining to fast food and the unhurried life unfolding around them. "Have you ever lived someplace like this?"

"Yup," he said. "You?"

"No. I mostly lived in the DC suburbs. My dad lived in Pennsylvania, but Mom lived in Northern Virginia. That was home, really. Where did you live that was like this?"

"It was someplace a long time ago…" The raw edge in his voice caught her off guard. "When I was in the Marines."

She shifted closer.

"You don't talk about the Marine Corps much." Or ever. That was fine. Some former members of the military did. Others didn't. Heartbreaking stories came from war. She'd learned not to ask questions.

Sawyer let out a long breath. "I don't."

And it was apparent that wouldn't change tonight. "Where did you live?"

"Annapolis." His thousand-yard stare lost its focus far beyond the fountains. "I lived in a little house there. Had a nice little life going for me…" He rubbed a hand over his face and then shifted his complete attention toward her. "I was married, Angela."

Her eyes widened. Of all the confessions he might make, that one wasn't on a mile-long list. Her lips parted, but nothing came out.

"I married my high school girlfriend." His jaw ticked in an almost painful, completely heartbroken way. "Her name was Penny, and we were married." The past clouded his eyes. He pinched the bridge of his nose and took a deep breath. "And she was pregnant with my son. I lost them both during childbirth."

Immediately, tears welled in her eyes. "Sawyer..."

He swallowed hard. "It was a long time ago. I was young." Sawyer hoarsely whispered, "So damn young."

Angela laid her hand over his. How did the food truck vendors, singers, and passersby continue as though life was normal when his pain was palpable enough to shake the streets? "I am so sorry."

He turned his palm upward and laced his fingers with hers. The fountains danced. Light caught the spray as it shot up and fell, splashing with an even pattern.

"Did you have a name for your son?" she asked, not sure if she should. Sawyer had decided to tell her his story, but it didn't feel as if he were finished.

"William Gregory."

Pain squeezed her throat; she squeezed his hand. "I like that."

"It's a good name," he said. "A strong name. My kid fought like hell. They both did." Sawyer licked his lips. "Medical negligence. Malpractice. That's what they call it when the doctor screws up."

My kid. Now Angela understood. His earlier words replayed in her mind. *If I could give you all of me, I would in a heartbeat, but I don't know how.* Sawyer didn't do long-term relationships because he had before and gone through hell. She wouldn't fault him for self-preservation.

"I'm not stuck in the past, Ange." He rolled his bottom lip into his mouth. "I'm not carrying a torch for Penny. It's been more than a decade since they passed. But the idea of hurting like that again..." He cleared his throat. "I told you earlier, I haven't been pretending. I'm giving you as much as I've got left."

Pretending had been such an awful lie. She couldn't even imagine how it seemed okay to say. She'd been guarding her barely wounded heart when he'd lived through hell.

Sawyer stood up and pulled her onto her feet. He wrapped his arms around her and pressed a long, lingering kiss to the top of her head. "Now that I've saddled you with that—"

"Don't." She shook her head and then rested her chin against his sternum. "You can share with me; it will never be a burden."

"All right. Understood." The corners of his mouth lifted as though he was tired enough to sleep for a hundred years. "Are you ready to walk back?"

"Only if you are."

His eyes closed. Sawyer hugged her tight again and then took her hand. Together, they retraced their steps past the food trucks and street performers. It took walking a block, maybe two, before the heavy hold of the past dissipated.

A light breeze skimmed over her shoulders. The wind was cool and clean. Life was ever-changing. A kaleidoscope. Their history would always be part of them. She couldn't forget her years in Pham's captivity. Sawyer couldn't forget his first love and son. Experience colored their path now, and she understood that more now that he'd opened up.

They arrived on their floor. Sawyer walked her to her door. "This was an amazing night," she said.

"It had its ups and downs." He chuckled. "Do you still want our..." Sawyer gestured between them. "Situation to continue after everything tonight?"

How could he even ask? She would have as much of him as he could give. No matter that heartbreak was looming, no matter what the logical part of her brain said, she needed to be with him. "Yes. You?"

"I can't give you everything you deserve."

Angela ran her fingers along the front of his suit jacket. "You give me more than enough." She tugged on his lapels as she had before they'd gone to dinner. "Is this when I invite you in?"

The corners of his lips flashed. "I would never say no."

She reached for the key card in her purse, but he paused her. Sawyer moved her toward his door and placed his arm above her shoulders, caging her under his hard chest. He feathered kisses from her cheek to her ear. "Spend the night with me, Angela. I need you in my bed."

The soft tickle of his breath morphed her already spaghetti-like legs into Jello. Sawyer's lips found hers, and without missing a beat, he let the two of them into his hotel room.

Only the desk lamp illuminated the tidy room. His bed was made, and there was no evidence he'd been in the room before now. He shucked off his jacket and loosened his collar. "Turn around."

He found the clasp of her dress at the nape of her neck then slowly slid the zipper to the swell of her ass. The beautiful velvet dress piled onto the floor. Just like earlier, he twirled her around. His fiery eyes drank every inch of her in the silky strapless bra and underwear, which matched the deep green of her dress. She had flaws that he didn't seem to see.

"I don't know what I was thinking." He tugged her close. "I knew exactly what was under that dress but didn't throw you over my shoulder and run back to this room after dinner."

A flush burned from her cheeks to her chest. "You were hungry."

"There are many kinds of hunger."

She reached for his shirt and unfastened the buttons then pushed it off his broad shoulders. "We're here now. What are you going to do about it?"

He stripped to the well-fitted boxer briefs that curved over his sculpted ass and hugged his powerful thighs. His erection bulged behind the dark fabric. Sawyer lifted her into his arms and placed her on the bed. Shoes and all.

Carefully, he removed Angela's undergarments until she lay naked, buzzing under his touch. The closer they came, the less oxygen they had to breathe. Longing twisted her insides. She craved Sawyer in a way that defied logic.

Sawyer tossed her shoes over his shoulder and lifted her ankle to his lips. The kiss seared her skin. This was so different than before dinner, when they'd been hot enough to spark a fire. Sawyer was taking his time with a slow-burn torture. His tongue snaked up the inside of her calf and teased upward until he nuzzled between her legs. The kisses continued rising, dusting over her belly, teasing the swell of her breasts, and caressing her nipples. He nibbled and murmured inaudible sweet nothings that sent her sky-high until his powerful body carefully covered hers.

Angela's eyes were closed. She soaked in sensation after sensation. Anticipation edged her close to losing her mind. "You are killing me."

His smile blossomed against her neck. "Good." Sawyer rolled to her side and urged her thighs apart. His fingers danced over her folds as his lips hovered just behind her ear. Breathy kisses made her squirm. "That's my plan, sweetheart."

His fingertips caressed her sensitive skin. Her delicate flesh was still tender from earlier, but arousal was quick to come. Sawyer touched her gently until a quaking tremble started deep inside her core. The intensity was almost too much.

"Easy, Ange," he whispered against her temple. "Relax for me."

Relaxing wasn't in the cards. Her hips wriggled. She needed more but didn't know that she could take it. God, she wanted it. Wanted him. "Sawyer, please."

"I've got you."

Angela arched. She couldn't escape from the desperate, rising climax brought on by his fingertip strumming her clit. He took her mouth in a kiss and growled for her to climax. It was as though he needed her to come as much as she needed to.

The understanding threw Angela into delirium, and her body convulsed. His name fell from her lips. She would never have enough.

Angela pulled him to her. She loved everything about them. How gentleness became cataclysmic and friendship became fire. "I need you. Now."

He smiled into a kiss. "Anything you say."

Sawyer slid on their protection and returned to her arms. His hungry mouth took hers again. Their tongues danced. His rigid cock pressed to her entrance, and she writhed for the pressure of him sliding into her tenderness. "Please."

He was careful as he eased inside. Sore but desperate for him to fill her, Angela angled for more as he delivered breathtakingly perfect thrusts. She cried for more. He loved her harder. Her nails bit into his back. His hips pinned her in place. She gasped and kissed and begged. Sawyer's full length was seated deep inside her, and he held her in place.

"Damn it, sweetheart," he whispered against her neck. "You are everything to me."

Emotion caught in her throat. Tears burned behind her eyes. Sawyer caged her against the pillows with such intensity and ferocity that she never wanted to leave his bed again. Their foreheads touched. His eyes squeezed shut. He was the most beautiful, giving man she'd ever known.

Then his eyes opened and showed the depths of his soul. Sawyer held her gaze, and they made love. He rocked into her again and again. Satisfaction pummeled her in a way she hadn't known could exist. She'd never been so cared for, so possessed, so absolutely well fucked within an inch of her life.

One of his hands laced itself with hers. He pinned it above her head. His shaft pumped into her, reigniting a frenzy. She had no more to give but climaxed again, and as she did, he stiffened, straining with an orgasm. Her name fell from his lips.

She was so in love…

Sawyer collapsed against her, gasping for breath. She never wanted to let him go. But his heavy weight was stolen away as he rolled onto his side. Sweet, sated kisses feathered her forehead and into her mussed hair. He gathered Angela to his chest. His racing heart slowed in beat with hers.

One thing was certain. For the rest of her life, she would never forget this man or this night.

CHAPTER THIRTY-ONE

THE SUN POURED through the sheer drapes. The aroma of French-pressed coffee wafted from the silver carafe. Angela speared another bite of pancakes as Sawyer called Parker on speaker and set his cell phone between them.

Pleasantries said, Parker got down to business. "I have an address for you."

Angela's eyes went to Sawyer's. "An address for what?"

"Mylene Hathaway."

She did a double take at the phone. "How is that possible?"

Parker blew out with an exhausted chortle. "You don't want to know how that kind of magic happens."

"Yeah, Parker. I do."

"Did you ever have a kid in an algebra class that asked, 'When are we ever going to need to know how to do this?'"

She briefly recalled the nightmare of SAT study guides and then envisioned Parker plotting slope-intercept formulas on a whiteboard. "I might've been that kid," she admitted.

"Math's nothing but a game," he replied. "Find the variables. Solve the puzzle. Finding Mylene has been like isolating the variables and reworking the equations."

How could Mylene have existed all these years in captivity, and no one did the math correctly? Her disbelief was giving way to anger. "Are you kidding me?"

"Don't shoot the messenger—and it's only an educated guess."

"One of Parker's educated guesses," Sawyer pointed out. "So there's a negative chance of his being wrong."

Parker didn't disagree. "You two will have to see what there is to see."

"Right." Something in Parker's voice needled under her skin. She glanced at Sawyer. He focused on his coffee. "Is there something else?" she asked.

"This is the thing, Angela," Parker said. "Given the variables and my analysis, I'm pretty sure she's alive."

Sawyer didn't look up from his coffee, and Parker's voice was still off. Her stomach bottomed out. "But…?"

"I don't know if she's held against her will or on Pham's payroll."

Parker's words landed like a wrecking ball.

Sawyer didn't share her jaw-dropping reaction. A moment later, he asked, "You okay?"

"That's insane." She recoiled. "Mylene didn't kill her husband and sister to work for Pham."

Sawyer pinched his lips but shrugged. "We aren't going to know anything until we check the situation out."

"Exactly," Parker confirmed. "Get eyes on the situation. Confirm it's her. Then we decide what's needed. An extraction plan or law enforcement."

Angela's mind whirled. She'd spent years with this woman in her head. After only two weeks of investigating, she was sure Mylene needed Titan's assistance. "I am here to help her."

"We're here to find her," Sawyer said quietly.

Find. Not *save.* This felt like a betrayal.

Sawyer scooted closer. "If this isn't who Pham's willing to give up in negotiations, then there might be someone still out there who needs help."

That elaboration didn't help her rushing thoughts. "Then the Feds might still cut a deal with Pham, and he won't stay in prison."

Neither man disagreed.

"You don't have to do this if you don't want to," Sawyer offered.

"Not find her?" She jerked back. "Like hell I'm not."

His lips quirked.

"You might not like what you see," Parker added.

"Where is she?" Angela asked.

"If it's her…" Parker's keyboard clicked. "She's about thirty minutes away."

She recalled when ACES exploded into the facility where Pham had kept her and Chelsea. It was such a barren place to live. With concrete bars and chain-link fences, she'd reimagined her surroundings into a livable house. The food was good. They tried to make sure she was never bored. But it was just an ignored commercial industrial depot. "Is she in a warehouse?"

"Actually, no. She lives in a regular house."

Betrayal hit again. She didn't know why. Pham kept Mylene in a house but not Angela? Or did Mylene live in a house as a traitor on Pham's payroll? Her stomach roiled.

Sawyer's gaze narrowed, but he said nothing to her. "Anything else we need to know?" he asked Parker. "Otherwise, we'll probably finish breakfast and game out our next move."

What was with all the game and puzzle talk? She pressed her fingers into her temples.

"I'll send over everything I have—and Angela?"

"Yeah?"

"No matter which way this goes, you figured out something major. The Feds should've listened to you years ago."

"Thanks," she managed before Sawyer disconnected the call. "You knew something already, didn't you?"

He crossed his arms and leaned back in his chair. "I knew there were possibilities that you might not like."

Her shoulders slumped.

"I've always known this could go a lot of ways." He studied her and added, "Yeah, I knew a few hours before dinner last night. Parker said it was possible, that he didn't know enough to say, and that he had more to look into."

"He knew enough to mention it to you."

"Yeah," he admitted.

"But you didn't say anything last night?" She shook her head. "I can't believe you."

After an overly long moment, Sawyer said, "There were two very different possibilities about Mylene. She was either a victim or a traitor. *Possibilities.* Working hypotheses that Parker had to figure out. Not intel. There was nothing we could do."

"So you didn't tell me."

"I figured, why fuck up a good night with a woman that was so damn excited about a pretty dress—when there was jack shit that we could do about it. I didn't burden you with news that could wait."

She wanted to yell. Angela pushed out her chair, stood up, and stormed toward the window. But her frustration with Sawyer wasn't there. He was right. There had been nothing they could do.

The person she was really upset with was Mylene.

Or maybe herself.

She rubbed her temples. Ibrahim would have some catchy piece of advice that would help. Something about realizing what was in her control. For all the therapy, she couldn't recall anything that would assist her.

Angela turned toward the table. Sawyer simply sat there, waiting for her to freak out or shut down. She didn't want to do either—but realized he'd been kind to keep the possibility of Mylene to himself last night. He'd been looking out for her. Always the bodyguard.

She walked toward him and crawled into his lap. Sawyer wrapped his arms around her and held her close.

"This is hard," she said. Her head rested on his shoulder. "I don't know if I can do it."

"Sure you can. It might not be how you envisioned, but it'll be done." He rubbed her back. "It's almost over."

A cry caught in her throat. It *was* almost over. Sawyer had meant to make her feel better. Now, she wanted to weep. Their investigation could be over by the end of the day, and where would that leave her and him?

He cupped her chin and turned her face to his. "Ange?"

She tried to look away, but that was no use. Tears welled in her eyes.

"I agree with Parker," he said. "No matter what happens with Mylene, you did something extraordinary."

The tears fell and burned down her cheeks. "I guess so." She was heartbroken. How could she lose this man so quickly? Angela rolled her lips together. He was never hers to keep. Maybe before last night, she could have walked away unscathed. But he'd made love to her. Before she'd fallen asleep in his arms, she'd imagined what it might look like if they had a different life. One in which they lived in a beach house with little kids to play football in the sand. Or a life in a coastal town where they could dress up, dine on tiny plates of haute cuisine, and then devour greasy burgers under the moonlight.

With his thumb, he swiped the tears from her cheeks. "When you first told Boss Man that you wanted to find Mylene, all I could think of was how it wouldn't work." Sawyer brushed back her hair. "I was wrong. Hell, you even came up with a signature question."

She shut her eyes and shook her head. "It all seems so trivial now."

"I'm proud of you, Angela. No matter what we find today."

There was nothing to say. She couldn't explain how her heart had already ached. Instead, she wrapped her arms around him and buried her face against his neck.

Composing herself took longer than she wanted. But after a few sniffly breaths, she returned to her chair opposite Sawyer. "I guess we should start our day. What did Parker send us?"

Sawyer took a sip of coffee. "Maybe you should eat first?" He speared a bite of pancake as if to remind her they hadn't finished their plates.

"I'm not hungry." After his disapproving look, though, she picked up her fork and played with her pancakes.

"All right, Parker says…" He scrolled. "Not much except an address and location summary." Sawyer chewed a bite of pancake, read, and added, "It's a small house owned by an untraceable shell company. Not a very big place. Overgrown lot. Minimal activity on the utilities. Water and electricity usage suggest a one-person household. No vehicle registered there." He took another bite and swallowed it. "No name history of note from the postal service and various direct mail distribution houses." He shrugged and set down his fork and phone. "I have no idea how Parker finds the places he sends us to, but he's rarely wrong."

"What are we going to do when we get there?"

"Knock on the door?" he suggested with a half laugh.

"I'm serious."

"I am too. Scope the place and see what there is to see. We can't have a plan until we check it out. Titan has US-based teams that could be there in a snap if we need backup. If we don't?" He shrugged. "We knock on the door? I pick a lock? We'll see what we see and make a game-time decision." He gestured to her ignored pancakes. "Finish those, and then we go?"

Some of her appetite had returned. She agreed.

Sawyer moved to his suitcase. "I'd feel better about all of this if I had a weapon and you had a vest."

"So let's stop somewhere and arm ourselves." She was somewhat surprised that Amanda hadn't arranged for weapons and security equipment. Still, it made sense given that they were trying to keep knowledge of Angela's location to as few people as possible. Especially if all they were supposed to do while at the safe house was wait. Since they'd left Emerald Isle, nothing had felt remotely dangerous.

"I'd be more comfortable if Titan made the arrangements."

"Do you even have a lockpicking kit?" She looked dubiously at his closet. The concierge who arranged for their clothes was likely not the same person Amanda or Parker would ask for weapons and surveillance equipment.

"You'd be surprised what I can use to get into places."

She snorted. "I doubt that." Angela took a last sip of coffee and pushed away from the table. "Will we come back here after we go to find Mylene?"

His shoulders lifted. "Another thing we'll figure out after we investigate the address."

"Gee, you know how much I love uncertainties."

He laughed. "Well, then, let's get you some information, sweetheart."

Fifteen minutes later, she was dressed, had said a loving goodbye to the green dress, and was out the door to find Mylene—and put an end to this romantic time with Sawyer.

CHAPTER THIRTY-TWO

THE NONDESCRIPT HOUSE looked exactly as it looked from the images that Parker had sent, though neither the satellite nor property record photos did justice to its disrepair. The gutters sagged. The fence had seen better days. Sawyer wasn't sure that anyone had lived in the building for years. Then again, the entire neighborhood felt ignored.

He circled the block again. Their newer-model rental car would stand out if anyone was watching too closely.

"What are you looking for?" Angela asked.

Two old work vans had caught his eye. One had darkly tinted windows. The other was overwrapped in worn signage from a plumbing and home repair company. "Anyone looking for us."

"Do you think this could be a trap?"

His gaze flicked to the rearview mirror. "It certainly got us here, didn't it?"

"Parker wouldn't have sent us into a trap unarmed."

Although they weren't entirely unarmed after their quick stop at Wal-Mart, he understood her sentiment. "I don't need a gun to keep you safe."

Sawyer parked behind the van with tinted windows. "Stay put a second."

He exited the rental car and carefully moved to the van for a closer inspection. The doors weren't locked. A quick peek inside revealed an overflowing ashtray, an old fast-food bag on the passenger floorboard, and not much else. Lookout vehicle, or was it owned by an untidy smoker? He didn't rule out either possibility. Sawyer opened the discarded fast-food bag. The receipt was paid by credit card and dated three weeks ago.

He returned to Angela's side of the car, and she rolled the window down. "Anything interesting?"

"I don't think so." He glanced at their surroundings. "Want to go for a walk?"

"Sure."

He led them in the opposite direction from Mylene's block. After they passed several driveways, she asked, "Where are we going?"

"I want to check out this van—"

A man in a maintenance-style uniform walked from the back of a nearby house.

Sawyer slowed their pace and kept his gaze straight ahead but watched the man proceed toward the plumber's van, open the rear doors, and rummage through a tool chest.

Another man in a matching uniform appeared from the backyard. "Hey," he yelled. "Never mind, I found it."

Sawyer and Angela walked by the plumber, who cursed his lazy, good-for-nothing partner.

They made a left at the end of the block then another until they were back on the same street. She took his hand when they turned toward Mylene's house.

Sawyer gave her hand a quick squeeze. "How are you doing?"

"Fine. Nervous. I don't know."

He scanned the area and stopped.

"What—"

After another quick study of their surroundings, Sawyer pulled her to his chest and gave her his full attention. "Do you want to go back to the car?"

"Absolutely not."

He grinned through a tightness knotted in his chest. Sawyer had only so many more times he could pull her close. Now wasn't the time or place to kiss Angela, but the rules of engagement were fuzzy when it came to her. He pressed his lips to hers. "We'll be careful."

The kiss left her smiling. "I know."

"There's no reason to be worried."

"First, that's not true." Her chin rose. "And second, I can be nervous and still want to keep going."

"*I know.*" After all, this was the same woman who slapped her would-be assassin. But Sawyer also knew that Angela's bravado was a crutch.

She pushed onto her tiptoes and smacked his lips with hers. "I can't wait anymore. Let's go."

He kissed her one more time because what the hell, why not? "Whatever you say."

They walked to the house next door to Mylene's, and Sawyer led them up the driveway. Her hand tightened on his.

"I'm just getting a better look," he explained.

They skirted behind the neighbor's house and saw Mylene's window shades were drawn. Carpenter bee holes pocked the fascia board along her roofline. The siding needed a good power washing several years ago. But he didn't see security cameras or telltale signs of booby traps, trip wires, or incendiary devices. He also noted that nothing on the exterior would keep a person inside who didn't want to stay.

"Do you think she's in there?" Angela asked.

"Not sure. Hang tight a second." Sawyer parked her next to a sun-bleached swing set that hadn't seen kids in at least a decade. He handed her the keys to the rental car. "If I'm not back in five minutes, get back to the car, and call Parker."

It didn't take Sawyer long to walk the perimeter of Mylene's backyard and get a closer look at the house. He tossed a couple of rocks at the windows. No alarms, and no one came outside.

He returned to Angela. "I don't see anything that worries me."

"So we're going to knock on the door?"

That still seemed like the best plan. His eyebrows lifted. "You game?"

"Of course I'm game." Her gaze danced over his shoulder. "If she saw you snooping in her yard…"

"Then we'll find out."

They returned to the sidewalk and proceeded onto Mylene's front stoop. Angela raised her hand to knock but froze.

Sawyer touched the small of her back. "Whatever we find out, we'll deal with."

She nodded then rapped on the door.

No one answered.

"That's a bit anticlimactic," Angela muttered.

"My turn." Sawyer banged hard enough on the old wood door that it threatened to fall down. "Keys." She handed him the rental car keys. Sawyer lodged them into the door jamb and opened the front door easily. "Probably could've elbowed our way in."

Cautiously, he called, "Hello?"

No one answered. Angela stepped into the house behind him and shut the door. The house smelled too clean.

"Do you smell bleach?" she asked.

"Yup." His Spidey senses screamed they had a problem. "Stay close." He eased farther into the small entryway. "Hello?" he called, knowing no one was home. "Mylene Hathaway?"

"*Holy shit.*"

Sawyer turned and saw what Angela had seen. She grasped his hand as they walked into the center of the living room. "Jesus Christ."

Slowly, they pivoted, taking in the walls. From floor to ceiling, framed pictures of Mylene's husband and sister covered every inch of space. There were family photos and crime scene photos as well as framed newspaper headlines and articles.

Sawyer pulled out his phone and called Parker. "Yeah, we've got a problem."

"What?"

He didn't know what to call it.

"Sawyer?"

"Something… wrong happened here." He didn't know what else to say. "This might be far beyond my pay grade."

"Huh?" Parker asked. "Did you find Mylene?"

Angela trembled, pulling away from Sawyer.

"Ange, wait—hey, Parker, I'll call you back."

"Send him pictures," she managed.

Parker asked, "Do you need a clean-up team?"

Sawyer agreed Parker needed to see this as soon as possible. "I don't know what we need, man. Give me a minute, and I'll send you some pictures." He ended the call and followed Angela.

They walked through this madhouse. He tried to understand why the walls were like they were. Every room except for a bathroom, a small bedroom, and the kitchen with a makeshift office area was covered with pictures and headlines related to Mylene's loved ones. They were even hung on the doors and taped onto the closed window blinds.

"He did this," Angela's voice shook. "That bastard did this."

Sawyer decided a video of each room would be better than photos. But even after he reviewed what he had filmed, nothing could do justice to the insane asylum they were exploring.

"Sawyer, we have to find her."

Mylene Hathaway needed help. It didn't matter if she had hung the photos herself or if Pham's people had papered the house with them. She would need a mental health evaluation and probably years of therapy.

CHAPTER THIRTY-THREE

MYLENE HADN'T LEFT her house since Pham had been arrested. The outside world was terrifying. She didn't know what to expect or who she'd see. Everyone hated her and what they had done. No one would ever believe what had happened. Pham had explained that so many times. Mylene was the reason Mark and Tabby were dead.

Now, they had forced her out of her home. She didn't know where they were bringing her or why.

"I'm not supposed to leave," she tried again.

They didn't listen.

They never listened.

She missed her house—and her husband and sister. Mylene hated seeing them and couldn't look them in the eye. But when she was home, they were still with her. Almost to keep her safe as much as to punish her.

Their faces had been Pham's idea. Their images were how he kept her in the house because she'd have to face them if she wanted to escape, and she never would.

But now that she had left and didn't know where she was going… Mylene needed them. They held up the walls and kept her safe.

"Can you take me back?" Tears slipped down her cheeks. The truth about what she'd done was so much more evident when there was nowhere to hide. Mylene pleaded, "Take me back home."

SAWYER PACED THE hotel lobby. Since the moment Parker had seen the video, sent it to the Feds, and told them to stand down and wait for Brock to arrive, Sawyer had been unable to sit still. That mind-fuck of a house would haunt his dreams. Angela had gone very quiet and stayed in her hotel room while Sawyer awaited Brock's arrival.

The hotel manager appeared for the thousandth time. "Is there anything else I can help you with?"

"I'm good." Wasn't his laundry list of supplies enough to make her think he was a crazy man? Cases of soda. Cutlery. Cookie sheets from their commercial kitchen. Duct tape. A football helmet—well, *that* she hadn't been able to locate.

She kept pace along his side. "Tea? A complimentary massage—"

"Look—" Did he look as though he needed a massage? "I'm waiting for someone."

The hotel lobby doors whooshed open. She took a step back. By the look on her face, Brock and whomever else he'd brought with him had arrived.

She skedaddled. Brock's all-business scowl matched those of the two men following close behind. They weren't from Sawyer's team, but they were Titan. That was all that mattered.

ANGELA'S HOTEL ROOM was as clean and organized as it could be after Sawyer had made a huge mess in his effort to protect her from unknown, nonexistent threats. She smelled like grape cola and felt almost as sticky. With her earbuds in and Amanda on the phone, Angela didn't know what more she could do to see herself busy. There were only so many times she could look at herself in the mirror or rehash the tale of Mylene's house of hell to Amanda. "I feel sick."

"I can't imagine," Amanda repeated.

"Yeah, you can. How are you feeling these days?"

Amanda snorted. "Better than Chelsea."

"You two will be through the worst of it soon." Angela didn't like to keep her girlfriends at arm's length from her recent drama, but with two pregnant best friends, she didn't want to bother them when they were both operating on ginger ale and saltine crackers. Then again, she needed to share and hadn't been able to connect with Jane. "You know what?

Sawyer's ability to compartmentalize is borderline scary."

Amanda chortled. "Why's that?"

"Well, he's all but locked me in a tower like I'm Rapunzel." Though this Disney Princess looked more like Humpty Dumpty crossed with the Tin Man from *The Wizard of Oz.*

"Bad example. The witch gets in, doesn't she?" Amanda asked.

Angela ignored her. "While he's downstairs, more or less unaffected." And not wearing a homemade, semi-bulletproof vest.

"I doubt that."

"Well, I'm stuck in my hotel room while he waits for Brock in the lobby."

"He doesn't want you in public. He has a reason to be overprotective. It's his job."

Angela looked at herself in the mirror and shook her head. "He might be going overboard at the moment."

"Why's that?"

Would Angela give away her relationship with Sawyer if she explained the list of rules he'd put in place when leaving her alone for under fifteen minutes? Not to mention how he'd duct-taped silverware to flattened soda cans, sandwiched them between commercial-kitchen cookie sheets, and called the result her makeshift chainmail suit.

"Sawyer cares for you," Amanda offered carefully.

Angela's cheeks flushed. "He's got a good heart. That's for sure."

"Have you ever thought about seeing him outside of work?"

"Seeing him?"

"Yes, Angela," Amanda said as though rolling her eyes. "As in dating. *Seeing him* outside of work."

Flames erupted at the back of her neck. "There is no such thing as outside of work. We live and breathe and work together around the clock."

"Hagan and I manage…"

Angela could not go there. She couldn't share how deeply she wanted more from Sawyer and wouldn't betray his trust. They had no future other than as co-workers and friends, and if Angela imagined the possibilities too many more times, she would have to walk away from her life at Titan.

A knot in her throat ached. Angela cleared it and changed the subject. "Do you think they killed Mylene?"

"Hm," Amanda offered, noting the abrupt change to the conversation with a knowing tone. "I don't know."

She pinched the bridge of her nose. "They'd stripped her personal effects and wiped the place down."

"That's what you said." Amanda sounded as if she knew precisely why Angela didn't want to discuss Sawyer.

"I don't think there's a stray hair or fingerprint for the Feds to find—I wonder what my mom thinks of all this."

"Do you think she knows?"

Angela scoffed. "What doesn't she know?"

Had her mom foreseen Sawyer before Angela had? Was that why she'd sent John Patterson? Did everyone have suspicions? Angela prayed Amanda wouldn't return to the possibility of her and Sawyer because they both saw how relationships could work in their world. If anything, they thrived. Hagan and Amanda. Chance and Jane. Liam and Chelsea. They were the gold standard of couples.

Amanda would never know that Sawyer had been a married father whose world was stolen. Angela would never press him to risk unfathomable pain again *because* of how much she loved him. That kind of selfishness wasn't fair. She swallowed hard. "They might have killed Mylene."

The line remained silent. Amanda certainly heard the rawness in Angela's voice. Finally, Amanda said, "I don't know. Mylene seems too valuable at this point to get rid of her."

"Yeah."

"Maybe they would have a few years ago, but given what we know now…"

Parker had updated Angela and Sawyer on the way back to the hotel: Mylene had been working for Pham. The cyber component of modern warfare was focused on civilians. Information wars. Deepfake videos. Bots and trolls that instigated fear. Angela was shocked and couldn't wrap her head around how a former army intelligence and communication specialist could go from serving her country to assisting enemy organizations.

She stared out her window. Pine trees surrounded the parking lot. Most of the parking spaces had been taken. People went about their everyday lives while so much ugliness existed. "You know that I first met Chelsea when Pham had her taken."

"I know."

"I remember telling her that everything would be all right. The food was great. I was never bored. No one bothered me, and when Pham came to visit, he was more like a sad grandpa than a scary terrorist. I even called him Gramps in my head sometimes."

"The mind can bend backward to make sense of the senseless."

She bit her lip. "Maybe that's what happened to Mylene. Maybe that's why she does what she does. Like a Patty Hearst situation."

"Maybe," Amanda said neutrally. "The questions will keep coming until someone finds her."

A knock sounded on her door. A muffled voice called, "Housekeeping."

Angela turned from the window. "No, thank you."

Housekeeping knocked again. Sawyer had said not to open the door. Had he also said not to say anything? Probably.

"What's going on?" Amanda asked.

"Housekeeping knocked." Angela peeked out the peephole. On the other side, an older woman was reading a clipboard beside a housekeeping cart. "I thought we'd hung the Do Not Disturb door hanger on my door."

"What time is it there? Angela, wait—"

She peeked through the hole again. The old lady looked harmless, but Angela's intuition issued a warning. She backed away from the door. "Maybe I should call Sawyer—"

Pain exploded in her chest. She lay on her back, unable to take a breath, and tried to sit up. Bullets splintered through the door as though the woman on the other side was aiming for the floor. Angela kicked herself back, still not catching her breath.

The locking mechanism clicked. One at a time, the lock tumblers fell into place. The door cracked open—and caught. The metal door latch caught. The metallic clang echoed in Angela's head. The woman tried the door one more time. It wouldn't move beyond the slight opening.

A thin string threaded onto the latch bar and looped around the bar's backside against the door jamb. Angela tried to sit up again. Pain rocketed through her ribs.

The string tightened around the base of the latch. The door shut.

She scooted back.

The string tightened. The latch jerked. The string tightened again.

The latch lifted and smacked free of the catch.

Angela dragged herself into the bathroom and locked the door. Her earbuds had fallen out. She had no phone and no weapon. She had nothing to save her except for the makeshift vest that Sawyer insisted she wear. But that wouldn't matter in a moment. She was a fish in a bucket.

CHAPTER THIRTY-FOUR

TITAN HAD SHOWN up in force, with the luggage to prove it. Sawyer helped unload the last duffel from Brock's vehicle. Somewhere in the mess of bags had to be enough weapons to arm a small country.

"That's it," Brock said. "Let's roll."

Their cell phones buzzed simultaneously. Sawyer's stomach dropped. He reached for his phone and hoped to read that law enforcement had more to share about Mylene Hathaway. It was a message from Amanda.

GET TO ANGELA

Sawyer's heart stopped cold.

Colby Winters swore. "What floor?"

"Tenth." Brock's face registered all the possibilities that message could mean while his mind appeared to run scenarios simultaneously.

"We'll get the stairs and back exits," Cash said, pulling his cowboy hat low before he and Roman peeled off.

"I'll man the first floor and lobby exits." Winters nodded at the elevators. "Go."

Sawyer and Brock ran toward the elevators. The doors opened. Sawyer yelled, "Get out," to the businessman pulling his rolling suitcase and then rushed in.

Brock pulled a Glock from his back. "You go. I'll clear the second elevator and get to you."

"Tenth floor. Room 1021." Sawyer smashed the button for the elevator door to shut.

He checked the magazine of his newly issued Glock and prayed the elevator would speed up. Years seemed to pass. The elevator chime dinged at his floor.

Weapon extended, he slid through the barely opened doors and saw no threats. Sawyer hauled toward their rooms. A housekeeping cart piled high with blankets blocked Angela's door. He knocked it out of the way. Bullet holes pocked the door.

He swiped the card and threw himself into the room. The door thudded against someone.

Sawyer side-tackled them to the floor. Their gun skittered out of reach; his pointed at their temple. "Don't fucking move a muscle."

The woman pinned under him seemed to know he wasn't a cop and didn't care if she died. The lady didn't struggle.

"Angela?" His guts twisted when he didn't see her in the room.

"Sawyer," Brock called from the other side of the door. "Open up."

Sawyer holstered his weapon and ran his hands over the mercenary, removing a backup pistol and plastic zip-ties. A loud bang sounded from the door. Brock walked in.

"Get this piece of crap." Sawyer threw the shooter on the bed and bounded toward the closed bathroom door. His heart hammered in his chest. Why wasn't Angela walking out or calling for help?

Bullets had blown off the bathroom door handle. Holes and dents cratered from the handle to the floor. Behind him, Cash and Roman walked in.

Sawyer knocked gently on the door, terrified of what would be on the other side. "Angela? Open up." He tried to open the door. It didn't budge. But he heard a metallic clang. "Ange?"

"Call Winters," Brock said. "Get him up here. He can get into anywhere."

Metal clattered on the other side. "Ange?" Sawyer peered through the space where the door handle had been and saw only the far wall. Metal clanged again.

"What the hell is that noise?" Roman asked.

Finally, the door cracked. Sawyer carefully pushed it open. A shaking, tear-streaked Angela sat crouched in a ball on the floor—surrounded by forks, knives, and a baking sheet.

His heart soared. Sawyer scooped her into his arms. She cried out in pain.

"It really hurts," she murmured against his shirt.

"You're okay." Carefully, Sawyer set her on the bathroom counter. His hands ran down her neck and over her arms. "Everything's okay now."

"We have to loop law enforcement in on this," Brock said from behind him. "What the hell happened in here?" Then he whistled. "Smart girl, Angela Sorenson. Smart."

Sawyer didn't know what Brock saw that was so smart but agreed they needed law enforcement and a hospital.

"I'm getting this piece of shit out of here," Winters called.

"Good riddance," Sawyer muttered. It would probably be best for everyone involved if he didn't set eyes on that woman again.

After a minute, Sawyer brought Angela to lie on the bed. Brock, Roman, and Cash milled around in Sawyer's periphery. He wouldn't take his eyes off Angela. How in the hell had this almost happened again? How had they found her? How—he stopped himself, emotion caught in his throat. If he started popping off questions, Sawyer wasn't sure he could stop. His judgment would be more clouded than it was already.

Cash sidled over and squatted eye level to the bed. "Brock's pretty impressed with you." Angela's tears had stopped, but she hadn't had much to say. Cash stood and eyed Sawyer. "But someone's gotta clue me in. What's up with the forks and knives?"

Somewhat embarrassed, Sawyer ran a hand through his hair. "A little improvisation."

The DIY vest might've absorbed some of the blow, but that didn't explain why Angela had torn the thing apart—or how she used it to keep the door shut.

Brock joined them. "She wedged the door in by the hinges. Didn't you?"

Angela nodded, slowly sitting up. She leaned against the headboard, wincing. "Yeah."

Sawyer marveled at Angela. Every time she was put into danger, from slapping her would-be assassin to barricading the bathroom door, her mind remained crystal clear.

"How in the hell did you think of that?" Roman asked.

As though the attention on her was too much, she downplayed the situation with a quiet laugh but winced again. "I have absolutely no idea."

Cash eyeballed the door to the hotel room as though doing calculations. "How far from the door were you when she fired?"

"Apparently not far enough." Her eyes rose to Sawyer's. "Sorry I gave you grief before you went downstairs."

His lips curved. Sawyer wanted to stomp around the room about all that had gone wrong but couldn't when she gave him that look.

"And," she added, "thanks for the silverware."

He laughed. Brock slapped him on the back. Roman and Cash rehashed the shot trajectory and circumstances, all agreeing that Angela was a genius.

Angela stood up. "I want to take a shower." She touched her arms. "I'm sticky and smell like soda and gunpowder."

"After the Feds talk to you," Brock said.

Sawyer understood this wasn't something a clean-up or black-ops team needed to handle. This had been the third attempted assassination of a federal witness. The realization hit as hard as a bullet to the chest. Angela needed to disappear into the Federal Marshal's Witness Protection program until, at the very least, she testified against Pham.

He hadn't met her when that suggestion had been made years ago, before Boss Man gave her a job and moved her to Abu Dhabi. Sawyer couldn't imagine the conversation would be any more successful today. He'd do anything to keep her safe. Hell, if she wanted, he'd disappear alongside her.

Witness Protection…? That would blow. New identities. Boring-ass jobs. But he might have a home to call his own again. A home with her. They could end up anywhere. The Pacific Northwest? A southwest desert town? They'd have regular jobs. They could do everyday things. They could get a dog.

"Thank you for not taking off that vest." Other than the impact contusions and maybe cracked ribs, she didn't have any wounds. Physical ones, at least.

"You told me not to," she whispered hoarsely.

His smile broke. "Yeah, and you told me I was crazy and that smelling like a Jersey Shore arcade wouldn't keep you alive."

Angela snorted. "Turns out I'm wrong every now and then."

Brock gave Sawyer a thumbs-up. "Cops are here. There's an ambulance downstairs, waiting. Feds will meet us at the hospital."

"I don't need an ambulance or doctors," she protested.

Sawyer shook his head. As much as he hated hospitals, Angela wouldn't wriggle her way out of a thorough checkup. "You have to get checked out. We'll drive you."

Her eyebrows arched. "But I only need someone with a little bit of medical knowledge."

God, she was killing him. He took her hand and led her into the hall. Police hustled toward them. Brock appeared behind Sawyer, ideally ready to run interference if anyone tried to separate him from Angela.

It only took a moment for Brock to work his magic, and they were able to leave.

The team took positions around them. Sawyer kept Angela under his arm until they reached the lobby, which was filled with the prying eyes of unsuspecting onlookers who wanted to watch. Some people even held up cell phones and took videos as if the spectacle was made for their social media feeds.

"Hang tight." Sawyer left Angela with Brock. Cash and Roman blocked the view from onlookers. Sawyer found the manager who was good for her word and willing to get Sawyer whatever he needed.

The manager had boxes stacked on luggage carts, and then, surrounded by bellhops and boxes, Angela was led to the back of the oversize SUV with blacked-out windows. Colby Winters was waiting behind the wheel.

Damn, Sawyer loved Titan, no matter what team or where they were. They always had one another's backs.

CHAPTER THIRTY-FIVE

THE OVERHEAD LIGHTS were too bright. The monitoring equipment was too loud. Angela couldn't find a comfortable way to remain in her hospital bed, but no one would let her get up and leave. "This is overkill."

"I heard you the first hundred times," Sawyer said from the chair by the foot of her bed. "But doctor's orders are doctor's orders. You're staying put for rest and observation."

She might have believed that more if there weren't two federal agents standing guard outside the door to her hospital room. On top of that, Sawyer's threat assessment was on a hair trigger. Doctors and nurses had to convince him they were who they purported to be before he let them near her. She apologized for the hulking muscleheads on guard-dog duty, but the situation never became any less awkward. Two nurses and a doctor had asked her a series of domestic violence screening questions while side-eyeing him. Each time, she'd reassured them that Sawyer was the reason she was still alive and that if they watched the evening news, there would likely be an interesting headline or two about her.

"Why did you choose Titan instead of Witness Protection?" he asked once the hospital personnel were gone.

The question caught her off guard. The offer of the Witness Protection program felt like eons ago. "How do you know they asked?"

His shoulders bunched. "Why wouldn't they?"

"Do you think my mother would be okay with that storyline hitting the press?" Angela scoffed but then softened and shook her head. "I say a lot of harsh things about her. But you know what? When I first saw her in Pham's warehouse before Titan blew the roof off, I ran and hugged her." If she were being honest, Angela wouldn't have minded a hug from *that* version of her mom, who had faced off against terrorists to save her daughter. But now the stakes and situation were different, and Angela didn't want the questions and demands that came with inviting her mother into the same room for a conversation. "She is many things…"

"She is," Sawyer finally agreed.

Angela sighed. "But she's my mother above all. I don't agree with her on much. Sometimes I don't even like her. But I ran to her when her arms were open." Angela offered a watery smile but laughed. "Still, Witness Protection wouldn't have worked for her."

"That's one reason not to accept a new identity, I guess."

"It wasn't because of her. I said no because I didn't want it. It didn't matter what my mom wanted. I trusted Jared Westin more than anyone else. He could keep me safe and let me be me. Boss Man thought of everything. He was ten steps ahead in planning: I wouldn't have to hide and lie. I wanted therapy. He introduced me to Ibrahim within the first few weeks after I arrived in Abu Dhabi. He arranged for you to keep me safe."

"Lotta good I've done for you, sweetheart."

Angela jerked toward him—and groaned at the aching twinge that the pain medicine hadn't blocked—and continued, dead serious. "Twice someone tried to kill me, and twice you were the reason I'm still alive."

He balked. "That's twice too many times—and three times if you count the beach house."

"I wasn't in Witness Protection, and a twenty-four-hour protection detail wasn't sustainable in the long term. I wanted a life. My life. I wouldn't change who I was then, and I won't now."

The muscles in his jaw ticked.

A slight but straightforward knock sounded on her door. It was different from the knocking of the medical staff and law enforcement, and Angela's stomach turned.

Her mother appeared. Had Angela just conjured her out of nowhere? "Mom? What are you doing here?"

Angela's mother greeted Sawyer politely instead of answering. With far less courtesy, she then asked for him to leave the room.

"No." Angela gestured to Sawyer that he was to remain by her side. "He stays."

As always, her mother was ready for a press conference, with hair blown out and makeup in place. But there was a tiredness in her eyes that Angela hadn't expected. "What's wrong?"

"What a question," her mother said, eyebrows raised. "I've been able to do most everything I want in my life, yet somehow, a decision I made years ago keeps hurting my daughter." She scorned. "What's wrong? *This.* I'm so tired of it."

Angela had never heard a defeatist word from her mother before. It unnerved her.

Her mom paced to the corner of the hospital bed and examined the monitor and IV bag. Her gold bangles clinked as she crossed her arms and then, turning on a high heel, moved to Angela's bedside. "What do you want to do?"

Angela's eyes darted to Sawyer and back to her mother. "What do you mean?"

"What do you want your life to be like?" her mother pressed.

Sawyer. Angela wanted Sawyer. That wasn't an option. It wasn't even a possible question. At least not in the way that she wanted. She closed her eyes and imagined her apartment in Abu Dhabi, how she managed the ACES team and went out for drinks with her girlfriends. She wanted to watch her friends as they brought new babies into the world—Angela wanted to be with her friends, the people she worked with so closely, as they navigated their unconventional lives. More than anything, Angela wanted to see Sawyer every day, knowing they'd once had a connection so hot it could burn Abu Dhabi to the ground. They'd return to normal but would always have a secret of their own. "I want life to return to normal."

"Oh, thank God." Her mother's gold-bangled hand pressed to her heart. "It's been so many years since we've had that." Theatrics finished, her mother squared her shoulders as if she'd done a good day's work. "That's perfect, and I was hoping that might be what you'd say. So, just in case luck was on my side, I brought Paul with me."

Angela choked. "What?"

Her mother didn't notice. "I'll go get him. He's waiting in the hall. Finally, everything can go back to normal."

"No." Angela drew back. "What are you talking about?"

Her mother frowned, hand resting on the door. She pulled back, eyebrows arched. "You said normal? Before Pham took you. Before you broke off your engagement. *Normal.*"

"We weren't engaged," Angela managed through clenched teeth. She looked at Sawyer, stoic and expressionless as a statue, then back at her mother, confidently over the top and wrong about everything. Incredulous, Angela shook her head. "My normal. As in: I go back to work. I go back home." No comprehension registered on her mother's face. "To Abu Dhabi."

Her mother's face remained frozen for a second too long as she evidently ran the calculations of the negotiation. Finally, she cackled, having apparently decided that ridicule was the right move. "Angela, that can't last forever."

"Why not?"

She composed herself and then turned to Sawyer. "Mr. Cabot, would you please excuse us?"

"Mother," she snapped, "if someone's leaving this room, it's not—"

"I'll step out, Ange."

"I don't want you to." But his discomfort was evident, and Angela relented. "Fine. Only for a few minutes."

The door quietly shut behind Sawyer. Her mother paced from one side of the bed to the other. "By the way, your father says hello and to feel better."

Angela's lips rolled together. "I'll call him later."

"He'd appreciate that." Her mother took a seat and rubbed her temples. "This isn't just about me."

Angela wasn't convinced.

"Paul misses you."

Angela snort-laughed. "Are you crazy?"

"He misses you."

"No, Mother, he doesn't. More importantly, *I* don't miss him."

"You've been focused on other things. How could you miss anyone when you're so focused on your job?"

"We weren't actually a couple. You should ask him about that. More like business partners."

"Exactly like your father and me. We have a fantastic partnership. Successful careers. Financial stability. A wonderful daughter."

"Did you ever want more, Mom?"

Her mom paused and blinked as if Angela had crossed a line into asking far too personal questions.

A nurse knocked on the door and breezed into the room. "Just here to see how you're doing."

Angela answered a slew of concussion-screening questions and had her vitals taken. Her mother paced, head down, forehead pinched as though she were mapping out various argument strategies.

A moment later, they were alone again. "Stop the strategizing."

"I'm not—"

"Yes, you are. But I'm not spending the rest of my life with Paul. I didn't even spend the last decade with Paul, if we're having an honest conversation. I had the title of girlfriend, and he had access to you."

"That's not fair—"

"It is, and it's the truth." Angela scrubbed her hands over her face. "Look, Mom." She closed her eyes and recalled the buzz under her skin whenever Sawyer touched her. "I'm not you or Dad, and the things that I want… they have to set my world on fire."

Crossing her arms, her mother scowled. "You shouldn't knock the fire that comes from success and stability."

Angela ignored her mother. "*Fire*. Passion. Romance. I didn't even realize that existed." A blush heated her cheeks. "But now I do, and I would never go back."

Her mother stopped pacing, and her eyes narrowed. She scrutinized Angela like a political opponent about to be dressed down. "The man who was sitting in here—"

"Sawyer. You know his name."

"Sawyer. He's the same one from our meeting in Abu Dhabi?"

"You already know that also." Could her mother see that Sawyer set Angela's world on fire? "We work together—you should thank him. He's the reason the attempts on my life have failed."

Her mother dropped into the chair by the top of Angela's bed. "I should thank him."

"He's important to me," Angela admitted. "And he's never come at me with an agenda."

Her mother crossed her legs, uncharacteristically fidgeting, and then relented. "Like I do…?"

"Yeah. You've had some doozies."

For once, her mother seemed to think long and hard before she spoke. "If I promise to drop the Paul conversation, would you mind if I stayed and sat with you for a few minutes?"

There was her mother. The person Angela had run to from Pham's captivity. "That'd be nice."

Somewhere out there, pigs were flying on a cold day in hell. Her mother didn't pull out her cell phone or lobby her agenda. She sat there, a mother with her daughter.

CHAPTER THIRTY-SIX

SAWYER HAD LEFT Angela's hospital room as though he didn't have a worry in the world. But under his closely managed exterior, he was fuming. He couldn't imagine the relationship Angela had with her mother. Hell, he'd heard the stories about Senator Sorenson, but to see them play out in real life was an experience he wanted to forget.

Just as the Senator had said, Paul waited outside Angela's hospital room. He leaned against the adjacent wall, taking a call while simultaneously typing on his phone.

Sawyer took a place next to one of the posted federal agents and waited. He had nothing to say to the guy, only because he wouldn't embarrass Angela by revealing Sawyer knew the top-shelf-level crap Paul had told her.

Paul's call ended. He briefly glanced up, did a double take at Sawyer, and then removed his earbuds. He stepped forward, hand extended. "Sawyer, is it? Nice to see you again."

What a politician. The two men shook hands. "You're here to visit Angela?"

Paul shrugged. "It's a good opportunity to rehash some plans."

"I didn't think you had any plans. Am I wrong?"

"Well…"

"Ya know, if I had an ex who showed up uninvited, especially after a shitastic day, I'd be irritated as fuck."

Paul flashed a megawatt smile. He'd go far in politics with that tool in his arsenal. "Angela and I have known each other since we were teenagers."

"I'll give you a tip. Knowing someone for an extended length of time means nothing if you don't bother to learn a damn thing about them."

Paul half laughed. "Man, what's your problem?"

"No problems—unless you bother Angela again. Do you understand me?"

Paul seemed to consider his next move.

"Does the Senator know how to get a hold of you?" Sawyer asked.

Again, Paul made another face. "I'm her chief of staff."

"Then why don't you and I go get a cup of coffee in the cafeteria? She'll find you when they're done."

He considered protesting but yielded. The guy wasn't an idiot in all things.

Nearly an hour later, the Senator contacted Paul. They'd agreed to meet at the visitor's entrance. Between Sawyer's conversation with Paul and Angela's with the Senator, progress had been made. Hopefully, she wouldn't have to deal with this guy or her mother's political planning again.

Sawyer had made it halfway back to Angela's room when he received a phone call from Boss Man.

"How's she doing?" Jared asked.

"About as well as can be expected. She doesn't want to be here but wouldn't leave against the doctor's advice."

Jared grumbled as though he and federal investigators had had something to do with her doctor admitting her for observation. Sawyer couldn't disagree with their sentiment. With guards posted outside her room in the secure wing of a hospital, Angela was safer than she'd been in years.

"I just received a phone call from the Senator," Jared said.

That was fast. But Senator Sorenson wasn't a mover and shaker on Capitol Hill for being slow to pull the trigger. "What'd she want?"

"To know more about you."

Sawyer's gut churned. He'd expected a complaint about the conversation with Paul. "Why's that?"

"I don't know. Why don't you tell me?"

Sawyer shrugged as he walked. "I was in the room when she arrived. Angela asked that I stay when her mother asked me to go."

Jared snickered. "Bet that was a fun back-and-forth. Well, I told Samantha to kiss my ass. If she has questions about you, she can ask you to your face."

Sawyer laughed, confident those had been damn near Boss Man's exact words.

"She'll probably do her own digging," Jared warned.

Probably. Or she would tell Paul to do it. Either way, Sawyer didn't care. There was nothing he had to hide. Boss Man let the conversation hang until Sawyer admitted, "Angela knows about Penny and William, if that's what you're worried about."

"Not worried. Just making sure you have as much control over your personal narrative as possible."

"I appreciate that."

"Look, Sawyer. Angela's mother is a pain in my ass. There's something screwed up in that woman's DNA. She's half-robot, half-asshole, and one hundred percent bloodhound. The lengths she went through to find her daughter... But..." Jared waited for a beat and then continued, "If she has a concern about you and her daughter, we're all going to hear about it."

Sawyer grimaced. He didn't want Samantha Sorenson inserting her nose into his relationship with Angela. "There's nothing to be concerned about, Boss Man." He stopped a few doors shy of Angela's room. "Anything else?"

"Not a damn thing."

Good. Because Sawyer was finished with everyone except his woman. He pocketed the phone and entered her room. The lights were dim, and her eyes were closed. He quietly took his place by her side.

Today could have gone so differently. There had been too many close-to-worst-case scenarios. He could have lost her. His throat ached.

"Hey," she whispered, slowly waking from her nap. Angela held out her hand. "When did you get back?"

He laced his fingers with hers. "A couple of minutes ago."

She tugged him closer. "I won't break if you lay down with me."

But he might. A distant, rational voice tried to tell him he was far too attached to the woman in this bed. That logic quickly disappeared, buried under his much more selfish, possessive thoughts.

Sawyer eased onto the side of her bed. She nuzzled close, groaning in discomfort but keeping him by her side. "I need you next to me."

Sawyer stroked her hair as she fell back asleep. There was nowhere else he would be.

CHAPTER THIRTY-SEVEN

MYLENE PERCHED ON the edge of the bed in her hotel room. The television remote weighed heavy in her hand. She didn't have a TV in her house. Even though she was a prisoner at home, she missed her bedroom and kitchen. She missed her routine too. While there were many places in the house where she couldn't lift her gaze and face Mark and Tabby, Mylene missed knowing they were close.

Without their pictures watching—scolding—her and without work, she didn't know what to do with herself. Mylene always worked. Even when Pham had forced her on vacations, the trips were work. For so many years, every minute of her life had been programmed. Now, alone and locked in a hotel room, she had only a television.

The autonomy was terrifying. She needed to block her wandering thoughts. Mylene turned on the TV. An advertisement for a hotel amenity appeared. The commercial was too bright and loud. She quickly pressed the buttons on the remote. The channels switched. Cartoons. The figures moved too fast. A headache pounded behind her eyes.

She changed the channel again and again. Commercials. Television drama. *The news.* Finally, something normal that she could stomach. Years had passed since she'd seen anything but the news. Reporters always talked in the same voice, using the same cadence as a lullaby. It was comforting and as close to Mylene's normal world as she could get.

The news report shifted from an earthquake overseas to a news conference led by Senator Samantha Sorenson. Sorenson was one of their archenemies. Mylene's nerves calmed. Listening to Sorenson was like her work, and maybe Mylene could handle the unexplained change of location as long as something familiar, like Sorenson, was at the forefront of her mind.

The screen chyron read, "2nd assassination attempt on Sorenson daughter."

Mylene didn't have to listen to the reporter to know who had been suspected of ordering the hit. The screen flashed to B-roll footage. Pham's arrest. The federal courthouse in Northern Virginia. Prosecutors posturing for the media. Mylene wanted Sorenson to suffer just like Pham.

Was the attempt on Angela's life the reason why they moved Mylene from her house? No one had known where Angela Sorenson had been, and then she almost died an hour away from Mylene's house?

The screen shifted to the last known photo of Angela Sorenson. She was about the same age as Mylene, whose stomach began to roil. She wanted to erase Angela's face but couldn't change the channel. Pham wanted to hurt the Senator. He wanted to make sure Angela wouldn't testify against him. How could she be a witness against Pham? Mylene saw time and time again how well Pham treated Angela.

But... Angela didn't deserve to die.

Did she?

Well, Senator Sorenson deserved for her daughter to die like Pham's daughter had died. Everyone involved with Quy Long's death was guilty and should be punished. That was why Pham had taken Mylene. She needed to be punished. She had done a horrible, terrible thing while following orders to relay messages. Pham had said so many times that his daughter would be alive if Mylene hadn't done her job.

So... Angela Sorenson should die.

Shouldn't she?

Yes? No? Both possibilities made sense. A headache thudded behind Mylene's eyes. She turned off the television and crawled onto the bed. They never should have taken her from her house. She didn't want to think about the real world that believed she murdered her husband and sister.

Again, Mylene's stomach lurched. Her thoughts raced. Angela would die or testify. But what if she didn't do either? Would Mylene be able to go back to her house?

She could go back home. Hope for the ordinary surged in her chest, and Mylene bolted upright on the bed. She could have her house back if Angela didn't testify. If Mylene could just speak to Angela and explain, then Mylene's life would return to normal again. If Angela disappeared again, if she promised not to testify… maybe Pham would be released.

If he was released, maybe Pham would recognize that Mylene's penance had gone on long enough. Perhaps they would take the pictures down in her house. She would like to keep one or two as a reminder of the family she loved, not the prison wardens they became.

Mylene would be free if Angela listened to her.

How would she find Angela Sorenson? She didn't have her computer to do research—but she did have a phone in her hotel room. They hadn't taken it away. Why would they? Mylene would never disobey.

But would they get mad at her for using the phone? Definitely—unless they knew how Mylene was helping.

She picked up and reached an outside line. It had been years since she had dialed a phone, but she knew the number by heart. She dialed it. The ringing echoed between her ears like a maniacal tennis match.

"Capitol Switchboard. How may I direct your call?"

Mylene's heart hammered. "Senator Sorenson's office."

"One moment, please."

The line beeped as the transfer was made. The phone rang twice. "Senator Sorenson's office. How can I help you?"

She could picture the intern assigned to take constituent phone calls. Or—her excitement grew—perhaps the person who answered the phone was on Sorenson's staff. Mylene was less than six degrees of separation from Angela now. Her pulse raced. "I need to get a message to Angela Sorenson. It's an emergency."

"I'm sorry?"

"Angela Sorenson. I need to speak with her right now. Can you please pass her a message?"

"Er, um, yeah. One second." Unintelligible whispers were just out of the reach of understanding. "What's your message?"

Mylene didn't know. Damn it. She'd been too certain of what needed to happen that she hadn't considered what to say. Her brain was trained on flame-worthy one-liners and rage-baiting memes. Articulating a message fit for a real live person...

"Hello?"

"Tell her not to testify," Mylene blundered. This wouldn't work. They wouldn't pass on a stupid message like that. "Pham. Because. You can't. Tell her to stay away."

Dead air hung on the line. She hadn't made sense.

"All right. Thanks—"

"Wait. I need you to listen. Tell her it's life or death. That she can't. Tell her I need to talk to her. It's important."

"And who are you?" the intern asked.

"I'm nobody anymore. But a long time ago, I wasn't." Mylene hadn't talked to anyone in years, and it was showing. Her tongue tripped and tied. "She and I are the same. We're trapped. But I want to go back home. I *need* to go back home. If she would leave and not testify... that would be best for everyone."

Mylene slammed the phone into the cradle. What the hell had she done? That wouldn't help Pham or get her back to her house. The headache punched in her temples.

The door to the hotel room unlocked. Mylene jerked the covers over her body and rolled like a hyperventilating burrito.

"Food."

She heard the sound of fast-food bags being dropped next to the television.

"I want to go home," she cried, face pressed into a pillow. Tears stung. "I want to go home."

They didn't bother answering. Footsteps retreated. The door shut.

She sobbed. All alone, mind fragmenting, Mylene wanted to die.

CHAPTER THIRTY-EIGHT

ROMAN AND CASH greeted Sawyer and Angela when they walked out of the hospital. Sawyer hadn't seen them since the incident at the hotel. Neither man's concerned scowl was friendly, but when they saw Angela, they tried their best to smile.

With an out-of-place straw cowboy hat, Cash opened the back door of a black SUV for Angela as though he were a chauffeur and helped her in. Sawyer slid into the back seat with her. Roman was at the wheel. Cash, the last one in the vehicle, did a once-over, monitoring their surroundings before closing himself in.

"Where are Brock and Winters?" Sawyer asked.

"They hightailed it back to headquarters," Cash answered.

"Where are we headed?" Angela asked.

Roman pulled out of the horseshoe driveway. "That depends."

Cash turned and faced them in the back seat. "The Feds were notified of a weird call."

Sawyer's eyebrow arched. "About?"

Cash tilted his head toward Angela. "Our bulletproof princess."

Roman's phone rang. The center console display read Titan HQ. He punched the button on the dash to answer the call.

"Got everyone yet?" Parker said through the car speakers.

"That's affirmative; we're all here."

"How you feeling, Angela?" Parker asked.

"Like I was run over by a water buffalo."

The corners of Sawyer's lips quirked.

"Are you up for a few hours' drive?" Parker asked. "Because the tables have turned, and I think your girl might be trying to find you this time."

"Mylene is looking for me?"

"I don't know. Maybe," Parker said. "There's a recording of a call made to your mother's office. The caller sounds like they might be in the midst of a mental health crisis, but—there's a Fed named John Patterson. You remember him, right?"

"Yeah, I remember him," she grumbled. "Who could forget?"

"Yeah, well, they sent the call to Patterson, and he thinks it's your girl."

Angela reached for Sawyer's hand. "Why would he think that?"

"I don't know. I heard the call. The call's pretty gibberishy, but it's clearly about you."

"Did they trace the call? Do they know where Mylene might be?" Angela asked.

"They have the location the call originated from and are going in shortly."

The black cup of hospital coffee churned in Sawyer's stomach. He hated unknowns and didn't love that Parker had called with so many. If Angela's doctors had kept her another day, they wouldn't be in this vehicle traveling toward all those unanswered questions. The operation would have been completed, and a report of findings could have been safely handed to Angela instead.

"If they find Mylene, are you game to see her?" Parker asked.

"Absolutely."

Sawyer made sure to keep his hands to himself. He wanted to tuck her protectively to his side. That wouldn't fly near their colleagues.

"All right, then," Parker said. "Roman will head this way. When we have confirmation that it's Mylene, we'll find out where to take you to see her. If it's not her, then I don't know. We'll come up with a Plan B."

Sawyer wanted Plan B to have a much more robust security component than what they'd discussed thus far: locate a new safe house and, until it was found, keep an eye on Angela at all times.

"Can I hear the call?" she asked.

"Yeah. Sure. Give me a minute."

Then the recording started with white noise and a standard congressional office greeting. The caller's voice was hoarse. At times, it rushed. Other times, it was stilted and garbled.

"Does that sound like Mylene Hathaway?" Cash asked.

"I never spoke to her. I only saw her."

"There's definitely a mental health issue in play," Parker added. "John Patterson will be able to sort through that."

"Will he be there?"

"I'm pretty sure he's already on the scene and will accompany her wherever they go."

Sawyer held his breath.

"John Patterson isn't on my list of favorite people," Angela admitted.

"Well, there's not much we can do to divert him from this project."

"I don't trust him," she added.

Sawyer agreed. "Yeah, I don't either."

"Is Titan assisting with her capture?" Roman asked.

"Nope."

"So all we have, intel-wise, is what they pass along?" Roman clarified.

"Yup," Parker said.

"That sounds promising," Roman added then looked at Angela in his rearview mirror. "Do you still want to do this?"

Angela reached for Sawyer and squeezed his hand as Cash glanced at the back seat. His gaze dropped to the handhold, and he averted his eyes. Sawyer's face didn't register either Cash or Angela. She was in a vulnerable state. He wouldn't violate their agreement's confidentiality, but he wouldn't leave her hanging when she reached out. He squeezed her back.

"Yes, no question." She gave another squeeze and pulled her hand back.

"All right, then," Parker repeated. "I'll see you in a few hours."

The call disconnected. Roman maneuvered onto Interstate 95 North. The back seat seemed smaller than it had a minute ago. Sawyer repositioned the seat belt digging into his shoulder.

"There was a gorgeous pair of earrings in my hotel room safe," Angela said. "They probably need to be returned to a local jewelry store."

Cash nodded, facing straight ahead. "Parker made sure we had a clean-up team get into your rooms after local PD processed it as a crime scene."

Both Angela and Cash sounded overly formal to Sawyer. He changed positions again. The back seat didn't have enough legroom. "How much longer?"

Roman snorted. "We've been driving for five minutes."

Cash and Roman were younger than Sawyer. They reminded him of Camden, the youngest guy on the Abu Dhabi team. Camden was cocky but had mellowed over the last few years. Sawyer wasn't sure the US-based team was very mellow. They rarely interacted. Sawyer wasn't sure how much Cash and Roman knew about the Abu Dhabi team. Probably as much as Sawyer knew about other teams based outside of the US. Jared Westin had one hell of an international network.

Angela closed her eyes and rested her head in the crook of her arm against the window. Would last night be the last time she and Sawyer fell asleep together? His chest ached. That couldn't be the case. He wouldn't let it. Once they'd found Mylene and negotiations over Pham had ceased and the fucker was safely in prison for the rest of his life, Sawyer and Angela could redefine their new normal. What would that look like?

Roman's phone rang again through the car's speakers. He answered, "What do we know, Parker?"

"It's her."

Angela jerked upright in her seat. "Are they certain?"

"Completely certain."

"Oh my God," Angela whispered.

"And," Parker added, "she's demanding to speak to you."

"Oh my God," she repeated.

"Apparently, much to John Patterson's chagrin, she'll *only* speak with you."

CHAPTER THIRTY-NINE

THE DRIVE NORTH took an eternity. Angela squirmed. Her ribs and stomach ached. She winced. Sawyer would change his position, dangerously close to hovering. She'd pull back, not needing anyone to see their personal business. Then the cycle would repeat itself, except in reverse. She'd move toward him, and he'd press away like she had the plague.

But that was far from her most pressing thought. Mylene Hathaway had her full attention. Why did she want to talk to Angela? How did she even know that Angela was nearby?

Roman exited the interstate. Anxiety and anticipation were a heart-rattling combination. Her hands shook in her lap. Angela wished her untrained status wasn't so apparent when surrounded by bombproof mountains of men. Then again, why did she care? She'd probably never see Cash and Roman again, and Sawyer had already seen her vulnerabilities.

Once again, her mind was back on Sawyer.

Roman made a few quick turns and then pulled the SUV toward a standard-looking office park surrounded by a very non-standard high metal fence topped with razor wire. The vehicle stopped at a security checkpoint.

"This looks very official," she said under her breath.

Roman rolled down his window and stated who they were. A man with a working dog circled the car. Another man with a mirror on a telescoped poll inspected the vehicle's undercarriage.

After the group had passed the mirror-and-dog inspection, the barriers in front of them lowered. Roman rolled over what she assumed were security spikes ensuring traffic moved only in one direction.

"Is this some kind of black-ops site?" she asked.

Roman nodded. "Something like that."

They parked in a space near the front of a building. Angela's nerves rocketed from her fingers to her toes.

Roman opened her car door, and Angela winced as she crawled out. "Do you think she's in there?" she asked.

"Yup. I do," Roman said.

They met Sawyer and Cash on the sidewalk. Cash led the way. Roman took the rear. Sawyer placed himself on the side of the street. They surrounded her like a security detail, not trusting their high-security surroundings. She couldn't imagine how someone who wanted her dead might penetrate the complex. Then again, she couldn't have imagined most of what had transpired recently.

"You doing okay, Ange?" Sawyer asked.

"Nervous." She ached to reach for Sawyer's hand. Professionalism kept her in check. Their lives would return to normal eventually. There was no need to bring her private life into the workplace. Somewhere in this building was a woman who Angela needed to see, who she wanted to save.

Could she still do that? Nothing had gone according to plan. Certainly, Angela hadn't imagined Mylene would be looking for her also.

They entered through heavily guarded double doors. The Titan men relinquished their weapons. They walked toward metal detectors while their belongings crept slowly down a conveyor belt and were viewed under an X-ray.

"Guess you guys aren't messing around," she said to the man who nodded for her to proceed.

Not messing around meant he didn't break his scowl even when escorting their group down a long hall that dead-ended with a single elevator. Their guard swiped a badge and stared into a retina scanner, and the elevator's large doors opened to reveal a compartment like an oversized freight cart.

The guard swiped his badge and scanned his eyes again before selecting their floor. The door shut slowly as though they were too heavy to move fast. Then down everyone went, past the first two underground levels, until they opened on the floor labeled Sub-Level C.

Armed security greeted them. None of the men with Angela balked at their high-caliber-rifle-bearing counterparts who led the way.

After a journey down a long hallway illuminated by fluorescent lights, the party was deposited in a small room that looked like a television police drama's take on an interrogation room. The metal table was bolted onto the cement floor, and the air smelled like despair.

An armed man gestured to the chair. "Ma'am."

Angela took a seat. No one else did. The metal chairs were as uncomfortable as they looked.

Cash and Roman posted behind her. Sawyer stood across from her, his back to a painted cinderblock wall.

"This is cozy," she said.

Sawyer's lips curved.

The door swung open, and Special Agent John Patterson joined them. "Angela, it's great to see you again."

She didn't fake the same enthusiasm, but she kept her interaction with him professional. They shook hands, and then he introduced himself to Titan's men. Titan remained where they were as John joined her at the table. His chair scraped on the floor as he made himself as comfortable as possible.

"I'm sorry about our conversation in Abu Dhabi," he said.

She glanced over John's shoulder. Sawyer's face was unreadable. "I guess you had a job to do," she said.

"Not all my jobs are fun and games all the time." John frowned contritely. "But I am sorry. I know I didn't put you in a great position."

She didn't want to rehash their meeting. "Do you really work on Pham? Or just my mother's projects?"

"All Pham, all the time."

"Except when dealing with me," she pointed out.

He took a pen from the interior pocket of his suit jacket. "You are intrinsically connected to Pham."

Angela wished that weren't true.

"This is what we know." John click-clicked his pen. "Mylene Hathaway called your mother's office and demanded to speak with you. She called from an easily traceable phone number and hadn't done anything to hide her tracks."

"She wanted me to come to her?"

John shook his head. "Given her mental clarity, I don't think that was at the forefront of her mind."

"What is?"

A hint of frustration on John's face was quickly hidden behind a controlled, closed-lipped expression. "I haven't had much time with her. She will only speak to us after speaking to you."

"Does she have a lawyer?"

John's gaze shifted around the room before he crossed his arms. "She hasn't been arrested. This isn't a law enforcement facility."

What type was it? Military? DNI? CIA? NSA? Mylene was here as a terrorist. They—whoever ran this facility—weren't interested in the murder of her husband and sister. They wanted intelligence. "All right. She wants to talk to me about Pham."

"As she indicated on the phone call to the Senator's office." John nodded. "She doesn't want you to testify."

Angela recalled the recording of the phone call. The chaotic voice had mentioned testifying against Pham, but the caller hadn't made much sense.

"We have Mylene in a nearby room. She's secured at a table. She cannot get up or move around. You're safe. She's not a threat."

Angela hadn't considered that Mylene would want to hurt her. "Will you be in there?"

"I will escort you in, but I don't plan to stay."

"You'll be watching from another room?" she asked.

Again, he clicked his pen. "Yes. There will be two armed men immediately outside the door. There will be two men posted behind her."

"I don't think she wants to hurt me. She might not want me to testify, but I don't think she'll physically try to stop me."

"Maybe not. But that's protocol."

"Protocol for a woman who was kept hostage by a terrorist?"

"Are you referring to yourself or Mylene Hathaway? Because we don't understand her role yet."

Angela hated John Patterson. "She's a victim."

"She's a woman who wants leniency for Pham, a terrorist."

"I know who Pham is," she snapped.

"What you don't seem to understand is that Mylene has been intimately involved in a foreign-based misinformation campaign," John replied equally coolly. "Not to mention, she's part of his network, which understands that if you're eliminated, you won't be able to testify—and the case against him crumbles."

"That's bullshit. There's plenty of evidence of exactly what he did to me. What he's done to everyone."

"You still don't understand the threat you're under."

Anger flashed down her spine.

"Pham's a billionaire with a network of killers and a legal firm of A-plus lawyers working around the clock on his defense. To prosecutors, you're the golden ticket. Angela…" John drew in a deep breath and let it out. "Simply put, the case would be easier to plead down if you were dead. So pardon me if I want you to understand why we have this woman at a black site, chained to the table."

Angela rubbed her temples. "Can Sawyer come in with me?"

John's eyebrows arched. "He can watch from where I am. We'll be less than five feet away."

"I'd rather he was in the same room."

John looked over his shoulder and studied Sawyer's face. Sawyer didn't offer the behavioral analyst anything to decipher. John pursed his lips. "I don't think it's a good idea." He pulled his cell phone from his pocket. "Mylene isn't in a good headspace. Adding another person to the mix might not help with our end goal."

She bet their end goal wasn't the same as hers.

John held up his phone. The screen showed a paused video of Mylene. "This is her."

That woman was definitely the woman Angela had seen over the years, but the Mylene on the screen and the one in Angela's past were worlds apart. This Mylene was broken. "That's her?"

John pressed Play.

The video came to life. Mylene sat on the cement floor of a cell, moaning. Her arms wrapped around her knees. She rocked on the floor, occasionally releasing her knees and pulling fistfuls of her tangled hair. In a hoarse voice, she begged to go home. She cried and cackled and curled like a baby, moaning again.

Angela tore her gaze from the screen. "And now she's cuffed to a table?"

"Secured," John agreed.

Her pulse quickened. "She doesn't need to be here. She needs help."

"Actually," he countered, "she wants to be here. Remember? She wants to see you."

She hated John. He simplified—borderline infantilized—them both. Mylene needed psychiatric help, and just like Angela felt for Pham, she did for Mylene. Angela stood. "Then let's go." She moved to Sawyer's side, not trusting John. "Will you make sure you're on the other side of the door?"

"I'll be where you want me."

Her heart squeezed. Sawyer didn't give two shits about John Patterson's preferences. His only goal was hers. "Thank you."

They entered the hallway and followed John around a corner. Two guards were posted outside of a door. Angela's stomach dropped. She had so many questions for Mylene and felt that none would be answered.

John nodded to one of the guards. They unlocked the door and held it open.

Angela's heartbeat galloped, and her purpose for being there suddenly disappeared. All she could remember was when Mylene had watched Angela from the sidelines as Pham pretended Angela was Quy Long. Mylene didn't help. She couldn't. She was just there.

Angela forced her clenched jaw to relax and then walked in. There sat the woman she'd seen from afar. The pained face from John's video had nothing on the pain that radiated from the woman cuffed to the metal table.

The dark hollows of Mylene's eyes pleaded when she saw Angela.

That desperation punched Angela in the chest. "Mylene."

Mylene sniffed with her runny nose. "You know my name?"

"I know who you are. Do you know who I am?"

She nodded.

Angela inched toward the table as though her shoes were lead-lined bricks. "Do you want a tissue? Something to drink?"

Mylene's vacant eyes didn't register the question. "I need to talk to you."

Angela glanced at the armed man behind Mylene. "Can she have a bottle of water? A tissue box?"

He didn't move.

She looked from one security camera to the next. "Can someone get her a bottle of water and some tissues?" Nothing happened. This was ridiculous. "Sawyer? Please?"

Angela turned to Mylene again. She pulled her knees to her chest and rocked in her chair, as she had on the floor. Tears had swollen her cheeks and eyes. Her nose ran. She needed to sleep. Or probably take a sedative.

The heavy cell door unlocked. Sawyer appeared with two bottles of water and a handful of paper towels.

Gratitude squeezed Angela's chest. "Thank you."

Sawyer set them on the table, gave Mylene a once-over, and then eyed Angela with a quiet lift of his chin. Unspoken support strengthened her resolve to help Mylene once the headache with Pham ended.

"Anything else?" he asked.

She shook her head. "Not that I can think of."

"Just let me know."

The heavy door closed behind him. Angela offered Mylene the paper towels. She didn't take any of them. It was as if she hadn't seen Sawyer or what he had brought in.

Angela took one of Mylene's cuffed hands.

The guard stepped forward.

"I'm giving her a tissue," Angela snapped and forced one into Mylene's grip.

"Don't touch her again," he growled.

Angela ignored him and didn't know what to do. Mylene didn't wipe her face or even seem to notice the paper towel. Angela uncapped the water bottle. "Are you thirsty?"

The question didn't register to Mylene.

"If you drink this, I will talk to you." Angela nudged the uncapped bottle.

Mylene shook her head. "They're going to poison me."

This was why Mylene needed psychiatric help. Paranoia hadn't even occurred to Angela. She took two long glugs and re-offered the bottle to Mylene. "If you go, I go."

"They want you to die."

"They who? This wasn't from Pham."

"They want you to die," she repeated.

"Not everyone does," Angela forced a half joke. "Do you?"

Mylene shook her head. "No."

"Drink, Mylene."

Warily, Mylene released the paper towel as though she didn't notice it had been in her hand, and with her hands cuffed together, she took the bottle of water and drank. Water dribbled from the side of her mouth. She wiped at the drips and her running nose with the back of her hand. "I don't want you to die. That's what I've been trying to tell you."

"Okay…" Angela opened the other water bottle and sipped. "I remember you."

Mylene rocked in her chair.

"You came to the vacations," Angela said. "I saw you other times. I can't remember everything. It blurred together. But I know you were there a lot."

"Watching." Mylene's unfocused eyes skidded around the room. "I was watching."

Angela nodded. "Why?"

"Because I was supposed to."

"Why?"

"Punishment." Her face fell. "But that part's over now. I have my house. I have my room. No one brings me anywhere anymore." Her expression twisted then focused with laser-like precision on Angela. "Not until now."

"Mylene…" She swallowed hard. "I was looking for you."

Her eyes rounded.

"I think that's why they moved you. They knew I was coming."

Mylene rocked again. "Why would you do that?"

"I'm sorry." It was hard to find the right words. Hell, it was hard to find *any* words. Who knew how many people were studying them just then? The cell walls seemed to close in on them. The stale air stank like desperation and misery. Angela couldn't think. "I want to help."

Mylene shook her head violently. Wild strands of hair stuck to her damp face.

"I saw the place where you've been living."

"My house?" Tears streamed down Mylene's face. "No. No. You didn't see it."

"I did."

"No one knows about me. That's my house. I need to go home."

Why would Mylene ever want to return to the house of horrors? "You can go anywhere now." Except that wasn't true. Not with the handcuffs and the secret black-ops prison guards keeping Mylene right where she was. Angela shouldn't say what she couldn't promise, but she couldn't stop. "No one will make you go back there."

"I have to!" Panic flooded over Mylene. "That's my house." More tears fell, and she pleaded, begging, "I need to go home."

Angela glanced at the guard as Mylene's words turned into an incomprehensible soup of mutters and cries. She glanced at the security camera, helpless to know the right thing to say. John Patterson would know. He'd click-click his pen and say things to make Mylene spill her guts if he were in Angela's shoes. "Mylene."

Mylene tucked her knees to her chest again and rocked. "My house."

Damn it. They weren't getting anywhere. Angela wasn't helping, and Mylene was still losing her mind. She needed Mylene to understand that they were on the same side—at least in some ways. Frustration gripped her chest. Angela didn't have the skills to help. A growing helplessness squeezed her lungs. "I know you didn't kill your husband and sister."

Mylene jerked. The shock had left her slack-jawed, as though Angela had slapped her, and the rocking, muttering woman suddenly became sharp as a tack. "That's not true."

Words had broken through Mylene's fog. Angela leaned into it. "Did you pull the trigger?"

"*No.*"

"Did you see them die?"

Once again, tears spilled down Mylene's cheeks. Her bottom lip quivered. "No, but—" She threaded her hands into her hair. Her fists knotted into the disheveled mess. Mylene pulled until she cried out and slumped. "It's my fault."

"You did not kill them, Mylene."

"I did. Not in the way you're thinking."

"I know you didn't," Angela pressed.

"You can't know that."

"Why can't I?" All she had was a theory based on toothbrush placements and Pham's need for revenge. Still, she was certain Mylene hadn't killed them.

"I'm responsible even if I didn't pull the trigger."

Angela ached at the thought of the hell this woman had been through. She ached for the hell she was still living in. If only Ibrahim were in the room. Angela tried to remember how Ibrahim would speak to her. She searched for anything that he'd said to her over the years, but her mind filled up with panicky white noise. "Whatever Pham told you, it's not true."

Mylene's brows furrowed. "Don't—"

"I can't tell you how many hours of therapy it took to be able to say that."

Mylene's lips parted, as though she was ready to defend Pham, but the defense didn't come. Maybe a memory of Angela came to Mylene's mind. Maybe Mylene simply didn't have it in her to jump from the responsibility for the deaths to defend the murderer of her loved ones.

No matter what gave Mylene pause, Angela jumped in. "I know what he did to me was wrong. I know he wasn't this old grandfather who really cared about me. But it still feels that way when I think about what happened."

Mylene closed her mouth and tried to defend Pham again, but just as before, nothing slipped through her lips. Angela remembered the anger and defensiveness she had after she'd been rescued. No one understood her mindset, and now she couldn't understand Mylene. "No one in the world understands the pain he put you through."

Mylene grimaced, and a watery glassiness flooded her eyes.

"But," Angela whispered, "I have a small idea."

"No… You don't." The other woman's chin dropped. "You can't."

Angela reached across the cold steel table and wrapped her hand over Mylene's. "Abusive relationships don't make any sense." She held on when Mylene yanked. The handcuff chain clanked against its attachment to the table. Angela loosened her grip but didn't let go. "There's no logic to them." Her throat knotted. "And I don't know what you have gone through, but I know that your brain—at least my brain—tried to make sense of, literally, living in hell."

Mylene looked away. She pulled her hands from Angela's and balled them together. After swallowing several times, she rasped, "You can't testify against him."

Angela rolled her lips together. Empathy was hard when the situation was so damn frustrating. She would never be able to convince Mylene she understood, just like she had never understood when others had tried their best to relate to what she had gone through. "You told my mother's office that *you and I* are the same. That we're trapped."

"You can't testify against him," Mylene repeated.

"I was trapped. You were trapped. But not anymore."

Mylene snorted. "Until he says different, we belong to him."

"I don't, and you don't anymore."

Desperation rolled over Mylene. "You don't understand. But you have to listen. Don't testify. Then we will both be free."

"That's not how it works." She reached for Mylene again. Mylene shirked. "We're both free of him now."

"No. If you disappear—you don't even have to die. No one has to kill you. You just have to go away. Not testify. He'll know that I helped him.

Don't you see? That I took care of his problem"—her voice broke—"and maybe he will see that I've suffered enough. That I've done my penance. I can go back home. That's all I want. I want my house. To be alone in my house."

"That's not how you separate yourself from him. Whatever forgiveness you're looking for… it's not in him to give." Angela chewed on the inside of her cheek. "I'm going to testify, Mylene. Because I need the same thing you need. Release, and I'm going to be able to find it by saying what needs to be said."

"No."

"It's what I have to do to survive my past."

Mylene squeezed her eyes shut and shook her head tightly.

A lump knotted her words. "Mylene… it will be better one day."

Mylene simply shook her head.

The door opened. John Patterson strode in. "Sounds like a good chat."

Angela ground her molars. The door opened again, and Sawyer entered apologetically. "We should go, Ange." He placed a hand on her shoulder and squeezed. "You two can talk later."

Reluctantly, Angela followed. Her ribs and muscles ached. More than that, she felt defeated. Not that she had any expectation of how this meeting should have gone. But it didn't feel like it should have ended this way. "Why the sudden interruption?"

"He took a phone call and said the meeting was over."

"Who called?"

Sawyer shrugged. "I doubt we'll ever know."

"Unless it was my mother," she muttered. "What are they going to do with Mylene?"

Sawyer shrugged again. They reached the elevator. A uniformed man stood at its side and swiped his keycard to call it. Five minutes later, Roman drove them from the black ops site. No one in the vehicle said a word.

CHAPTER FORTY

TITAN GROUP'S US headquarters, situated in Northern Virginia, was very different from its headquarters in the Middle East. Both areas had pockets of immense wealth, but Abu Dhabi's was far vaster and more apparent. The US headquarters was an obvious fortress. Their offices in Abu Dhabi were surreptitiously hidden inside a luxury hotel skyscraper—two, actually, both towers connected by sky bridges every few floors.

But the offices were nearly interchangeable. Both war rooms contained imposing conference tables and high-tech communications equipment. Parker's US-based tech lair was similar to Abu Dhabi's nerve center, where Amanda and Shah held court.

Angela seemed at home in the conference room and spent the afternoon arranging for her necessities, clothes, identification, and whatever else she deemed necessary. Sawyer had felt far less comfortable. Sure, he had access to whatever he needed, but the longer he stayed in the US without an agenda, the longer he felt the pull to escape.

He wandered to Angela's conference room. The door was ajar. He knocked and stepped in. She was on the phone but beckoned him in, whispering, "Give me a minute."

He walked to the windows. Everything was so green here. He hadn't realized that green trees and bushy shrubbery could make him nostalgic.

"I'm glad you're starting to feel better—uh-huh." Angela laughed. "All right. I know. I'll check in later." She hung up, still smiling in a way that made Sawyer feel like he was intruding. "That was Chelsea."

"You didn't have to get off the phone for me."

Angela's eyes twinkled. "We were done."

"Why do you look like that?" He studied her expression. She needed time off to relax with her girlfriends. Angela spent most of her time in the office, where she was surrounded by friends. Not like her current gig, stuck with him. Working ops could be lonely. "You need time off."

"No, I'm fine. I was just checking in on her. She was feeling a little headachey and pukey."

"Chelsea? Or Amanda? I thought Amanda was sick before we left?"

"Yup. Guess it's going around."

"Maybe Titan should invest in masks and hand sanitizer." It wasn't like Chelsea or Amanda to orbit their coworkers when sick.

"They're not contagious." Angela shrugged and wouldn't meet his eyes. "Nothing a little ginger ale and crackers won't fix."

Something in Angela's expression wasn't the least bit concerned about her friend being ill for several weeks. Then again, Sawyer couldn't stand hospitals or doctors. He wasn't a germophobe, but why tempt fate? It would be better for both women to be out of the office, recovering, than to spread the flu. *A noncontagious flu.* The thought stopped him cold. "What kind of sick?"

Angela shrugged and returned to her phone. "Something they picked up, I guess."

Sawyer didn't remember Amanda coughing and sneezing, but he did remember a few queasy looks.

"They're both sick?"

"Think so." Angela's evasion said far more than her denials.

"Are one of them—" Cold needles crawled up his spine. "Is one of them pregnant?"

Surprised, Angela peered over her phone. "What would make you think that?"

His eyebrows arched. "Someone's having a kid?"

"I didn't say that," she added too quickly.

No. She wouldn't because people didn't talk about pregnancies in the first trimester. Penny had made him keep his mouth shut when they first found out. Not that it made a difference on their last day. Sawyer had walked out of a labor room and into the maternity floor's waiting room filled with family. He'd never been more alone. Ruined for life.

Angela moved to his side. "Sawyer?"

His heartbeat thudded. "You should tell me."

"They both are," she whispered, scrutinizing his expression. Worry pinched in her eyes.

The answer hit him like a punch. He swallowed hard and forced a grin. "That's really great. Exciting news." So many things could go wrong. Chelsea and Amanda pregnant simultaneously? Double the trouble. Sawyer crossed his arms over his galloping heart as though he could rein in his worries.

"Sawyer." Her hand rested on his bicep. Concern darkened her beautiful eyes. "I'm sorry. I shouldn't have said anything."

He wanted to run away—or, better, shake Hagan and Liam to remind them of all that could go wrong. But it wasn't as if Liam hadn't already started a family. "Don't be, Ange. It's great news." He rubbed the back of his neck, trying to tamp down his own worry. "I can be happy for my friends without..." He gestured blankly. Without what—freaking out? Recalling the day Penny and William died? He would always remember that day.

Time healed. What a fucking cliché. But it had. Life had moved forward. Still, cold panic nestled in his chest.

Angela squeezed his arm. "I should've thought—"

"Tiptoeing around me doesn't change anything." Her palm was so warm. Sawyer needed more of her touch. If only they could be alone. He didn't need to share feelings or talk. Sawyer wanted to curl against Angela and breathe easier because she was in his life.

Jared threw the conference room door wide open and strode in. His laser gaze landed on Angela's hand grasping Sawyer's bicep. "Everything okay in here?"

Angela jerked away. "Yeah. I—" She took another step back. "Making sure everything is okay with his arm."

"Right." Jared snorted. "He was shot in the other arm."

She glared.

Sawyer rubbed the well-healing wound, which didn't hurt unless he messed with it. The dull bite of pain was nice. He gave the muscle a quick squeeze to clear his head.

"I have some news." Jared pulled up a chair. "It answers a few questions but—" He gave Angela an apologetic glance. "It's a little personal too." He nodded to Sawyer. "You want him to go?"

"About me?" she asked.

Boss Man lifted his shoulders. "Yeah."

"What kind of personal?"

"About the ex."

Sawyer didn't want to leave. He didn't think Paul Bane would be a problem anymore, but damn if he wasn't sick and tired of hearing about that guy. "I'll give you a few minutes," Sawyer offered.

"No," she said, stopping him. "You can hear whatever Jared knows."

Angela took a seat. Sawyer posted against the wall across from her.

"The ex…" Jared cleared his throat. "You're probably better off without him."

"You already know that I'm aware of that."

"He was seeing someone." Jared paused as though Angela might react.

She looked unfazed. "I know there were women." She smiled tightly. "One of the things I discovered the day he proposed."

Jared assessed her again and continued, "There was one he'd recently met." His jaw ticked. Sawyer sensed the mutual desire to kick Paul's ass to kingdom come. The two men exchanged looks. Jared continued, "The woman he was bedding was a mole."

"Wait—what?"

"Your mother didn't directly give away your location in Abu Dhabi and in North Carolina. Paul did. During pillow talk."

Stunned, Angela remained still as a statue. Then her head tipped back. "That fucking asshole." She gaped like she couldn't believe how stupid Paul had been. "Well, he can kiss his senatorial campaign goodbye."

Jared looked to Sawyer to make sense of Angela's reaction. He didn't know what to say. That wasn't the first thing he would've considered.

"Does my mother know?" she demanded.

"I think she's finding out right about now also."

Angela pushed from the chair and stomped toward the window.

"Angela?" Jared pushed out of his chair. "You okay? You need anything?"

She stared at the same trees that had left Sawyer mesmerized. "I need a break." Slowly, she turned around. "I want to get out of here."

"Parker is working on a safe house you can stay in until the trial. But it will be a few hours."

She shook her head. "No, not a safe house. Something different. And really, I don't even need a safe house if no one tells Paul where I am." Her lips pursed. "Maybe my parents' house in Pennsylvania...? No. I don't want to see them and their performative bullshit."

Jared's brow furrowed. "Like a stay at a resort? With spas and stuff."

"No. Something real. With pictures on the walls and leftovers in the fridge."

Jared faltered.

"Does anyone on your local team have a family?"

"No..."

"Do they have relatives that live nearby? Maybe I could borrow their house and just sit in it for a few hours—"

"Angela, you still have a target on your back. We can't—"

"Don't *you get it*? I want to pretend my life is normal for one minute!"

Sawyer had never heard her shout or even seen her lose her cool. Angela was too controlled. Jared eyed Sawyer as though he should know what to do. He didn't.

"I just got a puppy," Jared offered.

Sawyer almost laughed.

"A bulldog. Cute as hell. Gnaws on steel."

Fat tears welled in Angela's eyes. "What's its name?"

"Thelma," Jared answered, unsure how to handle the situation.

The tears rolled down Angela's cheeks. Sawyer didn't have a clue what to do.

"I think I need more than a puppy." She swiped at the tears and returned to the window.

Jared beckoned Sawyer. "Take your girl and the dog—"

"She's not my girl."

"Shut up for a second and listen," Jared growled. "And go visit your family's place. Take a minute, say hello to your folks, and then put them up someplace nice. Like a resort with a spa. Tell them it's a work thing. Titan will foot the bill. Then let Angela sit in your house with its leftovers and laundry or whatever and hold on to Thelma."

"I—"

"Have you ever seen her cry and shout like that before?"

"No," he admitted. Not two minutes ago, Sawyer wanted to be alone with Angela. To curl up with her, just the two of them. Now Boss Man was suggesting that kind of privacy. Sawyer ran a hand over his face. He and Angela had crossed too many lines, and throwing them into the place where he grew up would only entangle them further.

Jared inched closer. "She's been shot at—*on two different continents.* Her family is a piece of work. The ex is a piece of shit. Hell, she lived in a cage for years. Take Angela home and let her soak up normal."

Take her home. Sawyer wanted to run away with her and pretend. His heart would break when their time-blocked romance ended anyway. Funny how guarding his heart was the reason he avoided relationships to begin with. Never once had he been tempted to fall in love again. Yet here he was.

Jared glared. "I'm not asking, Sawyer."

He studied Angela at the window. "She's not going to say yes."

"Make it happen," Jared demanded under his breath and then left Sawyer to figure out the hard part.

He ran a hand over his face again and approached Angela as though she might be a bear. "Hey—I'll be back in a second."

She jumped as though she'd forgotten he was there. "I'm fine." Angela sniffed, still staring out the window. "Really."

That didn't ring true. He stepped into the hall and called his mother. "Hey, Ma."

"I wasn't expecting your call today—Sawyer's on the phone," she called to his dad. "Give me a second. Dad's coming." She put it on speakerphone. "How are you?"

"Good."

"You don't usually call weekday mornings."

"I'm nearby and thought I'd—"

"Nearby? You are? I didn't know you were in the US. Can we see you?"

"Actually…" He rubbed the back of his neck. "I thought I could swing by."

"You don't have to ask. Show up, son," his dad announced as though referring to high school football tryouts.

Sawyer paused. He wasn't going to hide Angela in the car, and his parents would never leave for a resort in general, much less if he was in town. "I have someone with me."

"That's fine. Bring whomever."

"She's having a hell of a hard time and needs a break."

"What better place than out in the middle of nowhere with us?" his mother asked.

Sawyer chuckled. As if his family could have had any other reaction. If Angela needed a taste of hunky-dory ordinary, she would find it in the house he grew up in. "We might have a dog with us."

"I love dogs," Mom added.

"A puppy."

"Even better."

Sawyer dropped his head back and stared at the ceiling. He couldn't remember what pictures were in their home. He almost asked if they could take down anything with Penny in it. And it killed him that he couldn't recall if they had already. More than ten years had passed. Still, his mother had lots of framed pictures and photos stuck around the house. There was a one hundred percent chance that his high school years—with Penny center stage—would be somewhere on the walls. "All right. We'll be there tonight."

CHAPTER FORTY-ONE

ANGELA COULDN'T EXPLAIN the tears. She was far past caring that Paul had cheated on her. She wasn't surprised that he'd been stupid enough to let one of Pham's flunkies into his bed and share her location. Learning that had been the straw that broke the camel's back. Everything had suddenly been too much to keep inside. So embarrassing.

Especially after Sawyer explained Jared's brilliant idea and how his parents were expecting them later that night. The only reason this crazy notion came to fruition was because Thelma was too cute to say no to.

Thelma's tiny body and oversized head followed Angela around as soon as Boss Man pointed the pup in her direction. And that was how Angela ended up with a wrinkle-faced bulldog puppy in her lap as she rode southwest from Titan's headquarters and into hilly rural Virginia.

Thelma squirmed as Sawyer pulled off an old state road onto a gravel driveway. Rocks kicked into the truck's wheel wells. "When's the last time you were at home?"

"The holidays. My mom does a whole thing for December."

"What is she like?"

"Tough as hell. Funny. Tenacious to boot. But incredibly sweet."

Angela liked how he described his mother—and based on the description, she would like her too. "So she should work for Titan?"

"No, she has a much harder gig. Librarian in an underfunded rural county." He slowed in front of a modest split-level home with flower boxes at the windows and an oversized covered front porch. "That woman would wrestle a bear for funding if it helped stock her shelves with books and board games."

Angela's nerves raced. "What about your dad?"

"Great guy. Coached my football team from peewees through high school. Loves his life. Loves his wife." He shifted the truck into park and scanned the small front yard that backed into the woods in the distance.

"Wow, Sawyer." She gazed at their little piece of heaven. "Why would you ever leave this?"

"Seemed like the thing that needed to be done." Absentmindedly, he drummed his thumbs on the steering wheel. "I come home from time to time."

As she watched his face soften, though, Angela could almost hear a wistful *but not nearly enough.*

Thelma yipped.

He reached over and gave the pup's head a good scratch. "We'll stay out of your hair and let you decompress."

Angela bit her lip. For all her tears and dramatic demands to sit inside a normal, happy home, she didn't want to be far from Sawyer and didn't know what his parents would make of her.

The front door opened. His mom and dad walked out and waited.

"They look nice," Angela said.

He glanced toward the house. "About as nice and normal as you can possibly want." He gave her a reassuring nod. "Come on."

Butterflies fluttered in her stomach. She exited the truck, set Thelma on the ground, and walked with Sawyer up to his front porch.

He wrapped his mom in a bear hug as his dad slapped his back hello. It was quite possibly the most wholesome, most genuine family interaction she'd seen in her life. Emotion caught in her throat.

A moment later, Sawyer pulled her into the conversation. "This is Angela Sorenson." The puppy yipped for attention. "And my boss's dog, Thelma. And"—he gestured to his parents—"these good people are Susan and Sam."

Sawyer's mother wrapped Angela in a hug almost as fierce as the one she'd given her son. His dad gave Angela a hearty pat on the back at the same time. "Welcome."

And Angela was done. She'd fallen in love with his family.

SAWYER BROUGHT THEIR bags in from the truck and dropped them in the living room. The heavenly smell of a homecooked meal filled the familiar space. He couldn't help but relax when he was under this roof.

His mom met him by the window overlooking the backyard, where Angela had sat on a lawn chair. She was watching Thelma chase moths, grasshoppers, and whatever could hold the puppy's attention.

"She seems sweet."

He nodded, wondering how much his mom would instinctively know or question.

"You want to tell me about this?" She lifted the sleeve of his T-shirt. "I thought I saw a bandage—and I was correct."

He pulled it up so she could see it wasn't bad. "Nothing but a little flesh wound."

"You were shot?"

"Grazed," he corrected. As she had always reminded him, he reminded her, "The right word's important."

She laughed good-naturedly but covered her heart with her hand. "I don't want to know, do I?"

"I was trying my best to keep her safe." He pointed his chin toward Angela.

"Looks like you succeeded."

He rocked back on his heels. "Dinner smells great."

"Chicken and potatoes. It won't be ready for another thirty minutes, give or take. But Dad's out in the garage. He could always use a hand."

Regardless of what project Dad had going on, he always had a task for Sawyer to do, especially when Sawyer was at odds with himself.

Sawyer made a pit stop in his old bedroom and hooked an old football from a shelf. He gave it a squeeze. The ball hadn't deflated much from the last time he'd been home. Tossing the ball to himself, he walked out the front door and followed the well-worn path to the old garage. A basketball rim hung without a net. He chucked the football toward the rim. The ball bounced off the backboard and shot to the side.

Dad stepped out. "I could use a hand."

"That's what I hear." Sawyer retrieved the ball. "I'm ready for you to put me to work."

They walked into the familiar space, with its scent of lawn clippings, motor oil, and wood projects. Tools lined the wall behind a tidy workspace. "What are we working on?" Sawyer asked.

"Your mother wants new shelves for the laundry room."

"What's wrong with the old shelves?"

"Exactly." Dad chuckled. "But a happy wife is a happy life." He pointed at the ten-foot lengths of white oak. There would be no particleboard in this man's house, at least not as long as Dad was in charge of its creation. "Mark those for me. I want two five-foot shelves for over the washer and then five three-foot ones to line that little wall that juts out and serves no purpose other than to irritate your mother."

Sawyer knew exactly the wall he was talking about.

They got to work in silence. Sawyer penciled off the wood. His dad cut them to size with the miter saw. They finished in no time and piled them to the side. "Tomorrow, you want to help me prime and paint them?"

Sawyer tossed the football again. "Nothing else I'd rather do."

Angela popped her head inside the garage, holding Thelma close to her chest. "I'm supposed to tell you it's time to wash up for dinner."

"Thanks," Dad called, and after Angela turned, he muttered under his breath, "Yup, bet there's nothing else you'd rather do."

CHAPTER FORTY-TWO

A NGELA HAD NEVER told anyone to wash their hands before dinnertime, and her family had never eaten dinner together. She'd done both tonight, starting when Sawyer's mother asked her to call the men to dinner with instructions to remind them to wash their hands. That made Angela laugh. Sawyer too.

When she was young, Angela ate mostly meals prepared by a nanny. As she grew old enough to take care of herself, she ate alone unless at a friend's house.

It fascinated her how the Cabots fell into place when Susan said it was time to sit down. The meal was served family-style. Clearly, they were used to company, folding Angela into the serving, passing, and talking as though she were any other friend of Sawyer's.

"There was this time in"—Susan paused to think back—"Sawyer was in eighth, ninth grade. I don't know. But he and his best friend Jimmy had these inflatable wrestler guys. Nearly life-sized."

Sawyer shook his head. "This whole night can't be about me."

Sam slapped the table. "Oh, I remember that—"

"He and Jimmy would blow these things up. Get all the kids in the halls chanting, 'Fight, fight, fight.'"

"The teachers, the principal, they'd all run in, blowing whistles, breaking it up."

Sam howled. "Old Mrs. Jessup had to be a hundred years old, throwing kids to the side to break up these fights."

"You weren't even there," Sawyer pointed out, trying to keep a straight face.

Sam clucked. "He's acting so innocent—and speaking of blowing whistles—"

"What did I get myself into?" Sawyer dropped his head back, barely hiding his laughter. "I should've warned you."

"No, no, no. I want to hear," Angela shushed him. "Don't stop, Sam."

"Now, first, you have to understand that I'm the football coach. Always was. So Sawyer knew what he was doing."

Susan beamed. "He and Jimmy—if you see a theme, you're right—Sawyer and Jimmy, all the time, always in trouble—"

"The good kind of trouble," Sawyer asserted.

Sam made a face. "The boys ran laps all summer to stay ready for football. I was proud of them."

"But," Susan took over, "what we didn't know was—"

"Bear in mind," Sawyer interrupted, "this was all Jimmy's idea."

Sam and Susan both pooh-poohed him before Susan continued, "Those boys ran laps around the football field with pockets full of birdseed and whistles around their necks. They blew the whistles, tossed the birdseed—they must've run a hundred miles that summer, whistling and throwing seed and making quite a group of feathered friends."

"Then I show up," his dad said, "ready for summer drills, ready for tryouts, blow my darn whistle and"—Sam raised his arms toward the ceiling—"it was like birds fell from the sky. They rained onto the field. I'd blow my whistle again, and you'd have thought I was a pile of peanuts."

Sawyer held up his hands. "Harmless prank."

"I could've died from bird flu."

"But you didn't." Sawyer filled his mouth with the last bite of his potatoes. "And you got a hell of a story to share."

Susan pushed from the table. "Who wants something sweet?"

Both men raised their hands. Angela laughed. Everyone got up from the table to clear their plates.

"I have a new box of Popsicles in the garage freezer. Sawyer, go get them."

"Not the ones with the cartoon on the front of the carton. They're terrible," Sam said. "We need to throw them out."

"I like them. Let them be."

"I'll find the right box," Sawyer said over his shoulder as he went to find their dessert.

"We shouldn't have told stories." Susan groaned. "My Popsicles are in danger."

Laughing, Angela followed Sawyer. "I'll make sure they're safe."

They walked out of the happy house and into the sweet smell of a warm summer breeze. The sun hung heavy just behind the trees, leaving long shadows on the grass and a sky filled with oranges and reds.

Sawyer hooked his arm over her shoulder. "I really should have warned you."

"Nothing you could've said would have prepared me for dinner with your parents. They are fantastic."

"I know. They're good people." He kissed the top of her head and then led her into the garage.

She wandered toward the tool wall and oversized saw on the workspace. "What were you doing in here with your dad?"

He opened the deep freeze and examined a box of Popsicles—held up the one Sam had banned—but tossed it back in for the less offending box. "Making new shelves for the laundry room."

"Of course you were." The far wall was an altar to Sawyer's youth. Pictures of sports teams and trading cards, fading from over the years, papered the wall. Laminated headlines celebrated youth league wins. "Oh my gosh. You were so cute." All that blond hair and those blue eyes screamed mischief. "I bet you and Jimmy kept your mother up late at night."

Interspersed with the sports pictures were school photographs and candids with friends. The same little boy appeared over and over with Sawyer. "That's Jimmy, huh?"

He laughed quietly. "Yup."

Then she saw the same girl over and over too. Most of the pictures were casual. But, in a few, Sawyer wore a suit. The beautiful girl in stunning dresses was always by his side. They looked so young and terribly in love. "That's Penny."

"Yup," he said in a much quieter voice.

She studied the old photos, all faded after so many years in a garage. "You two made a gorgeous couple."

"She was the pretty one." He stepped close to the wall of pictures, letting his gaze drift. "It's funny how, when you're growing up, all you want to do is be a grown-up. And then you're a grown-up, and life isn't the fairy tale you'd thought it'd be."

"That's the truth."

"But it's great to look back at those memories." He shook the box of Popsicles. "Let's go before they melt."

Angela thought she ought to say something more, but the silence was oddly comfortable. Sawyer hooked his arm over her shoulder again. When they returned inside, Sawyer doled out the Popsicles, and if Sam and Susan had noticed Angela and Sawyer were the slightest bit muted, they didn't let it show.

Thelma yipped from her crate. Sawyer scooped her out and cradled the little wriggling mess of wrinkles in the crook of his arm.

"We need a dog," Susan proclaimed.

Sam choked. "Have you lost your mind?"

"Sawyer, back me up on this. Tell your dad we need a dog."

"I don't need my son to tell me anything about a dog unless my son plans to move back, wake up each morning, walk the dog, feed the dog, and do all the dog things that I have no desire to do."

Susan cocked her head. "It would be nice to have you home."

Sawyer snorted. "So you can get a dog? No, thank you."

"Angela, tell him to stay." Susan held her Popsicle stick between her praying hands. "I really want a dog, and I really don't want to take care of it."

"I wish I could," Angela said. "But I like him back in Abu Dhabi."

"Oh, you're out there too. That's great. We never meet Sawyer's friends anymore when they're on the far side of the world."

"Gee, I wonder why, Mom. It wouldn't be the night's worth of stories at my expense."

"There are no secrets in this family," Susan replied. "Besides, funny stories are like oxygen. You need them to breathe."

"That's her plan for longevity," Sam added. "She'll outlast us all."

Susan collected the Popsicle sticks and tossed them in the trash. "Sam, help me with the dishes."

"I'll help," Angela volunteered.

"Not a chance. I'm not making you work on the first night under my roof."

"What am I?" Sawyer asked. "Chopped liver? I had to help Dad with shelves."

"Not your first night under my roof. Go take Angela outside. Show her the stars. You can't see them like this where you two live."

Angela's heart warmed at the family banter. If her parents were one end of the spectrum, the Cabots were all the way at the opposite end.

"I love your parents," she said as she slipped outside with Sawyer. Angela took Thelma from him and waited for him to return from the garage with a blanket. "They're the best people."

"I know," he agreed.

"I'd be mortified to bring you to visit my parents. Not that they're ever around each other."

He threw the blanket on the ground. "This probably smells like a campfire. Sorry."

Seriously. Who were these people? She couldn't get enough.

Thelma ran on and off the blanket before deciding to bite a corner. They sat down and watched the little pup growl and tug.

"I keep trying to get her to play fetch, but I think tug-of-war will be her thing." Sawyer jiggled the corner of the blanket and sent Thelma into a fit of growls. "It's still too early to see all of the stars."

Angela rolled onto her back. The sky had become a moody purple black. "Where's the moon hiding?"

He scanned the night sky. "Maybe we'll luck out. It'll be even darker."

Thelma ran across the blanket and attacked another corner. Sawyer lay next to Angela, folding his hands behind his head. "There's a bat."

In the air, a dark blur skittered this way and that before Angela lost track of it. She bet Sawyer had lain in the yard and stared at the stars, watching the moon and bats so many nights before. "Do you know what we did in high school for fun?" she asked.

"What?"

"Nothing. Absolutely nothing like this."

"I bet you did something."

"Not a chance. I racked up extracurricular activities for my college application and practiced for SATs."

He laughed. "That can't be all you did."

That was what she mainly remembered. "I certainly didn't experience life the way you did."

"That doesn't make it bad."

"But maybe not as memorable." She pursed her lips and searched for bats. "Ever since I moved to Abu Dhabi, I have been figuring out how to live my own life."

"How's that going?"

She smiled at the sky. "Pretty good lately."

Thelma wriggled between them and curled into a ball. Angela petted the puppy. "Kind of crazy that Jared has a dog."

Sawyer chuckled. "Right?"

"Even crazier, he gave me his puppy and told you to take me here."

"Boss Man has an unconventional sixth sense. He knows what works."

"That he does."

Sawyer chuckled. "Like his secret notes."

Angela glanced over, trying her best for a dubious expression. "I don't know what you're talking about."

"Sure you do. You're the woman behind his plan, aren't you?"

She didn't want to play games tonight. "What would you say if I said yes?"

His chest rumbled with laughter. "I'd want to know why he does it."

"Oh, you can figure that out. He was forming a new team in a foreign country and needed you guys to get behind a common problem. Bro it out and all that good stuff."

Sawyer laughed. "Unconventional."

"Just like you said. Boss Man has a sixth sense."

A bat zigzagged overhead. She pointed. "There's another."

The bat jerked from side to side and disappeared. The dark purple night was now an inky black. The sky was so different here from anywhere she'd ever lived.

"Are you going to be okay when we get back?" Sawyer asked quietly. "When life returns to normal."

She wouldn't need an occasional bodyguard much longer. Angela would return to the administrative helm. They would hang out as friends. No, her heart would not be okay. But after knowing about his past and seeing the pictures of the life he'd started with Penny, Angela wouldn't ask him for more. He'd been crystal clear. He couldn't give what he didn't have. But that wouldn't prevent her from being truthful. "I'll miss us," she admitted, scared that if she looked at him, her voice would break. "But I'll be fine."

She waited for him to say something. For the longest time, he didn't. "Follow my finger." He pointed toward the stars right above the tree line. "That's Deneb." His hand moved to the right. "Altair." Sawyer pulled her attention high. "Vega." He pointed at the area where he first started. "And back again to Deneb. It's the Summer Triangle."

"I thought the constellations had names like Orion and the Little Dipper."

"It's an asterism. Not a constellation." Sawyer sat up and retraced his fingers along the stars. "The three brightest stars in three different constellations: Cygnus, Aquila, and Lyra. Focus on the brightest stars you see."

Angela propped on her side, studying what had so easily popped out to him. She pointed. "Right there?"

"Yeah. Deneb." He guided her hand. "And this is Altair."

She focused on the bright light. "Oh, I see it now."

Sawyer guided her hand up. "Vega." Then, they went back to where they started.

"Deneb," she said.

"That's right." Sawyer pulled her back onto the blanket. His arm slipped under her neck. Angela moved closer to him and rested her head on his chest. "There looks like a million little stars between those two bright ones," she said.

"A river of stars."

"Yeah."

"The Milky Way."

How had she gone this long in life without ever looking for the Milky Way? She couldn't believe that she had known it existed and hadn't run outside on a dark night to search the sky. "Talk about awe-inspiring."

He stroked her hair. The even cadence of his breathing soothed her soul. If she was smart, she'd yawn and say it was time to go to bed. But when it came to Sawyer, she was hopeless.

CHAPTER FORTY-THREE

SAWYER COULD HAVE watched the stars with Angela in his arms all night. But the longer he stayed on that blanket, the more he hated how their bond would end. The more he hated their ending, the harder he tried to pretend he hadn't fallen for her. On and on, logic and emotion fought until he brought Angela inside from their night of stargazing.

Their bags were identical tactical duffels from Titan headquarters, though Sawyer hadn't packed his nearly as full. He walked down the upstairs hallway and past his old bedroom to the guest room, where he put Angela's bag on the bed.

His mom had set fresh towels on the bed and left a bottle of water on the nightstand. He wondered if his parents had any clue that it pained Sawyer to sleep across the hall from Angela as though they were only co-workers.

He tossed his bag into his familiar bedroom and returned to the living room, where his mom held court, walking Angela down memory lane with a photo album spread between them.

"You're boring her to death," he said.

Angela looked up. Her laughter and smile were too big, and her eyes were threatening to water. "Not a chance."

"But it's late." His mom shifted the album onto the coffee table. "I think your dad's already asleep." She touched Angela's shoulder. "It has been so nice to meet you." Then she glided by, giving Sawyer a knowing look that he would rather not have seen.

"Night, Ma." He kissed her cheek. "See you tomorrow."

After they were alone, Angela asked, "You played Puck in your high school production of *A Midsummer's Night Dream*?"

"God." He dropped his head back and groaned. "There are some memories that need to stay buried."

"I bet you were hysterical."

He refused to see if any photographic evidence was waiting to embarrass him on the coffee table. "No wonder I jumped headfirst into the Marines."

"Speaking of which, did I mention you were a perfectly adorable jarhead?" She flipped toward the back of the photo album. "You look so young."

He ran his hand through his scraggly locks. "I was."

Angela studied the picture and then him. "I like it better longer." She squinted. "Then again, if you still had that baby face…"

"I did not have a baby face." Sawyer sat next to her on the couch. "Give me a break. This is just after boot camp. I was a hardened Marine."

She snorted.

He rolled his eyes and turned the page—there he was with Penny. Sawyer had completely forgotten that day. He leaned closer for a better look. "God. We were so young." He tried to remember that day's details. Maybe it was one of the first days after he'd survived Parris Island. Funny how he could study that picture and not feel sad or even nostalgic. He just couldn't get over how young he and Penny looked.

"I'm sorry. I wasn't trying to be nosy—"

"No, don't be. I'm not." He tapped the picture. "She's not a secret. I'm not pining over my dead wife." Though he had avoided speaking of Penny and William for years. "She was an important part of my life." He waited for the guilt or misery or fear to drive daggers into his lungs. No such sensation was there, only a semi-odd feeling that he wanted Angela to know more about Penny. The two women were nothing alike. He didn't want to compare them, yet it was hard not to remember that past and wonder about his future. "You would've liked her."

"I bet I would have," she said with quiet hesitation, as though she believed him but didn't understand it was okay to feel that way.

Sawyer ran a hand through his hair instead of reaching for Angela. He hadn't done enough to comfort her in a house where Penny had been more than comfortable. He needed to fix that. They couldn't stay in this house tonight if Angela were looking over her shoulder for a ghost.

Sawyer nodded toward the photo album. "You want to know how young we were?" He shook his head at what now seemed so absurd but, at the time, only made sense. "We got married on our senior skip day. Right before we graduated." His chest rumbled with laughter. "And my nice, sweet parents? They nearly killed us both."

Angela's mouth fell open.

"Yup." He laughed. "You and I had very different extracurricular activities in high school."

She kept gaping.

"Oh, come on, Ange. It's not *that* crazy."

"Yeah, it is." She blinked hard. "You were so responsible. Enlisting. Getting married—and I was—"

"—doing what you needed to do, sweetheart. Don't compare."

"It's hard not to. You've always been so responsible. Such a caretaker."

"Trust me when I tell you, responsibility wasn't what was driving me at the time."

She shook her head. "You have no idea how mature and responsible you were—and still are."

How could that be true when he was actively avoiding a future with Angela? The mental barriers he'd built long ago were part of his life. That was the opposite of being responsible and mature. He'd been hiding. But, damn, when she was with him, he saw past the self-imposed rules, the barriers. He almost wanted to knock them down.

Would it be such a bad thing if they fell away?

Sawyer waited for anxiety to thread through the fibers in his heart and chest. It had done so recently when he learned Amanda and Chelsea were both pregnant. But right now, fear seemed slow to arrive.

Angela shut the photo album and stood up. "I should go to bed."

"Don't go." He snaked his arm around the back of her legs and pulled her in front of him. Sawyer held her in place and tilted his head back. He needed to say so many things, but his mind drew a blank. Instead, he dropped his chin, damn near like he was praying, and pressed his forehead against her stomach. "Not yet."

Now Angela brushed her hand through his hair. He couldn't move, paralyzed, prostrating himself to the woman he loved.

"Sawyer," she said in a voice that showed she understood she was his world. "I'm going to miss this when we're home." Angela kissed her fingers, pressed them against his cheek, and left him alone on the couch.

If things could be different, if he were that strong, responsible man who Angela saw, Sawyer would be a happy man with a very different life.

CHAPTER FORTY-FOUR

A PHONE CALL from Parker interrupted a lovely breakfast after a fitful night of tossing and turning and thinking of wishes and dreams. Angela was almost glad to have work to focus on as she and Sawyer retreated to the living room to take Parker's phone call.

"Two things," Parker said. "First, Angela, you'll be happy to hear that Mylene Hathaway has been transported to a first-rate mental health facility and will be reunited with her family."

Angela's heart jumped into her throat, and tears burned at the back of it. She was a ball of emotions. None had been focused on Mylene, but they were all about to be. "Really?"

"Really," Parker confirmed. "Hang on—"

"Angela?" Jared barked, joining the call.

"Yes, sir?"

"You did it. Mission accomplished."

She did, didn't she? Her fingers pressed to her throat. Angela couldn't speak and looked to Sawyer to say something. If she had to talk, she might cry in an over-the-top kind of way and embarrass herself.

He read her loud and clear. "Angela's the kind of happy where nothing's coming out of her mouth."

Jared and Parker chuckled.

"Thanks," she mouthed.

"Was there a second thing?" Sawyer asked. "Or should we just throw ourselves a little congratulatory party?"

"Yeah, there's more. Federal prosecutors told Pham's lawyers to shove it. Negotiations are off. They're sticking to the trial schedule. The judge says they have time to make up for."

Her eyes opened wide. A whole new level of emotion made her head spin like a Tasmanian Devil. White noise roared in Angela's ears. The trial had seemed years away. Ibrahim had tried to prep her as those years had ticked by, but she'd pushed reality away. The trial would always be next month, next year. Pham would always be the good guy and bad guy and person she had to testify against. Violent, stomach-churning nausea made the room feel too warm.

"Which means," Parker continued, "opening statements could be as soon as next week."

Angela tried to focus on Sawyer as though he were a lighthouse in a tumultuous sea. Strong and tall and capable. But worry tightened on his face. That didn't bode well for her beacon of stability.

"What does that mean for witnesses?" Sawyer asked.

Good. He was asking questions to get the answers she needed. Angela hadn't even thought about when she was supposed to testify. No, her panic was stuck at square one. The trial would start. After years of building this court case, it was time for action.

"It's the prosecution's prerogative as to who's called when. Opening statement and then they'll be off and running. Angela, they'll want to speak with you soon."

Her head swam. She tried to nod. Panic blanketed her chest, compressing until each breath was a shallow, racing mess. Parker continued talking, but she couldn't hear him. White noise and a little screeching voice in her head yelled that she would see Pham next week.

Oh, God. If not next week, then very, very soon. Bile rose into her throat. "I'm going to see Pham," she tried to say but wasn't sure that any words came out of her mouth.

"Angela?" Sawyer put his hand on her shoulder and gave her a little shake.

She couldn't focus on him. Her tongue felt thick. Swimming through the nausea, she swayed.

"Guys, we'll call you back." Sawyer hung up. "Ange, hey? You okay?"

Years had passed since she saw Pham. Her mind had been so screwed up then. He abducted her! How had she ever thought of him as family?

Her stomach roiled, twisting and tying into revolting knots. Cold sweat and confused memories prickled over her skin.

"Ange, look at me." His hands squeezed her shoulders. "Focus on me."

As her head swam, her eyes pinched shut. "I'm gonna be sick."

Sawyer half carried, half hustled her to the bathroom. Her legs gave out. Gently, he laid her on the cold tile floor. She curled into a ball, pressing her pounding temple to the tile.

Sawyer remained close. She could hear him speak but wasn't sure of what he said. Thoughts of testifying bore down on her with strangling force. Pham had stolen her life and pretended to care about her, but he didn't. She was a wealthy man's plaything, used and abused without a finger laid on her.

At one time, she'd almost loved him, or at least thought she had, desperately needing the attention that Pham had given easily.

But it wasn't real.

Knowing that made it better *and* worse.

A damp, cold cloth was pressed to her forehead. Angela moaned. It felt so good.

"There you go." He held the cloth against her skin. "Take a couple of slow breaths."

She hadn't realized how fast her heart was racing. Angela tried to slow her pulse. She inhaled through her nose, dragging in deeper, longer breaths.

"There you go," he repeated soothingly. "Nice and easy."

The heart-racing nausea slowly ebbed. Angela propped herself against the bathtub.

Sawyer sat on the tub's edge and smoothed his strong hand over the back of her head. He brushed her hair off her cheek and the washcloth and resumed stroking the back of her head. Finally, she'd caught her breath.

"Are you good for a minute?"

"I'm fine," she managed, sounding hoarse and unbelievable.

Sawyer kissed the top of her head. "I'll be back."

Angela turned the cloth over and pressed its cooler side to her forehead again. With her head between her knees and her arms crossed protectively over the top of her head, she tried to steady her racing thoughts.

Sawyer returned. "Take a drink of water."

She peeked up and took the glass. Her hand trembled, and deciding it was better to use two hands than to let the glass shatter on the tile, she sipped.

"Good, sweetheart." He returned to his perch on the tub's edge. "It will be okay."

She wasn't sure if that was true.

"Do you want me to call Ibrahim?" he asked.

She shook her head. "There's nothing he will tell me that he hasn't told me before."

Sawyer frowned but didn't try to convince Angela that she was wrong. He didn't have to. She knew it, but that wasn't what she needed.

"Have you seen Pham since Titan rescued you?" he asked, though she understood he knew the answer.

She shook her head. "Only in the news."

He slid down beside her and put his strong arm around her shoulders. She folded into him. *This* was what she needed. Him holding her. Protecting her from the world as he always did.

"Pham doesn't freak me out." But saying that ratcheted her nerves into a tsunami again. "I just—"

Sawyer squeezed her close. His lips pressed to the top of her head. "Whether he does, or he doesn't..." He inched back and lifted her chin with his fingers. Sawyer waited until he had her focus. "You're not going to face that monster alone." His thumb swept across her cheek. "You've got me. All of us."

She had Sawyer. She always had him. Angela nodded. When he looked at her like that, she felt invincible. She folded the damp washcloth and hung it on the side of the tub. "I couldn't do this without you."

"Sure you could." He smiled. "But you wouldn't have had as much fun along the way."

God, she loved him. She loved him so much it hurt.

Sawyer tipped her chin up again and kissed her lips softly. After an eternity of feather-light kisses, his forehead pressed to hers. Angela crawled onto his lap and traced her fingers down his temples, his cheeks, and his chin, carefully studying every millimeter of his face. This bond would be gone before too long.

"What's on your mind, Ange?"

She couldn't tell him. "Your parents probably think I'm nuts."

She didn't miss his scrutiny, but after a moment, he shook his head with a quiet laugh. "My parents are in the middle of a hot debate about what color to paint the laundry room shelves. They didn't notice."

That made her laugh. "Liar."

He crossed his heart. "Scout's honor." Sawyer slid her from his lap and stood, holding out his hand and then pulling her to her feet. "How do you feel? Better?"

"Eh..." Angela made a face. "I've started my day with better phone calls."

His lips quirked. "You probably need food in your stomach."

"Probably right."

Sure enough, when they reached the kitchen, Sam and Susan were shuffling paint chips in various shades of white and wheat. Susan barely paused to ask if either Sawyer or Angela needed more pancakes—the two had barely touched their plates.

"Told you." He smacked a kiss on her cheek. Neither Sam nor Susan noticed that either. Such was the paint debate.

Five minutes and a generous heaping plate of pancakes later, Angela was ready to finish the conversation with Parker. She finished her orange juice and decided that nothing would knock her down like that again. They returned Parker and Jared's call. The conversation continued without panic attacks or meltdowns.

"The only thing left to decide is where you wait it out," Jared said. "I'm sure Casa de Cabot is lovely, but a safe house is the way to go."

Not imposing on the Cabots was understandable, though she hated to leave a house that felt like a home.

"We need to be on high alert," Sawyer said, agreeing. "This is Pham's last time to keep Angela from testifying. I'm not heading anywhere that isn't stocked with enough firepower to protect a battalion."

That didn't worry her. Maybe it should have, but the only thing that would tie Angela into knots was facing Pham in court.

Jared let out a long breath. "We've been down the safe house road already. It didn't work as it should have."

"And we know why," Angela snapped. "I used to date an idiot who slept with Pham's—"

"I know, Angela," Jared said. "But it's safer if the Federal Marshals can stash you somewhere temporarily—"

"No," she and Sawyer said simultaneously.

Couldn't Boss Man see how close Witness Protection felt like Pham's abduction? Basic needs would be met, but she'd have to walk away from everyone until they let her go.

"I'm sorry to shit on your day, Angela," Jared said. "But your only option that everyone will agree with is a temporary stint in Witness Protection."

"Who is everyone?" she demanded.

"You know the laundry list."

She looked to Sawyer for answers. His hard-set jaw didn't show he had any. "Jared, I can't."

"We don't have much say—"

"Yes—"

"Angela," Jared interrupted, "I don't want to be the asshole. But you know that I'll be that guy. There are a lot of people trying to do right by you, by this trial—"

"Don't you get that the idea of someone bringing me to an unknown place where I can't contact my loved ones is too much to ask of me again? It's too similar to when Pham imprisoned me." The choking memories stole her rationality. "Don't you get that? Jared, please. I can't."

"I'm saying you don't have a choice."

Tears welled in her eyes. Angela shook her head. She tried to find safe harbor in Sawyer. His tight expression was one she couldn't read. Her stomach knotted. "Sawyer?"

Tension flexed in his jaw, but he shook his head. "Jared knows the players, the situation… He knows everything and is working from a clear-headed perspective." Sawyer ground his molars. "We're not."

Maybe Ibrahim could give her some kind of pass. A doctor's note that would excuse her from Boss Man's demands. But in her heart, she knew Ibrahim wouldn't ignore her physical safety—especially when it seemed as if they had exhausted all other options.

A tear escaped. Her arms felt lined with lead. Angela couldn't manage to wipe the tear away before another fell.

Sawyer noticed. His lips pinched, and his nostrils flared as he pulled in a deep breath. But he didn't contradict Jared.

Her world spun. The floor had been pulled from beneath her feet. Witness Protection had always been a distant, unexercised option, but she didn't think it would ever happen. It was happening. Angela's chin dipped.

"Parker," Jared said, "give me the line. Alone." A moment later, he said, "Angela, let me talk to Sawyer. Alone."

Her eyes flashed to Sawyer's. Sawyer lifted his chin.

Trepidation sprung in the pit of her stomach. What was there to say to Sawyer that Angela couldn't hear? Her throat knotted. The two men she trusted above all others wanted her to leave so they could talk about her. Slowly, she stood from the table and found herself in her bedroom.

Knowing that she was the topic of conversation needled under her skin. She shut the door and sank onto the bed. Every second crawled by. She tried to imagine their discussion and didn't like any of her thoughts.

Finally, Sawyer knocked on the door. She opened it, partly thrilled they were finished discussing her, partly hurt that they didn't think she could hear or handle what they had said.

"Your turn," he said. His face was unreadable, and, though he stood inches away from her, Sawyer felt miles away.

Angela rolled her lips together and found where Sawyer had left the phone. She picked it up and pressed it to her ear. She swallowed hard, suddenly unsure of her voice. "Boss Man?"

"Hey."

Her throat constricted. Jared sounded almost apologetic, almost... She wasn't sure. His voice wasn't patronizing or patriarchal. But it was something that made her insides feel like sludge. "What did you say to

Sawyer that you can't say to me?"

Jared let out a long, foreboding breath. "You said you had a problem with Witness Protection."

Her teeth clenched. "You know I have a problem with it."

"You said it kept you from your loved ones."

"Yeah," she said cautiously.

Silence hung on the call.

"That's never what you told me before. Years ago, when Witness Protection was on the table. Before I offered you a job with Titan."

She couldn't recall that exact conversation. "I don't remember specifically what I said."

"You told me that you didn't want to cede control again. I understood."

"Then why—"

"The situation has changed, Angela. You know it, and I know it. Look, here's what you can control. Your beliefs. Your values. Your thoughts and your perspective. But you can't control your loved ones."

"If this has to do with what my mother has said, I'm done with her weighing in on my life."

"I wish it was that easy, Angela."

"Why isn't it?"

He remained silent for so long that she checked to see if the call had been dropped.

"Jared?" she asked.

"I don't have experience on my side, but when I tell you this, you gotta know that I believe it."

"And you have to know that you're starting to freak me out."

"Great," he grumbled. "This was easier with Sawyer."

"*What was?*"

"I think your loved one is sitting in the other room."

Her stomach dropped. Her mouth did too.

"And judging by that stunned silence you're giving me, instead of a world-class Sorenson rebuttal, I'm not off base," he continued as Angela's heart seesawed. "Take a vacation. Let it be in Witness Protection. And if you need your loved one with you, bring them with you. No questions asked. Disappear together. When it's done and time to show up to work again, that's what you do. Together."

Heat crawled into her cheeks. Her heartbeat raced. Jared was talking about Sawyer. "I…"

"You don't have to manage a safe house or your safety. Neither does anyone else you bring along. If that's what you meant about not wanting to leave your loved ones."

Angela's mouth had gone dry. Had Jared told Sawyer she loved him? He couldn't know that. Still, not knowing something wouldn't stop Boss Man when his instinct spoke up.

Jared chuckled. "And if I'm wrong a hundred different ways, ignore me." She could almost see him shrug and crack his knuckles. "But I don't think I am."

"I can't be in love with him," she whispered.

"Why's that?"

Angela shook her head. "You know his past better than I do."

Jared released a soul-reaching sigh. "The shitty thing about this job is all of the ugly that I have seen over the years. Ugly conditions. Ugly humanity. Ugly, ugly grief. The kind when life's not fair, and it's hard to keep going. But this is the thing, Angela. Something changed in Sawyer the day he met you. You never saw him before."

"We're just friends."

"Good. You both needed that when you first moved to Abu Dhabi."

"We're still friends."

"Again, good. 'Cause rumor has it that's the basis for a lot more to build on."

"Jared—"

"I don't give two shits if you two are friends or fucking or in it for the long haul. But I do care if you ignore me when I say it's time for Witness Protection."

Jared wouldn't force her, but until this point, he had let her take the lead on where she was. That sank in. So did the points he had made about Sawyer. "Is this the same conversation you had with Sawyer?" she asked.

Jared snort-laughed. "No. Not a chance."

She had to laugh, relieved and more than a little curious. "Should I even ask?"

"I wouldn't say anything even if you did."

"Fair enough." Angela bit her bottom lip. "What now?"

"Sit pretty and let the Marshals whisk you to the unknown. I'll be waiting for you at the trial."

"And Sawyer?"

"Talk to him. He either disappears with you, or he'll make his way back to headquarters."

"No matter if he goes with me, can he also be at the courthouse when I testify?"

Jared scoffed. "Don't waste your time asking questions you already know the answer to."

That reply made her smile. Of course Sawyer would be wherever she needed him to be. All she had to do was ask.

CHAPTER FORTY-FIVE

THELMA, THE BULLDOG puppy, growled, wrestled, and attacked Sawyer's foot as he sorted through the stack of photos that had been kept in the top dresser drawer. In one after the next, he saw what his future had been. Then it was gone. Penny had been his world, and they'd had great plans. Their child had been a promise of what he hoped was the first of more.

Reverently, he returned the photos to the keepsake container and picked up Thelma. Jared had had a lot to say about safe houses. The best ones were rarely the most obvious. They weren't the ones with the best security systems or weapons stashed around every corner. The best ones were the comfortable ones, the ones that met unanticipated needs and provided a sense of safety beyond simply securing their occupants.

Boss Man wasn't known for talking in code, and when Sawyer had asked if they were really discussing the philosophical aspects of safe houses, Jared had simply said, "What do you think, dipshit?"

They hadn't been talking about safe houses. They weren't even talking about Angela. At one time, Sawyer thought he had it all together. Life had punted that plan to kingdom come. When the pain stopped, he stopped. It wasn't that he didn't live or feel. Working for Titan packed enough adrenaline for a dozen lifetimes. But Sawyer hadn't tried to live again.

Then Angela came along. Everything changed. The transformation hadn't been abrupt. Hell, until today, he hadn't noticed how long their situation had been in the making. Now that his eyes were open, he understood that if he didn't take a leap of faith and love Angela the way she deserved to be loved, his soul would shrivel and wither. He'd return to the shell of a person he'd been after Penny and William died.

Sawyer didn't know what that leap would look like. But he was done hiding from the risk. Fear wouldn't determine his future—their future.

ANGELA APPROACHED SAWYER'S bedroom. The closed door offered a layer of privacy that didn't abound in the cozy house. She appreciated it, but at the same time, as she closed in on the threshold, her heart hammered. All she had to do was find the right words.

Angela knocked on his bedroom door.

"Come on in."

She twisted the doorknob and crept in. Nervous energy swirled in her stomach.

Sawyer held the puppy to his chest, and Angela wished it was her who held Thelma. The squiggly little pup would keep her heart from jumping as she walked closer. "Hey."

A wary expression clouded his beautiful face. Something—maybe caution or carefulness—stormed in his blue eyes.

She bit her lip. "That was a weird phone call."

"Did Jared talk in codes and metaphors?" Sawyer repositioned Thelma in his arms.

"Not really." She inched closer and wished she could decipher his body language. "Should we compare notes?"

"Did he talk to you about various weapons stashes and the makings of a good safe house?"

Her brow knit. "No."

Sawyer nodded as though that made perfect sense.

If it did, Angela didn't get it. She asked, "Did he mention rumors and the trial to you?"

"No." Thelma squirmed to be let down. Sawyer set her by his feet. She scampered to the bed and grabbed hold of the dangling corner of the bedspread. A little growl and head-shaking attack ensued.

"Don't," he scolded her and redirected the pup to a rope toy. After ensuring Thelma wouldn't chew on the covers again, he returned his focus to Angela. "What rumors?"

She remembered how Jared's infinite wisdom included relationship advice. Friendship was the basis of so much more. Her heart tripped over itself, but Angela wasn't ready to explain that to Sawyer, so she changed the subject. "I'm going to let the Marshals tuck me away until the trial."

His expression flipped. With knitted brows and a scrutiny she wasn't expecting, he managed a tight, "That's the right thing to do."

"Yeah," she agreed.

His lips pressed together. "You worked out the details?"

She shook her head. His about-face didn't make sense. Her nerves were already sky-high and tangled. Now, they faltered.

"What's going on?" he asked.

Angela studied Thelma for an unnerving moment and licked her lips. This was Sawyer. She could tell him anything. Ask him anything. And, sure, they'd set up rules and had their reasons, but Boss Man wouldn't lead her astray. *Sawyer* wouldn't. He was her everything. "Come with me."

Now his lips parted. His expression changed again as though he didn't understand and was about to ask where she wanted to go.

Angela prayed she wouldn't lose this man. "Come with me. As Sawyer. Not as the man who keeps saving my life. But as the man in my bed. Who I—" There was so much to say, and most of it would send him away. She wanted him to know how much she loved and needed him, but she couldn't. "I know I can't ask you for more—"

"Wait." His voice had dropped to a bottom-of-a-barrel rumble. Its vibrations rolled over her skin, and goose bumps spread down her arms and back. Her frenzy of electrical sparks contradicted what he'd said. Cut off, she closed her eyes to whatever he would say in his best, most caring way to let her down.

Sawyer wrapped her into his arms. Her eyes pinched tighter. His lips dipped to her temple, her cheek, and finally, her forehead. She couldn't help but lean her softness into the rock-hard protection of his hold.

"Look at me, Ange."

Her reaction to this was something else she couldn't help. Her head tipped back. If only they could stay like this forever.

"You can ask me anything," he whispered in a way that made his chest rumble again. "Always."

"Maybe." Her voice trembled. She was terrified, and he could see it.

Sawyer cupped her chin and then eased back until he sat on the edge of his bed. He held her between his legs, eye to eye. "You can. And you know why? Because I have been in love with you since... I don't know. Since I first met you? When we first became friends? Or I first kissed you?" The corners of his lips curled into a sexy, soul-stealing smile. "And I keep falling in love with you. Over and over again. In so many different ways. So you can ask me whatever you need to ask of me."

Her heart raced. "*Sawyer...*"

"But you have to know this. I will *always* be the man willing to save your life, Angela." Sawyer cupped her chin in his hand. His thumb caressed her cheek. "I didn't think I could have a woman in my life again. When I told you that, I believed it. But I was wrong. I couldn't share my life with anyone again until I did so with you."

"*Sawyer.*"

"You deserve the world. You deserve to feel safe and loved."

Tears slipped down her cheeks.

"I want to be the man who gives you everything." He swiped away a tear. "I love you."

More tears spilled as her heart exploded. "I love you too." She wrapped her arms around his neck and buried her face against it. Relief and excitement raced through her veins. She laughed, and Sawyer draped her over his chest as they fell backward onto the bed.

He threaded a hand into her thick hair and pulled her face close. Their lips tangled. He rolled over and caged her to the bed. "You are my everything."

A flood of tears returned. "Stop making me cry."

He laughed, shaking his head.

She caught his cheeks between her hands. "You'll go into Witness Protection with me? It shouldn't be for very long."

Gently, he kissed her lips. "I will go anywhere with you. Always."

CHAPTER FORTY-SIX

W ITNESS PROTECTION WASN'T exactly like Angela had seen in the movies. She and Sawyer wouldn't be in the Marshals' protective care long enough to establish new identities in a new community. They simply had to stay put. No job. No communication with the outside world. No responsibilities other than staying within the secure confines of a federal safe house that was planted in the middle of nowhere. Truthfully, she didn't even know what state they were in, only that they were within a day's drive of the federal courthouse in Alexandria, Virginia, where Pham's trial would take place.

Sawyer and Angela only had each other, a closet full of board games, a pantry and kitchen full of food, and a huge, inviting bed. Witness Protection had been very nice in the lots-of-orgasms, lots-of-snuggling kind of way.

But their time together hadn't just been orgasms that could set the world on fire. Sawyer wanted her to be comfortable when they returned to the outside world, and he'd made it very clear that things would be different when they resumed their ordinary lives. There'd be no hiding that he was her man. Angela loved that in a way she didn't know she could.

Rain poured through the thick forest of trees that surrounded their little house. She'd tried her hand at video games that morning and discovered that she wasn't too bad with the old-style NES games that she'd only wished she'd been allowed to play as a child, but the games du jour gave her motion sickness. After that, they'd raided a closet full of board games, dice, and cards.

She watched her man shake the dice in the cup and roll them. Sawyer scrutinized the dice and smiled in the way that only a larger-than-life superhero of a man could while playing Yahtzee. Four of a kind. He marked his score sheet.

She tried to see his tally of points. "I'm going to lose, aren't I?"

His smirk was one part don't-give-up-yet and two parts you-better-catch-up.

She hated to lose games almost as much as she hated to play games based on chance. They gave her the same feeling as jumping headfirst into a public, serious relationship. There was only so much she could say and do to control their debut and future. Angela hadn't needed to discuss anything with her ex because they hadn't had a real relationship. Not one that she invested herself in or planned for the future. With Sawyer, she was crazy enough to envision growing old together. But she still needed to know some details. "So, I have a question."

Sawyer hummed as though he understood she wasn't clarifying the rules to Yahtzee or asking what they should do for dinner. "I was wondering when this would happen." His brows rose. "Will you throw your dice first?"

Angela paused. Her spine straightened. "When what would happen?"

"What's about to." He gestured to her cup. "Throw."

"You can't read my mind."

"That's not entirely true, sweetheart."

She shook her dice haphazardly and threw them onto the table, not looking at what she rolled. "What was I going to ask?"

"We've already figured out logistics in Abu Dhabi."

"Yes." She warily studied his casual nature. Moving in together was a big step, but it was hard to imagine any other option after Sawyer said he wanted to fall asleep and wake up next to her whenever he wasn't on assignment. "My place, temporarily. Until we get one that's ours."

Jared would let them choose a hotel suite that was laid out like an apartment. Interior decorators were on the house. It was all a part of the perks that came with working for Titan and living in a luxury hotel.

"But now you want to plan the details," Sawyer offered. "Responsibilities. Expectations."

He wasn't wrong. "Most relationships fail because couples fight over money and who takes out the trash."

"That sounds like a symptom. A lack of respect and communication being more of the problem."

"Hence, I want to talk about some things."

He grinned. "Give me your laundry list of questions, and I'll do my best."

She crossed her arms. It wasn't as if she was giving a quiz. "I just want to plan."

"Ange, you plan everything to a tee. I know that about you, and I'm not saying it's wrong. All I said was I wondered when this would happen."

Her lips flattened, but she tried to see it from his side. So, she was a buttoned-up control freak. That part of her had loosened since they'd set foot on the jet and she'd fallen asleep in his arms. It had been nice to let go of holding the world together.

"I'll start," he said. "I do my laundry. You do yours. I don't know what will shrink or melt or whatever else if I throw it in the washer with my jeans. Your wardrobe likely costs more than my collection of weapons, so I'm not going to screw with it."

Her eyebrow arched. "Can you put your laundry in the hamper and not next to it?"

His lips pursed as though he were considering the mental and physical requirements of depositing laundry twelve inches farther than where he usually tossed it. "I don't want to make promises I can't keep."

"Sawyer, seriously—"

"But we'll use housekeeping," he offered. "You won't even know I've piled everything on the floor. Or, you won't for long."

"You're a grown man, Sawyer Cabot."

He laughed and pulled her into his arms as he lay on the couch. "What else is on your list?"

"I like brightly colored furniture."

"Fine. I don't give a shit about the furniture, so long as it's comfortable."

That was fair. "Who cooks?"

"I'm a better cook than you," he said.

"That's because you coat everything in butter and oil and salt."

"Basic chemistry, sweetheart. You gotta season food."

"If I eat like you all of the time, my butt will not fit in my skirts."

The corners of his lips curled. "Or you'll fit *better* into your skirts. 'Cause, I'm not going to lie, I love your ass. More of it won't be a bad thing."

A blush shot from her neck into her cheeks. "Sometimes the chicken has to be skinless and the vegetables steamed."

He shook his head, his smile deepening. "The things I will do to make you happy."

"I'll cook sometimes."

"And I'll eat it. Sometimes."

Playfully, she shoved him. "I like to bake."

The corners of his eyes tightened. "I didn't know that."

"See. There are many things we don't know about each other yet, even if it seems like we know everything."

His hand ran up her spine and into her loose hair. "What are you going to make me?"

"Whole-grain bread."

Sawyer laughed and rolled on top of her. "What if I ask for something sweet?"

"You'd have to ask nicely."

His hips rolled between her legs, and his lips dipped below her ear. Sawyer took his time whispering, "I always ask nicely."

That was true. "I'm pretty sure I have everything to make cookies."

Sawyer asked her to bake them, and he did so *very, very* nicely.

CHAPTER FORTY-SEVEN

ANGELA WOKE TO the sound of a phone ringing. It wasn't either of their cell phones, and it took her more than a minute to place. Their safe house had a landline. She'd registered it as a relic from years gone by or maybe a necessity of living in a remote part of somewhere within a forest. Either way, the thought had been fleeting.

"Sawyer." Angela nudged him. "The phone is ringing."

He slapped the nightstand as though he were trying to snooze an alarm. "It's not."

"The kitchen. The phone on the wall."

With tousled hair and sleepy eyes, he inched off his pillow. She saw the mental gymnastics of who might call the landline that hadn't rung once since they'd arrived, then Sawyer lumbered out of bed, walking his naked self out of the bedroom.

He returned with the cobwebs seemingly cleared out of his sleepy thoughts. "It's time."

"That was them?"

He nodded and searched the floor for the clothing they'd discarded before falling into bed together. "Yup. You're scheduled to testify this afternoon."

Her stomach dropped like a boulder pushed into the sea. "Today?"

He nodded.

"How do we know it's them?" She gathered the sheets up to her chin, hiding as Sawyer walked around the room, gathering his belongings.

"They said they'd get a hold of us. They identified themselves the way they'd said they would."

"I thought that was if they knocked on the door."

"Or, apparently, if they called." He paused, took her in as she hid under the sheets, and sat beside her. Sawyer brushed her hair off of her face. "You're ready for this."

"I know."

"You can do this," he urged.

"I know." But she still didn't set foot out of bed. "But I'm not ready."

"Sweetheart, you've been ready for years," he said quietly. "The sooner you do this, the sooner you're done with him."

All of this she knew. Still, she was stuck under the sheets. "I don't know if I can."

It wasn't as if she was going to have a panic attack like she had at the Cabots' house. But her frozen limbs weren't moving. She didn't know how to jumpstart her derrière into action.

"Angela." Sawyer crawled over her and under the covers, pulling her into his arms. "I am ready to start my life with you. I am ready for everything. All of it. But it all starts with you taking this step and ridding yourself of this baggage. I can't do that for you. I would in a heartbeat, but it's not my burden to release."

An ache throbbed in her throat.

"I'm going to spend my life with you. I'm going to marry you. Have kids with you. Anything that you want, Angela. And all of that starts with testifying." He tilted her chin up, forcing her gaze to lock onto his. "Give me that, and I will give you the world."

Once more, tears threatened to fall down her cheeks. They had talked about their future, but when he put it like that, their future made her heart explode. She couldn't say anything except, "I love you, Sawyer."

"Love you too." He pulled her onto his chest and kissed the top of her head. "If I could do this for you, I would."

She knew that and nodded. And that was all she needed. "All right. Let's do this."

SEVERAL HOURS OF driving later, the blacked-out SUV rolled into the underground parking lot. Somewhere above them was the federal courthouse, brimming with reporters and Tran Pham.

Angela wore a black pencil skirt and cuffed white blouse. She channeled her inner badass with a stack of gold bracelets like her mother's and a vivid red lipstick that made her feel like a rock star.

Sawyer sat next to her, silent and holding her hand as the Marshal rolled to a stop. An armed gaggle of marshals waited outside the SUV to escort Angela into the building.

"When you're ready," the federal agent in the front passenger seat said.

Her heart galloped twice as fast as it had when they exited Interstate 495 toward the federal courthouse complex. She squeezed Sawyer's hand even tighter than she had as they slowed in the garage bay.

"Ready?" Sawyer asked.

Angela inhaled slowly through her nose and exhaled through her mouth just as slowly. "Yes."

Sawyer nodded to the agent in the front seat. The woman got out and opened Angela's door. Fluorescent lights from the parking lot flooded into the back seat, as did the murmur of voices, greeting her and setting them into action.

Updates were given. Directions commanded. Angela relied on Sawyer to hear everything and ensure she did what was needed. The protective gaggle hustled her into an elevator.

Two minutes later, she sat in a private conference room, a bottle of water at her right hand and Sawyer standing next to her left, waiting for the assistant district attorney prosecuting Pham's case to make their appearance.

The ADA didn't have much to say. She looked younger than Angela expected, but she also looked smart, savvy, and hungry for a conviction. The one-sided conversation ended with an utterance of "We'll call for you when we're ready."

Then Angela was alone with Sawyer and her bottle of water. She looked up at him. "I'm ready for this to be over."

He nodded, in bodyguard mode, scanning the empty room like a threat hid in the wood paneling. "Same, sweetheart."

One minute passed. Then five minutes. Finally, fifteen minutes had crawled by. "Maybe we should ask—"

The door swung open. A new face greeted her. "They're ready for you."

Angela's stomach lurched. She reached for Sawyer's hand. He took it and held it until they reached the door. "You've got this," he whispered.

She did. Forget the number of interrogations over the years and the amount of prep work the federal investigators and district attorneys' offices had put her through; Angela was beyond ready to leave Pham in her past.

They moved into the courtroom. A jury waited to hear from her. The judge reigned from the dais in the middle of the room. People filled all the other available seats. There were no news cameras, but reporters huddled at the back wall, ready to get their sound bites and run them out of the courthouse to wherever their computers and cell phones waited.

Then she saw Pham.

White noise and rushing blood pounded in her head. He didn't turn to watch her walk in, but she could have picked him out of the lineup if everyone had their back to her. For years, he was one of the only people she'd seen.

Sawyer was forced to stay with the crowd lining the benches. Whatever had been said to call her to the witness stand had already happened. A uniformed man directed her toward the elevated platform and empty chair. A microphone and a glass of water waited for her there.

Her palms sweated, but Angela didn't rush. She held her head up and strutted to the witness stand in her killer shoes. Out of the corner of her eye, she saw Pham as she passed, and at that moment, she decided to meet his gaze from her spot next to the judge.

Angela took her seat. The members of the jury watched her. Some looked curious. Others appeared to be exhausted by what thus far must have been tedious with savvy lawyers searching for loopholes.

Another uniformed officer approached. "Raise your right hand," he directed, "and repeat after me."

She swore to tell the truth and then noticed Sawyer at the back of the room. His tight jaw and stoic expression were unreadable to anyone but Angela. But, in his ice-blue eyes, she saw the words he'd promised. Their future.

With that, a calm settled over her. This chapter of her life would close. The next one waited minutes away. She couldn't wait.

Angela testified. She looked Tran Pham in the eye and said her piece. After she spoke, it was as if a weight had been lifted from her shoulders. Even when the defense crossed, she didn't care. There was only so much they could do to assassinate her character, since she had been Pham's captive for years.

"You may be excused," the judge said.

Angela met Sawyer's eyes and almost smiled. She was ready to go home and start their happily ever after.

A glass window shattered.

Bright lights exploded.

Hissing smoke instantaneously filled the room.

"Sawyer!" she called for help as pandemonium broke loose. She could barely see. Tears poured from her burning eyes.

The judge was pulled from his chair.

Gunfire popped. Screams tore into the chemical haze.

Angela ducked. Smoke burned her throat and nose.

A scurry of shouts and orders and rushing feet ricocheted in the melee. She covered her eyes. Rough hands grabbed her arm and shoulder, dragging her out of the chair and over the front of the witness stand.

"No!" Angela choked. She struggled. She lost a shoe and fought for freedom. Gunfire popped again. She threw herself away from the sound. Pain exploded in her shoulder.

Another set of hands reached her. *Sawyer.* She didn't have to see him to know it was her man. He roared, swung her into his arms, and, just as fast, rescued her from the gas-bombed room.

CHAPTER FORTY-EIGHT

"**Y**OU DID IT. You're done," Sawyer soothed against the side of Angela's head. He wasn't finished holding on to her, even though the threat had been neutralized. Once again, he'd found himself lying in a hospital bed with Angela. This time, he wasn't fucking around and told the world that she was his. Paramedics. Nurses. Doctors. Anyone who had suggested that his role wasn't to be right by her side had been told in no uncertain terms that they could fuck off. Sawyer was staying by his woman. His *very* medicated woman.

"I did it." She curled into him, agreeing, "I'm done."

No matter what happened with Pham's trial, Angela had sat at the witness stand, chin up, and given one hell of a testimony. The defense didn't have a leg to stand on other than a series of objections that judge had shot down.

As for what had happened in the courtroom, Sawyer didn't know who or why. The timing made no sense. But truthfully, he didn't care. Angela was safe, and she was done.

A woman in scrubs with a cheery disposition was allowed into the room, introducing herself as a radiology tech. "Ready to go to X-ray?"

"It's not broken." Angela, a little dopey from the recent painkiller, sat up with help.

"Then that's what we'll confirm." The cheery tech positioned a wheelchair next to the bed. "Can you get down or—" She smiled at Sawyer. "Can you get her down?"

Carefully, Sawyer placed a groaning, protesting, somewhat giggling Angela in the wheelchair. He thanked his lucky stars she was entertaining, which kept him from recalling how much he hated hospitals.

Angela held out a foot. "Do you think I'll get my missing shoe back?"

"No."

"Ugh, that's a tragedy."

The tech rolled Angela toward the door. "We'll be back in about twenty, thirty minutes or so."

"If you don't mind," he said in a way that brooked no discussion, "I'll tag along."

The ensuing trip to the radiology lab was quick. Waiting for the results was not.

Angela had the benefit of painkillers. Sawyer sat beside her, vigilant and growing slightly bored. That was preferable to the panicky feeling hospitals usually gave him.

Finally, a doctor walked in, brisk and hurried. He logged into the computer attached to the wall as he introduced himself. After a few keystrokes, the X-rays appeared on the screen for Sawyer and Angela to see. "Great news. A simple dislocation."

Her arm and shoulder had been immobilized pending the X-ray, but now the doctor moved to the bed and started to unfasten the bandages and harness that the paramedic had tied her into.

Sawyer knew this process would hurt like hell. If Angela did, she was too medicated to worry.

"This part won't be fun," the doctor warned him. "But then it's done." He ran his fingers up her shoulder blade and down her collarbone until he gripped the joint. "Take a deep breath." She did, and he popped the bone back into place.

Angela screamed.

"All done," the doctor said.

Sawyer retook his spot by Angela's side. Her eyes were wide, and though she looked like she might kick the doctor in the groin, she also seemed to notice relief in her shoulder.

The doctor warned about arm weakness, directed them to see a physical therapist, and promised that a nurse would follow up shortly with their release paperwork. Sawyer settled back into Angela's bed, certain that wouldn't be happening soon.

To his surprise, the door swung open. Jared Westin, not the nurse, strode inside.

"Boss Man," Angela said with a slight slur. "What are you doing here?"

Jared shook his head. "Looks like I have another couple on my hands."

Her goofy smile brightened. "We're going to get married."

Jared stepped back as though Angela had swung a bazooka his way. "What?"

Sawyer laughed but didn't dispute what Angela said.

Jared pinched the bridge of his nose. "Jesus fuckin' Christ, I can give one hell of a pep talk." After a long moment, with deep lines creasing his brow, he added, "Congratulations."

"Where's Pham?" Angela asked.

"Sitting in a prison medical unit. They needed to check him out before transporting him back to whatever hole they've been keeping him in."

Sawyer raised his eyebrows. "What do we know?"

"Other than Angela wrenching her shoulder while trying to escape a federal agent?" Jared shrugged. "Best guess is they've given up trying to eliminate testimony and are simply trying to break him out of custody."

"From a federal courthouse?"

"He wasn't behind bars. They knew where he was, and there were a shit ton of civilians for officers to protect once shit went down. I can see the tactical advantages—and the desperation."

"Yeah," Sawyer said. "But she's testified. She's done."

"I'm done," Angela repeated.

"Agreed. Short of retribution, their attention has been turned elsewhere."

Sawyer didn't like that. For years, Pham had made retribution his calling card, but not much of that had occurred since he had been arrested. Still, Sawyer's guard would never go down completely.

"I said what I needed to say. That's all I care about," she said.

The corners of Boss Man's lips quirked, and he asked Sawyer, "When are they releasing her?"

"Soon as the paperwork arrives."

"I have a doctor near headquarters. Doc Tuska. She should see him for any follow-ups needed. I'll make sure Parker sends the contact information your way."

"I want to go home." Angela leaned against Sawyer. "All the way back on a jet."

The corners of Jared's eyes crinkled as if he were trying not to laugh. "We'll make sure that happens soon as Doc clears you." Boss Man turned to leave but caught himself. "Marriage doesn't mean you share trade secrets. You hear me, sunshine?"

"Oh, no." She crossed her heart. "I wouldn't dare tell your secrets."

"Yeah, I wouldn't want to know about your psych training the team or anything," Sawyer muttered under his breath with a chuckle.

Jared dropped his head back and shook it. "People falling in love right and left. What a headache."

"Give it a try, Boss Man." Angela laughed. "I think you should do it, too."

"It takes two to tango." Sawyer snorted. "And I can't imagine the woman who would put up with you."

"Yeah, no. I like my life the way it is. Camden and I will hold our own on Team Bachelor."

"Don't forget you have the US team," Angela added, her eyes a little goofy. "If Sawyer wasn't the best-looking man ever, I might have noticed you employ seriously good-looking commandos."

Again, Jared dropped his head back and stared at the ceiling. "That's about all of this that I can handle." He managed a rough laugh. "See you back in Abu Dhabi."

The door shut, and Sawyer retook his spot beside Angela. "When are we getting married?"

"Soon as you put a ring on my hand."

His heart squeezed. "I'll make sure that's arranged. Anything else you want?"

Angela wrapped her good arm around him and laid her head on his shoulder. "Nothing but you."

EPILOGUE

TWO YEARS LATER

"I AM NOT sure that I have visited anyone else in the hospital more than I have visited you two," Jared grumbled, but Sawyer could see the humor in Boss Man's eyes.

"Life's tough, big guy," Angela said quietly.

Sawyer gave her a quick once-over, smoothing his hand over her hair. Life was tough. That was for sure. But it gave just as hard as it took. Life was hell as much as it was precious, and he would never take that for granted.

"Is it a good time?" Jared asked.

"Yes, but they're not—"

The door opened again. Jared stepped to the side. A cautious nurse scrutinized Jared but then instructed him to hold the door. Boss Man obeyed, and the nurse rolled the little bed into the room and parked it next to Sawyer at Angela's side.

Sawyer scooped his daughter into his arm and adjusted the little cap over her tiny head before handing her to Angela. Then he picked up his son and cradled him in the crook of his arm.

Jared let out a long, slow breath, shaking his head. "Hearing about twins is one thing." He took a cautious step closer. "Seeing them is another."

Angela, barely semi-rested but glowing, grinned. "I just said the same thing about carrying them versus holding them."

Sawyer approached Jared and shifted his son into Boss Man's gentle hold. "This is Alexander. Alex for short."

"One hell of a cute kid," Jared said, surprising Sawyer with his ease at holding a newborn. "What about Princess over there?"

"Grace." Angela kissed the top of their little girl's head and looked up at Sawyer, radiating warmth. "Alex and Grace."

Jared offered Alex back to Sawyer, and after a careful handoff, crossed his arms and nodded approvingly. Sawyer held Alex and perched on the edge of the bed next to his wife.

"Good names. Strong ones." The corners of Jared's lips lifted.

"They could call you Uncky Jared," Angela offered.

"Was that baby talk?" Jared lifted a hand. "Don't push your luck."

"Uncky Boss Man," she suggested, trying not to laugh.

He retreated a step. "All right. Congratulations. But I've gotta head out before all of this domesticated bliss gives me a migraine."

The door quietly shut behind Jared. Sawyer focused on his wife. He remembered the first moment he saw Angela. Now, he stared at everything she'd given to him. A life. Children. *Salvation.* He might've kept her alive, but she had saved his soul.

ABOUT THE AUTHOR

New York Times bestselling author Cristin Harber packs her military romance, romantic suspense, and new adult romance novels with steam, sizzle, and action of all types. Whether you want fireworks in the bedroom or a hunky ex-military team that saves the day, her bestselling romance novels will make you swoon and smile.

The ACES Series:
Book 1: The Savior
Book 2: The Protector
Book 3: The Survivor
Book 4: The Guardian
Book 5: The Defender
Book 6: The Bodyguard

The Titan Series:
Book 1: Winters Heat
Book 1.5: Sweet Girl
Book 2: Garrison's Creed
Book 3: Westin's Chase
Book 4: Gambled and Chased
Book 5: Savage Secrets
Book 6: Hart Attack
Book 7: Sweet One
Book 8: Black Dawn
Book 9: Live Wire
Book 10: Bishop's Queen

Book 11: Locke and Key
Book 12: Jax
Book 13: Deja Vu

The Delta Series:
Book 1: Delta: Retribution
Book 2: Delta: Rescue*
Book 3: Delta: Revenge
Book 4: Delta: Redemption
Book 5: Delta: Ricochet
*The Delta Novella in Liliana Hart's MacKenzie Family Collection

The Only Series:
Book 1: Only for Him
Book 2: Only for Her
Book 3: Only for Us
Book 4: Only Forever

7 Brides for 7 Soldiers:
Ryder (#1) – Barbara Freethy
Adam (#2) – Roxanne St. Claire
Zane (#3) – Christie Ridgway
Wyatt (#4) – Lynn Raye Harris
Jack (#5) – Julia London
Noah (#6) – Cristin Harber
Ford (#7) – Samantha Chase

7 Brides for 7 Blackthornes:
Devlin (#1) – Barbara Freethy
Jason (#2) – Julia London
Ross (#3) – Lynn Raye Harris
Phillip (#4) – Cristin Harber
Brock (#5) – Roxanne St. Claire
Logan (#6) – Samantha Chase
Trey (#7) – Christie Ridgway

Each Aces, Titan, Delta, and 7 Brides book can be read as a standalone (except for Sweet Girl), but readers will likely best enjoy the series in order. The Only series must be read in order.

Made in the USA
Middletown, DE
14 July 2024

57302328R00198